Bendis' book
re - children in war

Sunpath

Sunpath

Michael Maryk

Library of Congress Control Number: 2008904548
ISBN: Hardcover   978-1-4363-4397-8
               Softcover   978-1-4363-4396-1

This book was printed in the United States of America.

To order additional copies of this book, contact:
Xlibris Corporation
1-888-795-4274
www.Xlibris.com
Orders@Xlibris.com
49084

For
Gretha, Sten and the wonderfid Wallin Family
My Gratitude and Love

In the summer of 1943, the country of Finland faced certain annihilation at the hands of an enraged Russia, Finland's ancient enemy. A phone conversation in Stockholm, Sweden between two women, Maja Sandler, the wife of Sweden's Foreign Minister, and Hanna Rudh, Director of Sweden's philanthropic Bremmer Foundation, created a plan for neutral Sweden to temporarily adopt Finland's children until the war's end. Within three months, the operation, called FINSKA KRIGSBARN, became the greatest exodus of children in recorded history.

The *Sunpath* saga begins when the idyllic wilderness world of ten-year old Aimo Kekkenan is shattered by roving bands of marauding Russian soldiers when they invade his unsuspecting settlement in eastern Finland. The boy's parents lead him; his six-year old sister, Anna; and his traumatized eight-year old cousin, Pehr, to a children's refugee train. There they join hundreds of other children bound for the sanctuary of Sweden. Most of the adults avoid explaining the terrible possibility that, once apart, they may never see each other again.

The perilous journey takes ten days through Finland's wilderness countryside. Upon reaching the Swedish border, the children are transferred to a modern, electric train that deposits them to hamlets where they will stay with Swedish families who first cope but then bond with each other until the war's end. The train bears the old Viking name SOLVEIG (*Sunpath*).

Sunpath is the story of the indomitable courage of young Aimo Kekkenen. We follow his heroic journey within northern Sweden's spectacular landscape and discover the triumph of the human spirit together with the eternal love that, in spite of war exists among people all over the world.

Sunpath is a creative work of fiction based on actual events. Names and places are fictitious and solely the responsibility of the author.

Chapter One

Aimo Kekkenen celebrated his tenth birthday in abject misery, having just learned he and his sister would have to leave their parents. It was the worst birthday present the boy could imagine. He trembled in fear as he struggled for some new excuse to change his parent's mind. He had to make them realize how terrifying it felt to be sent away. The consequences were terrible. What if they should never see each other again, he worried.

He did not want to leave home and go to Sweden, but his parents said all the children of Finland had to go. The country was in trouble and faced dangerous times. That's why children had to be sent away, he was told. The unwelcome news angered the boy. He was now ten, and as far as he was concerned, he was old enough to solve whatever problems his parents faced.

He stomped across the kitchen of his small rough-hewn timber house and stopped at the doorway to the bedroom he shared with his sister. His mother was frantically packing suitcases and Aimo chose the moment to try one more time to explain how he felt, but she exploded.

"Enough!" His mother thrust the palm of her hand directly in front of the boy's face and glowered through tense and weary eyes. The strains of the coming war and her desperate preparations for her family's escape had changed her once-pretty face.

"Not one more word of complaint, Aimo. Do you understand? Go to the barn and help Papa with the horses," she ordered. She returned her attention to folding clothes into a suitcase.

Defeated once again, Aimo stared silently at his mother then quietly turned away and walked outside. He loved his parents and he knew they loved him. Why wasn't that enough reason to at least talk. but no one listened to him, he grumbled. None of his impassioned pleas or serious attempts at *grown-up* conversations could change his parents' mind. Aimo, Anna, his friends and most of Finland's children under ten were to be sent to Sweden for the duration of the war. He would have no say about the decision.

Aimo suppressed the uncomfortable urge to cry, frustrated by his impotence to determine his own destiny. He cast a longing glance at the nearby sheltering forest. It had always been his sacred sanctuary where he could turn for solutions to his troubles. But even there, he found nothing to help him with his present dilemma. He sauntered across the snow-covered ground, then turned to look at the building that was not just wood and daub. It was his home, all the home the boy had ever known.

Aimo sighed heavily in despair. Rumors of war with Russia had been part of the boy's life ever since he could remember. Now those rumors included Finland fighting the Germans. The gossip left Aimo both confused and frightened.

He vividly remembered the day three years earlier when the entire community of Lake Jarvii learned that Finland had joined Germany in attacking Russia. They welcomed a column of smartly-dressed Nazi soldiers passing through the village on their way toward the eastern front. The Germans called it Operation Barbarossa and they had come to fight the hated Russians, Finland's ageless archenemy.

The mood in the community was joyous. People gathered along the earthen main street amid a wild celebration. Nazi flags were on display everywhere. It was unlike anything the boy had ever seen, and he huddled next to his mother holding her hand. Father stood closely next to her, one arm protectively around his wife's shoulders while the other cradled Anna, Aimo's little sister. Aunt Leena and her six children stood with them. All the people of the village cheered as the military columns approached.

The rumbling sounds of motorized vehicles heralded the army's arrival, and Aimo stood mesmerized with youthful fascination as the Germans entered his once-tranquil village. A division of storm troopers sat at attention within armored open half .tracks. All wore swastika armbands and held neatly polished automatic weapons.

Aimo stared in awe, but the display disturbed him greatly. Ignoring his cheering neighbors, he searched the soldiers' faces for clues to his country's new ally. The boy saw nothing to suggest compassion or friendship. Instead, he found a frightening specter of fierce, ageless-looking men. All of them armed with the latest weaponry.

The boy viewed the apocalyptic sight through billowing clouds of choking dust thrown high above Jarvii's narrow unpaved main street, bathing the entire scene with an ominous ochre-colored light. The midday sun, glowing warmly in a clear June sky, paled into a riveting, surreal image of war that Aimo never would forget.

Now, three years later, the Aryan army had been defeated. The once-proud swastika soldiers, bloodied, battered, and in full retreat, were themselves pursued by enraged Bolshevik fighters who savagely drove the Germans westward toward the Baltic Sea, an escape route which took them directly across Finland. As a result, the Finnish population lay defenseless in between the warring armies. They knew they would be harshly dealt with, both from their ancient enemy, the Russians, and their former allies, the Germans.

Sweden is a wonderful, peaceful place, Aimo was told. Everyone lived in big houses with electric lights. Food was plentiful. His parents promised that in a few weeks, even they would leave for Sweden, but Aimo worried nevertheless. He did not understand why the family could not stay together. Instead of answers, Aimo was told children would be better off in Sweden. Period! Then he was reminded, swiftly and firmly, to obey his parents and to do so silently.

The midmorning sun, still low in the sky, glowed over the newly fallen snow with a light golden sheen, typical for late October in eastern Finland. In a few weeks, the sun would scarcely clear the horizon. Each passing day brought a growing darkness, inexorably engulfing the land in haunting shades of grey. The chilled autumn air, not yet cold enough for ice to form on the many lakes surrounding Aimo's village, heralded the fast-approaching winter. Six bitterly frigid months lay ahead before anyone would feel the warmth of the sun again.

His father's footprints, made earlier that morning, led away from the house. The clearly marked trail headed directly toward their barn that lay out of view within the pine forest that encircled the village. Aimo followed the trail, kicking angrily at the snow.

Suddenly, a subtle movement beneath a snow-laden pine branch jolted him to an abrupt halt. A low growl guided his sight to a large gray-furred head. A pair of glowering eyes, set between pointed ears, lay back in warning against the animal's skull. The eyes stared ominously at him.

"Tark!"

The boy called out the name of cousin Pehr's Malamute husky. The huge wolf-dog exploded from his concealment in a blur of white powder. He reached the boy in two bounds and braked to a stop, plowing a wall of snow with his skidding chest. He barked in excitement, his head between his front paws, and his rump high in the air. Tark's tail wagged furiously in a frantic signal of his desire to play, and the boy swiftly obliged.

Aimo dove for the dog's hindquarters, sending them both tumbling in the snow. Tark broke away, sprinting around the boy in a circle. Aimo jumped to his feet and raced down the hill leading to the lake. Tark, twice the boy's size, was on him in a flash. He jumped on Aimo's back with a force that sent them both sliding down the hill.

Suddenly, the loud raucous sounds of hundreds of ducks and geese simultaneously taking flight brought the game to an end. Aimo and Tark stared in the direction of the lake as flocks of birds took to the air. An instant later, the alarming echo of automatic gunfire reached them.

Aimo looked around nervously, trying to get a bearing on the origin of the sound, and fixed his gaze on the calm blue surface of the lake. A flock of ravens, high in the upper canopy of the pine trees above him, left their perches in alarm, their flight loosening a cascade of powdery snow to glisten brilliantly on the slanting rays of midmorning sunlight.

Aimo cautiously slinked to the water's edge, then slithered onto a rocky point of land facing eastward. Tark followed warily. The boy led the dog onto a weatherworn boulder jutting pugnaciously over the water. He flattened his small wiry body over the point and, ignoring the chill of the frigid stone against his chest, slid forward until he could peek at the distant shoreline. Concentrating intensely, they hardly noticed the cacophonous calling from V-shaped columns of geese flying overhead. Whatever sounds Aimo had heard, the frightened birds had heard it also. Rapidly gaining altitude, they made a noisy exit for the warmer climes of southern Europe.

Aimo's attention shifted to a movement on the hill above him. Cousin Pehr jogged unhurriedly over the crest of the hill, then pulled himself to a stop next to Aimo's boulder. He looked curiously at his dog lying by his older cousin's side. Tark's head was flattened, and his ears stood alertly erect while Aimo shielded his eyes with his hand and breathed heavily. Both stared across the lake.

"What are you looking at?" Pehr asked, bewildered.

"Shhh!" Aimo hissed. "Get down!"

Pehr dropped onto the rock and slithered next to Aimo.

"I heard shooting. Soldiers, I think," Aimo whispered.

As was his custom, Pehr mimicked his cousin. He shielded his eyes with his hand and stared at the distant peaceful shoreline but saw nothing unusual.

"Are you sure?" Pehr asked.

Aimo had more important things on his mind and did not answer him. Several other settlements bordered Lake Jarvii, each with fewer than thirty homes. Aimo concentrated on one of his favorite villages, Kaava, which lay directly across the water from him. When the lake froze in the winter, he often crossed the kilometer-wide expanse to play ice hockey with the older boys who lived there

Lake Jarvii was one of the dozens of various-sized lakes in the surrounding area, but Aimo considered it to be his property. His own home, perched on a tree-covered bluff, provided a clear eastern view of the water and glorious sunrises. The boy loved this scene as far back as he could remember.

Cousin Pehr's mother, Aunt Leena, and her six children lived next door to him. She had last seen her husband four years earlier when he left to fight the Russians in the Winter War of 1939, but he never returned. Nevertheless, the woman continued tirelessly with her life despite the hardships caused by his loss. The entire village recognized Aunt Leena as a talented baker, and the aroma of her freshly baked bread wafted down the hill and onto the rock where Aimo lay.

Nearby, Papa's moored rowboat floated serenely on the calm waters next to the shoreline. Soon it would be time to weigh it down with large stones and sink it where it would lie sheltered beneath winter's thick ice until next spring. The cold water protected the wood from rot and simultaneously sealed the seams to guarantee its seaworthiness the next season. The sight of the rowboat brought the boy fond memories of the many fishing trips he shared with his father, and he sighed loudly.

This nearly unspoiled wilderness was Aimo's world, and he could never think of leaving it. The volley of gunfire, so discordant to the familiar sounds of nature, violated all that the boy held dear and alarmed him deeply. He recognized rifle reports from hunting trips with his father, but these concentrated bursts of automatic gunfire were not those of hunters.

"What are you looking at?" Pehr insisted.

Aimo regarded his cousin's round cherubic face. Pehr wore a continual smile, an outward sign of his easy, if not slightly slow, nature. Pehr was definitely Aimo's opposite. He lacked his cousin's athleticism, and he accepted the older boy as the acknowledged leader. It did not bother him that Aimo was the best skier, the best hockey player, or the fastest runner in the community. Pehr had his beloved dog, Tark, and nothing else mattered to him.

Aimo ignored the younger boy's question, a habit he had recently picked up from the one-sided conversations with his parents.

"What do you have that on for?" Aimo indicated an official-looking identity tag held by a ribbon around Pehr's neck.

"I'm supposed to wear it when I go to Sweden. Where's yours?"

"I'm not goin'," Aimo said.

"I have to go. My sisters too," Pehr answered. Then he received a thought and patted the dog's head. "Aimo, if you're not goin', can you take care of Tark for me?"

Almost on cue, the husky focused his multicolored eyes, one grey the other blue, on Aimo. The boy's ruddy complexion reflected his outdoor life. A coarse mat of straight dark hair and dark blue eyes set deep within his wide cheekbones attested to the boy's Laplander background. As far as Tark was concerned, he and Aimo were one of a kind.

"Sure!" Aimo said. He sealed the contract by giving the dog a hug, then returned his concentration to the distant shoreline and willed his sight to discover the origin of the gunfire. He was so bent on finding the source that he nearly slipped from the boulder at the shrill call of his name.

"Aimo! Aimo! Come home now!" the voice yelled. Startled, the boy sat upright and looked in the direction of the caller.

Anna, his six-year-old sister appeared, dressed in the ankle-length red outfit grandmother had just finished for her. She moved quickly with short swift steps that made it appear she was floating over the snow-covered ground. She called again at the top of her voice.

Aimo cringed at the sound. He sensed something was wrong. Their survival depended on stealth and quiet. He was certain they were in danger, and the shouting girl was going to reveal their position. He jumped from the boulder and sprinted to his sister, pressed a hand over her mouth, and gestured for her to be still. The girl allowed Aimo to lead her to the big boulder where Tark and Pehr waited silently, but Anna had to whisper the reason for calling.

"Mama wants you to come home right now," she said, affecting a peevish tone.

"Shhhh!" Aimo hissed.

"Papa took our suitcases to the sled with the horses," she continued.

"Be quiet," Aimo said. He pointed across the lake. "Look on the other side."

Anna had learned an effective behavioral skill when it came to her big brother, discovering she was most effective when being persistent. Then her little girl's voice whined with an irritation that drove Aimo mad. There was no stopping her once she set it into motion.

"We have to go to the train. Mama said we're going to Sweden."

"Shut up! Lie down here and look," Aimo growled.

"I have new clothes, and Mama doesn't want me to get dirty," Anna protested. She placed her closed fists against her waist and stared defiantly.

Aimo gritted his teeth and uttered an unintelligible sound. His sister had become his daily responsibility and his most hated chore. Try as he might to please his parents, she always did something to get him into trouble.

Occasionally Aimo's patience gave out, and he would physically establish his position as older brother, and now was one of those times. He grabbed his sister's wrists and forced her down on the boulder.

"I said sit down," he growled.

Anna obeyed, taking a cross-legged position on the husky's rump.

Aimo had just celebrated his sixth birthday when the winter war with Russia broke out in 1939. His youthful face tensed as thoughts of war swept over him. He remembered the ruthlessness of the Russians that spring when the warmer weather allowed the Bolshevik hordes to return with their artillery and motorized equipment. The Finnish army was overwhelmed, and Aimo's family hid in the forest while marauding soldiers swept through their hamlet. The Russians spared no living thing, burning whatever they did not steal.

The idea of war, of soldiers firing weapons and terrified people screaming and hiding, sent a wave of panic through the boy. He regretted having thought of it and struggled to purge the memory from his mind. Suddenly, a new volley of shots erupted, this time much more concentrated. The children again looked in the direction of Kaava, no longer doubting the type of gunfire. Aimo's worst fears were realized. Soldiers were shooting at each other.

The children saw the flash of the explosion before they heard it.

A large phosphorescent light leapt over the pine trees on their side of the lake. A blast followed; and a moment later, the shockwave rushed over the children, knocking them off their feet. Tark barked furiously in the direction of their village.

A column of black smoke spiraled upward no more than one hundred meters away. A loud chatter of automatic weapons reverberated from the stricken area. Aimo grabbed his sister's hand, yanked her from the rock, and ran toward the safety of their house. Pehr remained where he lay, his arms clutched tightly around Tark. The husky barked furiously in the direction of gunfire coming from somewhere near Pehr's home.

"Pehr! Come with us," Aimo shouted.

Pehr implored his dog to follow him, but the husky would not move. His eyes had fastened on his home at the top of the hill, and he growled angrily. Pehr released his grip of the dog's neck, then joined his cousins in a wild dash for the safety of Aimo's house. Tark remained, barking uncontrollably, seemingly unable to decide if to follow the children or go to the defense of his property.

Aimo's mother appeared at the top of the hill, her weatherworn face twisted in a worry that described an age far beyond her thirty years. She gestured frantically for the children to join her and pulled them tightly against her body when they reached her.

"Are you all right?" she asked breathlessly.

All three children spoke at once, trying to explain what they had seen. Above all, they hoped the woman could somehow return the chaos to normalcy.

"There's a war!" Aimo shouted. He nudged his sister with an elbow for confirmation. When he got none, he continued his story excitedly. "There was a big explosion. We saw it."

Anna directed her mother's attention to a smudge mark on her red coat that she brushed vigorously with her hand.

"Aimo made me lie down and get my coat dirty," she complained.

The woman was not listening. Russian invaders, her worst nightmare, murdering and pillaging again, through their village. She agonized for being caught so off guard. Why had they not known of the soldiers' presence before? How could the Russians have come into their settlement without being detected? Where was her husband? An hour earlier, he had gone to fetch the sled to take all of them to the safety of Jyväskylä, twenty-five kilometers westward. Had he been surprised as well and possibly killed?

The closeness of the nearby Russian soldiers returned her thoughts on the immediate safety of her family, but the woman had not considered that their cottage was more than unsafe. It literally was a boxed-in trap. Unaware of the danger she was placing them in, she rushed everyone inside and moved quickly to a window, her eyes searching the surrounding forest warily. A movement near her sister's home fifty meters away caught her attention. Gun-carrying soldiers approached her sister Leena's property in a quick trot.

"Quiet! Soldiers are coming!" she whispered. "Aimo! Get your things. Pehr! Stay with Aimo!" She led Anna into her bedroom and continued her instructions. "We have to get out of here *now*. We'll meet Father in the forest. He's hitching the horses to the sleigh."

The boys crossed the main room to one of the two small windows flanking the fireplace that provided a clear view of Aunt Lena's house. The sight froze the boys in terror. Five soldiers methodically took positions outside the structure.

Aimo trembled uncontrollably as the leader of the five-man group shouted orders at Leena's house in Finnish, but the accent was unmistakably Russian. Aimo shook with fear, yet he could not keep from staring in terror-stricken fascination. He wanted to run to the forest and hide but stood frozen to the spot. Pehr stared at his house. He dug his fingers into the windowsill and began to whimper loudly.

The leader was a wide grizzled man with a red star-emblazoned fur hat that melded into his full beard, which gave his face a bearlike appearance. He held an automatic pistol in one hand and, with the other, gestured to his squad to take defensive positions. The soldiers pointed their machine guns menacingly at Aunt Leena's house. The leader called for the occupants to come out. He promised no harm would come to them if they obeyed his commands.

Suddenly, Pehr saw the pewter-colored blur of Tark race across the snow, rapidly closing the distance on the soldiers. The dog had disdained the safety of the children to come to the defense of his home, and he hurled himself furiously at the invaders. His jaws clamped powerfully on the leader's hand. It erupted in a shower of blood.

"Tark!" Pehr yelled. "Come back! Come back!"

A loud burst of automatic gunfire brought a sharp yelp of pain from the dog, and Tark somersaulted into a lifeless heap in the snow. Pehr cried out in agony; then his voice trailed off into uncontrollable sobs.

The Russian voice called again, this time stronger and angrier. They only wanted German soldiers, he shouted. He warned that unless everyone voluntarily came out, the house would be burned.

Mother entered in a panic, clutching Anna tightly. "Come! We have to run," she called, gesturing for Aimo and Pehr to follow.

Before Aimo could move, the loud chatter of automatic weapons, followed by human screams, pulled his attention to the window. The boy gawked in terrified horror at the spectacle of Aunt Leena, her five daughters and his grandmother grotesquely crumpled on the blood-spattered snow. They had heeded the commands of the Russian leader, naively accepted his promise, and came out of the house as ordered. Trust had cost them their lives.

Mother pushed Aimo brusquely aside. Taking hold of Pehr's shoulders, she looked through the window and shrieked—a long tortured wail that exploded into an agonized scream.

"NO!"

The bear-faced man spun in her direction, then signaled one of the men to follow him to Aimo's cottage as the other three set to the task of torching Aunt Leena's house.

Mother drew back from the window, pulling Pehr with her, but something had happened to him. The slaughter of his family was too traumatic. The boy's tongue seemed to have fastened to the roof of his mouth, and he made a continual noise that sounded like humming. Aimo grabbed his mother's free hand while Anna clung to the woman's side.

Suddenly, the back door opened noisily, and the fall of heavy steps tramped ominously toward them across the mudroom floor. Everyone stopped where they stood. Mother clasped a hand across Anna's mouth while Aimo held his breath. The terrified group watched and waited in frozen silence as the large inner door was slowly pushed open by the barrel of a gun.

Father, dressed in his white winter uniform and carrying his military rifle, burst into the room. Mother uttered a muffled cry of relief and rushed to him, burying her head in his chest.

"Two Russians are right behind me," he reported. "There's no time to escape. We have to try to surprise them."

Father pulled Anna and Aimo to the fireplace and scattered the stacked firewood, exposing random-sized pine floor planks. He searched for several loose boards against the wall which concealed a small hiding place he had created years earlier for such an emergency. He swiftly crammed his children inside, but there was no room left for Pehr.

Father shouted down into the hiding place. "Aimo! Take care of your sister! Keep her quiet, and don't come out until I tell you!"

Mother helped him replace the firewood over the hiding place; then she grabbed Pehr and followed her husband to the dining room. Father overturned a large oak table, creating a defensive barrier. Then he gestured for everyone to be quiet.

"They're here," he whispered.

Except for Pehr's humming noise, the room became unnaturally still. Mother placed a hand over Pehr's mouth to muffle his voice. Time seemed to stand still as everyone waited breathlessly for the accented voice to order them from the house.

Aimo twisted his body within his cramped hiding place, the movement allowing him to peek through the cracks in the floorboard. He tried to control his legs from shaking, but the trembling continued unabated. He had a clear view across the main room to the door leading to the mudroom and his attention flashed to a large center window on the adjacent wall.

Like some shadowed apparition from a nightmare, a Russian soldier suddenly appeared. He looked into the room quickly, then ducked his head out of view before peering inside again. He had cold gray eyes, and he focused his attention on the scattered logs in front of the fireplace. He stared directly at Aimo's hiding place, a sinister sneer *spreading* across his face. He shifted the machine gun in his hands and aimed.

Aimo's shout of warning was swallowed by the explosion from the noise of machine gun fire. Bullets tore indiscriminately through everything within the room. Shattered glass flew wildly, and the large grandfather clock, which sat in a corner of the room for as long as Aimo could remember, fell with a resounding crash. A moment later, the inner door was kicked open with a violent force. Once again bullets sprayed wildly over the area heralding the appearance of the grizzled man with the fur hat. He entered first and played his pistol around the room. A blood-soaked makeshift bandage was wrapped tightly around his free hand where Tark had attacked him, but it did not stem the bleeding. As he moved toward the fireplace, he stopped directly over the children's hiding place as drops of blood dripped quietly to the floor. A moment later he was joined by the machine gun—toting Russian.

Aimo held his sister tightly, unaware that the little girl's eyes had fixed on a rivulet of blood trickling through the floorboards. She followed the course of a thick red blob of liquid oozing inexorably into her hiding place. Anna could do nothing to prevent it from spilling onto her arm. It splattered softly onto her coat, and the girl shrieked loudly.

The bearlike man jumped into the air as though he had just stepped on a cat, then turned his attention downward to the scream. An instant later, a rifle shot rang out, sending a bullet through the bearded man's head, sending his star-emblazoned hat flying across the room. The second Russian was too slow to notice Father kneeling from his position behind the overturned table taking aim at him. The Russian turned to face the danger, but Father's next shot felled him instantly.

Mother frantically pushed aside the firewood. She pulled Anna from the hiding place as the little girl cried hysterically. Shouts of approaching Russian soldiers reverberated beyond the walls, calling in alarm for their comrades in Aimo's house.

Father crouched low to the floor and rushed to the fireplace window. The revenge-driven man uttered a low animal-like growl that rose from his throat. The glow from Aunt Leena's blazing house flickered on his face, and his eyes glowered in hatred as he surveyed the three charging soldiers. They came at a dead run, their excited voices loud and harsh, their figures nimbused by the flames behind them.

Father poked his rifle through the window, shattering the glass. He aimed carefully, fired, swiftly bolted a new shell into the rifle chamber, and rapidly fired a second time and then a third.

Aimo heard the agonized cries of the mortally wounded men outside as Father reloaded his rifle. He took careful aim and fired three more rounds into the downed men. Then there was silence.

Chapter Two

The sky on the southern horizon beyond Jyväskylä's train station glowed as though set aflame. Like the work of a frenetic artist, the heavens had become a celestial canvas of war and, ironically, foretold a rapidly approaching early winter snowstorm. The entire landscape, painted as it was in dramatic firey tones, provided a fitting backdrop to the tumult below.

Jyväskylä's town square heaved as large crowds of people milled about—creating a haphazard traffic jam of people, horses, sleds, and wagons—to form an impenetrable barrier. Aimo's family sled could no longer move forward.

Mother jumped from the sled and called frantically. "The train leaves at sunset. We have to hurry!"

The woman tucked Anna tightly in her arms, then turned and disappeared into the crowds. She sprinted wildly for the platform, shouldering her way through the chaotic crowds of people. Father was right behind. He grabbed the children's suitcases, took cousin Pehr by the hand, and called for his son to follow, "Come, Aimo!"

Aimo hopped from the sled and ran to stay as close behind Father as he could. The boy was overwhelmed by the state of near panic all around him. He looked fearfully to see if Russian soldiers were approaching, the image from the horrors at his home still strong in his mind. Noise raged all around him. Parents shouted to their children already on the platform, and children shouted back. Many simply cried as loudly as they could, children and parents alike. A group of harassed women in white kerchiefs and Red Cross armbands, together with a few Finnish soldiers, worked feverishly on the platform.

Behind them, a string of ten white boxcars stood as still, silent sentinels. An antiquated wood-burning steam locomotive coughed billows of smoke into the air, waiting for the signal to move. Large Red Cross flags fluttered from the front of the engine to the rear car on either side of the train, the signage of an internationally recognized noncombative vehicle of mercy.

The elevated platform teemed with crying children, many of whom still held their parent's outstretched hands. Aimo watched as Mother swung Anna up among them, and his sister's instantaneous wail reached a pitch louder than the background noise. The little girl gripped her mother's hands desperately.

"Aimo!" Mother shouted impatiently.

Father arrived first, pulling the stumbling Pehr behind him as Aimo dodged through the pressing masses, trying to keep pace. His father placed the burdensome suitcases and then Pehr onto the platform. Finally he took Aimo in his arms, clutched him desperately to his chest, and held him tightly. He snuggled the boy's head against his neck lovingly, the pain of losing his son overwhelming.

He struggled with the overpowering need to finally admit the truth to the boy. He had to tell him they would probably never see each other again, yet he could not find the words to say it. After years of hostilities with Russia, the boy's father knew the evils of war well. The Bolsheviks did not distinguish between Finnish soldiers, women, or children. Everyone was a target of their hatred, and if the children of Finland had a chance to survive at all, it could not be in their homeland. Sweden was more than just a sanctuary to the people of Finland. It was their only option. Father patted his son on the back, holding the boy in front of his face for one last look before placing him on the platform. Anna instantly clutched her big brother tightly while Aimo regarded his parents in bewilderment. He planned to offer one last plea to stay home but never got the chance. One of the Red Cross women maneuvering through the throngs of children placed her hands on Aimo's shoulders.

"You cannot go on board without identity cards," the woman scolded. She turned her attention to Pehr, his identity card firmly in place around his neck. "This boy is wearing his. Where are your cards?" she asked.

Aimo answered by blinking silently.

"Here they are," Mother called.

The volunteer checked the information on the cards. Satisfied to find everything in order, she placed the cord-held cards around the children's necks.

"Never take these off," the volunteer directed. "Children will be boarding the train in a few minutes." She turned abruptly and continued her job of checking identification tags with mechanical efficiency.

Aimo squeezed Anna's hand absently. He felt light-headed. A sensation of inexorably tumbling downward swept over him. The din from the surrounding throngs faded to a distant murmur, and his tear-filled eyes blurred his vision. He exchanged distressed glances with his mother, desperate to say something but could only contort his face in confusion.

Everything seemed to be happening so quickly. Protesting was useless, yet there was so much he wanted to say. His gulped air into his heaving chest, but his taut jaw muscles did not allow his mouth to open to produce words. Suddenly, a voice from the loudspeaker instructed the volunteers to help the children board the train.

Crying on the platform rose to a new crescendo, and Mother reached for Anna one last time. She took the little girl's hands in hers and kissed one, then the other. Mother released her grip on Anna, then pulled a ribbon-bedecked military medal from her pocket. She handed it to Aimo.

"Father wanted you to have this," she said.

Aimo recognized the medal at once. It came from his father's military uniform. A single gold bar, embossed with crossed swords, hung from a blue ribbon. Beneath the gold bar, two vertical stripes of white linen tapered down to a suspended gold cross. Papa had received it when Finland defeated the Russians in the Winter War of 1939. It was the very medal the boy dreamed of earning when he was older but was never told of its significance.

Aimo's eyes swept the crowd searching for his father, but there was no trace of him. Mother turned to look as well, but he was nowhere to be found.

"Where is Papa? I don't see him," Aimo's voice was desperate.

"I'll get Papa. Wait for us," Mother shouted. She turned, plunged into the crowd, and quickly disappeared into the mass of anguished people. Somehow, the boy knew it was the last time he would ever see his parents again.

Aimo watched in disbelief. Every fiber of his being told him his survival depended on jumping from the platform and reuniting his family before it was too late. He grabbed Anna and Pehr by the hand as Red Cross volunteers shepherded the hordes of crying children onto the waiting train. He was too late. A gaunt older woman wearing a Red Cross armband reached Aimo and instructed him to move with the others.

"Move along, boy," she ordered, nudging him away from the platform.

"Mama wants us to wait here," Anna said.

Aimo was furious. He wrenched himself free from the woman's grasp. "No!" he shouted. "We have to wait *here*."

The volunteer would have none of it. She placed her hands against the children's backs and shoved them firmly into a clutch of sobbing children.

It was too much for Aimo. He had been told by his parents to wait and was doing what he was told. Now a stern-faced stranger was forcing him to disobey. As far as Aimo was concerned, that was more than enough reason not to go to Sweden.

Dropping the suitcases, he took a firm grip of Anna and cousin Pehr, turned toward the platform, and plowed headlong into a strapping Finnish soldier. The soldier's duty was to oversee the orderly flow of children onto the train and he especially watched for unruly children presenting unnecessary problems. In front of him stood a defiant boy fitting that description. To make matters worse, he was leading two other children away from where they had been directed.

Recognizing Aimo as the ringleader of the rebellious group he grabbed the boy by the collar, picked up the discarded suitcases, and carried the boy as a cat carries a kitten. The soldier dragged the children into a car, then placed them onto a makeshift passenger seat next to a window.

"You can see your parents from here. Wave like this," the soldier demonstrated. Then he turned and abruptly left.

Anna looked out at the sea of waving hands through the window, oblivious to the rough handling her brother had received. "I don't see them. I don't see Mama or Papa."

Aimo slouched in his seat, staring at his boots glumly. He lifted his eyes and cast a glance at Pehr on a bench across from him. His cousin's knees were pulled up to his chest, and he covered his eyes with both hands, humming an incessant noise. Aimo found no solace there.

Anna pressed her face against the window and called to her brother again. "I don't see them Aimo. I don't see Mama or Papa."

"They're not coming back," he answered, his voice choking.

As the train lurched forward, Aimo placed a comforting arm across Anna's shoulders but avoiding her sorrow-filled eyes. He struggled with his own despair, overwhelmed with the fear of abandonment and struck with his inadequacy to do anything at all about it. Tears rolled freely down his cheeks as he nervously twisted the military medal in his free hand. He searched for some comforting thing to say to his little sister.

"They didn't even say good-bye" was all he could manage.

Chapter Three

Rebecca Filsson pulled the door of the railcar shut behind her and sighed deeply. She allowed herself a moment to gain her composure and surveyed the car full of traumatized children.

The train gathered speed, the rhythmic chugging of the steam engine slowly increasing the distance from Jyväskylä. The interior of the car was poorly illuminated by two kerosene lamps positioned in compartment doors at either end. Wooden benches had been installed to serve as seats. Beds were nothing more than blanket-covered planks placed across the benches.

The twenty-nine children assigned to her compartment, whose ages ranged from one to ten, collectively wailed in despair. Rebecca moved to the center of the car, clapping her hands to gain everyone's attention. She put a forefinger to her lips, held up both hands as a signal for quiet, and gave everyone a final moment to settle down.

Rebecca was twenty-four years old, a second-year medical student in her hometown of Wasa, and a widow of four years. The government-directed evacuation of Finnish children required many volunteers, and those with a medical background were of special value. She was among the first to respond to the call for Lotta Svärd volunteers, and she wore her white kerchief together with the International Red Cross armband proudly.

She began her address to the children by asking them to close the curtains tightly over the windows then, in a carefully modulated voice, described their journey and its perils as benignly as possible. Their greatest threat was discovery by enemy soldiers. Both the Germans and Russians had fired on similar trains, disregarding the large prominently displayed Red Cross flags.

"Everyone must be quiet at all times," she began. "No crying, no shouting, no loud talking." She lowered her voice to a whisper. "I want you to speak to each other like this. It's a game, so I want everyone to try."

24

Obeying the request, the children turned to the others in their cubicles and began to whisper.

"What should I say?" a boy asked loudly. Rebecca was quick to remind him to whisper even to her and to raise a hand if anyone wanted her attention. She then whispered the answer to the boy's question so all could hear.

"Tell whoever is next to you your name, and that you are very proud of them because they are so brave."

With the rules of the game in place, the whispering began. Slowly at first, then fortified by their own voices, the children engaged each other in earnest conversation. Several of the more extroverted children quickly began an animated sotto voce dialogue with whoever sat next to them. Descriptions of bravery flew within the wagon.

Rebecca circulated throughout the car and marveled at the children's resilience. They were typical of the other refugee children she had attended on previous trips. She discovered most children were eager to communicate with each other even if they had just met. She encouraged them and noted those she felt would require added support later.

Rebecca kept the arduous facts to herself. The twelve-hundred-kilometer journey to Sweden would take at least ten days since they were forced to travel only at night to avoid detection. Chances of being attacked if discovered were great. Their limited food supply would be replenished at scheduled community stops along the way, provided food was available. Water, stored in wooden barrels one per car, would be no problem because their northward course took them through the sparsely populated region of western Finland and the many rivers and streams along the eastern shores of the Gulf of Bothnia. Their final destination was the border town of Tornio, where the Torne River bridge crossed over to Haparanda, Sweden. Whatever happened to the children then was in the hands of the Swedes.

Rebecca noticed one cubicle from which no movement or sound came. A boy held a little girl dressed in a red coat. She sucked her thumb amid occasional shudders but otherwise sat quietly. Behind them, another boy seemed to be softly singing. She stepped in among them and smiled hopefully, but her smile was not returned. None of these three children were playing the whisper game. Rebecca spoke to the first boy.

"What is your name?" she asked.

"Aimo!" the boy replied.

"Is this your sister?" Rebecca continued. Aimo nodded.

"Does she have a name?"

"Anna," he answered.

The singing boy lay on his back and had not shifted his position. His hands were cupped tightly over his eyes, and Rebecca leaned forward to listen to the musical sounds he was making.

"What are you singing?" she asked.

"He's not singing," Aimo answered.

"Oh! I thought since you weren't whispering to each other, he must be singing."

"And he doesn't want to talk to anybody, not even to me," Aimo added.

Rebecca straightened herself and studied the children.

"Are you all right?" she asked Aimo directly.

"My sister's scared. We want to go home," he answered.

"What's your brother's name?"

"He's my cousin. His name is Pehr, and his mother's dead."

Rebecca shook her head in sad recognition. There was no emotion at all in Aimo's voice. The children were in shock, and it would require time to adjust from their trauma. She put her hand on Aimo's head, tousled his black hair gently, then stroked Anna's face.

"My name is Rebecca. If you need me, remember to raise your hand and whisper." She smiled warmly then moved on to the next group of children.

"These little areas with your beds are your own houses," Rebecca announced. "The oldest person in each house has to help the younger children. If you need help, ask me. The most important things are these." She pointed to the ID tags. "Don't ever take them off."

This was Rebecca's third trip as a volunteer. On her first trip six months earlier, there were four volunteers to each railcar, but the savage fighting in Finland was taking a terrible toll on civilians as well as soldiers. Now they were reduced to one volunteer per car. Rebecca took a deep breath and resigned herself for the grueling trip. She alerted the children to the location of the water barrel and how to find the bathrooms. Finally, she demonstrated with a group of four children how to snuggle together for extra warmth.

The locomotive, its ten whitewashed cars bedecked with Red Cross flags flapping in the wind, wound into the thick pine forest west of Jyväskylä like a fleeting, ghostly specter against the snow-covered landscape. Each car was equipped to hold thirty evacuees, a rule that fluctuated with the numbers of siblings, relatives, or community of origin. Every effort was made to keep these families together as this system of evacuation seemed to offer the least amount of stress.

A converted boxcar in the middle of the train served as the dining car. This meant all the children were served food in the same place. The main hazard was foot travel between cars. A safety barrier of heavy gauge fish netting stretched strategically between the cars as a precaution.

Rebecca herded her group between the cars for their dinners. No one had eaten a thing since morning. The overwhelming aroma of an appetizing stew filled the air, and the prospect of a warm meal was met with salivating anticipation by nearly all.

The dining car itself was crammed with children, all of them eating hungrily but quietly. Only an occasional inaudible whisper blended with the sounds of metal spoons scraping food from metal trays.

Aimo's attention was drawn to one of the wooden benches that served as a table, most particularly to a familiar noise of slurping that came from a bench near a wall. A reed-thin boy of Aimo's age ate with abandonment, his body hunched over his tray as though he were defending it. Clutching a large spoon in his right hand, the boy shoveled a continual flow of soupy stew into his mouth. To cap his uncivilized appearance, an unruly shock of auburn hair exploded from his head in all directions. He lifted his face, allowing it to hover a few centimeters above the tray, providing Aimo a clear view of a profile he knew all to well. If there were any remaining doubts to the eater's identity, the boy's huge nose, draped over a piece of bread, gave it away.

"Mooseface!" Aimo whispered in surprise. "What are you doing here?"

Aimo made his way to the generous space Mooseface's tablemates had given him. The boy was remarkably ugly and his near-primitive life with his two uncles had never prepared him for dining etiquette or little else considered civilized. He had one true friend with whom he shared almost all his boyhood adventures and smiled broadly as that person stood before him.

"Aimo!" Mooseface answered, equally surprised. Partially chewed food spilled from his mouth. "Come here and sit down."

Aimo placed his tray on the bench next to his friend.

"Are you gonna eat that?" Mooseface asked.

"Yeah!" Aimo answered "I'm starved."

"Me too!" Mooseface replied.

"You're always starved," Aimo noted.

"I thought you were gonna stay home," Mooseface said, returning his face to its position above the metal tray.

"My mama and papa made me go. I have to take care of Anna. How about you? You said you were gonna run away before anybody would send you to Sweden."

"Remember? You and me promised we both were gonna run away . . . together," Mooseface reminded him. "How come we didn't do it?"

"I didn't think my parents were gonna send me away. I thought they'd change their mind," Aimo continued, his voice flat. "Anyway, Russian soldiers came to the house this morning. They killed Aunt Leena and all my cousins, except Pehr.I think he's crazy."

Mooseface swiped at his mouth with his sleeve. He suddenly disregarded his food and stared at Aimo in disbelief, genuinely shocked. Finally he uttered an oath, "Fee Fon! They're all dead?"

Aimo nodded his head, a signal for Mooseface to resume eating.

"My uncles shot six Ruskies yesterday," Mooseface mumbled proudly. "They cut off their ears . . . they showed me . . . promised to give me one too . . . but they forgot."

Aimo cast a glance at Rebecca, who sat between Anna and Pehr. She ate the stew hungrily in spite of having to help Pehr feed himself. Aimo returned his attention to Mooseface. "What are you gonna do with *Rusky* ears?" he repeated.

"I dunno. I was gonna save 'em . . . for good luck maybe . . . anyway, my uncles said it was too dangerous for me to stay in Finland."

"The Ruskies are burnin' houses too," Aimo added as his friend rapidly consumed the contents of his tray.

"They're burnin' everything . . . even food . . . there's supposed to be plenty of food in Sweden though," Mooseface mumbled.

"I don't care! I hate the Ruskies! I'm gonna go back and kill all of 'em."

"I'll go with you, Aimo," Mooseface assured him.

The hungry boy searched his metal tray for any last morsel that might have escaped his detection. Finding none, he gazed hopefully at Aimo's tray, but Aimo's scraping spoon against bare metal signaled there were no leftovers to pass on. The boy's dark eyes gazed across the empty trays from among his neighbors. Nothing there either.

"You know," Mooseface continued, "maybe we should go to Sweden. They have a lot of food."

Aimo felt a tug on his sleeve and found Rebecca, Anna, and Pehr standing behind him. "We have to go back," she whispered. "There are others who have to eat."

"OK!" Aimo replied. He pushed himself from the table, the timely meal welcome. Aimo felt especially happy to find his friend sharing the same train. Suddenly, the glum apprehension that hung over his life the past several hours seemed to lift. Aimo was convinced that together with Mooseface, it would be much easier to return to Finland and fight alongside his father against the hated Russians.

"What car are you staying in?" Aimo asked.

"I dunno," Mooseface answered. "But it's near the front."

"I'm near the back. I'll see you later, all right?"

"All right!" Mooseface answered. He stood to watch his friend leave, then spied an abandoned tray that still held some traces of stew. He rushed in that direction.

Chapter Four

Reverend Bjorn Blixdal sat uncomfortably in one of the two armchairs in Bishop Levander's poorly heated office in Nilstad, Sweden. He pressed his tall bony frame against the cold leather backrest and shuddered. Blixdal preferred the chair in the shadows near the fireplace, but the bishop himself had offered him the seat next to the window. The reverend dutifully accepted it without complaint.

The floor-to-ceiling window normally provided a clear view of Lake Valdemaren and the epic mountains of northern Sweden, but a heavy overcast obliterated the picturesque backdrop. Low puffs of beige-colored clouds scudded over the choppy waters, spitting wild flurries of snow in the blustery north winds. Cold gusts rattled the window, sending shards of icy air to invade the room through invisible spaces in the window frame. The reverend eyed his preferred, and vacant, seat wistfully.

Reverend Blixdal was always ill at ease when visiting the bishop under any circumstances. He crossed his legs uncomfortably and drew his arms tightly across his chest, hoping the bishop would think his discomfort was created by the drafty window, which, to a great degree, it was. But he dared not run the risk of complaining or displeasing his sixty-nine-year-old superior.

The bishop held a Turkish cigarette between his thumb and forefinger, his palm turned upward. He drew in deeply and exhaled the pungent smoke, adding to the already overwhelming odor of burned tobacco that filled the room. Levander leaned back into his oversized leather chair, the warming fire crackling behind him. He gazed at the wintry scene outside the window. "Here it comes again!" he declared, referring to the returning season of cold, darkness, and ice.

Blixdal glanced through the window at the few people scurrying across the town square below him. They already were layered in the bulky clothes that would envelop their bodies for the next six months. The streets were white with snow, and the wind whipped furiously around the corners of the scattered buildings of downtown Nilstad, creating growing drifts.

The reverend adjusted his weight to dislodge the woolen long johns bunched against his buttocks. He was too damned uncomfortable to think clearly, and he strained to hear every word uttered by his host. Then, as though having a prayer answered, the bishop offered Blixdal a thankful solution to his plight.

"Care for a whiskey?" Levander asked from behind a column of blue haze. Blixdal catapulted to his feet at the opportunity. He crossed to the cabinet next to the fireplace where the bishop kept his liquor.

"May I get one for you as well, sir?"

"Just a small one, thank you, Bjorn. We both have much to do today, you know," the bishop answered. Blixdal filled the glasses, handing one to his superior.

"Skoal," Levander toasted before taking a sip.

"Skoal," Blixdal replied, bowing respectfully in Levander's direction. The bishop offered a weak smile in return as Blixdal raised his glass in salute. He swallowed half the drink in one gulp and shuddered as the ninety-proof alcohol burned its way down his gullet. He then resettled himself quickly in the second chair, feeling far more comfortable in his shadowed position near the fire.

The bishop took a letter from the top of his desk and offered it to Blixdal who read the document quietly without comment. He was next in line to become bishop of Jamtland County upon the old man's retirement. Levander's endorsement of him was critical, and the reverend behaved as though he were in obedience school.

Blixdal completed the reading then lifted his eyes. He sighed deeply, very aware that less than a year remained before the position he so coveted was his. He rolled up the paper and nodded his head as a signal that he had digested the letter's contents. The bishop studied his guest's expression carefully.

"The exodus has begun, Bjorn. Our government has decided to take all of Finland's children. The first group are due to arrive in Nilstad within ten days. Hopefully, you and your volunteers will have enough time to get everything prepared."

Blixdal held the rolled letter batonlike and waved it in Levander's direction, overwhelmed by the information he had just read. "I had not realized there would be so many. The original estimate was for twenty-five thousand children distributed throughout all of Sweden. This says it may be four times that number. A hundred thousand immigrants to add to our welfare roles. Over two hundred assigned to us right here in Nilstad. I don't think it's possible we can take so many."

"Stalingrad has changed everything, Bjorn. The Russians are in full pursuit of the Germans. They're driving them through Finland, and things have already become very difficult there." He exhaled another cloud of smoke in the reverend's direction.

Blixdal downed the remainder of his whiskey. Feeling more comfortable in spite of the smoke, the reverend's gray steely eyes could not mask his displeasure. He shook his head at the prospect of Sweden housing one hundred thousand Finnish refugee children for the duration of the war.

The bishop took notice immediately. "You seem upset, Reverend."

Blixdal took the invitation to express himself freely, which unfortunately meant pontificating, one the reverend's worst habits.

"This idea is typical of the problems of our social system. What starts out as a reasonable idea is then taken over by a group of bleeding-heart socialists. In this case, a couple of women of all people. Then it becomes national policy." The ninety-proof was making Blixdal's voice stronger.

"And it is the Church of Sweden's responsibility to assist in the administration of that policy," Levander injected.

Blixdal shifted his weight again, this time pulling at the tight collar beneath his full beard. He was now too close to the fireplace, and he was becoming very warm. His eyes wandered absently about the room. "The dictum calls for every Swedish family to take at least *one* child. Some of these families have difficulty making ends meet as it is. Everything is rationed. Winter is upon us, and now Swedes are being asked to give part of the little they have to care for someone else's problems. I apologize, Bishop Levander, but you expressed these same views to me yourself only a few months ago." Blixdal's views had become very much in favor of fascism. Sweden's socialist government had become intolerable to him. It was a view the bishop himself had once shared.

"Bjorn, I told you, everything has changed. You and I must understand that two years ago, Germany seemed invincible. Now I'm not so certain," Levander injected

"I pray to God you're wrong. Can you imagine what Europe will be like if the Bolsheviks win?"

"Probably exactly as that in Finland today," Levander answered. "Chaos! . . . retribution! . . . mass murder!"

"But it's Finland's fault. They became Germany's ally when it suited them, then withdrew when the Reich needed them most. So what does socialist

Sweden do? We offer to take care of their kids until the war is over, however long that may be."

Blixdal moved to refill his glass but noticed the bishop eyeing him judgmentally and returned to his chair empty handed. He swept his long silver hair back from his face and leaned forward. He carefully framed his message of displeasure into parameters he believed were familiar to both men. "Germany offers the world a Christian society with industry . . . education . . . science . . . morals . . . and purpose. Exactly the opposite of communism. If the Bolsheviks win, we all lose. It's that simple."

Levander shook his head in disagreement. "Look at the larger picture, Bjorn. Sweden has escaped the ravages of war because of its neutrality, yet we supply Germany with iron ore. Our major manufacturers make and sell war machinery to the Reich at a rate that provides our little country with one of the highest living standards in the world." He offered his empty glass to Blixdal as a sign that it was time to refill it. The reverend obliged both the bishop and himself.

"Skoal," the reverend said, but this time Levander ignored him. He had more to say about an issue that had bothered him for some time.

"There is the matter of personal effects that I have received . . . from friends in Germany. I've been asked to store them in safekeeping until the war is ended. I'm rewarded with cartons of Turkish cigarettes and the lovely Irish whiskey we're enjoying. I wonder how many others in our profession have received similar requests?"

"Why is that wrong?" Blixdal asked.

"Because they are stolen items! When this war is over, most of Europe will be devastated, and Sweden will be viewed as profiteers . . . or worse . . . collaborators. Should Germany lose, and they may, we will not be viewed too kindly by the rest of the world."

Blixdal already knew of the personal effects hidden within the bishop's house. He accidentally came upon the secreted cache himself and discovered a dozen secured cartons in a little-used room. Curiosity had driven him to open one of the crates, and he was astonished to find it filled with stolen jewelry and rolled canvases of rare art. The naive bishop had no clue of the value of the purloined material, but Blixdal did and plotted to help himself when the opportunity allowed.

The reverend also discovered the name of the German officer, Major Reynold Hulsman, who had sent the items. Blixdal wrote the major a letter, expressing his personal support of the Third Reich and his willingness to be of assistance whenever Hulsman needed. The major was quick to reply.

He had just come into possession of some priceless Vermeer paintings as well as nearly three million Deutsch marks from a bombed German bank. He struck a business deal with Blixdal. One hundred thousand Deutsch marks for the reverend should the clergyman find a buyer for the paintings, and an additional 10 percent or three hundred thousand Deutsch marks if Blixdal would hide the money until war's end. All Blixdal had to do was find a suitable place within his church. If he played his cards just right, Blixdal would become a very wealthy man at war's end.

The reverend emptied his glass. The thoughts of his life of wealth had invigorated him. The bishop was right. The Irish whiskey was delicious. In fact, it was the best he had ever tasted. He settled more comfortably in his chair and decided to inform the bishop that it was too soon to give up hope for Germany.

"The Vatican?" Blixdal intoned. "How about the world's view of Pope Pius XII, who, as everyone knows, is on record as favoring the Reich?"

The bishop dropped his shoulders, unable to offer an answer. But Blixdal was slipping back to delivering a sermon and was not yet finished. He stood and stretched his arms outward. "How can our taking a hundred thousand Finnish children into our homes help anything at all? Particularly these children whose backgrounds and standards are so beneath ours! They are more like wild animals than what we know as children."

Levander had heard enough. He jumped to his feet and pounded his fist into his hand. "Benevolence!" the bishop erupted. "Christian charity! Societal conscience! Generosity! Forgiveness!"

The older man plowed the stub of his cigarette into the ashtray. He leaned forward and lowered his voice. "It is how we want the world to remember us. I want your total cooperation in this matter. Is that understood?"

"Yes," Blixdal replied meekly.

There was no use in getting the old man riled any further. The reverend had many uses for the bishop's good graces. He had to bide his time and nodded his head obediently.

"Use your wife," the bishop continued. "She's a great asset. Charming, ambitious, and more energetic than anyone I've met. And you, Bjorn, we're both princes of the church and God's conduits to our flocks. Use your pulpit. Deliver the message of benevolence as only you can. We both know you can do it."

Blixdal clutched his knees uncomfortably with both hands and pressed the small of his back against the chair. "Rest assured. You will have the complete cooperation of both my wife and myself," he promised.

The bishop sauntered to the window and began drumming his fingers noisily on the glass while pensively studying the near-empty town square. Both men remained silent, but the rhythmic tapping of the bishop's fingers triggered unhappy memories for Blixdal. It reminded him of his father, a stern and unloving minister who inflicted frequent beatings on his only son with a shaving strop. His mother never came to his defense and disdained any signs of affection for her only child. Both his parents openly admitted that his birth was an unwanted accident and regretted the burden that parenthood placed on them.

The rural church in the province of Smaland in which Blixdal was raised was as bleak and poor as the windswept area of the stone-filled soil. Farming was difficult, but the plucky denizens toiled in the mud and drove their horse-drawn plows tirelessly through fields laden with ice-age deposited rocks. Blixdal was never able to forget the odors of spring when farmers fertilized the land and the stench of pig manure reeked throughout the county.

Both of his parents dedicated themselves to leading their son to a future career beyond any impoverished ministry. Their goal from the beginning was that Bjorn attain the level of bishop, and they set themselves to that purpose when their son was still a toddler.

Blixdal had been out of divinity school two years when his parents introduced him to Karen Skalgard, a poor local farm girl, but a remarkable Scandinavian beauty. Marrying Karen would enhance his career they told him. His best opportunity at becoming bishop would be in the unpopulated regions of northern Sweden. He was told to eliminate the large cities of Gothenburg, Malmo, and Stockholm as too competitive. When the opportunity presented itself in Nilstad, Bjorn Blixdal was told to discount the remote vastness of the northern region and concentrate on the fact that Jamtland County did have a bishop's seat.

As for his wife, Karen, the girl was overjoyed at the opportunity to marry the Reverend Blixdal. It meant freedom to leave the wretched life she had suffered on her parents' bleak farm for nineteen years. Her new husband was tall and handsome. He had striking features. His piercing gray eyes however, usually made her nervous, which she dismissed as sexual arousal. She complimented him by saying he reminded her of Rasputin, the wily holy man of Czar Nicholas's court. But the man did genuinely excite her, and she envisioned a family of beautiful children who would be a remarkable combination of the two of them. Most of all, she was prepared to work as hard as she could to live a life filled with the material things her family never had.

Blixdal was a born orator, and he quickly developed an ability to deliver a sermon that riveted the attention of his parishioners. Soon he learned to cultivate favors from the most influential of his community, especially those wealthy families who controlled the huge forest industry surrounding Nilstad. Now, as the man neared his fiftieth birthday, he had nearly attained his goal.

The bishop stopped his drumming at the window, leaned against his desk, and peered directly into Blixdal's face. "When I told you everything has changed, it includes my opinions of the Third Reich. I was wrong about them, and so are you. They no longer have my support."

"Why?" Blixdal asked.

"Many reasons. The recent photographs that were smuggled from Polish concentration camps have exposed the Nazis for what they are."

"As bad as the Bolsheviks?" Blixdal wondered aloud.

"Worse!" Levander said emphatically. "Much worse. I no longer look at the politics of these matters. I simply view them in Christian terms of right and wrong. You and I are powerless to do anything to change the course of those events that are yet to come but"— Levander extended his forefinger and pointed it directly at Blixdal's eyes—"we *can* and we *will* help those Finnish children. I am dedicated to that cause. I want you to swear an oath that you will cooperate."

Bishop Levander had never been more forceful. Tears welled in his eyes. In no uncertain terms he had put Blixdal's future and the reverend's personal relationship with the bishop in jeopardy.

Blixdal definitely was not going to allow his access to the old man's treasure trove elude him so easily. In one year, he would attain his life's ambition of becoming bishop himself and, as a bonus, great wealth. All he had to do was wait.

The reverend had only one response. He took the bishop's hand in his. Bowing his head, he kissed the back of Levander's hand. "On my oath," Blixdal swore.

Chapter Five

The train stood concealed beneath a stand of pine trees, allowing the children a welcome break to play briefly outside. Two days earlier, a warm air mass has moved over the region to melt most of the early season's snow exposing patches of darkened soil. The white cars of the train blended naturally into the background even with their clearly visible Red Cross identification flags. The refugees had traveled six days without incident, and the train engineer was pleased to be on schedule for their arrival at the Swedish border.

The old wood-burning engine stood like an old tired sentinel. It rhythmically coughed a pulsing belch of steam at one-minute intervals from the bare minimum supply of wood being fed into the furnace. With each soft *chug*, the smokestack sent puffs of white vapor skyward to rapidly dissipate into Finland's coastal wilderness. To the west, the blue expanse of the Gulf of Bothnia glimmered in the waning sunlight beyond a shallow stand of birch trees.

Rebecca surveyed the children from her vantage point at the back of the train. Six days earlier, these frightened and confused children felt abandoned. To a person, they believed they were being severely punished for something they did not understand. Yet in less than a week, they had settled into routines and were drawn to the security Rebecca provided.

Children gathered in groups to play quietly near their assigned railcar. Aimo was among the few exceptions, and Rebecca watched him with interest. He spoke with his friend Mooseface, and both boys busied themselves with something they held in their hands. Anna and Pehr stood close looking on. To Aimo's great relief, his sister had replaced him as his cousin's hand-holder. Both younger children were fascinated with the older boys and followed their activity closely.

Aimo and Mooseface had taken their treasured bone-handled knives and whittled industriously on small sections of white birch wood. The knives were among the boys' prized possessions, and they used the sharp blades to deftly chisel the soft wood into recognizable shapes. Even Pehr seemed to take an interest, and in less than five minutes, both boys had completed their projects.

"This is for you, Anna," Mooseface said.

The girl eagerly accepted her gift and held it lovingly, her large blue eyes beaming with delight. Aimo glanced from his work, pleased to see his sister smile happily again.

"A rabbit! Thank you, Mooseface!" She turned her attention to her brother. "What are you making, Aimo? Is it for me?"

"Almost finished," Aimo announced. "I need one more thing." He looked in Pehr's direction, cut a small lock from his cousin's hair, then returned to his project. He sliced a tiny split into the wood and wedged an end of the hair lock into it. Aimo proudly held up his craft for all to see. The likeness of a bushy-tailed dog was remarkably evident. "This is Tark!" Aimo declared.

He handed the sculpted figurine to his cousin. Pehr smiled weakly, his fingers closing tentatively over the wood. He lifted his eyes to speak. A garbled series of unintelligible sounds conveyed the afflicted boy's gratitude; then he returned his attention to the carving and resumed his humming. Aimo and Mooseface regarded each other quizzically, both completely puzzled by Pehr's reaction.

Suddenly Aimo's attention focused on the sounds of a rushing river that lay east of the train out of the boys' sight. In order to find it, Aimo saw he would have to scale a rise of jumbled boulders and moved in that direction with Mooseface at his side. Rebecca noticed the movement at once and called to him in hushed tones.

"Aimo! Where are you two going?"

"I'm just going to look at the river."

"Me too." Mooseface added.

"All right! But come right back. Tell Anna and Pehr to stay with me."

Rebecca knew Aimo's sister and cousin would listen to him before they would take directions from her. Six days of living together had taught the nurse what worked and what did not. Delighted to be unencumbered, Aimo obeyed the request and ordered Anna and Pehr to remain with the nurse. The younger children dutifully joined Rebecca and a group of others at the rear of the train.

A hill of moss-covered boulders formed a challenge to the boys, but they jumped with the grace of mountain goats until reaching the top of the rise.

The rocks below dropped off in a vertical cliff to a gorge carved by a turbulent white-water river cascading noisily among a series of rapids. A flattened, snow-covered area on the opposite side of the river spread away from the banks before merging into a small meadow. Towering above the meadow, a series of granite shelves rose to a high plateau. Aimo loved this wild scene. His home was the wilderness itself and nothing could raise his spirits more than the freedom he felt in this environment.

"Wow! What a place!" Aimo exclaimed. Mooseface nodded a grimy-toothed grin of agreement.

"Great trout water," Aimo continued.

"Maybe not," Mooseface stated mater-of-factly. "We're too close to big water. There's probably a lot of big pike in the pools."

"You know what this reminds me of? That trip we took in my father's boat on the Elf Creek. We almost drowned," Aimo reminisced.

"I thought your father was gonna kill you anyway for rowin' us into the rapids while he was asleep."

Aimo laughed at the memory. They had been fishing on Elf Lake, a small body of water teeming with arctic char. They had started early in the morning, and the fishing had been good; but by midday, the warm sun made everyone drowsy. Aimo's father fell asleep in the quietly bobbing boat while Mooseface held his fishing pole dreamily. Aimo, not fully awake himself, had rowed absently in the quiet afternoon, unaware his course led into a swift outlet that quickly became a white-water river.

His father awakened with a jolt as the rowboat rushed between large boulders. Fearing for their lives, he took the oars away from Aimo, all the while screaming a stream of invectives. Finally he maneuvered the boat into a calm pool. Aimo was prepared to receive the full wrath of the irate man when Mooseface, who had fished through the entire episode, felt a solid strike and reeled in one of the largest perch any of them had ever seen. Aimo's father forgot the unwelcome boat ride and joined the boys in hauling one large perch after the other into the boat.

"Remember when my father smoked the fish?" Aimo asked. "And you ate the ones he was saving?" Aimo laughed uncontrollably with the vivid memory. "And my father chased you with a stick!"

Mooseface's laughter joined Aimo's. "I ran like hell, but he still broke the stick on my back. That made him even madder."

"You looked stupid," Aimo giggled. He pointed a finger at Mooseface and laughed wildly. "He was beatin' you . . . you were runnin' . . . and screamin'."

Aimo rolled onto his back as his friend's extraordinary face caused him to laugh even harder. Turning completely around, Aimo faced upstream in time to see a movement among the granite shelves. He instantly became quiet.

A small herd of caribou descended at a gallop from the ledges above them. Reaching the river bottom, they bolted downstream in front of the wide-eyed boys. Aimo recognized the animals' behavior at once, a frightened herd in full flight. He retraced their retreat, searching for whatever had panicked them. Craning his neck upward, he detected a new movement on an upper ledge high above him. Shielding his eyes with his open palm, he made out the figures of four men. Three were involved with a pipe of some sort while the fourth held a pair of binoculars focusing on the train. Around his arm a red band with a large white circle stood out clearly. Within the circle, Aimo saw the unmistakable swastika.

"*Soldiers,*" Aimo exclaimed under his breath. The thought froze him motionless as Mooseface followed his friend's upward gaze.

The SS officer studied the train through his field glasses. He and his group of three infantrymen were the remnants of an original squad of twenty-five who had escaped a Russian ambush a week earlier. The four men retreated westward toward the Baltic Sea, sneaking through the forest at night with the hope of finding a coastal port where they might find a German ship to take them to safety. The SS troops discovered they no longer could count on Finnish people as allies, having been fired on when they approached a settlement. Destroying a Finish train seemed like a fitting punishment.

The lieutenant allowed his glasses to play over the train, the red crosses on the cars, clearly visible, and unfazed that the passengers were only a group of children. Without turning his head, he gave the command for the mortars to be set at four hundred meters.

In an instant, Aimo jumped down among the boulders, calling out loudly.

"Soldiers! Soldiers!" he shouted while racing toward the train.

Mooseface stumbled behind, his long spindly legs stretching to keep pace with his sprinting friend.

At Aimo's piercing warning, many of the children instinctively turned for the sanctuary of the train; but most stood still, curiously watching the wildly running boys.

"Soldiers! German soldiers!" Aimo called desperately. He spied his sister and cousin Pehr. They were together with Rebecca, all of them standing at the rear of the train. They seemed frozen in place, and he raced in their direction.

Meanwhile, Mooseface reached a group of children being hustled onto the train by the volunteers. Screams of panic had replaced the once-tranquil scene, and the wail of crying children spread over the pristine countryside like a human siren. The slumbering steam engine awakened, belching back to life with puffs of black smoke while the engineer and fireman frantically stoked wood into the furnace. The men knew full well the fate that awaited everyone if they were captured.

Rebecca hurried the children back to the cars, but she was not quick enough to stop Anna. The little girl ran blindly toward her brother when the first mortar struck fifty meters behind the train. The concussion knocked her to the ground, sending her sprawling across the snow in her red outfit. She rolled across the gravel, losing Mooseface's wood carving in the process.

Rebecca and Aimo sprinted to the stricken child and reached her simultaneously. The stunned girl focused on her brother, and she broke into a piercing cry.

"Are you all right?" Rebecca asked anxiously, lifting the girl in her arms.

"She's all right when she's crying," Aimo volunteered.

Rebecca handed Aimo his sister and ordered him to get on the moving train. The boy quickly obeyed, and Rebecca scanned the area one last time. Pehr stood dumbly in the middle of the tracks, pointing the little wooden figurine in the direction of the blast. Rebecca rushed toward him without hesitation just as a second mortar round passed over head. It sailed over the train and into the birch trees beyond, landing in a shattering explosion. A shower of debris rattled over the cars, jolting the children into renewed hysteria.

Rebecca grabbed Pehr with two hands and carried him like a disobedient puppy to the moving train's platform. Pushing him through the railing, she jumped in herself without a moment to spare. The train had gathered speed when the third mortar landed on the tracks in a bright orange cloud thirty meters directly behind them. The concussion violently lifted the rear cabin, spilling everyone inside; then the train settled back onto the track as heated debris pelted the car's exterior. Shaken but unhurt, Aimo crawled forward, pulling Pehr with him.

The noise of shouting, crying children filled the cabin. Aimo managed to guide his cousin through a pool of water from a ruptured water barrel, and he finally reached Anna. She lay on her side next to Rebecca, both of them stunned but otherwise unhurt. No one among them had been seriously injured although Aimo bled freely from both nostrils. Anna spotted Aimo's bloody nose at once, but she had a more pressing question.

"Did you find my rabbit?" She asked.

"I'll make you another one," Aimo promised absently.

"Your nose is bleeding!" Anna sobbed.

Aimo swiped at his nose with his sleeve. "It's OK," he said simply.

Pehr remained quiet during the entire ordeal and had resumed his peculiar humming while still holding his treasured piece of carved wood. Throughout the car, children cried loudly, and Rebecca moved among them to provide as much comfort as she could. Aimo managed to pull himself to a window, offering an unaltered view of the sea, a wide expanse of water greater than any the boy had seen in his life. The shock of the terrifying experience settled over him, and he shook uncontrollably. He clutched Anna tightly in his arms as the day's horrific experience rapidly penetrated his being, and he held his sister with a renewed purpose.

Chapter Six

The Torne River swept swiftly southward, draining the frigid waters of Lapland and serving as the northern boundary between the two countries of Finland and Sweden. Here the land rose into a high bluff, and the river narrowed, forging a deep canyon. At this juncture, a bridge linked the hamlet of Tornio, Finland, with the Swedish community of Haparanda.

This region of the far north, a scattering of tiny settlements seemingly carved from the wilderness, lay less than one hundred kilometers south of the Arctic Circle. Most human sounds were swallowed by the northern vastness, and at 8:00 a.m. in early November, the area remained in total darkness. A light snow fell, sifting downward like confectioner's sugar, presenting a familiar scene to the refugees. The train slowed to a stop in Tornio.

The children strained to see the wonders they were told they would find in Sweden, but only saw a shrouded area of nondiscernible shadows of white on gray. Dutifully, they packed their belongings in their suitcases, secured their identity cards around their necks, and waited.

Aimo was frustrated. Dressing Pehr was a little more difficult because the boy would not release holding his toy dog. Anna, meanwhile, complained because she could still see blood stains on her coat. As for himself, Aimo wore his oversized coat and his cap jammed over his ears. He had given a thought of pinning his father's military medal to his coat but changed his mind, deciding to hide it deep inside his pants pocket instead. Events that were about to occur made him glad he did.

The doors to the train slid open. Finnish soldiers instructed the children to follow them across the bridge leading into Sweden as quickly and quietly as possible. Aimo jumped from the train, and Rebecca handed him Anna, cousin Pehr, and their suitcases. Then the volunteer disappeared into the car. Aimo never again saw the young woman he had grown to admire and respect.

The group trudged through Tornio's knee-deep snow. Soldiers, positioned on either side of the queue, guided them to a bridge where the Finnish flag, a blue cross against a white background, hung limply from high atop a wooden pole. Muffled sounds of other Finnish refugees also escaping into Sweden greeted the children. Horse-drawn sleighs carried families and their belongings while people carried children or personal goods tied to their backs. A girl of fifteen nervously led a small herd of five caribou onto the bridge toward the sanctuary of Sweden.

"Soldiers are coming," she announced to no one in particular.

"Who?" asked one of the volunteers. "German or Russian?"

"Soldiers," she replied simply and followed her herd across the bridge.

The children reached the far side of the river where they were greeted by new soldiers, new volunteers, and a new flag fluttering above them. It bore a yellow cross against a blue background.

Finally after ten days and nights of cruel and grueling travel—where laughter did not exist and conversations could be nothing more than frightened whispers, a trip where each night brought terror-filled dreams and pathetic whimpering from their beds of cold, hard wooden planks—the children of Jyväskylä, Finland, who collectively did not know what they had done to be abandoned by their parents, arrived in Sweden.

Chapter Seven

Dr. Ulf Haraldsson stood at the window of the administration offices of a Swedish military compound recently appropriated from a logging company. He observed the Finnish children trudging through the snowy haze and absently fingered the stethoscope encircling his neck. Gathering his resolve, he sighed heavily in resignation, turned from the window and entered a huge open room.

Hundreds of cots topped with pillows and blankets were meticulously arranged into groups of ten. Glass-encircled electric light bulbs hung from the ceiling, illuminating the room for forty volunteers dressed in white nurse's uniforms bustling busily among the cots. Some of the volunteers busied themselves at a narrow cafeteria that stretched against a far wall.

Dr. Haraldsson entered his clinic through a door marked by a large red cross. His staff of eight nurses—clad in long white smocks, stethoscopes dangling from their necks—greeted the doctor with formal curtsies, then continued their task of preparing solutions for hypodermic injections. The Finnish children were about to enter an environment even more foreign than their ten-day train trip and every bit as frightening. Inoculations against mumps, measles, and tuberculosis were mandatory; and no refugee was allowed entry to Sweden without them. For most of the children, it would be their first look at electric lights, their first visit with a doctor, and their first inoculations.

The staff placed small flashlights, tongue depressors, and oral thermometers in their smock pockets and braced themselves for the anticipated chaos. The children entered the building, and volunteers descended upon them with purposeful efficiency, separating the children by sex. Aimo, however, was determined not to be moved from Anna's side but several equally determined volunteers changed his mind.

"I'm not leaving my sister," he shouted to no avail while being carried away.

Anna cried desperately, but a nurse came to her aid at once, placing her with a group of girls her age. Aimo was unceremoniously deposited with a group of older boys.

A soft female voice over the public address system came from somewhere in the ceiling and subdued the commotion as though a ghostly specter had entered among them. The voice welcomed the startled children to Sweden.

"Everyone is so glad to see you!" the voice announced, and a sprightly recording of a happy children's song erupted loudly from the speakers. The refugees regarded each other curiously. Only a few of them had seen or heard a radio or a Victrola record player. And no one had heard a song as insipid as that which blared from the loudspeakers:

> Now we're walking down the lane, down the lane,
> Now we're walking down the lane and see the happy cows.
> Good morning cows . . . Moo! Moo! Moo!

The children's song continued, adding other farm animal sounds. The refugee children were encouraged to sing along, and the decibel level of the music increased when the children joined in the new game. They sang reluctantly at first, but eventually, they all shouted out their versions of animal sounds. Volunteers meanwhile circulated among the children, removing clothing down to underwear and draping military-issue wool blankets over the children's shoulders. A volunteer discovered that most of the boys carried sharp knives, and once again, the volunteers descended saying it was against the rules to carry knives in Sweden.

The rest of the exercise ran with practiced precision. The voice on the PA informed everyone the lights would be dimmed, and a new game with lots of shouting would be played. Meanwhile, teams of volunteers began escorting groups of children into the clinic, beginning with the older boys.

Aimo stood fifth in his row, thoroughly confused, but emboldened by the military medal he clutched tightly in his fist. The room reeked of the strange odor of isopropyl alcohol; and the uniformed nurses began their examinations of throats, teeth, eyes, and ears. Then, without warning, the boys were jabbed in each arm with hypodermic needles. They yowled in a chorus, but before any could protest, the inoculations were complete.

Mooseface yowled hysterically until comforted by a volunteer. Stroking the boy's head, she recoiled suddenly. She played her flashlight beam into his thickly matted red hair and, near the occipital bone, discovered a large clutch of tiny white eggs.

"Lice!" she shouted in distress, her eyes searching the room for help.

Lice! The word itself swept the compound like an alarm. In the Swedish world of neatness and order, hygiene stood at the top of the list. Lice, that dreaded affliction where little insects built hives of egg clusters on one's hair, represented filth itself and literally made Swedish skin crawl.

Dr. Haraldsson ordered haircuts for all the children while volunteers moved about quickly in the main room gathering clothes. Assistance from the Swedish military garrison in an adjoining building was requested, and nearly two dozen soldiers arrived, prepared to battle the lice. Clothes were collected and taken outdoors to be burned. Meanwhile, the flow of children into Dr. Haraldsson's office continued unabated. Now, in addition to inoculations, hair was cut nearly to the scalp, followed by a tar-soap shampoo. With conveyor-belt efficiency, the children were led to the shower for a tar-soap lathering over their entire bodies, followed by an isopropyl-alcohol head massage.

The din of howling children drowned out the tenacious "happy" music over the PA system, and the well-intentioned plans of Dr. Haraldsson and his staff unraveled before their eyes. For these children, a little insect that enjoyed the ambiance of a head of human hair had succeeded in destroying in moments the exaggerated myths of Sweden they had been told.

By 7:00 p.m., the children and Dr. Haraldsson's staff were exhausted. Games of tag, relay races, and musical chairs, chosen for high physical exertion, had the planned effect. Hypodermic needles, shorn hair, and burned clothing were temporarily forgotten. With a pent-up need to simply run loose and shout after ten days of fearful travel, the children exploded with running, cheering, and noise.

Two-piece grey woolen warm-up uniforms replaced their burned clothes. The uniforms allowed easy movement, created a visual team identity, and provided a comfort to know they were not alone in their misery. At 7:30 p.m., lights were extinguished and banter among the children subsided swiftly. Snuggled beneath flannel blankets on comfortable cots, sleep came quickly to most with few exceptions.

Chapter Eight

Aimo lay on his back, happy to have spared the military medal from his clothes before they were confiscated. He studied the object carefully in the light cast by the weak glow of exit signs over the doors. His thoughts returned to the well-being of his parents. Could they have gone back to Lake Jarvii? Would their home still be there? If the Russians burned their house, where would Anna and he live when they returned?

Anna!

The sudden thought of his sister sent a wave of panic through him. He had not seen her since they arrived. He sat upright and scanned the cavernous room frantically; his sore arms from needle punctures a reminder of what the Swedes had done to him. If this is what Sweden had in store, he wanted no part of it. He put on his newly issued woolen warm-ups, stuffed the military medal into a pocket, and pulled on his boots. Draping the flannel blanket over his shoulders, he moved quietly among the sleeping children in search of his sister.

Dr. Haraldsson sat at his desk in the administration office, sipping his third cup of coffee. He relit his pipe and studied the pile of documents stacked in front of him, grateful to have the help of three of his assistants who stayed with him into the night. The papers had to be completed and signed in triplicate. Each Finnish child was then registered with a record, detailing age, birthmarks or scars, impediments, general health, and any anomaly that had been brought to the doctor's attention. The inoculations and the presence of lice, including the prescribed treatment of the day, were also listed. Dr. Haraldsson estimated the task for his group require three more hours of work. He drew deeply from his pipe and wearily continued the task of filling the many documents.

Sigrid Granade, a particularly large nurse who earlier led the children in exercising, loudly hummed one of the silly children's songs. Dr. Haraldsson shot her a steely glance, nearly demanding she remain quiet, but he thought the better of it. He needed all the help he could get. Unwilling to stifle the noise, the doctor himself joined in the humming of the silly ditty; and soon, two other assistants followed. Productivity within the room rose without anyone's knowledge.

Aimo entered the female section of the cavernous room. A frustrating search among the sleeping girls finally located Anna resting quietly on a cot. He shook her awake, covering her mouth with his hand.

"Ssshhh!" he hissed. "Get dressed. We're going home."

Anna sat up quickly and immediately vented her anger at being mishandled. "I don't like these people, Aimo! They burned my coat. Mama's gonna be mad," she fumed

"I don't like these people either. We're goin' home right now. Hurry and don't make noise."

Anna pulled on her warm-ups and boots as Aimo covered her shoulders with her blanket and led her quietly toward the exit door. Incredibly, they plowed into Mooseface hiding in the shadows, munching a loaf of bread.

"What are you doin' here?" Aimo asked in surprise.

"I was hungry and stole some bread. Where're you goin'?"

"Home!" Aimo hissed. "We're gonna go home."

"How about Pehr?" Mooseface asked.

"He can't come. Something's wrong with him," Aimo said.

"I'm gonna' get my boots and blanket," Mooseface announced. "I'm comin' with you."

Moments later, the small group exited the building and stepped into the dark night. Aimo followed a direction he thought would take them to the Tornio bridge. Once in Finland, he would ask the Finnish soldiers to return them to their home at Lake Jarvii. He led the way through a windless snow of tiny fluttering flakes, tinkling lightly as they fell. He followed the sound made by the rumbling of the Torne River in the distance and moved in that direction. After thirty minutes, the children had not reached the bridge or the river.

"It must be nearby," Mooseface called. "I hear water."

"I don't see houses, Aimo. Remember we saw them?" Anna added helpfully.

"We'll get there soon. We have to walk faster."

Aimo's direction actually led them eastward, away from the bridge. Unknowingly, the group traveled an upward-sloping peninsula that dropped precipitously to the ice-choked Torne River nearly one hundred meters below.

Everything was shrouded in white. Trees, ground, and sky merged into a gray shadowy mass. The children crested the hill, and the sounds of tumultuous water ahead grew much stronger. Aimo discovered a narrow trail that led downward. Luckily, they negotiated the steep, slippery slope to the banks of a fast-flowing, ice-choked river. There was no sign of a bridge, or for that matter, human habitation.

"I'm cold, Aimo," Anna whimpered.

"Me too," Mooseface added.

Aimo realized he had made a dangerous mistake. They were chilled to the bone and shivered miserably in the raw, frosted air. River moisture coated the trees with hoary frost, turning the branches into ethereal, ghostly specters coated in ice. Aimo looked through the grey darkness for shelter. Several unusual white mounds caught his attention. There they discovered three overturned rowboats covered in snow. They kicked at the snow of one of the mounds to create a space, allowing them to scramble under one of the boats. There they sat, hunched on a log in their newfound but refrigerated sanctuary, holding each other tightly for warmth.

The door to Dr. Haraldsson's office flew open and a volunteer rushed in anxiously. "Three children are missing," she said. "We checked everywhere. We found fresh tracks in the snow outside the exit door."

"I need volunteers," Haraldsson demanded.

Four soldiers joined the doctor for the search. Guided by flashlights, they followed the tracks made by the children leading toward the river and the treacherous hill above it. It would be easy to not see the cliff in the snow-filled night and fall to their deaths. Alarmed, Dr. Haraldsson broke into a jog with the soldiers following close behind.

The children huddled in the frosty darkness, cringing as frightening sounds of current-driven ice floes bumped against the bank. Suddenly, a flash of white light swept the area, illuminating a pair of black boots standing at the entryway like two giant smokestacks. Startled, Aimo shook anew in silent terror. Soldiers! But it was Anna who revealed their hiding place. At the sight of the boots, she gave a shriek that surprised Aimo as much as it did the searchers who stood outside.

Dr. Haraldsson and his volunteers anxiously pulled the children from beneath the boat, greatly relieved to find them alive. They covered the freezing children with blankets and carried them back to the military garrison.

"Why did you run away?" Haraldsson asked, trying to keep pace with the fast-striding soldiers.

"We want to go home." Aimo shivered.

The doctor asked nothing more. His main concern now was the children's health since he feared the children might have been exposed to the cold long enough to be frostbitten. When they returned to the compound, Haraldsson was satisfied that all three children were only cold, afraid, and tired. Otherwise they were free of any injury. But the fatigued man spent the rest of the night searching his mind for a new way to gain the trust of these frightened, homeless children that had been entrusted to his care.

All forty volunteers filled Dr. Haraldsson's office the next morning as he read aloud from a newly arrived communiqué confirming the presence of both German and Russian forces in northern Finland. The Haparanda Garrison could expect to receive hundreds of additional refugees and more work than anyone could have imagined.

Dr. Haraldsson looked up from the cablegram in despair. The time was nearly 7:00 AM, and his group of dedicated volunteers showed signs of fatigue. They had a trainload of three hundred children scheduled to leave immediately and would have to deal with new refugees and new challenges later in the day for which they were unprepared.

"One thing we cannot do is hunt for runaway children in the night. How are they?" Dr. Haraldsson asked. "Any evidence of frostbite?"

"No! None!" Sigrid Granade said. "We bathed them and gave them hot chocolate. They're sound asleep."

Dr. Haraldsson nodded his approval. "I've made a decision to tell all the children their parents will join them in six weeks. I know it's a lie, and I wish there were another way, but we don't have time to experiment. We must keep these children as calm and happy as possible. After breakfast, have them ready for the train. I'll make the announcement then."

The aroma of cooking porridge and freshly baked bread reminded Aimo he was very hungry. Pulling on his warm-ups, he retrieved the military medal from his pocket to verify its presence, then returned it to his pocket. *Perhaps it was good luck*, he thought, then realized it was worth much more than that to him. The medal and Anna were all he **had** left of his parents.

Dr. Haraldsson's voice came over the PA system.

"Attention, children. This is Dr. Haraldsson. Welcome to Sweden. You will soon be on a train that will take you to the community of Nilstad where you will stay with new families until the war is over." After a brief pause, the doctor continued, "And now, I have more good news for all of you. Your parents will join you at your new Swedish families in a few weeks."

A chorus of cheers reverberated within the converted gymnasium, drowning out anything more Dr. Haraldsson might have thought to add. Pleased with the reaction to his announcement, the doctor carried on with his other duties.

Aimo joyously embraced his sister, but Anna responded by crying.

"Anna! Shut up!" he said. "Mama and Papa are coming. You're supposed to laugh!"

The girl studied her brother's sincere face. Last night, he had gotten them into trouble with near fatal results. Now her brother's eyes sparkled with promise. It finally dawned on her that she soon would be reunited with her mother and father. She laughed happily.

The children once again bore their suitcases, now considerably lighter from the clothes that were burned, and were led toward Haparanda's train station. A breeze had blown from the north during the night, lifting the clouds and unveiling a sparkling clear, cold day. The glow of morning sunrise painted the southern horizon with golden hues, providing light but not warmth.

Finally, the children were able to see Sweden clearly. It was white to the north and south. To the east stretched the vast unfrozen blue expanse of the Baltic Sea, shimmering with pockets of frozen vapor mist. The greatest geographic change from the region's flatness however, lay to the west where ancient treeless mountains served as Sweden's epic border with Norway.

Aimo stared at the Baltic with awe, unable to see the opposite shoreline. He also had never seen mountains that weren't forested. Sweden certainly was different, but not the way his mother described. The giddy thought of being together with his parents filled the boy with hope. It no longer mattered that he was in Sweden. He had his friend Mooseface, and they had new territory to explore. Filled with those happy thoughts, he took Anna's hand as she took Pehr's hand. The three followed the line of children toward the train.

Haparanda's train station stood as a monument to modern Swedish civilization. Even a remote outpost such as Haparanda was linked by the most advanced and updated technology. Three platforms and several sets of stairs rose upward to meet a large two-story concrete building. Above the tracks, a series of symmetrical metal stanchions, connected by electric cables, stretched southward to the horizon. A magnificent electric-powered train stretched forward with a long series of reddish-brown passenger cars. The very front the cars were attached to a huge locomotive. Bold lettering on either side bore the ancient Viking name *Solveig* (*Sunpath*).

Volunteers herded the children into the clean, heated cars. Sofalike benches, covered in soft red material, ran below large windows, allowing unaltered views of the outside. Electric lights inside ceiling fixtures bathed the interior in a warm, welcome glow.

The children took their seats, happily stashing their suitcases in baskets above the windows. Joking, laughing, and hope for the future replaced the chaos of their exodus from Jyväskylä eleven days earlier. They were going to live in modern homes, with lots of food and caring families. More importantly, there was no war; and best of all, they soon would be reunited with their parents.

Aimo led his small group to the last sofa in the end car and stood on his seat to place the suitcases in the overhead basket. A volunteer saw the transgression and, using Aimo as an example, told all the children that in Sweden, everyone removed their boots before they entered a house; and never, ever, stand on the sofa unless in bare feet. Thus began the Finnish refugee children's introduction of Sweden as a place of muscle-bound rules and regulations.

The train lurched forward, gained speed swiftly, and moved smoothly toward the south. The engine sounded a long whistle of good-bye to Haparanda and began its journey toward the glow on the southern horizon. Gliding up a steep grade, it offered a vast view of the entire area from the summit.

Aimo looked behind him as the community of Haparanda grew smaller. Beyond the village and across the Finnish border marked by the Torne River, multiple fires spotted the landscape. War had come to all of Finland.

Chapter Nine

Karen Blixdal stood on the cold platform of Nilstad's train station craning her neck for some sign of the expected refugee train. She nervously buried her clenched fists deep within her ankle-length fur coat and flexed her toes in her fleece-lined boots to lessen the chill.

Her husband, the Reverend Bjorn Blixdal, stood by her side, gazing expectantly at the vacant tracks emerging from the forest half a kilometer away. He was chilled to the bone and needed to urinate but was unwilling to return to the throngs of community members waiting within the station and their inane questions about refugee children. There was another situation he had to worry over, however; and he cast a furtive glance at his wife, Karen. He prayed her tendency to make difficult promises hadn't created a serious problem for them today. He had prayed in vain.

This time, his wife had guaranteed their influential friends a first choice of refugee children by using his high rank in the church as a pledge. The two ladies sharing the platform with them, Fru Tornquist and Fru Falke, matriarchs of Nilstad's most prominent families, gave generously to the state-run Lutheran Church. If all went well, Blixdal would be their bishop in less than a year, and the offer to the women for a favored opportunity to choose the "two cutest girls on the train" secured their support of him as if it were written in stone. Provided of course, he did not wet his pants. He leaned toward his wife.

"Karen! I'm cold! Where the hell is the train?" he whispered.

The woman attempted an answer but stuttered instead. She learned long ago how important it was to please her husband of twenty-eight years as well as to obey him dutifully. She most certainly did not want to disappoint him now at this critical time in his career.

Her husband did not physically abuse her. In fact, he did nothing at all physical with her. They had not had sex together in years—he went elsewhere for that—and Karen's occupation with church community affairs kept her desires in denial. Her greatest fear was losing the prominent status she held in the community as the pastor's wife and, God willing, the soon-to-be bishop's wife. Divorce was not an option because the thought of returning to a hard-scrabble life on her parent's impoverished farm was a sentence she dared not to consider.

What Karen Blixdal did not fully comprehend was that her husband was equally dependent on her. A divorce from his very popular wife would end any chance of his becoming bishop and probably cost him his high position as head of Nilstad's church. So they each accepted their marriage of symbiotic convenience, and neither seemed to fully understand the control each held over the other.

There was another side to the clergyman that his wife actually did fear, his haunting eyes. Set deep within the pockmarked skin of his cheekbones, she had found them fascinating at first but soon learned they were devoid of human warmth. Instead, they burned with a self-righteous glow that controlled, judged, and condemned; and his eyes sent shivers through her body. She avoided contact with them always.

"Karen! I'm so cold I'm going to piss my pants," he hissed.

She kept her gaze on the railroad tracks and spoke rapidly, "Go inside, Bjorn. The train will be here soon." The woman's voice always rose several notches when excited, and now she nearly spoke in falsetto.

"When does the Reverend Blixdal think I should take my girl for christening? I certainly don't want a heathen child in my home."

The voice was that of Fru Tornquist, a tall, well-fed woman of forty. She and her dearest friend, Fru Falke, did everything together, including selecting wardrobes. Their long hair, coiffured in beautifully combed French twists, and held perfectly in place with elaborate, whalebone barrettes, complimented their outfits of Europe's latest fashions, making the emphatic statement that these were women of wealth.

The reverend regarded the woman curiously. The train had not even arrived, and here was Fru Tornquist, worrying over a heathen Finnish child they had not yet seen. His instinct was to lecture both of these irritating ladies as to why he disliked the Finns generally and why he particularly opposed Sweden's magnanimous invitation to receive their children in the first place. As far as he was concerned, the whole damn country of Finland consisted of heathens. But that is not what he told Fru Tornquist.

"They are Lutheran generally, Fru Tornquist. I'll want to see all of them . . . at catechism . . . eventually."

"What do you think Finnish children eat?" Fru Falke asked, not wanting to be excluded from an opportunity to speak to the minister. Blixdal pressed a fist to his temple and cast his wife a riveting look.

"Bjorn thinks they only eat wild game," Karen Blixdal added, avoiding her husband's stare. "But I—"

The shrill whistle of an approaching train instantly ended the meaningless conversation. A sleek electric locomotive emerged from the forest amid billows of swirling snow and glided toward the platform, sending out a series of piercing signals. Karen adjusted her coat, then nervously ran her fingers through a tangle of thick, wavy blond hair. She wanted to say something clever, but as the train approached, she was so overcome with anticipation she remained uncharacteristically silent. The huge engine came to a stop, and Karen swiftly led her procession into the first passenger car. The reverend followed close behind.

The scene before them was shocking. Fifty gawking children, dressed in warm-up uniforms and sporting shorn haircuts, looked like a group from an impoverished gymnastic camp. The children stared silently at the newcomers with large frightened eyes. There were no smiles, no endearing features such as flowing locks with sweet hair bows to set any of the children apart. They all appeared to be small, mute people.

"This must be the car for the . . . uh . . . unfortunates," Karen improvised. She led the way, hopefully, to the second car only to be greeted with a similar scene. She continued through the train, frantically yanking doors open, then rushing past startled children, completely dissatisfied. By the time she reached the last of the passenger cars, the woman was in a panic. There had to be two winsome girls somewhere on this train. She said a quick, silent prayer before pulling the last door open.

She entered the car then braked to a stop, her jaw dropping toward her chest. She stood in stunned silence, gawking upon the remarkable countenance of Mooseface, one of the ugliest human faces she had ever seen.

Although ugly, Mooseface was a happy-go-lucky type. A wide Cheshire cat smile beneath his enormous nose displayed the most disgusting set of yellow green teeth imaginable. Karen rushed past him to the center of the car and searched with desperate frenzy, feeling as though the walls of her world were crumbling around her. At first glance, there did seem to be a number of very young children, and her heart surged with hope. She moved through the car, her eyes sweeping from side to side, when the voice of Fru Falke rang out behind her.

"Oh! Karen! Look, how cute."

Fru Falke lifted a girl of three into her arms who had somehow escaped Karen's hurried scrutiny. Overwhelmed by her good fortune, the woman read the child's identity card out loud,

"Kasia Lillselet! She's adorable, don't you think?"

The little girl allowed herself to be picked up, but retained the firm grip of her twin sister's hand. Fru Tornquist went to her friend's aid and raised the other child in her arms. Neither of the frightened girls made the slightest noise. Instead, they both simply stared at the faces of the women who held them.

Fru Tornquist read the identity card. "Kisuri Lillselet," she trumpeted triumphantly. "We have sisters!" The women beamed proudly at one another.

Karen Blixdal exhaled loudly. She was greatly relieved and had every reason to be overjoyed. She should have left then and there, but fate had another plan. A child's humming voice, coming from somewhere in the rear, caught her attention. Her curiosity piqued, she decided to walk to the end of the car.

"Let's go, Karen!" her husband whispered over her shoulder,

"I just want to see the rest," she said, continuing her walk.

"We're not choosing kittens," he hissed impatiently.

But Karen was not to be denied. Childless against her wishes, she was drawn to three children grouped together at the very rear of the car, two boys and a girl. One of the boys hummed melodically, and his head swayed. She studied Pehr curiously until her eyes fell upon Anna. The woman uttered a gasp of approval. She moved to pick up the little girl who cowered in Aimo's arms. Unfortunately, she did not notice the boy viewed the woman's approach with a guard dog's glare.

"Look at this adorable child!" Karen shouted.

She placed her hands on Anna's waist in order to lift her up, and Aimo exploded. He leaped from the bench and pushed the startled woman roughly backward. Reverend Blixdal closed the distance to the stricken women in two giant strides and slapped Aimo hard across his face. The boy sailed backward onto the backrest, stunned by the blow. Anna's piercing scream brought a recoiling retreat from the Blixdals, and a volunteer came to the girl's aid.

The reverend backed away from the boy, his pale gray eyes glowering. "Heathen bastard!" he sneered, then turned and followed the women who, except for Karen, triumphantly carried their prizes.

Chapter Ten

The interior of Nilstad's train station teemed with throngs of milling people. Many had taken their own children with them to help select a refugee child. Dozens of notebook-carrying volunteers circulated among the community's citizenry, collecting names and addresses, checking the forms each family had filled, then fetching the child they had selected. A significant agreed-upon rule was to keep siblings together in the same family. So far, the selection process was going well.

Aimo, Anna, and Pehr were the last to leave the train, joining a stream of children being herded into a large circle in the center of the station's main room. The children pressed against each other like a school of frightened baitfish, overwhelmed by the number of people surrounding them. Anna clung to her brother, sobbing pathetically.

Constable Sten Vahleen stood out handsomely from the crowd. White gloves, white cap, and white epaulettes accentuated his official dark blue uniform. He stood tall with an athletic build and shook his head in dismay at the pathetic sight of the Finnish children. Next to him, his wife, Gretha, followed the proceedings with a wide-eyed stare. A nurse by profession and the mother of two small girls herself, she anguished over the terrible decisions these children's parents must have made. *How heartbreaking for all of them*, she thought. Then she spied Anna.

"Look at that poor child, Sten. She looks like our little Lisa. She's so frightened."

Gretha moved into the group of Finnish children and crouched in front of the crying girl. She placed a hand on Aimo's shoulder and another against Anna's face. Gretha smiled warmly.

"Please don't cry. You're too pretty to be so sad."

The woman's touch reduced Anna's crying to intermittent sobs. She raised a little fist to rub her tears away, and Gretha stepped forward to lift her. Once again, Aimo was quick to come to his sister's defense.

"No!" he shouted, shoving Gretha with both hands and sending her skidding on her rump onto the floor.

Gretha sat on the cold tile, embarrassed and surprised. The crowd of families looked on in silent disbelief, but Gretha remained calm. From her seat on the floor, she extended her hands and beckoned for the little girl to come to her.

"Come," she said coaxingly. "Come to me."

Slowly the girl responded, stepping tentatively away from her brother and into Gretha's arms. That was more than Aimo could bear. He moved angrily toward his sister again, intent on pulling her away, but was stopped cold by the grip of a powerful hand on his shoulder. Aimo twisted wildly to see who had hold of him, and he recognized the tall black form of the reverend.

"It's time somebody took care of a troublemaker like you. I'm going to teach you some manners," the clergyman threatened. He kept the boy in his viselike grip, his fingers like steel clamps on the boy's clavicle. The large group of onlookers gave the reverend a wide berth, but Constable Vahleen stepped forward and pulled Blixdal to a stop. Vahleen read the identification tag that hung from the boy's neck and looked at the reverend in the eye with a cold stare.

"We're taking the girl, Reverend. We'll take the boy as well. He's her brother. We'll keep them together," Vahleen told him.

Karen moved swiftly through the crowd and confronted her husband.

"Wait, Bjorn! We have no children of our own. This boy needs more than a good home. He needs a father figure like you."

Reverend Blixdal stood still, stunned by the message his wife had just delivered in front of his parish. Blixdal's arm was still held by the constable, and the reverend kept his grip on Aimo's shoulder. He gave the boy a long look and did not like what he saw. He especially disliked this little heathen, and he studied his wife's face for some sign she might not be serious. Instead, she smiled approvingly at the crowd.

"I think the constable's home is better suited for children," the reverend declared, releasing his grip of the boy. Karen stepped forward and took Aimo by the hand. She stared at the boy's face.

"Think of the good he can learn from you. Think of the love we can give him, Bjorn." She turned her attention to the constable, and Vahleen released his hold of the clergyman. Karen Blixdal turned to the crowd. They had become her audience, and she played to it. She continued with her plea to her husband. "A child in our home and in our church. It's as though God intended it."

Karen had given up on the idea of children early in her marriage. She remembered too well the misery of sharing her childhood with eight siblings where hunger and cold were her most lasting memories. Over the years, the sight of a newborn child, so wonderfully close to its mother, would always awaken a sense that a vital part of her life was missing; but her husband did not agree. Now the idea of bringing her own child home seemed like a life-fulfilling plan, especially now that she said it out loud. She maintained her hold of Aimo's hand and proudly walked him through the crowd of applauding onlookers.

Aimo turned once before being led through the door and saw Anna in Gretha Vahleen's arms. He was painfully aware that he had broken his promise to his mother to stay together, but felt powerless to protest any further. There was no one in the room to whom he could turn for help anyway, and he allowed himself to be led away.

The once-crowded train station lay nearly empty. A sharp contrast to the activity from an hour and a half earlier when it teemed with excited people brought together by the vicissitudes of war. Only a handful of volunteers circulated among nine remaining Finnish children, yet the drama within the quiet station was intense as it had been when the refugee train first arrived.

The volunteers knew the final destination of these unchosen few would be Nilstad's orphanage, an isolated area on the outskirts of town. Fröken Elsa, a sour spinster in her late forties, lived alone, serving as both director and staff in a large Victorian-style house that had become the orphanage.

Elsa's sharp Scandinavian features, a well-angled face held high on a long slender neck, were well postured upon a full-figured frame. She was potentially attractive but brusque and unfriendly. Disdaining small talk with the townsfolk, she drove to Nilstad in her small blue-and-yellow-painted orphanage bus whose ominous appearance was a chilling apparition to young and old alike. She shopped at the general store for rudimentary items then quickly left. Word around Nilstad was that the unsmiling Elsa would have been better suited as a mortician than the orphanage director.

The nine unchosen children remained clustered in a corner of the nearly empty room. Only Mooseface and Pehr seemed unaware they had been passed over by the families that surrounded them moments before. Pehr sat dumbly on his suitcase, humming at the wooden dog held firmly in his hand.

Mooseface, however, had been the recipient of an unexpected windfall. When the Swedish families circulated among the refugees, choosing those they wished to bring into their homes, a neatly dressed girl of seven stood transfixed, staring at Mooseface in awe, the boy's shaved head accentuating his remarkable nose. Mooseface had flashed a wide-mouthed grin, displaying his terribly stained teeth. The girl stared quietly as though she were at a zoo viewing some exotic animal from a distant land. She absently reached into a small white paper bag and plucked out a large chocolate-coated wafer, which she nibbled delicately. Mooseface followed every move wordlessly until the girl got the message that perhaps the boy might enjoy one of her delicacies.

She politely offered the bag to the big-nosed boy, identifying the contents as "mums mums." She expected him to take only one. Mooseface, on the other hand, was not quite so civilized. He accepted the entire bag and its contents as his own and grinned broadly. Not knowing what to do and totally embarrassed, the girl backed away silently into the crowd as Mooseface stuffed one of the tasty chocolates into his mouth. He groaned in delight having never sampled anything more delicious in his life. He plucked another chocolate from the bag for Pehr.

"Mums mums," Mooseface said, placing a chocolate wafer into Pehr's mouth. The boy stopped his humming, chewed the tasty morsel, and smiled for only the second time since leaving Jyväskylä.

Fröken Elsa entered the station carrying a leather briefcase. She presented herself to the volunteers and, after an exchange of documents, stepped over to the huddled children. She studied each of them carefully taking particular notice of Mooseface who had just placed another mums mums into Pehr's mouth. She approached the large-nosed boy and read the identity card that hung around his neck surprised to see but one name listed.

"Jounnii? Don't you have a family name?" Elsa asked

"Mooseface!" the boy replied.

"Jounnii *Mooseface*? That's your name?" she asked in disbelief.

The boy nodded his head as Elsa circled around him. She shook her head in amazement. "I can see why they call you Mooseface. What do you have in your hand?"

Mooseface innocently displayed the bag of chocolates to the woman but was not prepared for her actions. She snatched the bag, stuffed it into her coat pocket, and addressed the group of intimidated children.

"There is no eating or talking until I give permission. Is that understood?" The children remained silent except for Pehr whose humming continued. Elsa turned her attention to the boy still seated on his suitcase in the now-quiet waiting room.

"Stop making that noise," Elsa commanded. She gave the boy a moment to obey her directive, but Pehr continued unabated. She made a mental note to deal with him later, then addressed the unfortunate group of children.

"Get your things and follow me. Remember, no talking."

It was only a brief moment with Fröken Elsa, but the children already knew of their misfortune. Frightened, they followed the stern woman out of the station without a sound.

Magnus Olofsson stood outside the general store, loading provisions onto his flatbed Model B Ford. He followed the procession of refugee children moving past him under the threatening eye of Fröken Elsa. Lifting a brown-bagged bottle of home-brewed aquavit to his lips, he took a slug and smiled.

"Hey, Elsa," he called. "C'mon over and have a drink."

The woman shot a steely glance at the old man, recognizing him as the town drunk who lived on a farm near Lake Valdemaren. But there was another side to the old man that most did not know, including Elsa.

Olofsson was seventy one, string-bean tall, wiry, and tough. His cheery eyes described his happy, gregarious nature, and the man acted shamelessly. He said what he wanted, drank too much, and shared one idiosyncrasy with Elsa; they each lived alone by choice. Otherwise, the two could not have been more opposite. When sober, Olofsson was a warm and generous man. With his full white beard and white hair, he was a favorite to play the role of the Jul Tomten at Christmas.

"OK! If you don't want a drink for free, give me one of your kids," Olofsson joked.

"You old hermit! You're too unfit to have a wife or children," Elsa spat back.

"And how about you, dearie? When was the last time you got married?" Olofsson answered.

The insult struck a sensitive cord on the woman. She huffed haughtily, climbed aboard the bus, and made certain to avoid the old man's stare. She started the engine then turned to the children.

"I want all of you to sit still and remain quiet. Pehr! The boy making the noise! If you don't shut up, I'll wash your mouth with soap," she fumed. She regarded the boy in the rearview mirror whose humming continued unabated. "We'll put an end to this soon enough," she said to no one in particular then drove off.

Olofsson shook his head sadly as the bus pulled away. "Poor kids," he muttered, then climbed into his truck and drove slowly in the direction of his farm.

Sten Vahleen drove the official police car, carrying his wife and Anna onto the snow-covered lane leading to his home. They passed beneath rim-frost-coated limbs of symmetrically planted apple trees in the direction of the welcoming, warm yellow lights of the Vahleen house. Anna sat quietly on Gretha's lap, sucking her thumb, and perked up when the car came to a stop.

The Vahleen's two daughters, ten-year-old Meggan and six-year-old Lisa, bounded out of the house. Meggan opened her mother's door, smiling excitedly, but Lisa chose to remain on the porch.

"Anna! This is my daughter, Meggan," Gretha said.

"Hello," Meggan offered politely. "Welcome to Sweden."

The family entered their home with Anna in tow. The Finnish girl gazed wide eyed as the Vahleen family, with the precision of a drill team, removed their boots; stepped into wooden clogs; and meticulously hung caps, gloves, and coats on clothes racks hidden behind a curtain-shielded space beneath a flight of steps. Lisa stood next to her sister and stared curiously at their new visitor. Anna returned the stare.

The Vahleen girls were dressed identically in warm, colorful jumper-style dresses. Their straight shoulder-length blond hair sported large pastel pink bows, Meggan's on the right side and Lisa's on the left. Except for the difference in their height, they appeared like balanced bookends as they stood together.

"Who is she?" Lisa asked.

"This is Anna. She is a Finnish girl who is going to stay with us for a little while," Gretha answered gently. "You can pretend she's like a new sister."

"I want a dog instead," Lisa said and ran up the stairs to her room. Gretha turned her attention to her oldest daughter.

"Meggan, I want you to be her big sister. It's been a very difficult trip for all of the children who arrived here today." Meggan's attention focused on the little girl's shorn locks, and Gretha quickly added, "Anna might be embarrassed because her hair has been cut so short."

"I'll be right back," Meggan said.

She bounded up the stairs and returned moments later with an adorable white rabbit-fur bonnet. She presented the soft, cuddly cap to Anna who bashfully buried her face against Gretha's stomach. Undismayed, Meggan pressed ahead with the offering. "Look," she said, placing the white cap on her own head. Anna risked a peek.

The older girl seemed genuinely friendly, and the white cap did look pretty. Anna allowed the girl to remove her gray bonnet, and Meggan replaced it with the rabbit-fur cap, sliding it easily over her short-cropped hair. She led Anna to a large full-length mirror in the hallway, and a smile of approval spread across the little girl's face.

"Let me show you our room," Meggan said and led the Finnish girl up the stairs under the pleased look of both her parents.

Chapter Eleven

Aimo cringed uncomfortably in the backseat of Blixdal's black car, massaging his shoulder where the clergyman had pinched him. He shot a malicious glance at the back of Blixdal's head, silently promising himself that someday, he would make the brutish man pay for his abuse. For the moment, the boy listened to Fru Blixdal's incessant high-pitched banter and slouched into the farthest corner of the seat to avoid the sickening odor of her eau de cologne.

Karen knew all the homes of Nilstad's important people and directed the boy's attention to each one as they drove past. She called out the family's name, the father's job, the number of children, and little stories that Karen felt made the families special. Aimo was not listening. He was far more interested in their route instead, paying close attention of the landscape to remember identifiable landmarks as they passed. He already had concluded he was not going to stay with these peculiar people any longer than he had to.

They traveled westward, the neat, orderly community of Nilstad giving way to a dense coniferous forest. The road crested a hill overlooking the large lake of Valdmaren, and Blilxdal's church came into view, strategically situated on a bluff with a panoramic view of the surrounding valley. A tall conical bell tower of intricate handcrafted design, resembling overlaid fish scales, poked thirty meters upward. Next to it stood the church itself, a large steep-roofed building. Immediately adjacent to it was a two-story, somewhat foreboding, stone building serving as the reverend's family's living quarters.

Aimo's attention turned to a headstone-littered churchyard sloping downward to a large wooden boathouse at Lake Valdemaren's shoreline.

"What's that?" Aimo asked, pointing at the mortuary.

"Your home," Fru Blixdal exclaimed excitedly. She had not looked to where Aimo was pointing. The car came to a stop, and Karen jumped out, pulling Aimo with her.

"How do you pronounce your name?" she asked.

Aimo's silence immediately brought the black figure of the reverend to loom over him. Blixdal laid a huge hand on the boy's shoulder but, this time, did not squeeze.

"When Fru Blixdal speaks, you answer immediately, do you understand?" Aimo nodded his head yes then felt the grip tighten on his shoulder.

"Damn you, boy! Speak! Use that forked tongue of yours and tell Fru Blixdal your name."

"Aimo!" he squawked then squealed in pain. Karen immediately came to his defense. She removed her husband's hand from the boy's shoulder and led Aimo into the building. As they crossed the threshold of the church, Karen felt a warm flush coursing through her body. She looked down at the boy, his hand in hers, and decided right then and there Aimo was her biological child. There was no need for conception or pregnancy. Nor was there a need for the risk of a difficult delivery. In light speed, she had a child of her own and was overwhelmed beyond reason.

"We're going to make a few changes. A boy like you should have a name like . . . oh, perhaps . . . *Mikael!* I like that, don't you? *Mikael!* That's your new name, and this is your new home."

Aimo offered no protest. Everything was overwhelming, especially the interior of a church, a sight he never before experienced. Everything about it appeared mysterious and frightening.

Small red-glassed kerosene lamps hung from wall posts on ledges and nooks, providing the only source of illumination in the huge room. Large frescoes of stern-faced men scowled from the walls while equally stern-faced statues of men stood on alabaster pedestals. Aimo stared at the sights with wide-eyed fascination, terrified at having entered the most frightening place he had ever seen.

Karen led the boy down the aisle toward a small platform in front of the pews, their footsteps echoing eerily on the stone floor. They arrived at a door, which Karen opened dramatically, and they entered the building's living quarters. Karen's voice went up an octave, and she pirouetted in stocking feet on the wooden floor.

"This is where you always take off your shoes, Mikael. Use my clogs now, and I'll get you your own pair tomorrow."

She led him up a wide wooden stairway to the second floor and beyond a bathroom, which, at Aimo's quick glance, was a sharp contrast to the outhouses in his village. Finally they arrived at a guest room in a far corner of the house.

"I'm so happy you're with us! I've always wanted a little boy of my own. This will be your own room, and tomorrow we'll buy you new clothes. Well, Mikael, what do you think?"

Aimo crossed to a window and peered curiously outside at the dark, snow-covered scene. He avoided eye contact with the woman but understood she meant well. The reverend was another matter, and Aimo concluded he wanted to stay away from her husband at all costs. The boy remembered Dr. Haraldsson's promise that his parents would be joining them in Sweden in a few weeks. Aimo concluded that he could live with that and decided to obey the Blixdals' instructions. He did not know exactly where Anna was but remembered clearly who had taken her. He hoped his parents would understand he had done all that he could to keep his little sister with him.

The boy studied the lights of Nilstad, winking in the dark night, then turned to the woman and replied, "Thank you, Fru Blixdal."

Karen was overjoyed. She rushed to Aimo and embraced him generously, kissing the top of his head repeatedly.

"Oh! Mikael! You've made me so happy. I want you to call me *mother* from now on."

Aimo stuttered, unable to express his surprise at this new and outrageous demand. She moved closer to the boy and kissed the top of his head. The smell of tar and taste of isopropyl assaulted her nose and lips. She swiftly led him directly to the bathroom with a string of nonstop sentences.

"You poor thing! We're going to give you a bath right away. You haven't had a chance to clean up. You're probably starved."

The woman worked as she spoke, filling the tub with hot water, and adding generous amounts of scented granules to the steaming, bubbly liquid. Then she quickly began to undress him. Once again, Aimo tried to protest, but Karen was not to be denied. Soon she had the boy stark naked and sat him in the tub. She proceeded to wash him vigorously with a sponge from the head down. The warm water felt incredibly wonderful. In fact, the entire experience was definitely different from the galvanized tub and semiheated water from the fireplace he and Anna bathed in back home. Here, Aimo marveled, the Swedes did not even have to heat the water. It came directly from the wall!

The woman stood Aimo in the tub and continued her washing. She reached the boy's genitals and lathered purposefully. Unexpectedly, she realized she was enjoying the task in a way she shouldn't.

She allowed her eyes to look up at his face, seeking his approval, and she smiled warmly.

Chapter Twelve

Nilstad's orphanage stood at the side of a once-active paved road leading west to the Norwegian border. The picturesque highway rose gently toward the mountains of western Sweden and the ski resort of Storlien at the Norwegian border. Normally, the road was well traveled between the two neighboring countries, but German occupation of Norway brought regular travel to an end. As a result, Fröken Elsa's Victorian house stood isolated from any neighbors.

Elsa steered the bus down a sloping, snow-covered drive leading from the main road and parked in front of the unfriendly building. She searched for Pehr in the rearview mirror and found the boy sitting by himself, eyes shut and humming. The incessant noise had grown louder and became more irritating with every passing minute. Now, after the fifteen minute drive from town, she was annoyed almost beyond control.

Uttering an oath to herself, she called sharply for the children to follow her, leading them into a large glass-enclosed verandah. A row of wooden pegs stretched above an elevated boot rack against one wall.

"Always hang outdoor things here. Neatly! Never come into this house with boots or shoes on. Do you understand?"

Except for Pehr, the children nodded they understood, too afraid to utter a word of protest.

"Follow me," she told them and led the way up a flight of stairs to a second-floor landing.

A series of closed doors led to side-by-side bathrooms at the top of the stairs. On either side of the staircase, two large rooms had been converted to dormitories. Elsa led Pehr to the top of the stairs, directing the remaining children to the two rooms, girls on the left, boys to the right. She carefully observed the children like a predatory animal studying its prey. She watched with savage interest, both to see that her directions were followed and to identify potential problem children for special handling. All the while she held Pehr in her grasp.

"Take a cot, fix your beds, and arrange your clothes. Close the doors and no talking."

The children moved quietly as directed. Elsa turned her full attention to Pehr. The boy was idiotically humming at a piece of wood he held in front of his face. Had there been another sound in the house other than the monotonous ticking of an ancient grandfather clock, Pehr's humming would not have been audible. Now Fröken Elsa could take no more of it.

"Can't you understand me? When I tell you to be quiet, you be quiet! Is that understood?" Elsa glowered at the boy. She took him by both shoulders and shook hard. "Do you understand me?" she demanded.

Pehr clenched his teeth in an effort to form words but offered only what appeared as a toothy grin. He opened his eyes wide and pulled back his lips as the woman continued to shake him; then he raised the wood carving and spoke for the first time since the incident at Lake Jarvii.

"Tark!" he garbled.

Elsa slapped the piece of wood to the floor, breaking the fragile figurine in two pieces. She yanked the boy into a bathroom behind her, placed Pehr in front of a sink, then shoved a bar of soap into his mouth.

"You *will* obey me, damn you. Try to sing now!"

Pehr fought to push the woman's hand away, gagging as foam frothed over his lips and onto his shirt. Then he began to vomit. The woman shoved his head down into the sink bowl, and Pehr moaned in an agonizing wail.

"No!" he cried.

"Good!" Elsa said. "You're beginning to understand."

The door to the bathroom burst open, and Mooseface charged in, his shoulders squared and his head low. He plowed into the woman like a battering ram, burying his nearly bald head into Elsa's abdomen. The blow sent them both crashing into a wall.

"Leave him alone!" Mooseface shouted.

Mooseface realized his mistake immediately. Fröken Elsa was far too strong for him. The shocked woman swiftly regained her senses and brought the skinny boy quickly under control. She turned his back flush against her chest, then clamped an arm around the boy's throat and tightened.

Mooseface squirmed, desperately gasping for breath. The large woman dragged him into the hallway and down the steps to the first floor. She flung him through an open door, sending him tumbling downward over a short flight of wooden steps. He landed hard on the earthen floor of the dark cellar.

He lay on the dank soil, catching his breath, too stunned to cry out, and heard the door above him being locked shut.

He followed the woman's heavy steps from within the chilled blackness of Fröken Elsa's cellar as they pounded their way up the stairs to the second floor. Mooseface crawled to a potato bin and covered himself with a stack of potato sacks. He clenched his fists, wincing in pain from his many bruises. Fröken Elsa had made an enemy, and the boy swore he would find a way to get vengeance.

Chapter Thirteen

Lisa's favorite fairy tale was "Lille Basse," a children's story describing the adventures of a troll princess in the forest and begged for it to be read nightly. She lay next to her father, an arm familiarly draped over him, listening intently while enjoying her new position in bed. She had demanded to be separated from Anna, which placed Meggan between them. Now she slept closest to the wall on the bed the three girls shared.

Everyone seemed happy, including Anna, who still wore her rabbit fur hat. She remembered her mother promising that Swedish people would be kind. The promise appeared to have come true. She felt secure in the soft, warm bed with her new "sisters" with a sense of security she had not experienced in weeks.

Sten finished the story and kissed each of the girls good night on their foreheads. He walked to a set of glass-paned double doors leading to an outdoor balcony and blew his breath on the glass. The vapors slowly formed into feathery ice crystals, forecasting another cold night. He would have to put an extra coal brick in the furnace.

"Don't close the door," Lisa said to her father as he left the room. Sten allowed the door to remain ajar.

"Do you believe in trolls, Anna?" Meggan asked.

"What's a troll?" Anna asked.

"They're little people who live in the forest," Meggan answered. "They have homes made of moss and live under the boulders. They are friends of the animals and can even talk to them."

Anna was captivated. "What do they say?"

"Secrets! They tell secrets about the forest. Papa says he talks to them all the time," Meggan replied. "Do you have trolls in Finland?"

The Finnish girl gave the question her deepest thought. She never before had seen a child's fairy-tale book. The only stories she could remember were frightening tales of wolves that supposedly skulked in the shadows near her village waiting to snatch naughty children. "I don't think we have trolls. What do they look like?" she asked.

"They look old, have wrinkled skin, and wear animal skins for clothes." Lisa added. "Papa's going to show them to me the next time we go into the forest."

"Skins like my furry hat?" Anna asked innocently.

"Yes!" Lisa answered. "You look exactly like a troll," she giggled.

"I'm not a troll!" Anna shouted.

Meggan decided to bring her sister's hostility to an end. "Remember the story about the troll princess? She was very beautiful. You can be the princess," Meggan told Anna.

"I want to be the princess," Lisa protested.

"You can if you're nice," Meggan added with finality. "Now be nice and go to sleep, or we'll all wake up ugly."

Sten yawned loudly entering the kitchen. A sink full of Anna's soaking clothes filled the room with steam, and a large iron pot, gurgling with boiling water on the electric range, added to the billowing moisture. Sten poured himself a cup of coffee from a freshly made pot and heard Gretha moving about in the cellar. He walked down the steps to join her.

The cellar was partitioned into four fully functional rooms: a coal bin where firewood was also stored; a larder room with three hatch-covered potato bins on one side and neatly spaced shelves of fruit and vegetable preserves on the other; a third room used to store outdoor furniture, toys, and winter items, such as skis, poles, snowshoes, and sleighs.

Gretha stood in the fourth and largest room, surrounded by the most modern of electric appliances. Sten entered finding his wife hanging clothes on lines that stretched from wall to wall above a mangle, an ironing board, and a brand new Huskvarna washing machine.

"What are you cooking upstairs?" Sten asked.

"Water," she answered, continuing her chore. "Go up please, turn off the stove, and pour the water on the clothes in the sink."

"Why?" Sten asked curiously.

"The girl's clothes are filthy. They haven't been washed in weeks."

Sten was puzzled. "Why not use your new washing machine?"

"I'm not going to put filthy clothes in a new washing machine," she said emphatically. "Now please, just do as I ask."

Thoroughly baffled, Sten turned and climbed the steps. "Are you coming up soon?" He knew the answer but thought he would ask anyway.

"As soon as I'm finished. Then I can sit down and have some coffee with you."

Sten knew his wife well, and he treasured her dearly. They would soon celebrate their fifteenth anniversary, and he learned long ago that Gretha was a workaholic. There always were chores to do, and she rarely gave herself a moment to relax. She had no idea she was so driven. For her, getting things done on time was not only mandatory; it was Gretha's hobby.

Sten accepted his wife's commitment to keeping their lives and home in order, and, like some contagious disease, he rarely rested either. They both had full-time jobs: Gretha as a nurse in the acute section of Nilstad Hospital, and Sten as the local constable. He shared his jurisdiction with another officer whose territory lay east of Nilstad to the Baltic Sea. Sten handled everything west to the Norwegian border, an almost pristine region of old growth forest; undulating hills; and a network of rivers, streams, and countless lakes. Vast coniferous forests stretched for miles, contributing to the prosperous timber industry of the area. Nilstad, with its population of eight thousand people was, by far, the largest city in the area. All else were a scattering of tiny rural settlements.

Food and gasoline rationing was a way of life for everyone, and Sten was especially conscientious. He chose to use a sidecar motorcycle for economy and seldom drove the Volvo sedan that served as his official police car. There was always something for him to do at home. He felt guilty for not doing his share of family chores on the occasions when police duty kept him out late although he knew Gretha would handle both the household chores and the children without him.

They genuinely cared for each other and made love regularly, but not with the same frequency since Lisa's birth. Their two girls had taken a great deal of their time, and now there were three. Sten kept one area of his life to himself. There was a small amount of money to spare because both he and Gretha worked. Sten put exactly half of their savings in a joint account. With the other half, he bought trading stock with uncanny success. Everything he invested in made money, but he told no one, including his wife. One day, he promised himself, he would surprise Gretha and ask her to quit her job at the hospital. If the stocks continued to do well, they would have a prosperous retirement. He knew she would agree.

Chapter Fourteen

Aimo paced restlessly in his new room, unable to sleep. He pulled on his grey warm-up suit and stared through the window at the darkened landscape. Beyond the snow-covered ground, the unfrozen water of Lake Valdemaren stretched out—dark, cold, and huge. The yellow glow of lights on his side of the lake increased in number until they formed the town center of Nilstad. On the opposite shore, there was nothing but darkness. When and if the time came, escaping from the Blixdals was not going to be easy.

Aimo shifted his attention to the church grounds below him, focusing on the church cemetery. His gaze followed a row of headstones down to the lake's edge that ended at a boathouse.

A boathouse! That meant there had to be a boat, and a boat was exactly what he needed to get home to Finland. He reasoned that if the lake emptied somehow into the Baltic Sea, he could simply sail back home.

The boy twitched with excitement. He needed to discover what the boathouse contained and decided to find out right then. His instincts however warned him not to risk doing anything foolish. On the other hand, if he could at least satisfy his curiosity, he would be able to fall asleep; and that was motivation enough for him.

Aimo stole into the hallway in bare feet. Karen's voice came from behind a closed door across the hallway. She discussed a list of daily chores for Mikael, and Blixdal grunted his approval.

Satisfied that he knew where they both were, Aimo moved stealthily down the steps into the first-floor living quarters. He opened the door leading into the church, wedged his way into the room, and stood still.

The eerily silent place both dwarfed and frightened the boy. A red glow from the small scattered lamps filled the massive space with flickering shadows, creating a sense of movement within the darkened paintings. Statues of the apostles, mounted on their marble pedestals, stared at him threateningly.

Aimo exhaled puffs of white vapor and continued moving ahead, ignoring the chill of the cold stone floor on his bare feet. Extending his hand as a guide, he found a timbered wall. He crept forward but kept his attention riveted on the center of the room, fully expecting some sort of demon to be lurking.

Aimo stepped cautiously forward unaware of a darkened flight of steps leading to a subterranean chamber immediately in front of him. He stepped outward and dropped onto a stone step, then tumbled downward, landing with a thud against a door. Badly shaken but unhurt, he grabbed a wrought-iron latch handle above his head. He pulled himself up, the action causing the iron-bound door of the church crypt to slowly open. Immediately, a cold, penetrating breeze rushed over him causing new spasms of shivers.

Aimo's curiosity demanded he continue and led him further into a blackened chamber. Every fiber of his body warned him to leave and run back to the safety of his room, but the boy continued, moving cautiously down a spiral flight of stone steps and into a large earthen mausoleum. A cold, dank odor greeted him together with the sound of a creaking rope. Aimo moved in that direction, his eyes adjusting to the darkness.

The stubble of hair on his head stood even straighter as the boy became aware of the stone caskets all around him. Chilled to the bone, the unusual creaking sound urged him onward. A few steps later, he arrived at a huge open space in the floor. The boy turned to return to his room, deciding that was enough exploration for the night. Once again, however, his curiosity got the better of him. He had to discover what lay in the open space; then he would make a swift retreat to his room. He peered over the edge.

Directly beneath hovered the Nilstad church boat, hanging by ropes and attached to a pulley. It was enormous, larger than any rowboat he had ever seen, and covered with a canvas tarpaulin. It hung by ropes a half meter below the floor. The boat groaned from its weight, straining at the pulleys that had lifted it from the lake. A full meter beneath the boat, the unfrozen waters of Valdemaren lapped softly against the wood pilings.

Aimo stared at his discovery with disappointment. The boat was far too large for him to handle by himself. He definitely needed help rowing it. Perhaps together with Mooseface, then a new thought reached him. Perhaps the canvas meant it was a sailboat. That would be perfect.

Once again, Aimo believed he had seen enough for this first venture. Again he turned to leave, but his insatiable curiosity reminded him there was unfinished business. Was it a rowboat or a sailboat? He had to find out now.

Reaching down and stretching as far as he could, he was able to grab a corner of the tarpaulin and pulled. Simultaneously, a noise from behind alerted him. He lifted himself up from the floor and immediately felt another presence in the room. Someone, or *something*, breathed audibly in the darkness, sending puffs of exhaled breath drifting silently past his head. Terrified, he turned from the opening and rushed toward the door he had entered earlier. Unexpectedly, he plowed headfirst into something that was not there before. Someone large stood silently in front of him in the dark blocking his way.

Aimo shouted in fear as a blinding beam of a flashlight shone directly in his face.

"What in hell are you doing, boy?" the reverend demanded.

"I . . . I want . . . ," Aimo stammered, unable to speak.

The clergyman disliked this Finnish boy from the moment he first met him. Now, on his very first night and in the reverend's home, this heathen child was already causing him trouble. Blixdal held the light full on the boy's terrified face.

"I thought I heard a noise down here," the reverend sneered. "I thought maybe it was a wild animal—and it *is* a wild animal, isn't it?"

"I want to find my sister," Aimo said, finally able to see Blixdal's face through the glare of the flashlight.

"You want your sister? You want me to believe you expect to find her down here? Is that what you think?" Blixdal scoffed. Aimo remained silent, and the reverend continued, "You don't ask for permission, do you? Just like some wild animal, you decide you can walk around this house wherever you want. Is that what you think?" he repeated.

"We're supposed to stay together," Aimo blurted.

"You're a bad liar, boy. Come now. Tell me the truth. Why are you down here? Are you trying to run away? Is that it? That's a good idea, boy. I might even help you. But that's not the reason, is it? You tried to steal something from the boat, didn't you?"

Blixdal was justifiably nervous about the secrets that only he knew lay within the church boat. Did this boy discover something? The reverend intended to find out. There was no rush, and he was enjoying the situation since the boy had to be uncomfortably cold. *A just punishment*, the reverend thought.

Suddenly, a new light appeared from the steps at the far end of the room. Karen Blixdal hurried toward the reverend, a kerosene lantern in her hand. Then she saw Aimo, cowering in front of her husband.

"What's happening, Bjorn?" she asked, completely taken by surprise. She moved to Aimo. Without waiting for an explanation, she hugged the boy defensively.

"He's shaking all over. Mikael! My poor child. Don't worry mother like this." She clutched him to her chest then hustled the boy up the stairs and out of sight.

Blixdal watched wordlessly as the woman disappeared. He shone the beam of his flashlight across the room to the rows of stacked caskets. Certain he was alone, he played the light on the church boat that had held the boy's interest. He reached down and carefully lifted the tarpaulin. There, undisturbed, lay the cluster of three neatly rolled Vermeer oil paintings and, within the rolls, five stacks of German Deutsche marks.

The flashlight beam illuminated the plundered loot, revealing swastika-imprinted labels. German text bore the name of Maj. Reynold Hulsman, Dortmunder, Germany. The major had found an enthusiastic partner for his bounty in the Reverend Bjorn Blixdal and followed a typical German practice of stealing treasures from throughout conquered Europe. Finding a safe haven for the bounty until war's end was a challenge for everyone, but Major Hulsman got lucky. The unexpected letter from the reverend, a respected man of the cloth in conveniently nearby and neutral Sweden, was precisely the person he needed. The Vermeer paintings were the first shipment of treasure the major expected to skim from among the many crates of pillaged material the Reich had acquired. Both Hulsman and Blixdal expected to profit greatly from their enterprise. Of course, the reverend still had the bishop's cellar to purloin if given the chance. Blixdal was a happy man, and the episode with Aimo quickly forgotten. He replaced the upturned canvas, feeling quite rich.

Having satisfied himself that his secret treasure was undisturbed, Blixdal concluded that Aimo had simply stumbled upon the boat and never realized the significance of his discovery. Blixdal would now take precautions for the future. The reverend moved up the spiral staircase, closed the door to the mausoleum chamber behind him, and made a mental note to install a bolted padlock. That would prevent any further risk to his clandestine cache from Aimo, his wife, or anybody else.

The reverend stood silently within his dark church. Whereas Aimo cowered in fear within the unfriendly room, the reverend felt elated. This was his church, and he truly believed he was God's emissary to his parishioners. He was doing God's work, and in his mind, he was the truest of Christians. There were no feelings of guilt with the treasure of stolen goods within the church boat. He was not the one who had stolen it. The same truth held for the stolen material held by the bishop. Someone else had broken God's commandment, and they were the thieves. God had simply provided

Blixdal with an opportunity, and the reverend recognized it. If the Swedish authorities got a hold of any of the stolen items, they certainly would not travel throughout war-torn Europe to search for the original owners. No, Blixdal concluded, he was offered an opportunity as a reward for his duty to God; and he felt grateful.

He crossed to his altar, then carefully climbed the steps of the pulpit in front of the rows of empty benches. Raising his piercing eyes skyward, he mumbled the words of a prayer.

Chapter Fifteen

Aimo slept exhaustedly, his night's dreams of happy days with his family at home all ending in frustration. Throughout the uneasy night, important people in his life called for him impatiently, only to mysteriously disappear. Familiar places became strange and unrecognizable, reminding the boy he was hopelessly lost.

"Good morning, Mikael," Fru Blixdal greeted.

Aimo poked his head from under the blanket. There was Karen Blixdal, hovering over him and smiling broadly.

"While you've been sleeping, I've had a chance to get you some new clothes for school tomorrow." She put her hand on his head and tousled his hair.

Aimo took a few moments to recognize his new environment. The room appeared much different in daylight. He definitely was not home; and Fru Blixdal, a bundle of clothes over her arm, certainly was no dream.

"I said good morning," Karen repeated.

"Good morning, Fru Blixdal," Aimo answered.

"Remember! You may call me *mother*, all right?" She cupped the boy's face in her hands as Aimo nodded in silent affirmation. Karen embraced him strongly.

"You've slept a long time. We're going to dress you in these nice new clothes and have some lunch. It's already too late for breakfast. Then I'm going to take you through the church to show you some things you'll be required to do," Karen spoke with hardly a pause. She placed her burden of boys' clothing on the bed, anxious to see the transformation she knew the clothes would make. Patience, however, was not one of Karen's virtues. Unable to wait longer, she began to dress the boy at a fever's pitch.

The one-piece trapdoor flannel underwear and black wooden clogs were all the clothes Aimo could recognize. Everything else, from a pair of dark woolen knickers to a matching tweed long coat, were new to him. Stranger still were the striped kneesocks held up by garters. Worst of all was a wide-collared silken blue shirt and matching bow tie.

Fru Blixdal walked him to her room and stood the boy in front of a full-length mirror, beside herself with joy. The colors of the outfit seemed to enhance the boy's complexion, and she was pleased with her choices. She expected the selection of clothes for a ten-year-old boy would be difficult, but it wasn't. In fact, it felt as though she had been shopping for children's clothes all her life.

Finally, she had a child of her own and could not wait to show him off to her friends. She put her arms around him, tightly pulling him into her breasts. Years of being denied a child by her husband, coupled by his refusal of any physical intimacy, were a thing of the past. Through the good grace of God, she had a son.

Aimo, on the other hand, was convinced he looked ridiculous. He felt more ridiculous being clutched to Fru Blixdal's bosom. Rather than resist, the boy decided he would endure this treatment as well until his parents arrived. Thankfully, they would return his life to order.

"Tomorrow, you'll go to school, Mikael, and everyone will admire you. You will make Mother so proud. I just know."

Fru Blixdal led the boy into the church, stopping at a small closet where church vestments were kept. She searched among a number of maroon smocks and, finding one of appropriate size, she pulled it over Aimo's head.

"You must always wear this when you come into the church, Mikael."

"Why?" Aimo asked.

"Because this is God's house," she gestured to the statues and frescoes. "God lives here, and we never want to be disrespectful of him. Now, let's show you your duties."

Karen explained a series of chores she expected Aimo to perform, some daily and others weekly. One job immediately caught the boy's interest. He had to collect used candles in wooden boxes and take them to a small stone-walled room used for tallow-making that was dominated by a large black iron cauldron. His interest piqued considerably as Karen demonstrated the art of candlemaking to him.

She stood on a small step-up bench and dropped the used candles into the vat, then placed a wide-mouthed iron kettle beneath the cauldron's spigot. She turned the handle and filled the kettle with molten paraffin. Next, she looped three lengths of precut string over a wooden rod and dipped the string into the hot liquid. After several moments, she lifted the rod and allowed the paraffin to coagulate into a thin coat over the string that became wider with each dip. She repeated the process again and again until the desired candle width was achieved. She then placed the rod in a water-filled holder to cool down.

"When this cools, you may take these into the church. Would you like to try to make one, Mikael?"

Aimo's creative instincts were aroused. He loved handcrafting, but the only tool he had ever used was a knife for wood-whittling. Making candles seemed like fun, and the boy began his apprenticeship in earnest.

Hours passed and Karen felt the day was going beautifully. Whatever doubts she had regarding the rumored laziness of Finns were quickly eradicated by Aimo's industry. They both worked continually within the church until the fading November light surrendered itself to dark shadows, and Karen announced it was time to stop for the day. She was tired but pleased with the boy who never objected or complained.

"Thank you, Mikael," she said. "You've really done a lot of work. I can't wait to tell the reverend. He'll be home soon and will be so pleased to hear the news. He's a good man, Mikael." She offered the endorsement of her husband for Aimo's edification but hoped that by expressing it aloud, she might believe it herself.

The mention of Blixdal's name was not what Aimo wanted to hear. He did not trust the man and could never like him. Everything about him was threatening, and his eyes reminded him of wolves' eyes when, driven by cold and snow, they arrived at Lake Jarvii. They howled hungrily, searching for food, and their eyes shined menacingly. The children of the village were not allowed to leave their homes unattended by an adult.

Wolf Eyes! That's what I'll call him, Aimo thought, pleased with having the opportunity to think disparaging thoughts of a man he did not trust and was growing to hate.

Dinner did not get off to the start Karen had hoped. She planned to share the day's adventures with her husband, but the man seemed distant and preoccupied. He seemed to hardly notice the new place mats and colorful napkins that decorated the dining room table or the special roast-chicken dinner that filled the room with a delicious aroma. Finally, the reverend became aware of the changes.

"Are we expecting company?" Blixdal asked.

"No," she replied, "but I do have a surprise for you."

Karen ran up the stairs to Aimo's room and quickly returned with the boy. She proudly presented her creation to her husband for his anticipated approval.

Blixdal sat near the fireplace, a glass of brandy in his hand. He studied the boy as though an apparition had just appeared, then gazed at his wife who smiled radiantly. It had been years since she displayed such genuine warmth.

"Is this why we're eating in the dining room?" He shifted his attention to Aimo. "This boy is not to eat in this room until I allow it! He eats in the kitchen, and if you choose, Karen, we can all eat there together."

Momentarily crestfallen, she convinced herself the reverend had not really rejected the boy. After all, it was much more practical to dine in the kitchen even though she considered Aimo's transformation a reason for celebrating.

"That's a good idea, Bjorn," she said with composure. "Mikael, help me take these dishes to the kitchen table. We'll have dinner there."

Karen was skilled in handling her husband. He expected to be obeyed, and he expressed his decisions with no room for compromise. Years of listening to his bombastic pontificating taught her to understand his commands and to communicate in a way that never contradicted the man, but at the same time, it allowed herself to have her way. It was a skill she had mastered.

Aimo ate ravenously. Unfortunately for him, he only used his hands and a tablespoon, completely ignoring the knife and fork placed on either side of his plate. The shortcoming did not go undetected by the Blixdals. Karen made an urgent mental note to teach the boy proper Swedish table manners and hoped her husband was not noticing. She was wrong.

The boy sat hunched over his plate, his face barely above the mashed potatoes. He bit hungrily into a handheld chicken leg and ladled spoons of potatoes into an already-stuffed mouth. His cheeks bulged, and his lips smacked audibly.

"You damn pig!" Blixdal roared, his wolf eyes shining fiercely. "Go to your room! *Now!*" Blixdal directed a steely gaze at his wife and pointed his fork menacingly at the boy. "Get this animal out of my sight. The next time you have him sit with me, I want to see some sign of . . . of . . . *civilization!*"

Karen took the boy to the upstairs bathroom and out of the reverend's sight. She scrubbed Aimo's face and hands and assured the boy her husband was not as unhappy as he seemed. Returning him to his room, she added, "The reverend only wants the best for you, Mikael. One day, you will make him so happy he will want you to join him in the church."

Aimo lay in his bed, hungry and in the dark. He listened to the reverend admonish his wife loudly from downstairs in the kitchen, but was unable to make out what was being said. He changed his mind about calling the man Wolf Eyes. Wolves, at least, were honest in their behavior and had a purpose in nature. The reverend was a bully and a hypocrite and could never be trusted. Every fiber of Aimo's being told him he did not belong with these people and made a promise to himself he would run away within two weeks if his parents did not arrive.

Chapter Sixteen

Karen buttoned a white winter coat over Aimo's knickers outfit and placed a brown bag, lunch, and a pair of her wooden clogs into a knapsack. She helped the boy into a pair of her fur-lined boots, covered his head and hands with a matching set of mittens and ski cap, and stood back to take a long admiring glance at her creation. "Now! You're ready for school," she said and led him outside into early morning darkness.

A colder air mass had moved in during the night, bringing with it a heavy overcast. The first flakes of snow drifted downward, adding to the accumulation on the white landscape. Karen's high-pitched voice echoed with amplification beneath the lowered cloud ceiling, and the woman's ebullient energy seemed to have returned in spite of the exhortation she had received from her husband the night before.

Karen chatted continually about school. She excitedly named the families whose children would be in attendance, offering little anecdotes she felt Aimo needed to know. She ultimately mentioned Fredrik Pontilius, the headmaster. He lived alone at the rural one-room school, and from what she explained, the teacher had some mystery about him.

"Now there's a strange one," she said of Pontilius. "He was wounded in Finland. Now, isn't that a coincidence? Some say he's very stern because he has an artificial leg but"—she was quick to add—"everyone says he's a very good teacher."

His initial curiosity about the teacher was satisfied, and Aimo blocked out most of what else Karen Blixdal had to say. Aimo had already learned she had a habit of repeating the same subject, which she presented differently each time. If Aimo didn't feel like listening to her, she was certain to repeat it later anyway. Aimo concentrated instead on the network of forest trails. The beauty of discovering them in the falling snow felt very much like home to him. They had passed the halfway point of the four kilometer distance between the church and school when voices behind them called out loudly.

"Coming through! Look out behind you!"

Two boys—a little older than Aimo, both on cross-country skis—moved swiftly from a forest trail that fed into the main path where Aimo stood. The boys skied expertly and disappeared from view at a turn in the path.

"Do you ski, Mikael?" Fru Blixdal asked.

Aimo thought the question silly. It was common knowledge that everyone skied in Finland since it was the major source of winter travel, but Aimo chose to answer simply with a yes.

"Good!" she exclaimed emphatically. "I will get you skis of your own." Karen smiled at him again with genuine warmth.

Aimo was stunned by the statement. Getting anything new in Finland was a major event and usually required lengthy discussions, preparations, and, of course, saving or even sacrificing. Yet here in Sweden, people were so rich they simply bought whatever they wanted, whenever they wanted it. Nevertheless, the boy regarded the offer with welcome surprise. He looked up at the woman and gave careful consideration as to how he should reply.

"Thank you!" Aimo said genuinely. "Thank you . . . very much."

Chapter Seventeen

The island of Gronö jutted upward from the depths of Lake Valdemaren, then rose to become a fifteen-hundred-meter-high mountain peak whose wide base spread over seven kilometers. A two-lane bridge connected Gronö to the mainland, but by mid-December, lake ice became thick enough to support motor vehicles.

There were numerous extraordinary features on Gronö, but three man-made items—a ski run, a ski jump, and Gronö's charming little church—stood out. The ski run was a wide serpentine course carved into the mountainside facing the community of Nilstad. Traditionally, skiers took their final evening run, carrying a flaming torch as they coursed down the slope. The procession of the skiers bearing torch lights in north Sweden's midwinter darkness was beautiful to behold, and many townspeople timed their evening walk to watch the spectacle.

In addition to the ski run, there were two ski jumps—one for children and the second, of world-class dimensions—attracting the most expert athletes from throughout Sweden and, on occasion, from other European countries as well. In fact, Nilstad's winter-sport building stood adjacent to the ski jumps. The building's glass-covered trophy cases contained plaques and photos dedicated to each year's outstanding athletes. The name and photographs of an athletic young man figured prominently for the years 1937 and 1938.

Fredrik Pontilius, whose handsome features were as well known as his skiing record, was one of Nilstad's all-time leading athletes. His sinewy body allowed him to perfect a technique in which he cleared the ski jump, then jackknifed into a posture that brought his face to his ski tips. When he snapped into a gliding position, it allowed maximum air to build beneath his taut frame. Pontilius soared to a record jump in 1938 that still stood five years later. Many believed he would break his own record the following year, but fate had other plans for Nilstad's sport hero.

In 1939, Pontilius volunteered to fight alongside his Finnish neighbors in the Winter War with Russia. The young athlete was in Finland less than three weeks when a Russian artillery shell exploded next to him, the blast severing his left leg at the knee. Simultaneously, a hot shard of shrapnel struck his cheekbone, barely missing his right eye, and opened a jagged wound that would forever scar his handsome features. But the damage to the man's spirit was equally shattering.

He underwent a series of surgical procedures that ultimately had the doctors fasten a mechanical prosthesis to the stump of his left leg, but he could use it only to stand. He was unable to sit or bend the knee. Skin grafts covered the terrible wound on his face, and Pontilius grew a totally unflattering beard to hide it. It was a gesture that seemed to mirror his emotional damage as well. Only his full head of strawberry blond curls and ruddy complexion served as a reminder of the vital man he once had been.

Upon his return to Nilstad, months of therapy taught him to walk and speak, but did nothing to bring back the easy, charming smile that had been Pontilius's trademark. He seemed determined to bury the person he had been and added to his austere look by wearing round wire-rimmed glasses, making him appear much older than his thirty-one years.

He withdrew from friends and family, resisting the many opportunities that offered a new career. The many who admired him agreed to allow Pontilius time and space to heal. And in the summer of 1941, he accepted an offer to become headmaster at the rural school west of town. He lived alone in an apartment that was connected to the schoolhouse and took the teaching job seriously. Pontilius abandoned all attempts to return to his previous life.

He canceled his engagement to Solveig Olin, his childhood sweetheart. They had planned to marry in Gronö's church high atop the mountain. In the glow of summer's midnight sun, the petite timber structure, covered in cascading pink Cecil Bruner roses, was the overwhelming romantic favorite place for weddings.

His decision to break the engagement broke Solveig's heart as well and disappointed their many friends who thought them the perfect couple. Solveig matched Pontilius good looks and, in her own right, matched his athleticism. She was a quintessential flaxen-haired Swedish beauty whose sparkling blue eyes shone behind a freckle-faced smile. Pontilius refused her unconditional love, including sex, and asked her not to visit him at the school.

Solveig accepted the crushing disappointment with admirable dignity, but remained determined with a steel-willed tenacity to find a way to get Pontilius back. She worked at Nilstad's hospital in the ward for volunteer

Swedish soldiers wounded in Norway and sang in the choir at Blixdal's church. She kept herself as busy as possible, but she loved Fredrik Pontilius unconditionally. One day, she believed, Pontilius would awaken from his trauma and love her again.

Aimo stood in the snow, staring at the schoolhouse door. The class inside was already assembled, and the sound of children singing a hymn with a singsong prose flowed over the school ground. Going through the schoolhouse door was a daunting task to the boy. Inside the room were thirty-three children he did not know and, in fact, did not want to know. Perhaps school could be delayed until after Christmas. There were many good reasons why Aimo did not want to pass through *that* door which stood ominously in front of him and step into *that* schoolroom, but he could not find the words to express them. He turned to Fru Blixdal to tell her how uncomfortable he felt, but with customary impatience, Karen shoved the door open and pulled Aimo in behind her. A hush fell over the room as all eyes turned to the intruders.

"Forgive us, Herr Pontilius. I didn't realize we were so late." Karen shoved Aimo in front of her. "This is my Finnish boy, Mikael," she announced.

"My name is Aimo!" he blurted angrily.

Pontilius was taken completely by surprise. It was a widely known rule within the community that no one ever barged into his room when classes were in session. The teacher also knew the Blixdals were poor candidates to be surrogate parents. He cast a long gaze at Aimo. It was predictable that the Blixdals would give the Finnish boy a non-Finnish name, the teacher thought. What wasn't predictable was the Finnish boy's spunk to defend himself. Pontilius immediately liked the boy.

"Aimo!" Anna shouted from her desk across the room and rushed to embrace her brother, giggling loudly in delight. The scene brought peals of laughter from her schoolmates. In less than ten seconds, Pontilius's class descended from its orderly decorum to a raucous group of kids. The teacher quickly put an end to it by slamming his wooden cane across his desk.

"Silence!" he commanded, and the room turned still. Pontilius eyed the minister's wife warily then turned his attention to the class. "Everyone stand and say good morning to Fru Blixdal."

"Good morning, Fru Blixdal," the class sang in unison.

Pontilius bowed politely. "Thank you, Fru Blixdal."

"Thank *you*, Herr Pontilius. Good morning, children." The woman waved to the children, then gave an energetic good-bye wave to Aimo before walking outside.

Pontilius ordered the class to sit down then turned to Aimo.

"We begin our classes at 8:00 AM," he said, pointing his cane to a large round clock above the chalkboard wall. "And we take off our coat and boots before we enter this room. Please go to the closet next to the door and do so now."

Aimo moved to the closet, all eyes fastened on his every move as the room of children watched in attentive silence. *They're all looking at me*, he thought, the worst possible way to begin school. He unburdened himself of the knapsack, struggled out of his boots, and replaced them with Karen Blixdal's wooden clogs. Hanging his coat on a wooden peg he reentered the classroom and instantly knew he had done something else wrong. Aimo was greeted by a group of older boys who laughed loudly at his Little Lord Fauntleroy outfit but, a quick stare from the teacher in their direction brought a return of silence.

"Take the desk at the back of the room near the window," Pontilius ordered. Aimo quickly shuffled to the desk, plopped down, and wished he could disappear.

"What is your name?" Pontilius asked.

"Aimo," the boy replied.

The boy used his own name again, Pontilius observed favorably. A slight smile crossed the teacher's face, and he nodded his approval. He turned his attention to the class, then rapped his cane on the desk to signal them to continue their interrupted singing.

The children rose from their desks and began the hymn. Aimo stood dumbly, not knowing what to do. Suddenly, a movement outside the window caught his eye. A shadowy figure approached stealthily through the snow, heading straight for him. Instantly, the terrifying memory of being crammed beneath the floorboards in his home while fearing for his life swept over him.

For a brief moment, he had returned to that moment in his home at Lake Jarvii. The approaching figure outside the window had become the Russian soldier.

"Soldiers!" Aimo shouted in terror. He dove recklessly under his desk, his heart pounding.

Pontilius's eyes darted to the window. There stood Fru Blixdal, smiling sheepishly, unaware of the new confusion she had caused. She turned away, leaving the window vacant once more and Pontilius's class very much unsettled.

Aimo trembled beneath his desk, and Anna rushed to his aid. She knelt beside him and placed her pudgy little hand on her brother's arm in comfort.

Once again, Pontilius slammed his cane against his desk to bring order. The children returned to their seats, clearly frightened by Aimo's behavior.

Silence gripped the room, broken only by the mechanical sound made as Pontilius snapped his prosthesis into place. He straightened himself stiffly, pushed himself off the tall stool and addressed the class.

"Open your books! I want all of you to read the next chapter from your literature book . . . immediately," he ordered.

The class of thirty-three children, divided into rows by grades from one to six, reached for their respective books as Pontilius hobbled in Aimo's direction.

"Anna," he said gently, "please, return to your desk. Aimo! Come with me."

Pontilius led Aimo into the cloakroom and cast one last warning glance at the class before closing the door behind him.

"What's wrong, boy?" Pontilius asked.

"Nothing!" Aimo whispered.

"What just occurred in the classroom was not 'nothing.' Tell me what happened in there," Pontilius demanded.

"I thought I saw soldiers," Aimo answered.

"That was Fru Blixdal,"

"I know that now. I thought she was a soldier."

"Have you seen soldiers before?" Pontilius was beginning to understand the boy's behavior.

"Yes," Aimo answered tersely.

Pontilius could easily commiserate with the young refugee. He knew the terror of confronting enemy soldiers first hand. But the teacher needed to be able to manage the boy's behavior or risk losing control of his class. The law regarding the Finnish war children stated that if a Finnish child behaved intolerably, he would be removed from his Swedish family and placed in an orphanage.

But something else drew Pontilius to this dark-haired boy who had shown such spirit, and he felt a strange need to protect the child.

"There are other Finnish children that arrived with you in Nilstad, Aimo. Except for you and your sister, the others go to school in town. Would you like me to transfer you there?"

"My sister too?" Aimo asked.

"I don't think that's possible. She lives with the Vahleen family. Their two daughters are in this class."

"Then I'll stay here with my sister," Aimo answered.

"You're very welcome at this school, but I want you to understand me," Pontilius said carefully. "You cannot disrupt this class. If you do, I'll be forced to use my cane. Do you understand me?" It was a dire and distasteful threat, but Pontilius had to risk it. He smacked the cane impatiently in his hand.

"I said, do you understand?"

"Yes, sir, I do," Aimo answered.

At exactly noon, the teacher called a halt to classes and announced the lunch period. Children hurried to the clothes closet, donned their outerwear, then rushed outside.

Pontilius followed Aimo with a special interest as the boy moved to join his sister. She was not alone. Both Vahleen children stood with her, and as Aimo approached, Meggan became quite protective toward the two younger girls. Pontilius recognized the awkward situation. He hobbled toward the little group.

"Hello!" Pontilius said. The children froze in place. Meggan knew from experience that Herr Pontilius rarely approached the children unless he intended to admonish them.

Meggan hesitated before responding. "Good day, Herr Pontilius," Meggan replied with a polite curtsy.

Pontilius decided he would ease the awkward situation in which the boy found himself. "Welcome to school, Anna," the teacher said happily. He extended a hand, but the little girl stepped backward, seeking protection behind Meggan's back and bumped into Lisa who already occupied the space. Haltingly, Anna extended her hand as her lower lip protruded into a serious pout. Her face contorted, and she took in a deep breath that preceded a very loud wail. Aimo stepped forward and covered her mouth with his hand as Meggan looked on in surprise.

"She cries a lot," Aimo said. "She's my sister, and I'm supposed to take care of her."

"She's very lucky to have her big brother here, Aimo. Let me present Meggan Vahleen and her sister Lisa." Aimo stared at the girls, their matching hair bows set precisely on opposite sides of their heads. That's when he noticed that Anna was wearing one as well.

"The Vahleens are a very nice family. Anna is well cared for there," Pontilius continued. "Meggan, shake hands with Aimo and tell him about your home." The teacher turned away, limping toward the door leading to his apartment.

Meggan thrust her hand directly at the boy and offered a stiff handshake. Aimo took her hand in his. He thought about something to say but could think of nothing. With the exception of his little sister, he couldn't remember ever holding a girl's hand before. This was different. There was a wonderful softness to her touch, and he locked his eyes on to hers, definitely enjoying a very unusual feeling. He continued his grip for several long moments without realizing the girl's palm had turned warm and moist. Meggan made no effort to withdraw it from the boy's grasp. It also marked the first time she had held hands with a boy. She blushed then quickly took the initiative.

"Let's go outside and eat lunch," she said.

Aimo released his hold, but Meggan swiftly retook the boy's hand in hers, leading her little group, with Aimo in tow, to the cloakroom where they dressed for the outdoors.

Meggan was unexplainably excited. She spoke with hardly any interruption, talking about her parents, her friends, her home, and the lights she saw each evening on Gronö mountain. She completed her one-sided conversation declaring that one day, she would be married in Gronö's church. When Aimo finally spoke, she was not prepared for his question.

"How do you get to your house?" Aimo asked.

She volunteered detailed directions to which Aimo listened carefully until the girl lost his undivided attention. Aimo's interest had shifted to a group of boys his age who pushed handheld snow plows across the ice of a small pond. They placed two wooden crates, positioning them on either end of the pond as goals.

"They play bandy after school," Meggan informed. "It's like ice hockey. They use sticks and a little ball. Do you have a game like that in Finland?"

"Yes," Aimo answered wryly. "We call it ice hockey too."

Chapter Eighteen

At exactly 2:30 p.m., Pontilius gave each class their homework instructions and dismissed the children for the day. As usual, the older boys led the rush to the clothes closet, then hurried to the frozen pond where most of the children had gathered to view the bandy game. They followed the spirited play on the ice as the boys skated back and forth across the pond at breakneck speed. An occasional yell or cheer signaled a goal scored or an effective body check.

Arne and Lenne, the same boys who had skied passed Aimo earlier, were the school athletes and considerably bigger than the other boys. They took a special delight in demonstrating their size against the smaller boys who courageously competed with them, but took a punishment for their efforts. The rules of the game demanded the boys not complain or cry from the rough and tumble sport, but an unusually shrill shriek from one of the skaters caught everyone's attention.

Nils Holmgren, a spunky ten-year-old, had scored a goal while Arne defended him; and he paid the price moments later when a wicked body block severely twisted his knee. With the help of some classmates, Nils hobbled off the ice and removed his skates.

"Hey!" Lenne shouted. "We need somebody to take Nils's place."

The skaters surveyed their quiet classmates, but no one seemed willing to volunteer for punishment of their own. Then Arne spied Aimo standing on the hill beside Meggan.

"Hey, you! Finska!" Arne called. "Come over here."

Lenne skated alongside his friend and regarded Aimo curiously as he ambled toward them.

"He's the one with the sissy clothes," Lenne whispered. "I don't like him."

"I don't like him either," Arne sneered contemptuously. He shouted to Aimo. "Finska! We need another guy. Put on some skates."

"I don't have skates," Aimo replied.

"Do you know how to skate?" Lenne asked.

"Sure," Aimo said, "but I don't have any skates."

"I'll get Nils's skates," Arne declared. Moments later, he returned to Aimo with the borrowed skates.

"Put these on, Finska. You're on their team." Arne pointed gleefully to a group of younger boys Aimo's age.

The two older boys skated to mid-ice, chuckling to themselves in anticipation of beating up on the disliked Finnish boy. They showed off for the onlookers by strut-skating back and forth across the ice.

Aimo's teammates looked at him curiously as the boy tied on the skates. He removed his coat, bringing renewed laughter from the flamboyant outfit Karen had gotten for him, but Aimo ignored the laughter. He determinedly accepted a hockey stick and skated with his team to their side of the pond. His side would have the first chance to advance the puck and score a goal.

"OK!" Lenne shouted. "Let's go."

One of Aimo's teammates tentatively maneuvered the puck to the center of the pond and was immediately confronted by two of the older boys. The smaller boy turned his back and unwittingly offered himself for an open body check. The first defender plowed into him, sending the boy skidding across the ice. A second defender confidently stole the puck and skated arrogantly toward the goal.

Aimo had never seen anything so stupid. His years of ice hockey on Lake Jarvii taught him to use speed and attack aggressively. These Swedish teammates showed little finesse and had no idea of teamwork. No one had yet learned to pass.

Aimo eyed the boy with the puck lazily approaching the goal then bolted in his direction. Skating low to the ice, he stretched his upper body far in front of his swift skates. The boy with the puck raised his stick above his head and was set to smash home a goal when Aimo flashed from behind. He neatly stole the puck away a moment before the boy could swing his stick. Totally unaware of Aimo's move, the boy swung at the place where the puck had been. The momentum carried his feet from under him, and he collapsed in a heap on the ice.

The crowd of school children howled with laughter, then screamed in delight as Aimo raced up the ice, sprinting past everyone including his own teammates. Untouched, he flicked the puck into the basket while his schoolmates shouted, "Goal!"

Arne and Lenne were furious. Now it was their turn to attack. They skated up the ice in a defiant phalanx, determined to reestablish their superiority.

One after the other of Aimo's teammates was bowled over as Lenne pushed the puck in front of him. He bore down on the Finnish boy, standing alone in defense of the net. Lenne squared his shoulders preparing to skate over his antagonist. At the last instant, Aimo pirouetted in a nimble move, avoiding physical contact. He poked at the puck and sent it skidding behind a very surprised Lenne.

Aimo jumped on the puck in a flash just as two older boys tried to barrel into him. He ducked as the boys lunged, and they collided in midair, bringing more howls of laughter from the spectators. Aimo's path to the goal was blocked by two more defenders. With a burst of speed, he glided swiftly to the barrier of snow that marked the sideline. He looked for a teammate to whom he could pass the puck for a centering shot but saw only Arne, ominously skating at full speed toward him.

Arne had an angle, and he knew it. He focused on Aimo, preparing to slam him into the snow barrier. Aimo recognized his situation. He braked to a stop in a plume of ice crystals, then finessed the puck beyond his opponent. Arne tried to compensate for Aimo's maneuver but lost his balance instead. The surprised boy fell on the seat of his pants and skidded into the snow. Renewed cheering signaled the Finnish boy had scored his second goal.

Shouts of "Aimo!" brought Pontilius to a window overlooking the pond. He watched amused as the Finnish boy outmaneuvered and outskated the other players, skating so low that he appeared to touch the ice with his nose. Pontilus sighed loudly, exhilarated by the sight of the unusually gifted boy. It seemed like such a short time ago when Fredrik himself dispalyed the same talents. Here was a natural athlete with a special skill and Pontilius recognized the instincts as those he once had himself.

The game came to a sudden end when the tall figure of a man dressed in black clerical garb moved down to the pond, causing the children to scatter. Reverend Blixdal called for Aimo, and the boy dutifully obeyed. He immediately removed his skates, returned them to Lenne, and shook his opponent's hand. Then he pulled on his boots and coat, placed the knapsack over his back, and walked over to his Swedish guardian.

The wait had taxed the man's patience. Blixdal grabbed Aimo by the ear and, without releasing his hold, led him away from the pond to a black car parked at the top of the hill. The clergyman shoved the boy into the backseat and drove off.

Arne and Lenne stood side by side, breathing heavily from chasing Aimo over the ice but appalled by the reverend's harsh treatment of their classmate.

"I don't like that Blixdal," Lenne said.

"Me neither," Arne concurred then, as an afterthought, asked Lenne how many goals Aimo had scored.

"Five," Lenne replied.

"Next time, he's on our team!" Arne declared.

Pontilius made his way back to his desk and entered a note in his daily log regarding Aimo's dilemma. The boy's chances of a normal life were very poor with the Blixdals, he concluded. It was time to look into the possibility of sending Aimo to another family.

Potinlius' first challenge would be to separate the boy from his surrogate mother, unaware the woman had no intention of losing her child.

The reverend, on the other hand, would be more than pleased of being rid of Aimo and had already begun concocting such a plan.

Chapter Nineteen

Aimo set the last of the candles in the candelabra thus completing his morning chores. He stood before the reverend to ask for Blixdal's permission to leave for school and waited for a break in the clergyman's bombastic oratory as the man rehearsed a sermon from his perch in the elevated pulpit. His powerful voice reverberated off the walls explosively, and he chopped the air in front of him with both hands to emphasize his main points.

"Herr Blixdal, I must leave for school," Aimo said impatiently, not wanting to be late to Pontilius's class again. The reverend became silent then turned his attention to the small figure below him.

"What did you say, boy?" Blixdal growled. Aimo had forgotten he was to *ask* permission instead of making a statement.

Aimo corrected himself. "Your permission to leave, Herr Blixdal,"

"I want you to come here directly from school. Is that understood?" The reverend waited for Aimo to acknowledge him, and the boy nodded. "There is much for you to do. Sankta Lucia Day is next week, which means Christmas will be here before we know it."

Standing beneath the pulpit, the boy craned his neck upward and again nodded, anxious to leave the company of the clergyman.

"You may go," Blixdal said and returned to the sermon rehearsal.

Aimo rushed to his room, grabbed his knapsack, and sprinted down the stairs, two steps at a time, before plowing directly into Fru Blixdal. She had been waiting for him at the bottom of the steps, a large smile across her face.

"I have something for you," Karen said, reaching into a corner. She handed Aimo a set of new skis and poles and sang out, "Tra-la!"

Aimo was thunderstruck. He had not expected the woman to have kept her promise of giving him skis.

"Come, Mikael. Give Mother a hug. You may say *thank you*."

"Thank you!" Aimo erupted. He enthusiastically wrapped his arms strongly around the woman's waist. "Thank you! Thank you!"

Karen held him tightly. "Please say 'mother,' Mikael. 'Thank you, Mother.' Please! Please do that for me."

Aimo pushed himself away and returned the skis back to the woman. "You're not my mother. My mother and father live in Finland, and soon I'll be with them again."

Aimo had not intended his words to be hurtful. He thought he had simply stated the facts as he knew them, yet the message penetrated the woman as though she had been stabbed with a knife. Karen sobbed softly, and the boy attempted to move past her.

She held out her hands to stop him. "It's all right, Mikael," she said. "Please take the skis and hurry off to school."

Aimo rushed out into the morning darkness in a confusion of emotions. He did not want to be late again for Pontilius's class, yet he was forced to wait for several minutes before the reverend would even speak to him. He did not expect the surprise that Fru Blixdal had given him, and although he expressed his genuine gratitude, he found out it wasn't enough. Everything he did for the Blixdals came with a price the boy was unable to pay. Aimo could not wait to put as much distance in his life between himself and the dysfunctional Blixdals. He quickly stepped into the new skis and glided swiftly onto the forest trail leading to school, unaware that Karen cried disconsolately from behind the window curtains as he disappeared in the distance.

A starlit morning sky provided all the illumination Aimo needed to ski expertly in the December dawn. A few minutes later, he heard voices in front of him and recognized the figures of Arne and Lenne skiing their way to school. Aimo pushed himself forward with renewed energy, increasing his speed until he was directly behind the two boys.

"Look out! Coming through!" Aimo shouted.

He sailed past the surprised boys, but once they got their wits about them, they took off after him in hot pursuit; and the race was on. The trio sped swiftly through the forest like a pack of young wolves in full flight, but it was Aimo who led the boys from start to finish into the schoolyard. He braked into a snow-plumed stop. Arne and Lenne, their red faces lathered in sweat, were immediately behind him.

The boys all breathed heavily and scooped powdery snow over their heated heads to cool down, causing billows of steam to rise in the frigid air. Fascinated with their gifted Finnish friend, the older boys decided it was time to share their outdoor adventures together.

"Every Sunday, we go ski jumping on Gronö. Can you come with us?" Arne asked.

"There's a great ski jump there," Lenne added. "This year, we're going to jump from the big one."

"It's so high it's in the clouds," Arne added with some exaggeration.

"Can you ski jump, Aimo?" Lenne asked.

"Dummy! Aimo can do anything," Arne stated.

"I can," Aimo said softly, "but Herr Blixdal won't let me."

The older boys vividly remembered the incident with the clergyman from the ice hockey game a week earlier. Every day since then, the reverend's black car had perched on the road when school let out, like a waiting vulture to take Aimo away.

The trio entered the school, and Arne followed close behind. "I'm gonna ask my parents if you can stay with us. Herr Pontilius told me to ask them."

Lenne added, "My father says the priest is a jerk. Why does he drive you home every day?"

"Because I have to help Fru Blixdal get the church ready for Christmas," Aimo said.

"How come? Christmas is a couple of weeks away. We don't go to church anyway," Lenne admitted without waiting for Aimo's answer. "So? Do you want to stay with Arne?"

"My mother and father will be here soon," Aimo said, "Maybe even today. My sister and I will stay with them."

"Is the reverend still gonna drive you?" Lenne wanted to know.

"I hope not. Anyway, I have skis now, so I don't ever have to go in his car again." Aimo declared.

The sweaty boys entered Pontilius's classroom with ten minutes to spare.

When Aimo returned to the Blixdal's home, he found Karen in an animated conversation with the reverend. Her voice was agitated and tears streaked downward from the woman's swollen red eyes. She obviously had been crying for some time. Aimo entered the room, and the woman wiped her face with a handkerchief then welcomed the boy home.

"You have mail from your parents, Mikael. Would you like me to read it to you?" she asked, her voice was pitched an octave higher than usual. She offered the letter to Aimo. He grabbed the paper excitedly then noticed the letter had already been opened.

"No, thank you, Fru Blixdal. I'll read it myself," Aimo said. He glanced at the letter, quickly recognizing his mother's handwriting. His spirits soared. "Thank you, Fru Blixdal," he repeated enthusiastically, then sprinted up the steps to the sanctuary of his room.

Aimo fetched the military medal from its hiding place beneath his bureau and sat on the edge of the bed. He held the letter tightly in his hand for a brief moment, wishing it would bring him the good news that he soon would be rejoined with his parents. He opened his eyes and began reading.

My Darling Children,

How are you both? Father and I miss you so terribly. We think of you all the time. The Russians burned our house after we left, and we had to move to Jyväskylä where we are staying with our friends, Pekka and Jenni. Pekka and Father have been fighting the Russians and even the Germans. We don't know when this dreadful war will end. Everything here in Finland is terrible right now, and I am so glad you are safe with nice people in Sweden. Please take good care of Anna, Aimo. You are our little man, and we are proud of you. We count the days until we will be together again.

Love, Mother

Aimo got up and walked to the window and stared pensively at the yellow lights shining warmly from the houses scattered beyond him. Once again, questions without answers filled his mind, and he reread the letter again before returning it carefully to the envelope. Why had his mother not given an exact date for their arrival in Sweden? If Father were away fighting, how would it be possible for both of them to come to Sweden together?

It's so peaceful here, Aimo thought. Why does there have to be a war in Finland? Who made wars? How could men Aimo had never seen hate Finnish people so much?

The boy's reverie was suddenly interrupted when the door to Aimo's room flew open. Blixdal strode in angrily and threw Aimo's new skis unceremoniously onto Aimo's bed.

"Where did you get these?" Blixdal demanded.

Aimo was taken by surprise, his mind hundreds of miles away in Finland.

"Did you hear me, boy? Where did you get these skis?" Blixdal repeated.

"From Fru Blixdal," Aimo replied.

"Ah! . . . Fru Blixdal. She gave you brand new skis. It isn't yet Christmas. Is it your birthday?" he asked sarcastically. Aimo shook his head, and Blixdal continued, "Why did she do it, boy? Can you guess?" Aimo shook his head again, but Blixdal had a point to make. He grabbed Aimo's ear and gave it a severe twist.

"She did it, boy, because she loves you, God help her! All she asks is that you call her *mother*. Is that so difficult?"

Blixdal released his grip and pointed a finger directly into the boy's face. "From now on, you will call Fru Blixdal mother, and if you ever disappoint her again as you did today, I'll take you directly to the orphanage." Blixdal rushed from the room, leaving Aimo to rub his ear to soothe the pain.

Aimo returned his attention to his mother's letter. She was wrong! Sweden was not a wonderful place. It was a terrible place with terrible people. God only knew what was happening to Anna. She was always with the Vahleen girls, and it seemed she no longer cared for her own brother. He wondered if she were being threatened as well. If children were treated so awfully, what would happen to his parents when they arrived?

No, Aimo thought. It was up to him to take Anna back to Finland where they both belonged and to hell with Sweden. He opened the window, hurled his skis onto the snow below, and dressed for his return to Finland. He pulled on a pair of long-john flannel underwear and slipped into a new woolen warm-up suit. Finally, he stashed the military medal in a pocket and sneaked quietly from his room.

Blixdal had returned to practicing his same sermon for the umpteenth time, his voice penetrating the stone walls of the building. Sounds of cooking utensils in use in the kitchen told Aimo both Blixdals were too busy to hear him. He silently put on his boots, mittens, and a cap then stole into the night. Taking a moment to visualize the directions given him for the Vahleen's home, he headed in their direction determined to take Anna home to Finland with him.

Chapter Twenty

Gretha Vahleen guided a rolling pin over a thick length of gingerbread dough with determination. She flattened the balled mass into a buff-colored circle and, tasting it for flavor, allowed Meggan, Anna, and Lisa to cut out shapes with their assorted cookie cutters. The girls had been waiting in excited anticipation for Gretha's signal and jumped to the task with enthusiasm.

Gretha turned happily to her best friend, Solveig Olin, remembering baking Christmas cookies with her mother when she was a small girl. She smiled at the pleasant memory. Solveig had been invited by Gretha to share in the traditional Christmas baking, and she was pleased to see a smile on Solveig's pretty freckled face, a rare occurrence since Pontilius ended their engagement. Gretha was pleased the young woman accepted the opportunity to share Christmas with her family.

"Do you remember when we were that age?" Gretha asked. "I actually dreamed of making cookies." She nodded in the girls' direction. "They're cute, aren't they?"

"They're adorable," Solveig said. "Everyone seems to have accepted Anna."

"There's still an occasional problem with Lisa, possibly because they're the same age. Anna has become a part of our family in such a short time. It's amazing with children, isn't it? I don't know what we'll do when she leaves."

"Have you heard from her parents?" Solveig asked.

"Karen Blixdal told me Anna's brother received a letter, saying that things are terrible there. We've heard the Germans and Russians are not only fighting each other, they're also killing women and children in Finland. Thank God we have no war here."

Gretha felt embarrassed for allowing thoughts of war to interfere with their Christmas arrangements. She quickly embraced her friend in apology and called aloud, "Let's be happy tonight. Let's all sing Christmas songs."

Aimo skied swiftly to the outskirts of Nilstad, searching among the scattered pale lights glowing from within a curtain of falling snow. The directions Meggan had given him described a cluster of conifer trees followed by an orchard of symmetrically planted apple trees on either side of a lane. Her description was perfect in every detail, and the boy found it easily. The delicious aroma of baking gingerbread reached Aimo as he approached the house, and it reminded him he had not eaten for hours.

The sounds of singing drew him to a kitchen window. There was Anna, together with her new "sisters," singing loudly. Aimo took off his skis and prepared to knock at the front door, then thought the better of it. No adult Swede could be trusted, he thought. Swedish men were stern and without humor, like Reverend Blixdal. The women were overbearing and suffocating, like Fru Blixdal and her friends. If these people acted toward children in this way, Aimo reasoned, then it might even be worse for his parents when they arrived. He was not going to allow that to happen.

The letter from his mother brought back the gnawing uncertainty he experienced when he first learned of the plan to send Finnish children to Sweden. How long ago that seemed now. Aimo forced the unpleasant memory from his mind, concluding he had many good reasons to return to his home. He was far more valuable in Finland fighting the invaders of his country. It made more sense to help his family rebuild his home at Lake Jarvii than it did to clean Blixdal's spooky church.

Aimo quietly opened the Vahleen's front door and stepped into the darkened hallway. A stairwell space for storage of outdoor clothing lay concealed behind a curtain beneath the flight of steps leading to the second floor. He ducked in and peeked down the hallway from behind the curtain. The happy singing of female voices drifting from behind the door were interrupted by approaching steps coming up from the cellar sending the boy scurrying back into the racks of hanging coats. Aimo held his breath as Constable Vahleen ascended the stairs above Aimo's hiding place, singing as he went. Suddenly, the kitchen door flew open, and Meggan shouted happily.

"Papa's home!" she cried out and bounded up the stairs after him.

Aimo watched through the curtain as Meggan and Lisa rushed by. Trailing behind was Anna. Aimo saw his chance. Stepping quickly from behind the curtain, he grabbed his startled sister by the arm, covered her mouth with his hand, and pulled her behind the curtain.

"Quiet!" he whispered. "I'll get into big trouble if anybody finds me. We have to go."

"Why?" Anna whispered in surprise.

"We got a letter from Mama and Papa today. We have to go home before they get here."

"I don't wanna go, Aimo."

"We have to go. These are all bad people. Mama and Papa are gonna hate it here. Now hurry! Put on your coat and boots before we get caught."

Anna reluctantly followed Aimo's instructions, but she was confused. The Vahleens were wonderful people. She had grown very close to Lisa and Meggan, her new sisters. She even called Gretha and Sten *mama* and *papa*. Running away was a bad idea, and she had to tell Aimo but did not know how. She struggled with the allegiance bonding her to her new family and of the authority of her older brother. She loved Aimo but no longer had confidence in his decisions. Instinctively, she knew running away was going to lead them into trouble.

Aimo, fearing that at any moment he would be discovered, hurriedly buttoned Anna's coat. The girl opened a bureau drawer and began to sob softly. Memories of her own mother and father had not only faded, they had also been replaced by the Vahleens. The thought of leaving them was too much for the little girl to bear.

"I don't want to go, Aimo. I like being here." Tears streamed down her face.

He took Anna's hand in his. "If Mama and Papa say you can stay, then you can come back here. All right?"

Aimo's offer of compromise sounded acceptable. Once again, she allowed her big brother to lead her out into a cold, snowy evening and a new perilous adventure.

Chapter Twenty-one

Magnus Olofsson trudged out of the general store and plopped two cloth sacks of groceries onto the flatbed of his truck. Fitting a metal ratchet into the engine block of his Model B Ford, he cranked the magnetos and fired the motor to life. The simple machine sputtered courageously against the cold, and the old man pulled a flask of aquavit from his coat pocket. Taking a long swig of his homemade brew, he allowed his gaze to sweep the deserted street.

Lights from homes and businesses illuminated Christmas decorations which stretched along the street. However, all the colorful expressions of the season would soon come to an early end, possibly even before the Christmas holiday itself. An emergency ordinance was scheduled to go into effect designed to shield all lights from possible enemy aircraft.

Magnus Olofsson shook his head in dismay at the changes war had wrought. In all his seventy-one years, he had never heard of hostilities as savage as those that now raged throughout Europe. The Swedish parliament believed the fighting itself would spill into Sweden, and the country's neutrality would not last much longer. Germany had recently demanded Sweden continue to supply iron ore for its war efforts for which the Swedes were paid handsomely. But German demands on companies to pledge their companies as *Jew free* for the privilege of providing armament and war machinery was being met with increasing Swedish resistance.

The fortuitous surrender of Nazi armies in Russia made cessation of trade between Germany and Sweden an opportunity, albeit risky, the Swedes believed they had to take. Horror stories of German atrocities in Poland and elsewhere were confirmed, and the Swedes had good reason to prepare to defend themselves.

"It's only a matter of time," Olofsson thought out loud. He took another long drink from his bottle, crawled inside his truck, and waited for the engine to warm. He turned on the windshield wipers, and followed the blades' slow back-and-forth rhythm as they swept dry, fluffy snow from the glass. Encircling the steering wheel with his arms, he stared at the season's colorful decorations with sad, baleful eyes.

This Christmas season marked the fiftieth anniversary of his marriage to Dagmar Sommarfelt, if indeed they *had* gotten married. As fate would have it, the couple were making honeymoon arrangements in Göteborg when she met *the love of her life,* a visiting Portuguese sailor, and sailed away with him instead.

Olofsson returned to Nilstad a heartbroken man. His mother tried every scheme possible to introduce her handsome son to every available young woman she could find, but Olofsson would have none of them. Lengthy lectures on the virtues of marriage were routine even up to his mother's dying day. He was good looking, his mother reminded him, and wealthy since he would inherit the farm and all its considerable land. His mother insisted it would be sinful to deprive a worthy woman the opportunity to be his wife, but Magnus was adamant.

Dagmar did break his heart, but not his spirit. He attended Nilstad's dances and festivals that filled the calendar year. He was not a wallflower since he made quite a number of women, single and married, very happy to have his occasional attention. But Olofsson never went farther than that.

The old man could not remember any specific date or event that brought him to stay permanently on his farm. Here he was, surrounded by wild game and great variations of nature. Several streams on his property held brook trout, grayling, and arctic char. When ice broke on the rivers each spring, large lake trout left Lake Valdemaren to spawn in the streams. A few weeks later, they were followed by northern pike which, during spring rains, snaked across gravel-covered roads to lay their eggs in protective swamps, a tactic that offered the hatchlings an opportunity to survive their cannibalistic parents. Moose, caribou, and deer were abundant; and badgers, foxes, and wolves added to the enormous mix of wildlife. Once spring arrived, fields of wildflowers hosted dozens of colorful migratory songbirds, and Lake Valdemaren itself teemed with waterfowl.

So the farm became far more than Olofsson's home. It had become his sanctuary and his life, and he felt no need to share it with any woman. He held a deep mistrust for men as well, so he had few friends except for an occasional official get-together when Constable Vahleen made his rounds. Otherwise, he never entertained visitors.

The old man felt an overwhelming melancholy of late. At first, he dismissed these feelings, concluding he drank too much. Then, as autumn's chill and darkness settled in gloomily, he blamed the changing season for his depression. As Christmas decorations glowed over the deserted street in Nilstad and war raging in the countries around him, Olofsson concluded it was life itself that was getting him down.

He looked into his rearview mirror and was surprised by his own image. He saw an old man with white hair and a full beard. Aches and pains were numerous and lingered longer. He took another long drink, then decided to have his usual conversation with himself whenever he got into one of these troublesome moods. "You're tired of living, my friend," Olofsson muttered.

He grimaced into the mirror having more to say, but a sudden movement behind his truck caught his attention. Two children were sneaking up on him. Olofsson's first thought was they had come to steal the goods which lay on his flatbed. "So you want to steal from Magnus," he said softly. "Well, I'm ready for you, little magpies."

Aimo, on the other hand, had been watching the old man ever since he started the engine. The only thing he wanted to steal was a ride where Anna and he might find shelter for the night. The boy jumped into the flatbed and pulled his sister up behind him. The next instant, Olofsson jumped from the truck and grabbed Aimo by the collar, unaware that Anna lay shielded beneath the boy. The girl greeted the old man with a bloodcurdling scream.

"Hellvetta Fon!" Olofsson shouted in shocked surprise. Then he regained his composure. "What are you two doing in my truck?"

"We want to go home," Aimo said plaintively.

The old man immediately recognized the Finnish accent. Anna's crying, meanwhile, was reaching Wagnerian octaves.

"Can you get her to be still?" Olofsson yelled over the din. He released his hold on Aimo, and the boy gathered his sister in his arms. She shook in fear, and Olofsson felt terrible for frightening the children.

"Are you running away?" the old man asked gently.

"Yes," Aimo replied.

"Well, why didn't you say so? Come into the cab where you'll be warm," Olofsson added and helped the trembling children onto the seat. "This is the wrong time of the year to run away. It's too cold. Who're you living with anyway?" he asked.

"My sister's living with the Vahleens. I'm staying with Reverend Blixdal and his wife," Aimo answered.

"Son of a Bitchdal!" Magnus exploded. "That blowhard bastard! No wonder you ran away. I'd run away too." Olofsson regarded the now-quiet little girl. He leaned toward her and lowered his voice. "I know the Vahleens. They're very nice people."

"Meggan and Lisa are my sisters," Anna replied

"I don't understand why you ran away from them."

"Aimo made me," she complained.

Aimo lowered his eyes in shame. His sister was right. All he did was get them into trouble.

"So your name is Aimo," Olofsson said. He offered the boy his hand, and Aimo took it. Olofsson playfully gave his hand a heavy shake, exaggerating the boy's strength. "That's a strong handshake," Olofsson joked.

"You did it," Aimo replied quickly.

Olofsson became serious. "Look, I can understand why you don't like Blixdal. He doesn't even like himself. But running away won't do any good because you'll both freeze to death."

"I got a letter from my mother and father. They're going to come here any day."

"So . . . ? Why don't you wait for them at Blixdal's place? It's warmer there than out here."

The boy returned the old man's stare. He made sense, and there was kindness in Olofsson's eyes. It was stupid to risk freezing and, worse, to take risks with Anna as well. But the fury of Blixdal's temper came to Aimo's mind.

"Herr Blixdal is going to beat my butt," Aimo said.

"So . . . ? It's better than dying in the snow. Tell yourself you're going to get bigger and stronger, and one day, you'll kick his hypocritical butt."

Aimo smiled at the idea and Olofsson added, "How about I take you kids back?" Both children nodded in agreement. Olofsson shifted into gear, and the old truck chugged forward. "Did I tell you I don't like Blixdal?"

"Sort of," Aimo answered as the old man drove off.

Olofsson directed the Model B truck down the lane leading to the Vahleen home. The glare of a flashlight beam cut through the large heavily falling snowflakes across his windshield. The old man brought the truck to a stop under the snow-covered branches of an apple tree as Constable Vahleen closed the distance in a dead run. He was totally out of breath when he reached them.

The old man climbed out of the truck and confided the ordeal that Aimo and Anna had just been through. Olofsson asked Vahleen to understand Aimo's situation with the Blixdals as well as the boy's determination to return to Finland with his sister. "We'd do the same damn thing if it were us," Olofsson concluded.

"How do I get Aimo to understand the danger he put Anna and himself in?" Vahleen asked. "Not to mention he broke the law by breaking into my house. Think of that! I'm the law around here for God's sake."

"They're both pretty scared. I don't think this is the right time," Olofsson said.

"You're right, Magnus. Talk to the boy in your own way when you return him to the Blixdals. I'll take the girl." Vahleen opened the door to the truck and was met with Anna's open arms.

"Papa!" she cried out jumping into the man's chest.

Aimo kept his head bowed shamefully and stared at the floor.

The excited voices of Gretha, Solveig, and the girls descended on the truck. Everyone spoke at once. A myriad of overlapping questions finally ended when Meggan rushed to her father and snatched Anna from him angrily.

"How could you do this, Anna?" Meggan chastised. "Why did you run away?"

Anna threw her arms around the older girl. "I'm sorry. I'll never do it again."

"Never?" Meggan demanded, and Anna replied, "No! Never."

"Never, ever, forever," Lisa joined in, and the three girls jogged back to the house, hand in hand.

Vahleen shook Olofsson's hand vigorously. "Thank you, Magnus. We all appreciate what you've done."

"Magnus!" Gretha added with relief, "Do you have plans for Christmas?"

"No, Fru Vahleen," he replied politely. "I don't."

"Good!" Gretha said emphatically. "We want you to share Christmas with us and play the role of Santa Claus."

"It's a contract!" Olofsson said, shaking hands heartily then took notice of Solveig. The beautiful woman had silently witnessed the drama resolve itself, and she stepped forward. She offered Olofsson her hand without waiting to be formally introduced.

"Solveig Olin," she said.

The old man stiffened his upper body, took her hand in his, and bowed. "Magnus Olofsson, at your service," he said strongly.

"It's good to meet you," she said with a smile, then added, "I'm also sharing Christmas with the Vahleens."

Olofsson laughed loudly. "Then you can definitely count me in," he chortled.

"Magnus Olofsson! Behave yourself," Gretha scolded jokingly. "Bring Aimo to the house, and you both can have some fresh-baked gingerbread and coffee."

Olofsson entered his Model B and invited the constable to join him. The two men sat on either side of Aimo. The boy's eyes had not lifted from staring forlornly at the floor. Olofsson started the engine and drove slowly toward the Vahleen house.

"Cheer up, Aimo," Vahleen said. "I'll call the Blixdals when we get home so they won't be worried."

"He's gonna beat me anyway," Aimo said sadly, "and then put me in an orphanage."

"He can't do that, can he?" Olofsson asked angrily.

"Who told you about the orphanage?" Vahleen asked.

"Reverend Blixdal," Aimo answered.

"Why?" Vahleen continued.

"Because I didn't call Fru Blixdal mother," Aimo replied.

Vahleen faced a dilemma. Officially he was obligated to call Blixdal to report he had custody of his Finnish adoptee, and then return him. For all Vahleen knew, the Blixdals may have already tried to call him to report Aimo's disappearance when everyone was out of the house searching for Anna. The major concern Vahleen had was that Aimo's well-being depended on what he told the Blixdals.

"Why won't you call her *mother?*" Olofsson asked.

"'Cause she's *not* my mother," Aimo responded indignantly.

"What's gonna happen if you do call her *mother?*" Olofsson continued.

"Nothing . . . I guess," Aimo said.

Olofsson braked the truck to a stop and slapped the boy on the knee. "Then by god, call the woman *mother!* Call her *grandmother!* Hell! Make 'em both happy and call her *mother superior.*" The old man looked at Sten, "Listen, call the Blixdals . . . tell 'em you found the boy . . ."—he searched for a solution—"doing what? . . . Aimo, how did you get to the Vahleens?"

"I skied," Aimo replied, very interested in the old man's plan.

"OK! Sten, here's what I think you can say. Aimo was skiing . . . got lost . . . and you found him. How about that?"

"But I'm not supposed to leave the house," Aimo added.

"Why did you leave in the first place?" Sten asked.

"Because Fru Blixdal gave me skis, and I didn't call her *mother*," Aimo repeated.

"Here we go with *mother* again," Olofsson shouted out loud.

"Wait a minute," Sten added. "Here's what I'll say . . . Aimo was upset that Fru Blixdal was *upset* . . . because he didn't call her *mother* . . . he felt so bad he went out for a long ski run . . ." Sten lifted his eyes, searching.

Olofsson broke in, "Skiing on his new skis . . . that his *mother* gave him . . . and . . . and . . . he felt so bad he—"

"Cried," Sten interrupted. "He cried . . . got confused . . . and got lost."

Olofsson was enjoying the unfolding story. Now he became enthusiastic. "And I found him!" Olofsson announced triumphantly.

The three conspirators climbed from the truck. Sten took Aimo's skis and placed them on the flatbed. As they moved into the house, Sten turned to Olofsson. "If you found him, why did you bring him to *my* house?"

"Because you're the constable, and the boy was crying so hard he was incoherent, that's why," Olofsson offered simply.

"Good!" Sten said. "I think it will work. Let's go in the house. I'll call the Blixdals. You and Aimo can get some muffins and coffee."

Aimo had intently followed the two adults as they scripted a story to spare him from the reverend's punishment. His head swiveled back and forth between the animated face of Olofsson, and the deep, contemplative expression of the constable. Both were so involved they had completely ignored Aimo. Nor had they asked for his input. This was their story to create and convincing Bixdal was their mutual goal.

Aimo was elated. He never before had had two adults so focused on his well being that they would energetically invent an excuse for his behavior. The boy followed the old man into the Vahleen's home, a half smile on his face at the irony of being welcomed into the same house he had broken into earlier.

Olofsson drove Aimo back to the Nilstad church, both well fortified with freshly baked pastry and hot coffee. As they neared the road leading to the Blixdals, Olofsson rehearsed Aimo's story one more time.

"OK, Aimo! Fru Blixdal gave you skis, and you didn't do what?"

"Call her *mother*," Aimo replied.

"No! No! Not yet! You didn't show your *respect*." He emphasized the word.

"I did not show Mother my respect," Aimo said.

"And . . . ?" Olofsson waited for the hook to be set.

"And I felt so bad . . . I took a long ski run and cried."

"A lot," Olofsson reminded him, "You cried a lot."

"And I got lost and Mr. Olofsson found me and took me to Constable Vahleen."

"That's enough! Just remember, whenever you can't think of what to say, look at Fru Blixdal and say 'mother.'"

The moment Olofsson stopped his vehicle, the church door flew open; and Karen Blixdal, still ecstatic over the welcoming phone call she had just received from Constable Vahleen, rushed through the falling snow to the truck.

"Mikael! Mikael!" she shouted repeatedly.

"Go to it, Aimo," Olofsson coaxed. The boy jumped from the truck and embraced the woman at once.

"I'm so sorry, Mother," Aimo said. "I went for a long ski and got lost—"

"Mother!" Karen Blixdal cried out loud, "Oh! Mikael! Mikael! Bjorn! He called me *mother!*"

She danced the boy in circles on the snow as Reverend Blixdal strode purposefully to Olofsson's truck. He had little use for the likes of Olofsson and even less use for the Finnish boy who, he hoped, had indeed run away for good. Basically he was angry that Aimo had been found and now had to feign his gratitude to Olofsson, of all people.

"Thank you for finding the boy," Blixdal lied through clenched teeth.

"I'm glad I did. He was crying." Olofsson peered in the direction of Aimo and Karen. "Crying a lot . . . lots and lots of crying."

Olofsson watched bemused as Aimo allowed Karen Blixdal to hug him repeatedly. Olofsson put the truck in gear and drove away in the snow mumbling to himself, "Crying so much for his whacky mother . . ."

He broke into peels of uncontrollable laughter and did not see the rage building in Blixdal's face.

Chapter Twenty-two

The community of Nilstad settled into a frenetic pre-Christmas pace as it did each year on December 12, the day before the traditional Sankta Lucia celebration.

Gretha had the Vahleen household working full bore. Gaily colored materials of red, green, and white were found throughout the house. Newly washed and ironed curtains, tablecloths, bathroom linens, and bedsheets were placed in their appropriate places. A permanent aroma of freshly baked bread, cakes, and cookies permeated every room. Colorful knickknacks of straw, pewter, and wood depicting Christmas scenes and characters were everywhere. Candles of red or white protruded from a variety of candleholders.

Everyone had a job to do and Gretha, with a single-minded purpose, made certain each person did his job on time. Sten kept himself busy on a secret project, staying out of sight behind the closed doors of his cellar workroom. Tradition called for the man of the house to sleep a little later on December 13 and be celebrated by the arrival of Lucia, the legendary princess of light, usually played by the woman of the house or the oldest daughter, which for her first time, would be portrayed by Meggan. Everyone else in the house had to play a subordinate role of an attendant.

Gretha and Solveig completed baking a mound of traditional saffron buns, then collected the girls to finish the fitting of their Lucia costumes. The long-anticipated replacement of Gretha with Meggan as the Lucia princess would finally happen this year.

At Nilstad's Western District School, Fredrik Pontilius labored alone in the night, devoid of the gaiety and happiness in the community around him. Three days remained before the Christmas school break, and the teacher had to finalize each child's grades for submission to the district office of education.

The thirty-three students, in grades one through seven, required a full one-page evaluation per child. This year an added task required Pontilius to record psychological observations of each Finnish student as well as recommendations for their future in Sweden.

Pontilius's only company was his shortwave radio. He switched bands between Sweden's Melody Radio, playing Christmas folk songs from Stockholm and the BBC, with its classical music and English newscasts describing the course of the war.

Across frozen Lake Valdemaren, Magnus Olofsson, a master at making fishing lures of wood or metal, hung dozens of brightly colored plugs, wobblers, and spinners from their treble hooks throughout the cabin. All were painted in intricate colors and detailed patterns. Olofsson even decorated his Christmas tree with an assortment of fishing lures even though he was a week early for tree trimming.

He had built the cabin with no architectural plans, no real knowledge of construction, and no help. But he was pleased with the results. He especially loved the ceiling-high stone fireplace occupying an entire wall. A variety of blackened cast-iron pots hung from metal hangers fastened to the stone. Olofsson did most of his cooking simply by swinging a pot, suspended from a metal hanger, directly over the open flame of the fireplace.

Against another wall, Olofsson had built a potato liquor still in which he produced the strongest, if not the best, potato brandy in the region. Devoid of electricity, the cabin relied on several kerosene lamps to provide illumination and the fireplace to supply warmth. Three large windows offered wide-angle seasonal views of the countryside he treasured. As far as Olofsson was concerned, this was all the company he needed.

Christmas was the only time of year the Blixdals worked together as a harmonious team. As the church social director, Karen Blixdal's days and evenings were filled with preparations for the season. Immediately following the Lucia celebration, Karen planned to assemble her choir members to prepare for the very important Christmas-day service, the one day of the year Swedish churches were filled to capacity.

Reverend Blixdal in particular looked forward to the day with great anticipation. The Christmas service was held in the inky darkness of 7:00 AM. and worshipers traveled from throughout the region packing the church to overflowing. This was *the* day and *the* audience the clergyman needed to deliver his perfect sermon. He knew it and labored at editing and rehearsing the script continually in anticipation of the moment his parishioners would welcome him as their new bishop.

The job of preparing the church for the holiday season was Karen's; and this year, she worked at her chores with a newfound energy together with her compliant assistant, Aimo. The boy accepted Karen's requests with a string of "Yes, Mother" replies, leading the woman to mention her "beloved Mikael" in her evening prayers and thanking God for the boy's Christian rebirth.

For Aimo, keeping busy allowed time to pass quickly; and he awoke each morning, hoping it would be the day that would bring a reunion with his parents. He kept the military medal in his pants pocket at all times, making certain the treasured possession stayed with him each time he exchanged trousers. The nearly nonstop industry within the church provided Aimo with several benefits. The reverend was too busy with scriptwriting or voice inflection to notice him, except at dinner time. There, under the watchful eye of the clergyman, the boy ate in proper Swedish fashion as Aimo remembered Fru Blixdal's eating etiquette.

Fork in the left hand, knife in the right. Cut one, bite-size morsel at a time. Chew with mouth closed. Sit upright in the chair. Ask for food to be passed. Don't reach.

A second benefit was the fun the boy had in candle-making. He melted wax in the black cauldron in the tallow room and made candles at every opportunity; so many in fact, that boxes of candles began to stack up in the small stone-walled room. Aimo's industry resulted in the Nilstad church being better illuminated than it ever had been.

There also was a third benefit, a special surprise Fru Blixdal said Aimo could expect. This promise captivated the boy. Could it be, he hoped, there was an arrangement for his parents to arrive at Christmas? *What a present indeed*, Aimo thought. He silently thanked Magnus Olofsson for the advice in dealing with the clergyman's wife.

Dinnertime on Lucia Eve was the best meal Aimo had experienced with the Blixdals. Even the reverend seemed to be in a cheerful mood, very much out of character for him. Following the dinner, the reverend excused himself for some duty he needed to perform at the orphanage, and Aimo assisted Karen with cleaning up in the kitchen. Afterward, she produced a music sheet with the score for the Santa Lucia song, explaining how she would play the role of the Lucia princess for her husband in the morning.

"You, Mikael, will be the *Star Boy*, and you must learn these words."

She handed Aimo the sheet of music and instructed him to follow her lead as she sang, "Darkness the world besets, shadows prevailing, even the sun forgets, charity failing. Then in the winter night, she'll bring us hope and light, Sankta Lucia, Sankta Lucia."

They rehearsed the song together while completing after-dinner chores and continued the singing when going up to Aimo's room. There, Aimo's Star Boy costume lay stretched out over the bed, a white floor-length tunic and a high conical cap made of white drawing paper covered with golden stars held in place by an elastic ribbon fitted tightly under the wearer's chin.

Aimo stared at the concoction in disbelief. It looked exactly like the dunce cap Pontilius kept at school, and Aimo didn't want to participate in anything so silly. But he surrendered himself to Olofsson's earlier advice. That meant accommodating the relentless Blixdals.

"Come, Mikael. Let's try these on," Karen said. She unbuttoned his clothes until the boy stood in his underwear and allowed the woman to pull the white tunic over his head. Then she placed the Star Boy cap on his head.

"There! You look adorable," she said inviting Aimo to peek at himself in the mirror.

Aimo preferred not to. "When do I have to wear this? Just tomorrow morning?" he asked hopefully.

"You don't like it, do you?" Karen exclaimed in disappointment. "Well, let's take a bath. We have to be absolutely clean tomorrow. Then I'll put on my Lucia crown, and you'll see how beautiful we'll look together."

Karen sprinkled a hefty supply of bubble-bath crystals into the heated water, filling the steaming room with the pungent odor of sweet lilac. She called for Aimo to come into the bathroom, removed his underwear, and watched as the boy ducked playfully under the billowing mounds of bubbles.

"I think Mother will take a bath now too," Karen said. She removed her clothes, stepped into the bathtub, and faced Aimo.

The boy poked his head through a hill of bubbles, surprised to find the woman in the water with him. It was the first time she had joined him in the bathtub, and Aimo felt strangely uncomfortable. He accepted nudity as natural, but the idea of being in a bathtub so close to a naked woman aroused the boy in a way he did not understand.

The large white mounds of the woman's breasts seemed to float on the surface of the water, and her wide pink nipples looked like raw flesh. She took a washrag, lathered it in soap, and cleansed her face. She lathered a second time and washed beneath her arms then raised her eyes to see Aimo staring at her breasts in fascination. She lathered the washcloth and handed it to the boy.

"You may wash them if you want to," she said.

"No! That's OK," Aimo answered.

"Oh! Go ahead, Mikael. Wash them," she coaxed.

Aimo took the wash cloth, scrunched it into a ball, and rubbed the woman's breast as though scrubbing one of the wooden church pews.

"No! Do it gently, like this," the woman said. She placed the open cloth in Aimo's palm and guided his hand over her breast, moving his hand in a slow circular motion. Aimo's eyes riveted on his hand, and he allowed his fingers to close over the softest flesh he had ever felt.

Karen closed her eyes, adjusted her shoulders, and presented her second breast to the boy. Aimo dipped the open cloth into the warm water and prepared to wash the second breast as he did the first, but Karen had other requirements.

"Just use your hand, Mikael. Don't use the cloth," she said throatily. Her voice had lowered, and she kept her eyes closed.

Aimo's hand moved across the tip of her breast and was surprised as her nipple became turgid. Fascinated by the change, the boy poked the rigid nipple with a forefinger.

"It got hard," Aimo said in surprise.

Karen's eyes flashed open. She took Aimo's hand in hers and sighed deeply. Taking a deep breath, she pushed his hand away.

"Thank you, Mikael," she said quickly. "Now dry yourself and go to your room. I'll join you in a moment."

Aimo hopped from the tub, dried himself, and went to his room as instructed. He did not see the woman slide down into the warm water, spread her legs, and release the sexual tension that had built up in her loins.

Chapter Twenty Three

At six in the morning on December 13, Sankta Lucia Day found the Vahleen kitchen alive with activity. Solveig lit the numerous candles as Gretha placed cups of hot cocoa and baskets of warm saffron buns onto two trays. Gretha switched off the kitchen light and, in fluttering candle glow, gave a final inspection of the girls' outfits. Their reflections were clearly mirrored in the kitchen window against the black early morning darkness. Everyone was dressed in their white floor-length tunics. Garlands of gold tinsel encircled their waists and head, and Meggan wore her crown of flaming candles radiantly.

"Look how beautiful we all are," Gretha said in a hushed tone. Everyone took the moment to admire themselves as a group before Gretha directed them out of the kitchen. Silently, they climbed the steps to the second floor and took a position outside Sten's bedroom door. Gretha held up her hand, and at her signal, their five voices began their Santa Lucia serenade in harmony as they entered the bedroom.

Sten crawled from beneath the warmth of his down comforter, smiling happily at the heartwarming sight before him. Meggan, portraying the role of Santa Lucia for the first time, marked a family milestone radiantly. Flanking her were the sweet faces of Anna and Lisa, singing with the innocence of angels. Sten shifted his eyes to the extraordinarily beautiful women standing behind the girls, quite flattered by the honor his family brought to him.

Through every darkened door,
She's coming near. Defeating dread and gloom, Dispersing fear
Welcome the maiden fair, With candles in her hair,
Santa Lucia, Santa Lucia.

Fru Blixdal brushed her hair vigorously to effect cascading blond locks tumbling over the bodice of her white tunic. Having succeeded with her hair, she placed the scarlet sash around her waist, then positioned the Lucia crown of candles on her head.

She found Aimo in the kitchen, struggling uncomfortably in his Star Boy tunic and attempting to pull a batch of warm saffron buns from the oven. He placed them on a tray next to a pot of coffee, causing the cups and saucers to clatter in the process.

"Shh! Mikael!" Karen whispered. "We must be quiet. We don't want to wake the reverend yet. Light the candles on the tray then light these on my crown . . . *carefully*."

Aimo completed his candle-lighting instructions without mishap. He then lifted the tray with coffee, cups, and warm buns in preparation for climbing the stairs.

"Do I look beautiful?" she asked. Aimo nodded his head, but her smiling face twisted into a frown.

"Where is your hat, Mikael? The Star Boy must wear his hat."

Aimo hated the hat and wished she had forgotten it. Unfortunately, she remembered. It looked stupid and, worse, did not fit. The elastic band under his chin to hold the contraption on his head always slipped, snapping painfully under his nose.

Karen placed the Star Boy cone on Aimo's head, fixed the elastic band beneath his chin, and led him outside the reverend's bedroom door. She began singing and, Aimo followed her into the dark room. At the foot of Blixdal's bed, Karen sang earnestly while Aimo stood mutely by her side.

All corners of the world, No more obscure
Hope will become unfurled, She will assure
Days will again be bright, So speaks the Queen of Light,
Sankta Lucia . . . Sankta Lucia

Blixdal awakened from a sound sleep with a start. Startled, he sat upright in bed and stared at the apparitionlike forms who seemed to float like ethereal specters in the darkened room. Finally he recognized the face of his wife beneath the glowing candles and shifted his gaze to Aimo. The boy looked idiotic, and Blixdal might have laughed were it not for the expression on the boy's face. In the candles' glow, Aimo's dark eyes stared passively in the direction of the clergyman, but his face contorted through an assortment of grimaces.

Unknown to the reverend, Aimo was having great difficulty with the rubber band holding his cone-shaped hat on his head. The band had already begun to slip beneath his chin as they began climbing the steps to the reverend's bedroom. Inexorably, the contraption was slipping forward and would soon spring loose. Aimo's hands held the laden tray steady so he couldn't use them to help his dilemma. He contorted the muscles of his face in a desperate attempt to keep the elastic secure, but Blixdal misunderstood the boy's expression. In his mind, Aimo was brazenly making faces at him, and the reverend intended to deal with the unruly boy as soon as Karen finished singing.

The song came to an end, and Karen surprised the man by leaning forward and kissing his forehead.

"Happy Lucia, Bjorn."

"Happy Lucia," Blixdal answered.

"Mikael! Come! Join me," she commanded. Aimo, the tray loaded with muffins and filled coffee pot clutched firmly in his hands, walked to her side.

"How do we look?" She draped her arm around the boy, and the clergyman nodded in approval, deciding to hold his scolding of the boy until after his wife had completed her ceremony.

"Give the reverend the tray of coffee, Mikael," Karen instructed.

Aimo leaned forward offering the minister the tray. He realized his mistake at once, but was powerless to prevent what was about to happen. The elastic band beneath his chin snapped upward, sharply striking the boy beneath his nose. The timing could not have been worse.

Blixdal had stretched his arms to take the tray from Aimo. At that same moment, the boy's hands left the tray to clutch his face. For a millisecond the candlelit tray, loaded with saffron buns, hot coffee, and cups hung suspended in the air. Then it dropped onto the reverend's arms. The man recoiled swiftly in a reflective reaction that launched the tray and all its contents into a catapulting collision with his chest. Blixdal's agonized cry exploded across the room.

"Oowwww! . . . Jävla Fon! . . . Oowwwoo! You little bastard!" Blixdal yowled. The scalded man sprang from the bed, his nightclothes drenched in burning hot coffee. Karen stood screaming beneath her crown of candles as the reverend shoved her aside. He snatched up the serving tray and began pummeling the boy with it.

Amid a cascade of sparkling embers, Fru Blixdal shouted a prolonged "NO!" She wrestled the man to the ground as lighted candles tumbled from the crown-harness on her head. Both adults writhed on the wooden floor, smacking at the flame with their hands and plunging the room into inky blackness. Aimo scrambled out of the bedroom, bolting for the safety of his own room and leaving the minister and his wife to contort on the floor.

Karen cried uncontrollably, beside herself in disappointment. She had so looked forward to the Christmas season with joy, desperately wanting their Sankta Lucia tradition to be extraordinary now that it could be shared with a child. Instead it was a disaster. She buried her head in her husband's coffee-soaked nightshirt and cried bitterly.

The reverend held the shaking woman against his chest, stroking her hair absently while stifling the urge to erupt in rage.

This hated Finnish boy . . . this heathen child . . . this stupid, tragic attempt of providing a home for this unwelcome refugee . . . all of it . . . must come to an end. His own future depended on it. That meant placing Aimo in the orphanage at the earliest opportunity or, god help him, doing away with the boy entirely.

Chapter Twenty-four

The class labored silently at their final exam before the Christmas break. Pontilius looked up at the loudly ticking wall clock then gazed over the intensely concentrated children. Aimo caught his attention. The boy twisted uncomfortably in his desk, alternately scribbling on the paper in front of him and scratching his head. The teacher took careful notice.

"Two minutes," Pontilius announced. He snapped the prosthesis in place and limped in front of a window. The whitened countryside glistened pristinely beneath the clear blue winter sky. "Time," Pontilius called.

The quiet room stirred as the students expressed relief at having ended their ordeal.

"I want everyone to place their examination papers on my desk," Pontilius continued. "Meggan, please take some volunteers and make us all some hot cocoa. It's too cold to eat lunch outside. We'll stay indoors today."

The children moved freely through the room, fetching lunches from knapsacks and chatting nervously about their exams. Aimo remained seated at his desk dawdling.

"Aimo," Pontilius said softly, "I called time. Put your paper on my desk, then put on your coat and boots. I want you to come with me."

Aimo followed Pontilius into the school yard. They headed silently in the direction of the ice hockey pond, and finally, Pontilius spoke.

"Do you want to tell me what's bothering you?" he asked. Aimo answered by shrugging his shoulders.

"You've become very nervous these last few days. Why?"

The boy shook his head as a signal that he did not know.

"I want you to trust me, Aimo. I would like you to tell me what's bothering you." Again, there was no answer.

Pontilius recognized Aimo's behavior. He remembered the feeling of desolation when he discovered his leg had been amputated. He lay alone for days on a cold cot in a darkened Finnish field hospital. Morphine-induced sleep brought dreams of exhilarating triumphs on the ski slopes and passionate pleasures with Solveig. They all shattered to an end as he relived, again and again, the moment when the artillery shell exploded next to him.

He recalled the surprise of the nearby blast which threw him into the air. Slowly, the awareness of where he was and what had happened returned, and he felt the dull pain at his right knee. He screamed in agony at seeing the stump of what was left of his leg. Then he closed his eyes and wept, willing with all his being that somehow, he could simply open his eyes again and have the leg return.

Pontilius vividly remembered the day a young Finnish doctor came to his bed and strapped a mechanical apparatus to his thigh above the knee. Working meticulously, the doctor connected the smooth, skin-colored wooden replica of a human leg that required engagement to stand and disengagement to sit. But instead of a leg, there was continual physical pain.

The shame of being disfigured extinguished the ebullience of the young man who had volunteered to help his Finnish neighbors. He would never be the man he had been. Those who tried to help him were doing so out of pity, he thought. He was a curiosity at best, and he resigned himself to a life of loneliness.

"I want to show you something," Pontilius said. He lifted his pants leg up to reveal the prosthesis. It stood out, stark and artificial. Aimo gawked at the sight. "You knew, didn't you? All the children must talk about it," Pontilius added.

"Not all the time," Aimo answered. "And nobody makes fun."

"Well, I can't help that everyone knows. Sometimes, I feel I want to shout to people . . . I'm not *normal* . . . is that how you feel, Aimo?" Pontilius spoke with bare emotion, unaware that he was unveiling his innermost feelings to another human being for the first time since his injury.

"Yes!" Aimo said simply.

"I lost my leg in the war. It got blown off," Pontilius told the boy.

"Fru Blixdal said it happened in Finland."

"That's right. I was hit by a Russian shell."

"I hate the Russians."

"Is that how you feel about Reverend Blixdal?" Pontilius asked.

"Yes! I spilled coffee on him. I didn't mean to. He said he's going to put me in an orphanage," Aimo confessed.

"And that's why you're nervous?"

"Yes! If I go to an orphanage, my parents will never find me," Aimo said, relieving himself of his immense burden.

"Would you like me to find another family for you?"

"I have to stay near my sister," Aimo replied.

"I spoke with Constable Vahleen to see if you could stay with them. Their house is very full."

"Lenne said I could stay with them," Aimo informed.

"All right then. That's a good choice. If that's what you'd like."

Aimo nodded. Pontilius offered his hand. "Is it a contract? If it is, I'll arrange it."

"A contract," Aimo answered. He took the teacher's hand.

"You will not go to an orphanage, Aimo," Pontilius declared.

The quiet scene was suddenly disturbed by the discordant sound of a car horn noisily announcing Blixdal's arrival.

"Why is the reverend here? School hasn't let out?" Pontilius asked.

"I don't know, but I have to go," Aimo said, releasing his grip of the teacher's hand. "Maybe my mom and dad have arrived." He sprinted to the reverend's waiting sedan and disappeared into the vehicle.

The teacher relocked the prosthesis in place and angrily followed the path of the car as it left the school yard. "I promise, Aimo. You will not go to an orphanage!" Pontilius said aloud to himself.

Reverend Blixdal drove in detached silence, completely ignoring Aimo, sitting worriedly in the backseat. The boy watched the unfamiliar countryside, searching in vain for recognizable sights. They were not returning to the church where he expected his parents to be delivered. Could his parents be somewhere else? he wondered.

"Where are we going?" Aimo asked.

"You'll see when we get there," Blixdal answered while keeping his eyes on the road. He said nothing else.

Aimo's worst fears were realized when the clergyman's black sedan pulled off the road and braked to a stop in front of a large Victorian house. Over the door hung the dreaded sign, Nilstad Orphanage.

"Stay in the car and wait for me," Blixdal commanded.

The reverend slammed the door shut and trudged through the snow toward the verandah. Removing his boots, he entered the house in stocking feet then paused for a moment. He listened for sounds in the house, but hearing none, he climbed the steps to the second floor.

Both doors to the children's ward were shut, but whimpering from within the rooms told the man that Fröken Elsa was in one of her *disciplinary* moods. He reached a flight of narrow steps leading to Elsa's chambers, climbed the stairs, and put his ear to the door before opening it. He allowed himself to enter.

The peculiar heptagonal-shaped room offered a panoramic view of the nearly isolated countryside from its five large windows. A rose-shaded floor lamp illuminated the room with a hazy pink hue while a large floor-model radio softly played American contemporary music from the BBC. Elsa lay on her stomach in a black fringed housecoat, sleeping soundly.

"Elsa! It's me, Bjorn. Wake up," Blixdal called.

The woman rolled over sleepily then, recognizing Blixdal, she sat up quickly.

"I'm sorry," she said with a yawn. "These damnable kids woke me early this morning." She held her hand to her mouth to stifle a second yawn, which allowed the robe to fall open, revealing the deep cleavage of her breasts. "How long can you stay?" she asked provocatively.

"I can't stay. I've come to ask a favor."

"I'll grant it if you promise to stay with me a little while," she answered seductively.

Blixdal sat on the bed next to her. "What are your duties with the orphans? Do they go to school?" Blixdal visited the orphanage many times before but never to ask questions about the children.

Elsa rose from the bed, crossed to a cabinet, and filled two crystal glasses with sherry. She returned to the minister and offered him the drink.

Blixdal accepted it and quickly touched Elsa's glass with his "Skoal."

"Skoal," Elsa replied, and each took a healthy swallow of the sweet wine.

"School?" Elsa asked, wiping her lips with the back of her hand. "These are Finnish children. I have nine of them here. In addition to being idiots, they're too uncivilized to go to school."

"Good! Then you teach them here?" Blixdal asked.

"Bjorn! Why such a banal question? Part of my duties here are teaching. Their ability to learn is another matter. What are you trying to tell me?"

Blixdal stammered, "I have . . . that is . . . we have . . . my wife and I . . . have taken a Finnish boy into our home. Sometimes, I think I could kill him. I've even dreamt about killing him." Blixdal's voice trailed off. He fought to control himself then continued, "He is going to bring ruin to my career. I know it."

Elsa took another swallow of sherry and shot the reverend a steely glare. "You want *me* to take another damn Finska? You must think me mad. I keep records. I don't receive my stipend or ration stamps without records." Elsa moved to a window and looked over the darkening countryside. "I can't take some kid here because you hate him."

"Elsa!" the reverend pleaded. "It's worse than you think. In less than one year, I'll be named bishop. These next months are the most important of my life. I'll pay double your stipend . . . and I have ways of getting additional food stamps."

Elsa strode thoughtfully around the room draining her glass of sherry as she walked, then she refilled the glass..

"Where's the boy now?" she asked.

"Downstairs in my car," Blixdal replied.

"Downstairs!" Elsa exploded. "I'm so pissed at those brats that if you brought one more kid to me now, I'd kill him myself."

"I can't leave him now anyway. I just picked him up from school. The damn teacher saw us."

"When? When do you want to do it?" Elsa asked

"After Christmas. The boy has run away twice already. We'll simply declare he did it again."

"And what about your wife, Bjorn? How does she feel?"

"God, no! That's the problem. She can't . . . she can't ever know. She fawns over the child like . . . like . . . it's her own. It's so . . . ridiculous . . . it sickens me."

Elsa felt the control she had over the man returning. He always felt guilty when speaking of his wife and it caused him to stammer in disjointed sentences.

"My poor, Bjorn! The plot thickens. Your wife can't know. My superiors can't know, and I'm to take all these risks so you can become bishop."

"I would be . . . grateful . . . ," Blixdal stammered again. Elsa interrupted him. It was time to test the man further.

"Grateful enough to leave your wife?" she asked.

"Damn you, woman," Blixdal snapped, his voice rising. "I've told you from the start, there will be no divorce. You and I have what we have. It's all I can give you."

"Calm yourself, Bjorn." She crossed to Blixdal and kissed him passionately. "I love you freely. I've told you that." Blixdal returned her kiss, and the woman wrapped her arms around his buttocks, pressing her pelvis against him.

"Take me before you leave," she pleaded huskily.

"I can't. Not now. I have the boy in the car." Blixdal squirmed to free himself.

Elsa released her grip and moved to her bed, allowing her housecoat to fall to the floor. She spread herself provocatively over the blanket.

"Let him wait another thirty minutes," she said.

Aimo shivered uncontrollably. The outdoor temperature was well below zero, and the unheated car offered little comfort. He gave a thought to running away but realized there was no where to go. He would not last long in the frigid cold. Olofsson's warning that he would be of no value to his parents if he froze to death reminded him it would be foolish to try.

The windows of the car were covered in thick frost, and the boy rubbed the glass vigorously with his mittens, melting a small window in the ice. Aimo peered through the space in the direction of the house. At that moment, a boy his age emerged from the verandah, carrying a large metal bucket. The boy stumbled through the deep snow to the tree line at the property's edge. He emptied the contents of the bucket behind a drooping, snow-laden pine branch and darted back into the house.

Aimo recognized the familiar profile. "Mooseface!" he shouted as the boy disappeared through the verandah. Aimo jumped from the car and raced toward the large building. He pulled open the verandah door and stepped into the house without hesitation. Slowly, his body adjusted to the warmth, and he strained to see or hear anything that could tell him of Mooseface's whereabouts.

Sounds of soft crying coming from the second floor above him drew Aimo's attention. He climbed the steps cautiously, discovering the source of the noise came from behind two closed doors. Choosing the door nearest him, Aimo turned the handle and peeked inside.

The pungent odor of human waste wafted sickly over him. Grimacing from the stench, he slid inside the darkened room. The electric lights were switched off, and closed window shades prevented the penetration of whatever light a mid-December day provided. Aimo could barely make out five military cots placed vertically against a wall, but the sounds of sobbing children drew the boy closer.

"Mooseface!" Aimo called hopefully in a loud whisper.

"Aimo!" a voice replied from one of the cots. Aimo rushed to the sound of his name and stared at his friend shivering under his blanket.

"Hi, Aimo!" Mooseface whispered through chattering teeth.

"Hi, Mooseface," Aimo replied. "Were you outside just now?"

"Yes! That bitch makes me go out every day and empty the shit buckets. We're not allowed to use the toilets. I'm frozen stiff," Mooseface complained.

"How come you can't use the toilets?" Aimo asked.

"'Cause somebody pissed in bed," Mooseface answered.

"How come you gotta do it?"

"She hates me. She put me in the cellar as soon as I got here. She's a witch. She beats everybody, even your cousin."

Aimo was crestfallen on hearing the news that Pehr had been placed in the orphanage. During the past several weeks, he had been so consumed with his own worries he hadn't given his cousin a thought.

"Pehr?" Aimo asked. "He's here? Where?"

"He's in the bed next to me. He's really sick. He coughs a lot."

Aimo moved to Pehr's cot. The boy lay on his side beneath a woolen blanket, his incessant hum scarcely audible. Aimo put a comforting hand on his cousin's matted hair. Mooseface lifted himself from his bed but kept the blanket wrapped tightly around his neck.

"Anyway, that's why I have to empty the shit buckets. As soon as we got here, she stuck soap in Pehr's mouth and broke the wood dog you made for him. I was makin' him another one and got caught."

Mooseface and Aimo stared down at the sick child.

"Pehr! Pehr! It's me, Aimo," he whispered. The boy was burning with fever.

"He can hear," Mooseface announced. "Hey, Pehr! It's me, Mooseface. Aimo's here."

Pehr slowly turned to the voice, and Aimo gaped in disbelief at the frightful sight. Pehr's eyes were red and swollen, and two streams of mucous hung heavily from his nostrils. Gone was the robust boy who had shared Aimo's youth. In his place was an emaciated, seriously ill, and possibly insane child.

Pehr opened his mouth to speak but coughed instead. A heavy croup revealed the deep congestion in his lungs. He turned on his side, his body wrenching into convulsive coughing that ended with copious amounts of phlegm spattering from his mouth.

"He needs water," Mooseface declared. He moved to a dresser and returned with a water-filled glass. Suddenly, the sound of thumping from the floor above stopped him short.

"What's that?" Aimo hissed nervously.

"They're doing it again," Mooseface announced. He gave the glass of water to Pehr who drained the glass thirstily.

"What are they doin'?" Aimo asked.

Mooseface plunged his right fist repeatedly into the palm of his left hand. "You know . . . they're doin' it. Every time the reverend comes over, that's what they do. He's as bad as she is."

The thumping grew louder and more rapid, joined by the moan of Elsa's voice. With each thump, her voice rose until she cried out, "Bjorn! Bjorn!" Blixdal's voice joined hers in a loud, audible groan, and the thumping abruptly ended.

"He's finished now. He'll be comin' down the steps in a few minutes," Mooseface reported.

"I better get back to the car," Aimo said.

"Why did he bring you here?" Mooseface asked.

"I dunno! I think he's gonna make me come here though."

"Not if I kill that bitch first," Mooseface growled. "Someday, I'm gonna do it."

"I'm gonna get you out of here," Aimo promised. He turned to Pehr. "I'm gonna come back, so don't run away or nuthin', all right? It's too cold to run away. I'm gonna get help for everybody. Thanks for taking care of my cousin, Mooseface."

Aimo left the room and quietly exited the house. He stepped into the arctic air that smacked against his face, causing his eyes to water. He wrenched the car door open, climbed inside, and huddled in the backseat, awaiting the reverend's return but uncertain how he could get Pehr and Mooseface out of the orphanage.

Several minutes later, the reverend jumped into the car, started the engine and drove off, ignoring Aimo completely.

Chapter Twenty-five

Karen Blixdal pressed the telephone receiver to her ear, then sank into a chair in despair. Fru Falke's excited voice delivered the bad news. When the conversation ended, Karen replaced the receiver, clutched her head with both hands, and groaned out loud. Fru Falke's husband had laryngitis and could not sing the "Silent Night" solo on Christmas day, the focal point of Karen's Christmas program.

"Disaster!" Karen cried.

Desperate for a solution and deep in thought, she paced into the hallway. Christmas morning was but two days away, and Karen's tradition of featuring a baritone voice to sing "Silent Night" was in serious jeopardy. Fru Falke's husband, wealthy and blessed with a good voice, was Karen's ideal choice. None of the remaining male members of her choral group were good enough to solo. Struggling to think of a replacement, she entered the church to present the problem to her husband, but changed her mind when she saw the reverend, in full clergy vestments, rehearsing his sermon.

Then she spied Aimo at the far end of the church. He walked into the tallow room, carrying a box of used candles. A few moments later, he emerged with an empty container and Karen grabbed him. She put her fingers to her lips as a signal for the boy to be still.

"Mikael, can you sing?" she whispered hopefully. She harbored the idea that if she could not have a baritone voice, she might use the opportunity to introduce her son to the community.

"I don't think so," Aimo replied.

"Everyone knows 'Silent Night.' It's an easy song. I'm certain you can sing it," Karen added with conviction. Assuming the stance of a choir director, she positioned her hands in front of her and bade the boy follow.

"Silent night, holy night. All is calm—" Aimo squawked loudly.

"Quiet with that noise!" Blixdal shouted from the chancel.

Karen looked at Aimo in defeat. The boy's singing voice was terrible. She had to face the inevitable. "Silent Night" would have to be sung by a soprano.

"Herr Pontilius can sing," Aimo volunteered. "He sings all the time at school."

"Pontilius! Of course! He has a beautiful voice," she said excitedly. "He was in our choir before his . . . his accident."

Her voice trailed off when she remembered Pontilius never reentered the church since his return from Finland. But it was worth a try. She led Aimo into the kitchen, scribbled a note, then told him to deliver the note to Pontilius.

What good fortune! Aimo thought to himself. Not only was he to be relieved of the never-ending church chores, but he was also given permission to ski again for the first time since his failed escape from the Blixdals a week earlier.

"Yes! Mother," Aimo said with enthusiasm and was out of the house in moments.

The day was clear and mild, the temperature barely below freezing, very unusual for northern Sweden on December 23. Disdaining his ski cap, Aimo sped over the forest trail and onto the school grounds in less than thirty minutes.

A skier slalomed tentatively down the hill toward the ice hockey pond, and Aimo stopped to study the figure carefully. *Herr Pontilius*, he thought, overjoyed at recognizing his teacher.

"Herr Pontilius!" Aimo called excitedly. He skied swiftly to his teacher's side. "Hi! You really ski good," Aimo said, genuinely impressed at the man's ability in spite of his handicap.

"Ski *well*," Pontilius corrected. "You're a good skier . . . a very good skier."

"Thank you," Aimo replied.

"So you really think I ski well. I've got you to thank for that."

"I don't understand," Aimo replied.

"Someday you will. There are some lessons we ignore in life, but when we finally do notice them, we sometimes learn them too late. Let's just say . . . you've been my inspiration . . . and you've helped me a great deal." Pontilius smiled then changed the subject. "What brings you here, Aimo?" His voice pitched lower.

Aimo reached into his pocket and handed his teacher Karen Blixdal's note. Pontilius read it quickly then returned it.

"Tell Fru Blixdal I respectfully decline."

"She's gonna be mad," Aimo said, placing the note in his pocket. "Fru Blixdal said you used to sing in the church choir."

"Well, that was a long time ago . . . before my leg."

"But you don't need a leg to sing, Herr Pontilius."

Pontilius laughed heartily. "I know. What I meant was, I'd rather not be with people for a while. Not even in church."

"Why?" Aimo asked innocently.

Pontilius thought for a moment, groping for an answer to help explain the feelings he had had about himself and the changes he sensed he was now undergoing. He had come to admire Aimo, finding it strangely easy to speak openly to him. Subconciously there was something about the boy that reminded him of himself. He bore the same free spirit he once had and now so desperately sought to regain. Training himself to ski again was just the first step back in his self-styled rehabilitation, but he still felt insecure. The boy vigorously massaged a handful of snow onto his heated scalp and looked at the teacher, his tousled hair creating an impish appearance.

"I don't want to go back to the church either," Aimo added. "You can go or do whatever you want. Reverend Blixdal can send me to the orphanage, and I can't say anything."

"No, they won't," Pontilius scoffed. "I spoke with Lenne Senstrom's family. They would love to have you join them after the holidays. Is that all right with you?"

"Herr Blixdal took me to the orphanage already. I saw my cousin Pehr there. He's very sick, and the minister and the lady were doing . . . you know . . ." Aimo searched for the words, then opened the palm of his left hand as Mooseface had done and banged it with the heel of his right hand forcibly.

"He took you to the orphanage? When were you there?" Pontilius asked.

"Yesterday. Remember when he picked me up at lunch? I thought maybe he was gonna take me to my mom and dad."

"And you saw the Reverend Blixdal, together with Fröken Elsa yourself?"

"Herr Blixdal left me in the car. I was freezing, so I snuck in the orphanage. I went into a room and found my friend Mooseface and my cousin, Pehr. That's when I heard them doing it."

"Aimo, I want you to come with me and tell Constable Vahleen."

"No! I can't! Fru Blixdal said a surprise was coming for Christmas. I think it's my mother and father."

"I'm not so sure of that, Aimo," Pontilius said, shaking his head.

The teacher knew he certainly would have been alerted if any of the Finnish parents were arriving. But he had no proof they weren't already here either. The boy sincerely believed their arrival was imminent, and Pontilius did not want to disappoint him. But the teacher was determined to make certain Aimo's days with the Blixdal's would soon come to an end. He had to learn more of the reverend and Fröken Elsa. One way to do that might be in Blixdal's church.

"All right, Aimo. Tell Fru Blixdal I'll come to church and sing. But don't tell anyone what you told me of Herr Blixdal and the orphanage."

"Why?" Aimo asked.

"Because I'm going to do something about it. I want you to trust me. Don't tell anyone"

"OK!" Aimo extended his hand to the teacher. Pontilius took it, and Aimo bowed respectfully. "It's a contract," the boy said, then skied back into the forest.

Aimo was pleased with himself. Fru Blixdal was going to be ecstatic over the good news that Herr Pontilius had accepted her invitation to sing in the choir. She was sure to tell her husband who, in turn, might forget the orphanage idea altogether. His optimism soaring, Aimo dismissed the orphanage idea entirely since only two more days remained until Christmas and a reunion with his parents. Once his parents arrived, they would take Pehr and Mooseface out of the orphanage. All of them would move into a house so lovely that even Anna would want to leave the Vahleen's and rejoin her real family. Aimo's spirits could not have been higher.

The boy's happy thoughts carried him through the forest. He arrived at a trail junction between the school and the church. Arne and Lenne always came from the trail that led to town. Aimo wondered what lay in the opposite direction. There was no need to hurry back, he thought. The meeting with Herr Pontilius had been brief, and the news that he carried back to Fru Blixdal was good. No need to rush back to church and more unending chores.

Aimo followed the new trail, meandering through a series of rises and twisting drops beneath the heavy cover of conifer trees. At the top of a steep rise, the conifers thinned, allowing an uninterrupted view of Lake Valdemaren. The vastness of the lake before him reminded Aimo of Lake Jarvii, broken as it was by a series of ragged peninsulas and islands of varying sizes.

He stood at the elevated point for some time, scanning the frozen surface below him. Directly across the lake was the unmistakable bell tower of Nilstad church on a rise above the lake's eastern shore. A movement of a figure on the ice on the opposite shore, about a kilometer away, caught the boy's attention. The figure chopped at the ice with a hatchet, the sound echoing clearly up to Aimo's position.

"Ice fishing," Aimo thought out loud.

He descended the hill at breakneck speed. Gliding through a wide stand of white birch trees, he skied onto the ice. Aimo approached the figure quietly. The fisherman sat on a mound of snow, his back toward the boy, and fished intently with a carved piece of wood shaped like a long tapered pistol handle. The fisherman brought the end of the wood upward in swift, rhythmic jerks until a fish struck the jigging lure. Lifting the wood high over his head, he grabbed the fishing line in his free hand and hauled the struggling fish quickly onto the ice.

"Wow! That's a nice perch," Aimo exclaimed.

Magnus Olofsson, swiveled around and fell on the seat of his pants, Startled by Aimo's voice,,.

"Fon! Where did you come from?" Olofsson asked, thoroughly surprised.

"Up there," Aimo said, pointing in the direction of the school.

Olofsson studied the boy's face for a moment then smiled in recognition. "The Finnish boy! I thought I recognized the accent. What are you doing? Running away again?"

"No!" Aimo answered indignantly. "I'm on my way back to the church."

"How did it go with the Blixdals? Did the reverend cane your butt? . . . Wait a minute," Olofsson interrupted himself, remembering. "Do you call the old lady *mother*?"

"All the time," Aimo answered matter-of-factly.

"Then you didn't get your butt beat, I betcha."

Aimo was tempted to tell the old man about the orphanage, but remembered the promise he had just made to Herr Pontilius. The perch, lying still on the ice, became the focus of his attention.

"What's your name, boy?" Olofsson asked.

"Aimo," the boy replied.

"Aimo! That's right . . . I'm Magnus. Do you know how to ice fish?"

"Sure!" Aimo said.

Olofsson offered him the fishing gear. Aimo took the wooden handle and blew his breath over the frozen line to thaw it. He returned the jig lure, a small oblong piece of lead with tail feathers of white hiding a small hook, into the hole. He guided the rapidly sinking line with his fingers until it reached the end of the stick, then swirled the end several times. He snapped the rod upward, allowed the lure to drop, then snapped it upward again, this time setting the hook into a fish. Aimo quickly pulled up the line and dropped a perch onto the ice next to Olofsson's fish.

Olofsson laughed loudly. "Good job, Aimo," he shouted, watching with interest as the boy expertly unhooked the fish. Aimo then quickly returned the line to the water before it could freeze.

The activity reminded the old man of a grandfather and his grandson he met one summer's day a few years earlier. They fished from a rowboat; and the grandson, whose age Olofsson guessed as four, sat at the stern, a fishing pole in one hand and a small white blanket pressed to his face in the other. The old man rowed back and forth a short distance from the shoreline; and when a fish struck, the little boy shouted, "Granpa!" He would carefully place the blanket on his lap, reel in a wiggling perch, then returned the blanket to his face as soon as the fish was brought aboard. Olofsson watched with envy that day as their activity repeated itself, and he wished fate had allowed him to have a grandchild of his own.

"I like to use jigs like this one," Aimo said, "'cause the exercise keeps me warm. My father uses bait." Aimo's voice broke the old man's reverie.

"Minnows?" Olofsson asked.

"Maggots," Aimo said with disgust. "I hate to touch 'em."

"I always use lures. I make my own," Olofsson said.

"I love to make lures. My father showed me how to make a special plug, and it's great for pike."

"I know where we can catch some big pike. We'll go in the spring when the ice breaks," Olofsson promised.

"My mom and dad are coming to get me in a couple of days, so I won't be here, but thanks anyway," Aimo said, then set the hook into another fish. He pulled the perch from the hole and once again, dropped a wriggling fish onto the ice.

"Thank you for letting me fish," Aimo said, and returned the fishing rod to Olofsson.

"You can stay and fish with me if you want to," Olofsson offered hopefully.

"I have to go back to the church, or Herr Blixdal will get mad."

"Call him mother, too," Olofsson chortled. "Maybe that's what he wants."

Aimo stood straight, bowed courteously, then extended his hand to the old man who accepted the handshake. "Thank you again and Merry Christmas," Aimo said. He moved away and skied across the lake in the direction of Nilstad church.

Olofsson watched the figure grow smaller in the distance. He absently reached into his pocket and drank from a bottle of his homemade liquor. He wiped his bearded mouth with his sleeve as an unexpected wave of profound sadness settled over him.

Chapter Twenty-six

Gretha Vahleen removed the Christmas ham that had been curing beneath a mound of rock salt inside a ceramic crock. Quite satisfied that the centerpiece of her Christmas smorgasbord was in the final stages of preparation, she swiped at a lock of hair with the back of her hand. She surveyed the activity in her kitchen with the air of a military field commander at the height of battle.

Solveig stood at an ironing board, pressing several sets of red and green colored linen tablecloths. Meggan occupied half a table at the far end of the room, mixing dough for an almond cake. Anna and Lisa shared the other half, punching out gingerbread animal shapes with cookie cutters. Lisa transferred some of the raw dough animals onto a baking tray under the watchful gaze of Meggan who, from her self-proclaimed position of table supervisor, decided the dough was too moist.

"Add more flour," Meggan said.

"We already did," Lisa answered defensively.

"It needs more," Meggan declared with finality. She gathered the unbaked cookies into a heap, took the flouring can away from Anna, and sprinkled a new coating of unbleached flour over the mound of dough.

"Now! Knead it again, flatten it with the rolling pin, *then* use the cookie cutters."

"Mama!" Lisa called in protest. "Look what Meggan did."

Gretha witnessed the entire event with mixed feelings. Her oldest daughter was fast becoming a clone of herself. She was not about to violate the cardinal rule she herself had learned from *her* mother. There was room for only one *kitchen dictator* at a time. Anna's lower lip curled into a precursor of a wail, but Gretha was not going to allow her kitchen to be disrupted.

"Girls! It's time to get a Christmas tree. Let's get Papa Sten to take you out to the forest."

Within minutes, Sten and the girls were on their way to cut down a tree, and sanctity prevailed in the kitchen once again. Gretha returned to her chores

135

and began rolling small sections of ground meat into the traditional Swedish meatballs when the telephone rang.

"Can you take it, Solveig?" Gretha asked, displaying her messy fingers.

"Oh! Hello, Fru Blixdal," Solveig answered. Gretha waved her soiled hands in front of her as a sign she did not want to be disturbed by the chatty woman.

"Fru Vahleen is making meatballs. Can she call you later?"

Solveig's smile faded from her face as she listened to the voice over the phone. After several unsuccessful attempts to reply, Solveig managed to squeeze out, "Thank you, Fru Blixdal," then hung up the phone and plopped into a chair. Tears welled in her eyes, and Gretha rushed to her side.

"Solveig, what's wrong?"

"Fru Blixdal said Torsten Falke was unable to sing in the choir."

"Is that a tragedy?" Greta asked with incredulity.

"Fredrik is going to sing instead."

"My god! That *is* good news . . . isn't it? I mean, this is the first time he's doing anything socially . . . isn't it?

"Yes," Solveig nodded.

"When did you see him last?"

"Several weeks ago. He was still the same. He didn't want me to come near him. I so wanted to just hold him again . . ." Solveig's voice broke, and she sobbed softly. "I have tried, Gretha! God knows, I've tried. He keeps everything inside. He told me I should find another man, one who is whole." She wept and Gretha embraced her.

"We have to give him time to heal," Gretha said comfortingly.

"How *much* time?" Solveig voice rose angrily. "Fredrik has made himself clear he doesn't want me any longer. He told me he's releasing me from our engagement so I can continue with my life. Continue for what? I suffer from his wounds as much as he does. I suffer from being constantly turned away. It's as though our life before he was wounded never existed."

"You have to be patient," Gretha said softly.

"I don't have the courage for more patience, Gretha. I wrote my cousin in the United States. She told me there is a family who needs an *au pair* girl."

"You can't run away from love, Solveig. You'll still suffer, but you'll be thousands of miles away and unable to do anything about it."

"But I can't do anything about it here," Solveig said desperately.

"Does he know you may leave the country?" Gretha asked.

Solveig shook her head, "I didn't tell him."

"Well . . . I have an idea. Let me think about it a while longer."

Chapter Twenty-seven

Christmas Eve morning found the Vahleen house in a whirl of excited activity deliciously enveloped within the fragrances of baking food. The girls, giddy with anticipation, helped Papa Sten decorate the Christmas tree in the living room. A clear path was provided for Mama Gretha and Solveig who passed continually between the kitchen and dining room. The women set the tables with colorful Christmas linens and napkins, the Vahleen's best china and cutlery, then finally placed white candles on the numerous clear-pine candle holders.

The remainder of the house had been decorated several days earlier. Handmade straw ornaments, shaped into animal forms, hung from window muntins and doorways. Red and green cloth panels, covered with white needlepoint depicting Christmas scenes, were tacked vertically at every doorframe.

By noon, the work was done; and Sten lit the stack of logs in the fireplace, completing the transformation of their home into a replica of a Carl Larsson Christmas painting. In one magic moment, Gretha's month-long planning glowed in splendid Christmas warmth. She took her husband and Solveig by the hand and allowed herself a moment to absorb the beautiful traditional scene.

A pounding on the front door and the loud inebriated voice of Magnus Olofsson interrupted the festive mood.

"Merry Christmas," he shouted.

"Sten! Let Magnus in," Gretha lowered her voice to a whisper. "We're going upstairs to get ready."

Olofsson, dressed in a floor-length caribou-skin coat, stepped into the foyer, the odor of alcohol strong on his breath. He was definitely prepared to celebrate and obviously was off to a fast start.

"Merry Christmas, Magnus. If I didn't know better, I'd mistake you for a musk ox," Sten joked.

"Try to think of me as a wolf," Olofsson growled playfully. He shoved a large burlap bag at the constable.

"Hold on to that a moment Magnus and come with me," Sten said, leading the way to the cellar. They moved into a private workroom. Switching on the light, he closed the door behind him, then took the bag from Olofsson.

"Careful with that," Olofsson warned. He pulled out four flasks of his homemade aquavit. "One for you, one for Gretha, one for the house and"—Magnus removed the cork on a bottle—"one for us!" He put the bottle to his lips, took a healthy slug, then offered the flask to Sten. "Skoal."

"Skoal," Sten replied. He grimaced as the liquor burned its way down to his stomach. "Wow! Magnus! That is the strongest *brandvin* I've ever tasted."

"Have another," Magnus said, reaching for the bottle, but Sten pulled the flask away from him.

"One is enough for now, Magnus. Do you have the costume?"

Olofsson fumbled in the bag and retrieved a papier-mâché Santa Claus mask. He placed it over his face and scrunched a long red-stocking hat over his head. "Well! How do I look?" Olofsson asked.

"Like a Viking opera singer," Sten laughed.

Olofsson smiled at the thought. "Hell! It's starting to snow anyway. By the time I get to play Jul Tomten, I'll be covered in white. We're in for a storm," he warned.

Sten collected the carefully wrapped Christmas presents hidden in his workshop and placed them in the burlap sack; then he led Olofsson back up to the living room to await his wife's planned entrance.

Gretha led the girls in a dramatic descent of the staircase and found the men sitting next to the living room fireplace. She positioned the girls proudly in front of her. All three wore special Christmas dresses she and Solveig had made for them.

Greta and Solveig wore the traditional folk costumes of Jamtland county, floor-length Christmas-colored jumpers. The heavy wool material embraced their bodies in figure-enhancing style, fitting snugly over high three-button collar white blouses. They both wore their hair up in braided buns held in place by small white-fringed bows. The effect on the men was immediate. They stared in wide-eyed appreciation, and Olofsson jumped to his feet.

"Bravo!" Olofsson shouted as he and Sten clapped their hands vigorously. The girls radiated beauty, and each smiled knowingly.

Meggan stepped up to Olofsson, offered her hand, and curtsied. If ever there was a time for formality the girl knew, it was now. She knew that

Olofsson would be playing the role of the Christmas tomten and wanted to make certain she did not offend him. Calling the man *Uncle* Magnus made good sense.

"Merry Christmas, *Farbror* Magnus."

"Merry Christmas!" Olofsson replied.

Lisa and Anna followed Meggan's lead. "Merry Christmas, Papa. Merry Christmas, *Farbror* Magnus," they said and curtsied.

Sten hugged the girls happily.

"Thank you! Thank you! Thank you! You're all so pretty, I think Jul Tomten is going to be very generous."

To set the mood, dinner traditionally began with glogg, a heated spiced red wine, spiked this year with Olofsson's aquavit. The well-endowed table bore the traditional Swedish Christmas smorgasbord: an assortment of cheeses, meatballs, mustards, and pickled herring, all carefully spaced with measured distance from each other. Two salads—one of red beet, the other of cooked red cabbage—a bowl of apple sauce, and a sherry-laced strawberry gelatin mold bracketed Gretha's centerpiece Christmas ham. The daunting presentation beckoned, and the adults attacked the feast with gusto. The children's anticipation of the arrival of the Christmas *tomten* reduced their appetites to a few meatballs and most of the strawberry mold.

Olofsson offered frequent calls of "Skoal," followed by bombastic toasts on subjects varying from the beautiful women of Jamtland to the art of producing aquavit. According to protocol, each toast was answered with return calls of skoal by the others, followed immediately by another mouthful of the hard liquor. The continual drinking of the potent alcohol produced swift results. Soon Gretha and Sten offered toasts of their own. Then Solveig joined in, toasting the value of dear friends. As dinner neared its end, Olofsson's house bottle of aquavit stood nearly drained.

"I've got to make some strong coffee," Gretha said, pushing herself up from the table.

"May we see if the Jul Tomten is coming?" Meggan asked. Anna and Lisa looked on eagerly. Gretha offered a smiling nod, and the girls raced up the stairs, searching the darkened landscape from the balcony window in their bedroom.

"It's snowing too hard to see," Meggan called from the second floor.

"I told you a storm was coming," Olofsson slurred.

"The perfect time for Tomten to make his appearance," Gretha said. She cast an approving eye at the men, signaling them to begin their part of the Christmas celebration.

The men returned to the cellar where the old man donned his Christmas tomten costume. Sten rearranged the Christmas packages in the burlap sack, which Olofsson threw over his shoulder. He took another long drink from Sten's bottle of aquavit, grabbed a wire-handled kerosene lamp, and stepped out into the snowy night.

Olofsson continued a tradition played out in most Swedish homes for centuries. He circled the property, sneaking among snow-covered trees in the apple orchard, until he reached the lane leading to the Vahleen household. He then started walking toward the house, holding the lighted lantern in front of him. Trudging through the snow and singing loudly to the happy season, the old man drew ever closer to a house filled with three deliriously excited children. The dry, powdered snow fell heavily, creating a metallic tinkling from countless frozen crystals falling onto each other, harmonizing with Olofsson's Christmas caroling. He reached the house and thrust the lantern in front of him.

Meggan saw the tomten first shouting excitedly from the upstairs window.

"Look! See the light? Tomten is coming! Tomten is coming!"

The girls pressed their faces against the cold window. Meggan, consumed by the magical moment, returned to being a young naive girl again, and Anna snuggled against her.

Olofsson called from the hallway in a throaty voice he hoped disguised his identity. "Are there any good children in this house?"

The girls spilled down the steps, confronting Tomten in the hallway where he stood.

Olofsson attempted to peer down at the figures before him, but the poorly made eye holes in his mask, combined with the amount of alcohol in his bloodstream made seeing difficult. He cocked his head awkwardly to help his view while the girls stared back dumbly. They knew it was Olofsson but willingly suspended their disbelief, fully accepting him in his new role. They *wanted* Olofsson to be the tomten, and that was enough.

"Please come in, tomten," Gretha bade.

Olofsson stumbled into the living room to a large chair near the fireplace prepared for him. The girls giggled excitedly at the sack filled with gifts.

Olofsson reached into the sack with considerable effort and lifted three packages. He read the labels identifying Meggan, Lisa, and Anna with some difficulty; and the girls eagerly accepted their gifts.

Meggan's gift, a copy of Astrid Lindgren's book *Pippi Longstocking*, brought heartfelt thanks to everyone around her.

Lisa's package revealed a pink-skinned plastic doll with long curly hair that said mama when tilted forward. It was exactly the doll she had seen in a store window and wanted at first sight. She clutched it lovingly when suddenly, Anna's piercing scream followed by hysterical crying, brought the merriment to an end. The stricken girl backed away from the cause of her grief. A furry small-scale version of a white polar bear lay on the floor.

"What's wrong, Anna?" Gretha asked, holding the girl comfortingly.

Anna pointed at the polar bear. It stood on its hind legs, its front paws outstretched, and its tooth-filled mouth wide open.

Meggan picked up the gift, examined it, then shook her head in bewilderment, unable to see what had been so frightening.

"It's all right, Anna," Gretha said, maintaining her hold on the girl. "You don't have to be afraid. You see! Meggan is holding it!"

"But she doesn't know how dangerous it is," Anna replied, and the room erupted in loud laughter.

Lisa offered Anna her new doll and told her they could both play with her gift until the polar bear was tamed. Anna seemed pleased with the solution.

The celebration extended into the evening with gifts for everyone. Sten surprised Gretha with an Electrolux vacuum cleaner, then impressed everyone with a detailed two-story dollhouse he had assembled from a kit. Gretha had sewn a plaid wool robe for Sten and matching flannel nightgowns for the girls. Somehow, she had found the time to secretly knit a red sweater for her dear friend, Solveig.

Olofsson received Grieg's recorded *Lyric Pieces*, Opus 43 together with Lars-Erik Larsson's *Pastoral Suite* for his cabin Victrola from his hosts. Gretha jokingly told him he needed some uplifting music, living alone as he did.

Perhaps Olofsson had too much to drink, or the words regarding his lonely life were too close to the truth. He certainly had opportunities to marry and have a family. Sitting heartbroken across the table from him even now was an available beauty if ever he saw one. The realization of being a noncandidate for Solveig's interest, or anyone else for that matter, replaced his alcohol-driven joy.

Olofsson grew very sad, recognizing for the first time that life had passed him by. The gaiety of the day vanished, and he politely excused himself. Wishing everyone a good holiday, he ignored his host's efforts to stay the night with them. Olofsson tucked the recordings under his arm and walked out into the snow to his flatbed truck.

The old man drove drunkenly toward his cabin, a feat made even more remarkable because of the swirling snow. Somehow he reached his destination without incident and threw several new logs over the still-glowing embers in the fireplace. He opened a new bottle of aquavit, took a long drink, and immediately fell asleep.

Reverend Blixdal surveyed the Christmas decorations Aimo and Karen had prepared. To Aimo's surprise, the clergyman even approved of the extra candles Aimo had made, but was unwilling to allow the boy an opportunity to rest. He ordered him to check the tallow vat to make certain it was filled in the event more candles would be needed.

Aimo entered the tallow room and climbed onto a stool and peered inside the vat.

Blixdal was right. The bowl was half empty. The boy threw in several new bricks of wax stored in a corner bin and increased the flame beneath the vat. He brought the tallow to a boil, then stirred the bubbling, molten liquid with a long-handled wooden spatula.

Aimo struggled with the thick consistency of the molten liquid. He stretched his wiry body dangerously over the cauldron of bubbling wax, standing tiptoe on one foot. Unknowingly, the other foot extended backward; and he kicked the vat's spigot handle open, allowing a silent, steady stream of melted wax to spill onto the floor.

Aimo did not notice the accident. He closed the vat lid and, placing the wooden spatula on a hook, exited the room as a growing pool of hot liquid spread across the floor.

The boy joined Fru Blixdal in the kitchen, unable to control his excitement of the expected reunion with his parents. If all went as he expected, he concluded, he would be brought together with his parents for Christmas the next day. Fru Blixdal, however, was convinced the boy's excitement was due to the holiday. She teased him continually with hints of a "special surprise" as a reward for all his hard work.

"You'll be a very happy boy tomorrow," she said. "Now! We all have to get up very early in the morning, so give Mother a kiss good night."

Aimo kissed the woman quickly on her cheek and bounded up the steps to his room, passing the reverend nervously pacing the hallway while rehearsing his sermon. Once in his room, Aimo climbed into his flannel nightshirt and, in what had become a nightly ritual, dug the military medal from his pocket. He no longer said an evening prayer. Instead, he found comfort in the simple act of holding his mother's gift in his hand and thinking of their reunion. He peered through the window and searched for light from the distant houses, but on this night, the heavy snowstorm blotted everything from view.

Aimo jumped into bed and buried himself beneath the warm covers, his mind whirling with questions regarding his parents. Where would they stay? Certainly not with the Blixdals. How would they arrive? It had to be on the same train that brought all the Finnish children. What about Anna? His parents wouldn't be pleased if she chose to stay with the Vahleens.

Once again, Aimo found himself asking questions that seemed to have no answers. *Why did life have to be this way?* he wondered. The boy curled into a ball and fell fast sleep, exhausted from his workday.

Chapter Twenty-eight

On Christmas morning, Karen Blixdal awoke everyone at 5:00 as planned and immediately fell to the first of her many tasks in what promised to be a hectic morning. She had an hour and a half to prepare herself and breakfast, iron her husband's most formal vestments, and lay out Aimo's new woolen knickers outfit: vest, shirt, tie, and a seven-button jacket. She also needed to allow enough time to prepare coffee for the arrival of the choir at 6:30 AM. She was well aware that thirty minutes later, the Nilstad church would be filled to overflowing with faithful parishioners.

At 6:45 AM. Blixdal led Aimo out to the bell tower while Karen continued her chores. They both were greeted to a wild winter's sight. During the night the wind had increased, and snow blew horizontally across the landscape, a warning that the storm soon would develop into a blizzard. Swirling snowflakes drifted into a series of white waves whose crests launched plumes of powdery crystals over the deepening mantle. But the storm had not yet reached a total whiteout, and there was still a gauzy view of the forested valley below.

Blixdal shielded his eyes to scan the scene beyond the church. Excitedly, he pointed out the lights from torches carried by cross-country skiers and horse-drawn sleighs, their harness-mounted bells jingling. A myriad of fluttering yellow lights wove over forest trails, their pale lanterns leading people in the direction of the Nilstad church. Blixdal's spirits soared. His audience was on its way!

"See those lights, boy?" the reverend shouted excitedly over the wind. "They're coming to hear me! Now we're going to summon them. Follow me. Hurry!"

Blixdal rushed into the bell tower and led Aimo through a short lesson in bell ringing. Satisfied that Aimo was prepared, the reverend instructed the boy to wrap the rope around his arm.

"Pull!" Blixdal yelled, and Aimo yanked down on the rope. The bell answered with a long booming *bong.*

Nilstad church was one of the few churches north of Stockholm with dual bells in the tower. Both bells were of equal size but of different density with varied metal gauges. When rung together, they produced distinctly different tones. Additionally, one of the bells featured two strikers, which created dual notes, one quickly following the other. The combined result between the two bells was a deep, long *bong*, followed immediately by a quick-sounding *cling-clang.*

"Pull!" Blixdal shouted, and the Nilstad church bells rang out over the snowy countryside, beckoning the faithful to the one church service of the year most were certain to attend.

"Bong! Cling-clang! Bong! Cling-clang.

The ringing church bells ranged far over the white landscape. They blended harmoniously with the jingling of dozens of sleigh bells, creating a metallic symphony announcing the arrival of Christmas to Jamtland County.

A four-horse sleigh illuminated by twin kerosene lanterns and its harness-bells jingling, carried the Vahleen family to the church. Gretha snuggled closely against her husband who guided the horses. Solveig and the girls sat behind them, huddled beneath a heavy woolen blanket. Occasionally the young woman popped her head up into the wind to allow the snowflakes to cool her anxiety-flushed face. The idea of seeing Fredrik Pontilius at the church had seemed thrilling the night before, but as the sleigh drew closer to the church, Solveig's anticipation grew, and her body became damp with nervous perspiration.

In contrast, Anna's memory of the perilous sleigh ride with her parents when they escaped from Finland only months earlier had faded. She occupied herself with her new sisters, playing a game which the girls called "hunt the mama-speaking doll" that involved the now-tamed toy polar bear, amid continual giggling.

They entered the church with a stream of fellow parishioners, the vaulted room aglow from hundreds of flickering candles resulting from Aimo's handiwork. Sten and the children seated themselves on a bench several rows removed from the raised altar. Gretha and Solveig made their way to the choir section to take their places with other choir members.

Solveig's gaze darted about the large room searching for Pontilius, but he was not to be seen. Tension gripped her abdomen, knotting her muscles.

What if he doesn't come? she worried. He had been so final in his decision to end their engagement, declaring emphatically they should avoid each other. It was tormenting. She was certain she knew why Pontilius behaved as he did, but also knew he still loved her. She could help him if only he would permit her.

Solveig looked back at Sten and the children and discovered Meggan signaling excitedly to her. The girl pointed to the front of the church, and she followed Meggan's gesture toward the entry, then sucked in a deep breath. Pontilius had arrived. He surveyed the sea of parishioners filling the benches, then limped in the direction of the choir.

Solveig noticed a number of positive changes in him from when they had last spoken. He walked upright and no longer slumped. Although his limp was pronounced, he stood erect, his strong shoulders propelling him forward. He still supported himself with his cane, but the awkward hobbling step was gone. He had carefully trimmed his beard, the heavy, bushy mass reduced sufficiently to reveal a slightly discernible white scar that had been the terrible gash across his cheek.

Pontilius approached the choir section as Solveig's heart beat rapidly. He was dressed in his stretch ski pants that flattered his muscled legs and hid any sign of the existence of his prosthesis. A blue ski sweater hugged his upper body, and a white woolen scarf hung around his neck. He clutched a red-tassled ski cap in his hand, uncovering his bare head of curly blond hair still wet with perspiration. He had obviously skied the several kilometers from his school to the church.

Suddenly, Fru Blixdal was by his side, excitedly pulling the man to the head of the choir. He had no time to notice any of the choir members, including Solveig. Karen was not going to allow a last-second glitch now that she had Jamtland's best baritone voice in her grasp. She handed him a music book and animatedly whispered her plans for the choir. Satisfied with her instructions, she took her position next to the piano, picked up a triangular chime, and turned to the congregation. Beaming broadly, she struck the chime several times, and the restless murmuring within the church subsided.

She adjusted the candle to illuminate the music score and began the piano introduction to "Silent Night" with simple spaced chords that echoed across the expectant room. Softly, the gentle baritone voice of Fredrik Pontilius melodically drifted across the rows of worshipers. At the completion of the first stanza, the full choir joined voices with the soloist, an octave higher and a tone stronger into the second stanza.

Pontilius grew confident in the music and secure in the harmony he shared with the choir. Slowly he turned his head away from Fru Blixdal's piano direction and cast a glance over the choir members who sang together with him. The unexpected sight of Solveig, her face radiant, caused his voice to break off; and momentarily, the baritone soloist only mouthed the words. For a fleeting second, Pontilius heard nothing as all sound seemed to have vanished. His eyes fastened to Solveig, and she contorted her face to urge him on. A moment later, Pontilius regained his composure, his voice stronger. A smile of delighted recognition spreading across his face. Solveig smiled back hopefully through glistening eyes.

The song ended, and Karen Blixdal rose from the piano stool in satisfaction. She struck the chimes signaling the choir to sit. Pontilius attempted to whisper a message across the choir to Solveig, but Karen pulled the man to his seat. He struggled to straighten his prosthetic leg that stretched out uncomfortably in front of him, finding it nearly impossible to sit in the chair. He reached to unfasten the prosthesis but dared not risk the embarrassing noise. It was frustrating. He couldn't turn around to signal Solveig and had no idea where Constable Vahleen was sitting. He would have to wait until after the service to speak to the constable about the relationship between the reverend and Fröken Elsa. However, the sight of Solveig had set his mind in a turmoil. He now knew how much he loved her and how important she was to his life. He was determined to let her know, and he wrestled to formulate a plan to reunite them.

Karen Blixdal struck her chimes. Aimo, dressed in his long maroon-colored robe, took his cue and moved to the minister's elevated pulpit to light the candelabra.

"Look!" Sten whispered to Anna. He lifted the girl to his lap, enabling her to see her brother. "It's Aimo."

Anna stared curiously and at first didn't recognize him. Dressed in the altar-boy garb, his once-wild hair combed in a slicked-down middle part, the boy appeared much older than his ten years. Anna turned inquisitively to Sten.

"What happened to Aimo?"

"He's supposed to look as though he works in a church," Sten whispered.

"He looks strange," she observed unhappily.

"I like the way he looks," Meggan volunteered.

"I don't," Anna said with finality and sat back down on the bench.

Blixdal entered the room from behind a drape-covered doorway, moving to the lectern dramatically, his black robes fluttering with each stride. He came to a stop and allowed a moment to gain his captive audience's full attention; then he erupted into his sermon. For the next thirty minutes his voice thundered over the congregation. He spoke of the lack of virtue in the world and the dire consequences that would come to those who did not repent. The reverend's words touched on every vice he could think of. Not once did he mention love, a subject he had never been allowed to learn. His was a world of judgment, condemnation, and prosecution. There was no compassion, no understanding, no forgiveness. When at last he finished, he stood silently at the lectern, trembling with emotion.

Blixdal allowed his eyes to sweep over the rows of faces that stared silently back at him. The man was totally unaware the congregation had been deadened by the admonitions he had hurled at them. Yet he expected some reaction, a signal of some kind. Perhaps tearful eyes or a rush to the pulpit of contrite sinners begging for divine intervention in their collision course with eternal damnation. Instead, his congregation rose rapidly from their pews and headed for the exit. They departed hastily from the church into the snowstorm, disdaining the traditional handshaking as soon as the choir finished its final Christmas carol.

"Go to him," Gretha urged Solveig.

Pontilius was unable to avoid well-wishers from the community. They still worshipped their sports hero and were thrilled to hear his singing voice again. The crowd swept him away in the direction of the door.

"I don't know what to do," Solveig replied helplessly.

"Tell him . . ." Gretha struggled for an answer.

"That I love him? That I want to share my life with him? I've done that! I've said that!" Solveig sat down on the pew burying her face in her hands.

Gretha took the initiative. She worked her way down the nave and caught up with Pontilius at the narthex where she found him encircled by a large group of friends. She pushed her way through the throngs of people and, with a determined thrust, took Pontilius's arm. Upon reaching her objective, however, she was at a loss for words and did not know how to tell him about Solveig.

"Fredrik! You . . . you sang beautifully," she said dumbly.

"Merry Christmas, Fru Vahleen," Pontilius answered.

"Oh! Merry Christmas! Merry Christmas! Please, call me Gretha, Fredrik. I'm not so old that you should call me Fru Vahleen."

Pontilius tried to hold his position among the departing congregation, but his entourage remained circled about him. The entire mass moved him inexorably toward the exit. Finally, the crunch of surging people wrested Gretha's grip off the man's arm. Unable to move with the crowd, she flailed the air in Pontilius direction and called out.

"Sten and I . . . we'd like you to have Christmas dinner with us," Gretha shouted.

"We've got him first," a teammate declared from the teacher's ski jumping days. They reached the exit and stepped out into the snowstorm. Defeated, Gretha watched the group then shouted helplessly.

"Solveig's leaving for America. If you don't stop her, you'll never see her again." Pontilius dissolved in the swirling white haze, unable to hear a word of what she said.

Sten maneuvered the girls in the direction of Reverend Blixdal, who remained standing within the elevated pulpit. He eyed the constable's approach curiously since they alone had chosen to greet him and pay their respects.

"Merry Christmas, Reverend. Wonderful sermon," Sten lied.

"Merry Christmas, Constable," the clergyman answered.

"Say Merry Christmas," Sten instructed the girls.

"Merry Christmas, Herr Reverend Blixdal," Lisa and Meggan sang in unison. Anna remained silent, finding a more secure position behind Papa Sten's back.

"We'd like to invite Aimo to Christmas dinner with us if that's all right with you, Bjorn." Sten asked.

Blixdal peered at the small cluster of people remaining in the nearly empty church, then shook his head. "There's too much to do here today, Constable. Fru Blixdal has prepared a Christmas dinner for some of our friends. Aimo will be needed."

"But he's a child. Let him enjoy the day with his sister and schoolmates," Sten protested.

"He is having Christmas here with us. Fru Blixdal has planned on sharing this day with him, and it means a great deal to her. The Tornquist and Falke families are joining us with their Finnish girls, so the boy will have plenty of company." The reverend was firm.

Meggan stepped forward unexpectedly. She stood erect, her arms held straight at her sides, and she shouted angrily, "It's Christmas! He should be playing . . . not working. And he shouldn't have to spend Christmas with old people."

"Should he be ice skating?" the minister responded quickly. "You might be pleased to know that Fru Blixdal has gone to the trouble and expense of buying the boy ice skates of his own. It's Christmas for her also. Or are you too selfish to think she might not deserve to enjoy a child she genuinely cares for?"

Sten took his eldest daughter's hand and pulled her toward the exit. He knew she had violated every law of church protocol, and she could not have been more discourteous, but the constable was proud that she had the temerity to speak to Blixdal as she had.

He gathered Anna and Lisa and led the girls quietly to the sleigh where he found Solveig sobbing unhappily in Gretha's arms. He placed the girls in the sleigh and took the reins of the snow-covered horses. He shouted impatiently to the horses and guided the team away from the church, thoroughly baffled as to how the joy of the day turned to despair in such a short time.

Chapter Twenty-nine

Aimo sat quietly at the dinner table, making certain he followed the Blixdals' etiquette rules. He was hungry, but far too nervous to eat. He had been up and working since five in the morning, yet he felt very alert. He ignored the adults who ate their Christmas meal noisily while the two small Finnish girls fidgeted restlessly.

So far there was no sign of his parents; otherwise they would be eating with them. Unless of course, the Blixdals did not want his parents at the same table with the Falkes and Tornquists. *That made good sense*, Aimo thought. Fru Blixdal liked doing things dramatically. What could be more impressive than presenting his parents when the time came to open gifts?

Fru Blixdal rose from the table and raised her goblet of glogg.

"Merry Christmas, everyone. I want to propose a toast to our son, Mikael. He has become such an important member of our family, and Bjorn"—she turned to her husband and extended her cup to him—"thank you for your patience with us."

She returned her attention to Aimo. "You have been everything we have wanted in a son, Mikael. You have been a wonderful help to us, both in the house and with many of the church chores. Skoal," She toasted and raised her cup to her mouth.

"Skoal," her guests rejoined.

"Now, we have a surprise for you," Karen announced. She turned for the kitchen, and Aimo held his breath in the suddenly still room. He focused on the kitchen door in wild anticipation. All eyes were on the Finnish boy, all sharing a secret unknown to him. Even the reverend allowed the edges of his lips to turn slightly upward in a semblance of a smile. The room remained silent until one of the little girls whimpered uncomfortably, and Fru Tornquist pressed her face against her ample bosom.

"Tra-la!" Fru Blixdal announced. She reentered the room with a large beautifully wrapped Christmas package. Beaming, she offered the boy the gift. Aimo accepted it tentatively. He opened the box and found a gleaming pair of new ice skates. Karen Blixdal gasped audibly in approval and applauded energetically.

"Merry Christmas, Mikael," Karen exclaimed profoundly.

"Merry Christmas, Mikael," the adults repeated loudly.

"Give Mother a hug, Mikael," the reverend urged. He used the name Karen had given the boy for the first time. "Come now! Give Mother a hug," he repeated. His tone had become impatient but civil.

Aimo lifted his gaze from the skates and stared at Karen Blixdal. She stood before him, her arms wide spread. "Is this the surprise you promised?" he asked the woman, barely able to speak.

"Yes! Now you can skate against those other boys and beat every one of them," Karen replied.

"But you said . . . I . . . I thought . . . my . . . my mother and . . . father would be the surprise," Aimo stammered, his disappointment consuming him.

"*I'm* your mother now, Mikael," the woman replied.

Aimo jumped to his feet and hurled the package onto the table, splattering food in every direction. Both Finnish girls wailed simultaneously and Aimo continued to shout, no longer able to control the contempt he held for his overbearing hosts.

"No! You're not my *mother!*" the boy shouted. "And my name is *Aimo! Aimo! Aimo!* I don't want your damn skates."

"Bastard! Bastard! You heathen bastard!" Blixdal shouted. He slapped the boy hard across the face, and Aimo fell backward. His eyes fixed defiantly on the black-clothed man who, like himself, had lost all self-control. Blixdal seethed with venom and spouted a string of Swedish invectives unacceptable within a church. "Djavla Fon! Djavlar, och Helvetta ochsa!"

"Go to hell!" Aimo screamed, jumping to his feet. He raced up the stairs to his room, slamming the door behind him. He sat on the edge of his bed in despair, fingering his military medal and scarcely aware of the commotion raging in the dining room.

All the adults seemed to be shouting at once, and both Finnish girls cried loudly. Suddenly, Karen Blixdal released a long agonized scream, "No!" that she repeated continually as she rushed from the dining room and into the church. Moments later the guests left, marked by the loud slamming of the front door. Except for the howling winds of the blizzard, the house grew still.

Blixdal paced the hallway in confusion. The two most influential families in Jamtland county and the guests in his own home had been horribly insulted on Christmas Day. He was certain the Falkes and the Tornquists would complain to his superiors. That was certain to obliterate all chances of his becoming bishop.

He knew from the first moment he laid eyes on Aimo, the boy would bring trouble for him. Like some awful premonition, he feared an incident such as this to be inevitable. Why had his wife been so stupid to bring a heathen child into their lives? All his experiences with children warned him it was a bad idea. Yet *he* allowed a refugee child into their home and had to assume some of the blame.

If a chance still remained to retain his ascension to bishop, it would have to be with his wife's help. He planned feverishly, his balled fists grinding against his temples as he paced the floors of the dining room. Then he received a thought of a viable solution.

His wife, Karen. The bishop himself always expressed his admiration of the woman. Both Karen and he would meet with the bishop the next day and explain their version of the story before anyone else did. *A good, simple solution*, he mused. With these thoughts in mind, Blixdal entered the church and found his wife kneeling before a cross, her hands folded in prayer and muttering incoherently.

Blixdal knelt next to the woman, intending to share his idea of the plan, but the woman's distraught condition changed his mind. He patted her head comfortingly, realizing for the first time the great value she was to him. He thought to embrace her and confess that he indeed loved her but, at the last moment, decided the time was not right.

He raised his eyes to the rafters, and the howling wind remained in this position for several moments. *Suppose the meeting with the bishop did not go well? What then?*

His body trembled uncontrollably as the seriousness of his dilemma became clear. The reverend rose, clasped his hands behind his back, and stalked across the nave of the church, searching for answers, his gaze fastened to the floor. A pool of glistening liquid, oozing from beneath the tallow room door, caught his attention. He pushed the door open, stepped into the room, and was immediately stuck fast to the wax. He pulled his knees upward in a panic to free his feet from the gluelike morass and stepped out of his shoes.

It was the last straw. A low growl in his throat rose to a shout.

"Aimo! Aimo!" Blixdal howled.

Fru Blixdal rushed up the stairs crying uncontrollably while the reverend struggled across the befouled room, no longer able to control his anger. Rivulets of saliva streaked across his beard.

"Aimo! Come here at once!" he bellowed.

Aimo heard the reverend calling. He thought about finding a place to hide until the man could calm himself. Perhaps he could enlist the help of Fru Blixdal, then changed his mind. He no longer wanted anything to do with either of the Blixdals. He preferred to accept his punishment and get it over with. That would give him the night to escape from these intolerable people.

Aimo entered the church, prepared to face the beating he expected. He walked slowly among the pews toward the reverend, unaware of the large wooden ladle the man held concealed behind his back. The boy arrived at the doorway and noticed the wax-covered floor immediately. He lifted his face to the reverend in bewilderment.

The clergyman stood concealed just inside the entrance to the tallow room and chose that moment to attack. Blixdal sloshed forward as best he could, the wax-covered soles of his bare feet lifting and falling on the sticky morass with a large smacking sound. He held the wooden ladle like a club with two hands above his shoulders and swung wildly at the boy but missed. His momentum loosened the grip his feet had of the floor, and he fell forward. The cudgel struck the door frame, barely missing Aimo's head, the momentum causing Blixdal to crash face-first onto the wax-covered floor. He pulled himself up in a murderous rage, covered with wax.

Aimo ran at top speed to escape. He raced to the catacomb steps, jumped down the stairs, flung open the door, and entered the room. Terrified, he stumbled in the dark and hid behind a casket, his heart pounding wildly.

The reverend reached the open door, cursing himself for not securing it as he intended to do weeks earlier. Had he done so, he would have had Aimo trapped at the bottom of the steps. There he would bash his head in. As it was, the boy was in the catacombs. There was no way out except through the boat hole and certain death on the ice in the raging blizzard. He had the boy trapped anyway, and this time Blixdal would make certain the boy did not get away.

He entered the catacombs, closed the door tightly behind him, and pulled a wooden casket across the frame to block the boy's escape. Satisfied with his scheme, the reverend's revenge-filled eyes scanned the frigid surroundings wildly. In moments, he discovered billows of Aimo's hyperventilated breath rising from behind his concealment, revealing the boy's hiding place. Blixdal crept stealthily forward.

"You godless bastard," he hissed. "I'm going to kill you!"

The reverend lunged behind the casket and swung the cudgel mightily. The blow struck Aimo across his back, propelling him against the boat winch.

Whack! The cudgel struck the wooden rope pulley just above Aimo's head. The boy ducked the blow and fell heavily onto the tarpaulin-covered boat, causing the damaged pulley holding the weight of the boat to give way.

Aimo lay on his back, looking upward at the opening above him just as Blixdal's rage-filled face appeared. Out of control, the man raised the cudgel again, hurling it spearlike at the helpless boy. Aimo twisted out of the way as the wooden mallet tore into the canvas, but Aimo could not stop from toppling face-first onto the snow-swept ice of Lake Valdemaren.

Dazed and frightened, the boy knew Blixdal would kill him if he caught him. He rose to his feet and ran blindly into the snow. In a matter of steps, Aimo found himself swallowed in a cloud of swirling white flakes with no idea of direction. He sprinted wildly, unaware his course was leading him to the unsheltered center of the lake and unable to hear the groans of splitting ice as the lake heaved in the violent storm.

Blixdal's night of calamity held another unpleasant surprise for the hapless man. Jumping into the boat in a headlong pursuit of his quarry, his body weight was more than the broken pulley could bear, and the ropes gave way completely. Instinctively, the reverend tried to suppress his fall. Grabbing the torn tarpaulin, he ripped the canvas wide open.

The stolen art treasure spilled onto the windswept ice as he landed heavily on his chest, the force knocking the breath from his lungs. For a brief moment, the rolled paintings lay tantalizingly next to Blixdal, but he was unable to move his body. He lay on his side, staring as his dreams of wealth rolled forward and back in the treacherous wind. Suddenly, a strong gust lifted the priceless Vermeer paintings and stacks of German Deutsches marks into the air. In one brief moment, the swastika-labeled treasure disappeared into the stormy night. Blixdal gasped vainly in protest.

Oh, god! . . . Dear god! . . . Dear, dear god! . . ."

Chapter Thirty

Olofsson sat on the edge of a chair next to a cluttered table of emptied bottles of aquavit and stared drunkenly at the graying embers in his fireplace. Occasional gusts of howling wind swept deepening drifts of snow against the house, forcing snowflakes down the chimney to crackle loudly on the weakly burning coals. The cabin's temperature dropped steadily.

Olofsson was more asleep than awake. His mind drifted back in time to reflect on warm summer days with endless sunlight. He recalled the unbridled joy of being in love and planning a life and a family much like the Vahleen's. Now the old man regretted his behavior. He was not only alone but also old and alone. If he really wanted to face the truth, no one wanted him now. All anyone saw was an old man making a fool of himself.

He drained the contents of the bottle and dropped it absently onto the table. He staggered to the woodpile next to the fireplace. Five logs remained. A stacked woodpile lay outside against the house, but in the depths of his drunken despondency, the old man had already decided he would never need more than those within the cabin. He lifted a log and dropped it into the embers. Tongues of the new flames flickered upward, and Olofsson shuffled to the large window overlooking Lake Valdemaren. He saw nothing of the outside and moved his face closer to the glass. The old man regarded his reflection on the cold glass, confirming his advanced age. The cold radiated from his mirrored image, and he blew his breath purposely on the windowpane, causing the vapors to freeze into feather-shaped ice crystals. Pleased with the results, he exhaled several more times until the frost-covered window obliterated his image.

"Now is the time to end things," Olofsson slurred with conviction.

He turned his head slowly to survey the interior of the cabin that had been his lonely home for so many years. He extended an arm in front of him in an attempt to grasp *something* which he could pull to his bosom, anything that he could simply caress in recognition; but only imagined objects drifted by as if a reflection of his seventy-one years. They were absent of all substance.

Olofsson realized the winter had really just begun. Several months of frigid darkness lay ahead. And then what? What reasons could there be to continue? The only thing he had to look forward to was becoming older. *Now is the time*, he thought. No need to get any older. The man surrendered himself to his depression, sighed heavily, and simply gave up. He prepared to kill himself.

The light in the cabin brightened as the log burst into flame. Olofsson's eyes focused blurrily on a coil of rope laying next to a satchel of tools. He lifted his gaze to the crossbeams of the cabin's rafters where one beam buttressed the wall just above the door. He moved unsteadily to the rope, picked it up, and carried it to the entryway. Fastening one end to the wrought iron door latch, he then pulled a chair beneath the beam. Climbing atop the chair, he fashioned a crude square-knot noose and slipped it over his neck. Olofsson rocked unsteadily.

He was prepared to die, but only after he had one last drink. Removing the rope from his neck, he stepped from the chair and, stumbling to the table, drank heavily from a flask. Then he fixed his clouded gaze on the Victrola. The occasion of his death required somber music, and he chose Jean Sibelius's Fifth Symphony on the turntable. He cranked the handle until the band was tight.

The woodwinds of the symphony descended into a mournful melody that rose loudly. Scurrying strings blended with brassy drama, and Olofsson moved slowly back to the noose dangling above the chair. The symphony played ominously behind him like a prelude to a Strindberg play.

Aimo ran wildly across the windswept ice with no knowledge of direction, everything a swirling mass of white. Snow melted on the panicked boy's overheated head, then quickly refroze, accumulating against his skull like an ice-sculpted death mask. Occasionally, the wind abated; and Aimo thought he saw the hulking figure of Blixdal charging after him, and he ran on in renewed terror. He could not last much longer before he froze to death. He shivered uncontrollably, never so cold before in his life.

The howling wind swept the snow from the ice, and for the first time, Aimo felt the movement beneath his feet as the ice cracked loudly. A long fissure extended in front of him, and the boy knew of the danger he was in.

He had been exposed to the bitter cold for nearly fifteen minutes. His fingers and toes throbbed in pain, and he coughed frequently from swallowing the frigid air. He stuffed his hands into his pockets, his numb fingers tightening unconsciously into a fist around the military medal. He stumbled forward, driven by sheer will in what had become a life-and-death struggle to survive.

The crack in the ice widened, becoming open water. At first it was only a few centimeters, but as the ice heaved the boy knew much of the frozen lake would split. His father once told him that the first splits of lake ice usually ran perpendicular to the shoreline, and he ran with renewed hope. He followed the open water until at last, he saw the shoreline a few meters in front of him.

Aimo stumbled forward. The wind raced through the branches of the trees, creating a sound like one of Pontilius's furious symphonies the teacher played during the school lunch hour. Then Aimo realized it *was* a symphony, and it was coming from somewhere nearby. He struggled to locate the source of the sound when the glow of Magnus Olofsson's cabin beckoned directly in front of him. Driven by the subconscious instinct to survive, Aimo plodded toward the light.

Olofsson finally succeeded in holding himself steady enough to secure the rope around his neck. The old man swayed unsteadily on the chair. Nothing in the room was in focus any longer. Surrendering himself to his fate, he allowed his body to relax. Olofsson dropped from the chair.

At that moment, the door to the cabin swung open, creating a slack in the rope. Instead of ending his life, the old man crashlanded onto the floor. Olofsson's fingers tore at the tightened but ineffective noose around his neck. He rolled to a rest, his back against a wall just in time to see the dim blur of a small figure collapsing in a heap in front of the fireplace. The old man kicked at the door, slamming it shut, then crawled over to see who or what had entered his cabin. The frost-covered form of an unrecognizable boy, his body covered in snow, lay unmoving in front of the fireplace.

"Helvetta Fon!" Olofsson slurred aloud.

Summoning whatever sense he had left, the old man pulled the blankets from his bed and dropped them over his unexpected guest. Then he collected the remaining logs within the cabin and shoved them into the fire.

The effort proved too much for the liquor-obliterated man. He collapsed over Aimo, too drunk to recognize the boy, and began snoring loudly. Olofsson fell into an unconscious sleep, oblivious of the noose that remained fastened around his neck.

Neither Aimo nor Olofsson were aware that in the old man's simple cabin, on the day of God's gift to all people, Magnus Olofsson and Aimo Kekkenen had each given the other the gift of life.

Chapter Thirty-one

Constable Vahleen grabbed the jangling phone, more asleep than awake. He made a forced attempt to speak coherently.

"Constable Vahleen," Sten mumbled.

Reverend Blixdal's agitated voice blurted out the details of Aimo's disappearance onto the ice of Lake Valdemaren while Sten answered with a series of grunts.

"When did it happen?" Sten asked.

"Thirty minutes ago," Blixdal answered.

The howling wind already answered Sten's next question, but he asked it anyway. "Is it still snowing?"

"Yes!" Blixdal shouted. "A blizzard."

"And you're certain the boy ran onto the lake?"

"Yes, I'm certain. I followed his tracks," Blixdal replied.

"I'll come as quickly as I can," Sten said and hung up. He stepped out of bed, shivering in the chilled room. Gretha switched on her bedside lamp and regarded her husband sleepily.

"You'll go where? What's happened?" she asked.

Sten began dressing, his face masked in troubled thought. It was obvious to Gretha that something unpleasant had happened, and her husband's police instincts were hard at work. He turned to his wife.

"It doesn't make sense. Blixdal called to tell me Aimo ran away tonight. Only an idiot would attempt to run away in this type of weather. The boy knows better. And he'd never run onto a large lake. There's no shelter, and the wind is certain to cause the ice to break up."

"Perhaps he *had* to run away," Gretha offered, unaware of how near the truth her thoughts were.

"There's more. Blixdal said he followed Aimo's tracks onto the ice. This wind would obliterate tracks in seconds," he emphasized by pointing to a window rattling in a heavy gust.

"You can't go out, Sten," Gretha protested. "It's too dangerous."

"I regret I didn't help him the last time he ran away. Maybe he's hiding in the church somewhere and needs help now. I've got to go, Gretha. It's my job."

Gretha knew her husband well. However, she had an opinion on everything and never hesitated to offer it. Her gift was in her ability to present her thoughts unthreateningly, especially when she sensed Sten should apply caution to his impulsive nature. Every so often, however, the man pursued his purpose with dogged determination; and she resigned herself that now was one of those times. She glanced at the clock ticking loudly on the bureau, surprised to see the time was not yet 9:00 p.m.

"I'll call from the church," Sten said, kissing Gretha on the cheek. "Don't tell anyone about this, certainly not the children."

"Sten," Gretha called softly, "do you think Blixdal may have done something to the boy?"

"I don't know," Sten answered. "Aimo told me Blixdal threatened to send him to an orphanage."

A powerful gust rattled the entire house violently. Gretha stood by the window and peered out at the swirling snow. "You can't go out in this. You have to wait until morning."

Sten looked at Gretha's troubled face and joined her at the window. His wife was right. The likelihood of him getting lost or trapped in the storm was high. He shook his head in defeat.

"I'll make us some tea," Gretha said. "Climb back into bed, I'll be right back."

Gretha looked into the girls' room on her way to the kitchen and was comforted to see the mounds beneath the blankets where the girls slept. Satisfied that no one had awakened, she went downstairs and set a kettle of water on the range. She settled into an armchair next to the still-warm fireplace where ash-colored embers offered an occasional crackle.

How swiftly the time goes by, she thought.

Christmas had come and gone more quickly than she had ever known. She leaned her head wearily against the squared backrest of the chair and sighed audibly. She missed the company of her friend Solveig, who returned to her empty home earlier in the day. The great anticipation of Solveig's arrival, her two-week stay, all the fun they had in preparing for Christmas, and the companionable in-depth conversations only women can have with each other had also come to an end.

"How swiftly the time goes by . . . how swiftly . . . how swiftly," she repeated. She closed her eyes and fell asleep in the chair.

Chapter Thirty-two

Olofsson's eyes blinked open. Bewildered, he stared at the crossbeams of his cabin directly above him. He had no idea of time or place. He pushed himself up from the floor on wobbly legs, his head throbbing. He made his way unsteadily to the door unaware of the noose still fastened to his neck. He had to throw up and grasped for the door latch, but it was missing.

"Fon!" he sputtered. He dug his fingers into the edge of the door in an all out effort to open it, but it was frozen shut. Olofsson yanked mightily until it opened far enough to stick his head into the cold air. Without a moment to spare, he wretched uncontrollably, purging himself of the toxic bile that had accumulated in his system. He pulled his head back inside the cabin, shoving the door shut. He felt much better until he became aware of an unusual object around his neck and tried to loosen whatever was fastened there. His fingers informed his dimmed brain of the rope, and Olofsson nearly panicked, remembering he had tried to kill himself the night before. He tore off the noose and hurled it to the ground in disgust. Slowly, the events of the previous night returned to him. Someone had entered the cabin the night before.

Curiously, he moved to the blanket in front of the fireplace but could not remember what lay beneath it. What he did know was that he was terribly cold. If he did not bring firewood into the cabin immediately, he and whoever was under the blanket would soon freeze to death.

The storm had ended abruptly several hours earlier. The countryside lay buried in a half meter of new snow distributed unevenly by the fierce wind. Drifts five meters high were common. However, the section of the house facing the lake also faced the wind. Snow on that side measured but a few centimeters in depth, and the old man stepped outside easily. The lee side of the cabin was another matter. Snow had drifted to the roof, totally obliterating the view of the house from Olofsson's roadway. Beneath all the high snow lay the old man's truck, now buried until spring. Olofsson gave no thought to it at all. Instead, he dug for the firewood that lay against the cabin wall and staggered inside with an armful.

It took Olofsson a considerable effort to stack the wood properly in the fireplace, douse the logs with the flammable aquavit, and ignite them. The flames instantly erupted into a blaze, and Olofsson stood in its increasing warmth. Within minutes, the well-insulated sod-roofed cabin's temperature rose to a comfortable level, and Olofsson took stock of his environment. The first order of business had to do with whatever lay beneath the blanket, and he lifted the woolen cover.

Olofsson recognized Aimo at once. The boy was too poorly dressed to have survived without suffering serious frostbite, he thought. He shook the boy to wake him, and Aimo only moaned. The old man stripped off Aimo's clothing and dressed him in a pair of his own semiclean woolen long johns. He placed a pillow beneath the boy's head and covered him again with the blanket; then he filled a kettle with hot water for tea and porridge.

Suddenly, Olofsson began to shake uncontrollably. He made his way to the flask-covered table and picked up a bottle of aquavit. Filling his mouth with alcohol, he swished the contents around in his mouth and spat it into the fireplace. Tongues of alcohol-induced flame leapt toward Olofsson's face.

"Fon!" the old man joked to himself. "I damn near exploded."

During the next hour, Olofsson drank four cups of hot tea and consumed two bowls of oat porridge but resisted the urge to drink any more alcohol. He carried the boy to his bed, checking for signs of frostbite on fingers, toes, and ears. The white-skinned telltale signs of frozen flesh were absent. Still, the old man could not get Aimo to awaken.

Olofsson filled a cup with tea and adding a splash of aquavit, poured a small amount of the hot liquid into the boy's mouth. Aimo responded with a heavy, mucous-laden cough.

"Pneumonia!" Olofsson said out loud. He put his ear on the boy's chest and heard the telltale gurgling of fluids in the boy's lungs. Each cough resonated with congestion. The boy was seriously ill, but beyond two bottles of quinine and a bottle of iodine, he had little in the way of medicine in the cabin. He knew he had to purge the fluids from Aimo's lungs immediately, or the boy would die.

Olofsson set to his nursing tasks with determination. He soaked several cloth towels in hot water and spread them over the boy's bare chest. Aimo responded immediately with spasms of coughed-up phlegm. Olofsson again offered hot tea, and this time Aimo swallowed, and his body stirred uncomfortably. Olofsson placed the boy on his stomach and once again covered him with blankets, and the boy slept deeply.

Olofsson ran his hand through his hair wondering what else he medically could do. Coming up with nothing, the old man added additional wood to the fire, raising the room temperature considerably higher.

Olofsson's options were few. He was snowbound and his Model B flatbed buried under several meters of snow. Still, he could go for help if necessary. He would have to risk the cold and snowshoe across the lake to Blixdal's church. That idea he dismissed entirely. The old man knew the reverend had to have been the cause of the boy's flight. However, deep within the old man's conscience, another element kept Olofsson in his cabin. It felt good to be caring for another human being, a feeling he had not experienced for many years.

Large patches of blue sky signaled the storm's passing. Occasional passing snow flurries fluttered overhead as a lingering farewell to the potent blizzard, and the southern horizon glowed a sunrise of red and gold patterns. Importantly, the wind had calmed to a zephyr. But the calm was deceiving. As Olofsson scurried in and out of the house carrying loads of firewood, the cold air told Olofsson the temperature was at least forty below zero. It would be suicide to snowshoe anywhere in temperatures so low.

Olofsson perspired in the overheated room as he tended to creating order within the cabin with a newfound zeal. He began by clearing the bottle-strewn table and came upon the stack of records scattered around the Victrola. He replaced Sibelius's somber symphony with his Christmas gift, Lars-Erik Larsson's uplifting *Pastoral Suite* on the turntable. The old man found himself instantly energized by the inspiring music. He fell to his chores with a sense of purpose he had not experienced for a very long time.

Chapter Thirty-three

The constable paced about in his small office, continually stalking around a topographical map of Lake Valdemaren's shoreline. He poked his finger on the spot marked Nilstad church, then shook his head in dismay. There were no homes within a half-kilometer radius of where Aimo could have found shelter. It was highly unlikely the boy or anyone else could travel any farther than that in a blizzard.

Vahleen leaned back into his swivel chair, locking his hands behind his neck and taking stock of the events of the last twenty-four hours. He recalled the nearly one-hour drive earlier to Nilstad church where he found Fru Blixdal beside herself in genuine hysterics and quite unable to provide any pertinent information. She continually shouted the name Mikael. It took several glasses of brandy to allow her to mercifully fall asleep in exhaustion.

Blixdal, on the other hand, explained the entire evening's experience with great detail: the boy had become upset during dinner, Blixdal recounted, his behavior witnessed by both the Falke and Tornquist families. The boy was asked to thank Karen for his Christmas gift, a pair of skates. Instead, he unexplainably hurled them onto the dinner table. Then, after insulting everyone, he ran to his room. Blixdal and his wife tried to placate their insulted company; and while they were busy, Aimo spitefully stole into the tallow room and vandalized the cauldron, flooding the floor with molten wax. He ran down into the catacombs, jumped onto the hoisted boat, and caused it to break free from its fastenings. Then he ran onto the lake.

Blixdal assured the constable the boy took this route because the wooden mallet from the tallow room had been left on the church boat, and the reverend saw Aimo's clearly visible tracks leading onto the lake.

Sten searched the church for two hours. There was no sign of the boy or any evidence to refute the reverend's account. Nevertheless, there were at least three problems from the reverend's story that disturbed the constable.

Aimo's overcoat and boots were still in place in the mudroom together with outerwear belonging to the Blixdals. That meant Aimo had run away, in a blizzard, without coat or boots, all of which were readily available.

Secondly, if the boy were going to run away, why vandalize the tallow room first and then run through the catacombs and onto the lake ice?

Lastly, everything suggested Aimo had not prepared his escape very well, and this ran counter to his knowledge of the boy.

No, Sten thought to himself. Aimo either ran away in desperation, or Blixdal had kept his threat and somehow delivered the boy to the orphanage without Fru Blixdal's knowledge. Vahleen considered the latter concept the most likely.

Sten yawned loudly. He was dead tired, and there would be many reports to file. Letters for the administration committee overseeing the well-being of Finnish refugee children, documents in quadruplicate to the district police office, and a double-spaced typewritten account describing, in minute detail, the events and witnesses to Aimo's disappearance.

And that was just the beginning. He would also have to provide detailed documents for the Finnish authorities. Sten had no idea how much additional work that would be but feared it would be considerable. He rolled his official stationery into the typewriter, opened his note-filled booklet, and prepared to type, wondering again why Blixdal was lying.

Chapter Thirty-four

Reverend Blixdal sat rigidly next to the frigid window in Levander's office. He stared silently as the bishop read from the letter Blixdal had prepared, explaining his version of the events of the previous evening leading to Aimo's running away. Sensing Blixdal's nervousness, the bishop averted the reverend's stare and spoke to him without lifting his eyes from the paper.

"Help yourself to a drink or a cigarette," the bishop offered. Blixdal took a cigarette from the bishop's desk, placed it on his dry lips, lit it, then coughed uncontrollably. "They're Turkish," the bishop warned. "They're quite strong."

"I usually don't smoke, sir. The cigarettes are quite good, however," Blixdal answered nervously.

The bishop completed the letter, having made random notes on the margin. He arose from his chair, walked to a table containing several bottles of alcohol, and filled two glasses from an unmarked flask. He placed one in front of Blixdal.

"This is real Irish whiskey, Bjorn. Skoal."

Blixdal lifted his drink. "Skoal," he said, then drained the glass.

"We're quite lucky here in Sweden. The fighting has not touched us. Our industry is booming, and there are more jobs than people able to fill them."

He crossed to the window and drummed his fingers nervously on the frosted glass. Blixdal knew a lecture was on its way.

"My cellar is filled with priceless art and artifacts from our unfortunate neighbors on the continent who otherwise would lose it all to looters. There is a fortune just beneath my feet, delivered to me from Berlin by relatives I hardly know. I've been asked to store it in safekeeping until war's end. I must confess, I'm reluctant to even review their contents. But . . . I'm rewarded for storing it with Irish whiskey, French wine, and Turkish cigarettes." The bishop sipped at his glass as the reverend grimaced uncomfortably.

"We're very fortunate," Blixdal agreed.

"That's what troubles me about this, Bjorn." The bishop held Blixdal's letter in front of him. "All we need to do is tend to our business and avoid problems. Do you know what I mean?"

"I think so," Blixdal answered.

"I don't think you do." The bishop reached into a drawer and retrieved a folder. Blixdal froze in his chair, fearfully anticipating what sort of information the bishop might produce.

"You were next in line to succeed me, Bjorn. All you needed to do was your job." The bishop opened the folder. "I have already received letters from both Herr Falke and Herr Tornquist. Their recollection of the evening at your house differs greatly from what you've written. They said you struck the boy with force and used vile language. Your actions surprised and shocked them. They have concluded, and I quote from one of them, '*Unacceptable from a man of the cloth.*' They all have withdrawn their support of you to succeed me."

"No!" Blixdal shouted. "They can't do that. You can stop them. You can intervene on my behalf."

"Even if I could, they have told me they will petition Stockholm if I do not acquiesce."

"How can they do this? I have done so much for both those families!" Blixdal was near tears.

"Apparently, they were most appalled by how you physically abused the boy. They are willing to stand as witnesses, if needed, of course."

"Please, Bishop Levander, I beg you. Please! I *must* be made bishop. It is my life. I have devoted myself. I have suffered as Jesus suffered. I beg you," Blixdal sobbed openly.

"You may remain at your position as reverend of Nilstad church on a probationary basis. That is all I can do for you."

Blixdal regarded the bishop hopefully. "Suppose the boy refutes these charges? That would exonerate me, would it not?"

"The boy is dead, Bjorn," Levander reminded him.

"We don't know that. I saw him run off into the storm, that's all. I did not see him die, and neither has anyone else. Let's assume he's survived. If I bring him to you and he refutes these charges of my abuse, then surely, in fairness, you would reconsider. Please! I beg you. Give me hope." Blixdal's face was tearstained, and his nose ran freely.

The bishop shook his head at the pathetic scene before him. Blixdal was suffering profoundly, and Levander had no desire to inflict more pain.

"All right, Bjorn," the bishop said comfortingly. "All right. Find the boy. If he refutes, I promise to reconsider."

"Thank you! Thank you!" Blixdal gushed, earnestly kissing the backs of both of Levander's hands. "I will find him. I promise."

Blixdal bowed politely and left the bishops' chambers, elated at the possibility of achieving his life's purpose still existed. But he was wrong. Not only was he to be denied the bishop's position, Levander had already made up his mind to replace him as reverend of Nilstad church as well.

Chapter Thirty-five

Aimo lay drifting in and out of sleep for seven days, as Olofsson provided continual care. The old man disregarded time, waking when Aimo did, and allowing himself rest when the boy fell asleep.

Perhaps the need to care for someone other than himself was responsible for Olofsson's new behavior. Whatever the reason, the old man's waking hours were filled with nonstop chores. He thoroughly cleaned the cabin, stacked cords of firewood next to the fireplace, and warmed a previously prepared moose-meat stew. He added some new ingredients daily with frozen carrots, onions, or potatoes. After one week's cooking, the stew resembled a thick but tasty soup.

Without realizing it, the old man had not taken a drink of hard liquor since Aimo had entered the house. Now he used the aquavit to either spice his cooking or start his cooking fire.

Aimo's fever broke on the eighth day after he stumbled into the lakeside cabin. His once-ruddy complexion now had a pale green hue, and his dark eyes seemed to have sunk deep into their sockets. He was very weak, and his emaciated frame clearly revealed his rib cage.

On several occasions Aimo's fever-induced dreams had Russian soldiers chasing him through deep drifts of snow. Then a new figure would appear, sprinting wildly behind him. The black-robed figure of the reverend, armed with the wooden cudgel, always replaced the soldiers. In dream after dream, Aimo fell into the snow, unable to raise himself as the black hulk relentlessly descended upon him. Aimo struggled, writhing from the nightmare, his body bathed in perspiration. Finally, the fever subsided and brought the nightmares to an end. Aimo blinked his eyes open and stared at the bearded man whose grizzled face smiled back warmly.

"Hello there," Olofsson said softly. "How do you feel?"

170

Aimo struggled to place the unthreatening voice with the face, then allowed his eyes to sweep the interior of the unfamiliar cabin.

"Where am I?" Aimo asked.

"You're in my house," Olofsson replied.

"Herr Blixdal . . . he's going to kill me." Aimo said desperately, his eyes widening in fright

"The hell you say! He's on the other side of the lake. Is that how you got here . . . over the lake?"

"I don't know . . . I think so . . . maybe," Aimo tried to remember.

"Did you come from the church?" Olofsson continued.

"Yes."

"Then that's what you did, boy! And you're lucky, 'cause the ice broke in the storm. It froze back again . . . it won't break now until spring."

"I don't want to go back to the church, mister . . . I forgot you're name."

"Why don't you call me grandpa?" Olofsson said hopefully.

"'Cause you're not," Aimo's voice was agitated. He had had enough of people claiming they were his relatives.

"Take it easy," Olofsson said reassuringly. "My name's Magnus. Magnus Olofsson."

"Mine is Aimo."

"I know. We met before under similar conditions," Olofsson said smilingly.

"Now I remember. You told me to call Fru Blixdal mother."

"That's me. At your service." Olofsson's demeanor put the boy at ease.

"I'm hungry," Aimo said.

Olofsson refilled Aimo's bowl with another round of moose-meat stew. Aimo ate ravenously, ladling an unbroken string of spoons into his mouth. "This is the best soup I've ever had," the boy managed between slurps. "As soon as I get better, I want to go home."

Olofsson shielded his disappointment at hearing the boy say he wanted to return to Finland. He allowed Aimo to eat unencumbered and, cranking the Victrola again, allowed Lars-Erik Larsson's inspiring *Pastoral Suite* to fill the cabin. The inspiring music brought the man a ray of hope.

"I'll tell you what I think we ought to do. If Blixdal learns you're here with me, he's gonna want you back," Olofsson said scratching his beard.

"No he won't. He hates me," Aimo said.

"I think Fru Blixdal likes you."

"She's nice," Aimo answered.

"Well, do you want to go back?" Olofsson asked.

"No!" Aimo said, stuffing another spoonful of stew in his mouth.

"Well, it sure looked to me like his old lady wants you back."

"She's not mean or anything," Aimo added in her defense.

"But she's not your *mother*. I think we did this before."

"I want to go home to *my* mother and father. I want to go to *my* home," Aimo insisted.

"Well, that's what I mean," Olofsson said. "We can't let the Blixdals know you're here. If they find out, they'll either take you back or send you to an orphanage . . . and we don't want that either. So stay here with me until the snow melts. I promise. I'll help you get back to Finland if you still want to go. How does that sound?"

"I don't have to go to school?" Aimo asked. The old man shook his head.

"How about my sister? She's gonna be worried."

Olofsson shook his head again, "I'll tell the Vahleens, but we'll keep it a secret from everybody else."

"It's a contract," Aimo nodded approvingly.

"A contract it is," Olofsson repeated, lifting a cup of nonalcoholic berry juice to his lips.

Pontilius stood at the chalkboard scrawling a series of math problems, then became aware of Meggan, who stood silently next to him. She curtsied and offered Pontilius a letter.

"My mother told me to give this to you, Herr Pontilius."

The teacher slid the letter neatly into his jacket without opening it, and Meggan curtsied again before returning to her seat. Pontilius checked the rows of silent students counting three vacant seats.

"Who is missing?" Pontilius asked.

Several children identified two of the students as sick at home. Meggan raised her hand. "Aimo is missing," she added worriedly.

Pontilius marked his ledger and recorded Aimo's absence. Almost on cue, the door burst open, and the reverend stepped inside. He stamped his feet noisily to shake off the accumulated snow, then regarded the class while ignoring the teacher.

Blixdal scanned the rows of seated children hopefully. "Good morning, Herr Pontilius. I'm sorry to bother you," he said without looking at the teacher.

"Good morning, Herr Blixdal," Pontilius answered. "Children, please stand and say good morning to the Reverend Blixdal."

The children obeyed and rose together. "Good morning, Herr Reverend Blixdal," their voices sang in concert.

"Good morning, children. I'm looking for the Finnish boy who lives with us," he announced.

"Aimo?" Pontilius asked. He tried to get the clergyman's attention, but Blixdal ignored the teacher as he continued scanning the classroom.

"Herr Blixdal!" Pontilius said sternly. "May we speak alone?"

Blixdal turned his head violently, and Pontilius saw for the first time the reverend had undergone a transformation. A trickle of mucous had dried on his upper lip, and his clothes were wrinkled, suggesting he may have slept in them. But it was Blixdal's wolflike bloodshot eyes glaring menacingly that made Pontilius wonder if the man had gone mad.

"Where is the boy?" Blixdal demanded.

"I want you to come to my chambers to discuss this privately," Pontilius said. He took Blixdal's arm hoping to spare the children from the clergyman's irrational behavior and tried to guide him out of the classroom.

Blixdal pulled away. "Yes! Aimo! That's who I'm looking for. Where is he?" He faced the classroom. "Where is he?" the reverend shouted.

"He's not here, Reverend Blixdal. When we last saw him, he was with you in the church at Christmas," Pontilius said.

"And that's when he ran away . . . in the storm . . . on the lake . . . he could have died. Someone knows where he is . . . tell me . . . I demand it!" Blixdal raged.

The effect of the clergyman's voice on the children was as the teacher feared. A chorus of protests was joined by a piercing cry from Anna, bringing Meggan to the stricken child's side. Lisa joined her sister and draped an arm over Anna's shoulder.

"You awful man," Meggan hissed, angrily. "I hate you! I hate you!"

Pontilius smashed his cane hard across his desk, and the room quieted immediately. The teacher punched angrily at the prosthesis below his knee, locking it in place with an audible snap. He approached Blixdal again, this time raising the cane over his shoulder menacingly.

"Get out! Get out! . . . now!" Pontilius growled.

Blixdal spun on his heels and left the room quickly.

Pontilius calmed the class, then asked if any of the children had knowledge of Aimo's whereabouts. The room remained silent as the children searched each other's faces for a positive answer.

"He's in heaven," Anna said sadly.

"Who thinks that?" Pontilius asked the class, clearly upset by the statement. "Who thinks Aimo is dead?"

No one raised their hands, and Pontilius continued.

"None of us believe that," he said, speaking directly to Anna. "You don't either, Anna. You know Aimo better than all of us. He would never give up, and he would never leave his sister."

He turned his attention to the class. "I want all of you to go home . . . now. Get your parents and your neighbors and search for Aimo. Maybe he's hiding in a barn . . . someplace warm."

Pontilius held out his hands for silence. "Before anyone leaves, I want all of us to say a little silent prayer for Aimo while we're all together. Just bow your heads and close your eyes."

The room grew quiet. After several moments, Pontilius's soft voice broke the stillness.

"All right. You're all dismissed for the day. Your assignment is find Aimo. You'll be back in school tomorrow at the usual time."

Pontilius walked to where Meggan, and the girls stood forlornly. He took Anna's hand.

"Let's all go to your home together. I have to speak to your father," Pontilius said.

Gretha stood in front of the bedroom mirror, making final adjustments before leaving for her job at the hospital. She pushed several strands of loose hair into a neat bun behind her head and turned slowly, allowing herself a complete view of her reflection. She tucked at her sweater, pleased by what she saw, and nodded approvingly.

Outside, sounds of her children's voices brought her to the window, and she was surprised to discover her three girls unexpectedly returning too early from school. She was shocked to see Pontilius skiing with them. Alarmed, Gretha rushed from the bedroom and reached the open porch just as the girls arrived with their teacher.

"Aimo ran away," Meggan shouted. "We have to find him."

Gretha looked questioningly at Pontilius, amazed to see him skiing with no sign at all of a handicap.

"Hello, Fredrik! What on earth has happened?" Gretha asked.

"May I speak to you privately, Fru Vahleen?" Pontilius asked.

"Gretha . . . please call me Gretha," she reminded. "Of course. Come in. Meggan, make hot chocolate for everyone. Come to the living room, Fredrik."

Gretha led the teacher into the living room, still bedecked room in its Christmas splendor. She offered Pontilius the easy chair between the fireplace and Christmas tree, happy to see the man disconnect his prosthesis without embarrassment.

"What's wrong?" Gretha asked, and Pontilius recounted the visit from the distraught clergyman.

"I've never liked the man," Pontilius continued, "but everything about him was of a man who either has gone mad or soon will."

"He told the children Aimo might have died?" Gretha repeated incredulously.

"He simply blurted it out. He didn't care a damn about the effects on the children . . . not even Anna."

"We know about the boy running away. It happened on Christmas night. Sten was called to the house, but couldn't leave because of the storm. He went to the church the next morning but found no trace of Aimo. Sten didn't believe the reverend's story either. He told me Karen Blixdal was hysterical. My friends and I have tried calling her, but no one answers."

"*Christmas night!*" Pontilius blurted. "That was a week ago. If the boy didn't find immediate shelter, he couldn't possibly survive. What does Sten say?"

"He's very worried, Fredrik. If the boy did run onto the lake as Blixdal said, he probably was swallowed by the lake when the ice broke."

"He might have survived . . . if he found shelter. But a week in these conditions are impossible for any person," Pontilius added.

"It's worse than that. The boy ran off without winter clothing. No hat, coat, gloves . . . nothing."

Pontilius shook his head in despair.

"The roads are finally to be cleared of snow today," Gretha added. "Sten believes there's a chance Blixdal took him to the orphanage. Aimo told us he'd been threatened with being sent there."

"Aimo told me the same thing. That *must* be where he is. But I'm still baffled by Blixdal's behavior? I hope it's not a ruse to cover up something?"

The idea of foul play suddenly became a viable thought.

"Is Sten at his office? I've put off speaking to him about Aimo for too long," Pontilius admitted.

"Yes! Wait here. I'll phone him," Gretha said.

"Tell him I must see him as soon as possible."

Gretha turned to leave, then remembered the note she had asked Meggan to deliver. "Did you read my letter, Fredrik?" Gretha asked.

"No! Not yet," Pontilius answered. "I have it in my pocket. I haven't had the opportunity to look at it."

"It's brief, Fredrik . . . but significant. Read it while I call Sten. I'll tell him you're on your way."

Gretha left the room as Pontilius pushed himself up from the easy chair. A row of photographs on the fireplace mantle caught his eye. A photo of Solveig and himself taken at midsummer in 1938 had a prominent position on the mantle. He stepped forward to take a closer look.

Solveig wore a long white cotton dress with a wreath of wildflowers encircling her head. Both her arms were draped around Pontilius's shoulders, his tanned skin enhanced by a white shirt and white slacks. He faced the camera, an oak leaf laurel angled jauntily over his curly hair, and he smiled broadly as Solveig kissed his cheek. Pontilius shifted his gaze to the white slacks. There, sticking out from beneath the rolled up cuffs, were both his legs. Once again, pain and sadness overwhelmed him, and he silently cursed his bad luck. Pontilius turned away from the mantle and retrieved Gretha's letter from his pocket.

Dear Fredrik,

As Solveig's friend, I have watched her suffer the consequences of your injury. She asked me not to interfere, and during this time I have obeyed her request, but today, I risk violating the promise I made to her. She has never stopped loving you, and I don't believe she ever will. In her own way she is as wounded as you are Fredrik, but she cannot bear to suffer loving you as she does, only to be continually rejected. You should know this now because she has been offered a job with a family in the United States. If she leaves, I'm certain she will not return. I beg you, for both your sake and mine, if you still care for her, stop her before its too late.

Fondly, Gretha Vahleen

PS. I would like to offer you a wise thought from the Danish writer, Soren Kierkegaard: "Life can only be understood backward, but it must be lived forward."

Pontilius folded the letter and placed it in his pocket as Gretha returned.

"Sten would like you to get to his office as soon as possible. He's just learned the roads have been plowed. He's going to visit the orphanage at once."

"Thank you, Gretha," Fredrik said and made his way to the door.

"Did you read my letter?" Gretha asked curiously.

"Yes, Gretha. I should have acted sooner. I haven't had the nerve to ask her to forgive me. Thank you for caring."

Chapter Thirty-six

Constable Vahleen stabbed a forefinger on a map of Lake Valdemaren over the name, Nilstad church. "We've done this dozens of times, Fredrik. I can't see how the boy could have survived. There's not a house near enough to the church."

Pontilius brought his face closer to the map. "Suppose the boy didn't run away? He told me Blixdal had threatened to send him to the orphanage."

"He told me the same story," Sten said, "and I believe him. I arrived at the church just a few hours after he supposedly ran away."

Pontilius stepped back from the map in bewilderment. "Could the woman who runs the orphanage . . . what's her name?"

"Fröken Elsa . . . something or other," Vahleen said.

"Could she be involved somehow? I should have told you this earlier. Aimo told me she and Blixdal are having an affair. Blixdal took the boy to the orphanage about two weeks ago and ordered him to stay in the car. Aimo got cold . . . went into the house . . . and apparently, he heard them."

"That's the second time I've heard that rumor," Sten said. "Gretha told me many of the women in the area believed they were better than just friends. How do women get to know these things?" Sten joked.

"But how could he have driven in that storm?"

"I did, sort of. On my motorcycle. The road was drifted over and difficult in places. But I got through," Vahleen said. He rose to his feet. "I'm going to check on the orphanage today. It took the army a week to open the roads."

Pontilius placed his hand on the topographical map and moved it in a swirling motion over the area around Nilstad church. His fingers rose and fell over the diverse shoreline where dozens of islands and peninsulas of varying shapes and sizes spread over the region.

"Did Blixdal say he saw Aimo run away?" Pontilius asked.

178

"No! He said the boy left the church by way of the catacombs behind the boathouse. He said he saw Aimo's footprints on the ice."

"Nonsense!" Pontilius snorted. "The wind was so strong it would have obliterated tracks in seconds."

"I know! I have no doubt Blixdal was lying," Vahleen exclaimed.

"But if Aimo did go onto the lake, he'd have drowned when the ice broke, unless he somehow crossed to the other side." Pontilius looked at the map's expanse of blue, indicating Lake Valdemaren's irregular pattern. "How wide would you say it is across here, a kilometer?"

"About that," Vahleen agreed, "but it's unpopulated. It's unlikely he'd find any type of substantive shelter." Vahleen moved to the door and pulled on his coat. "Stay here for as long as you'd like. I want to get to the orphanage before it gets dark." Vahleen paused for a moment. He had news of a personal nature regarding Pontilius but questioned the timing. He surrendered to his instincts. "By the way, Gretha told me Solveig will be leaving for America," Vahleen said.

"I know. Gretha told me when I was at your house," Pontilius answered sadly.

"I'm sorry, Fredrik. She and Gretha have grown very close. She stayed with us at Christmas for two weeks. We had Olofsson over, also. He played Jul Tomten for the kids but didn't stay sober very long. Olfsson left a little early, right after Christmas Eve dinner. A few hours later, Solveig left for her home, so the place got kind of lonely."

Vahleen slapped his hand down quickly onto the map.

"*Olofsson!* By god he lives on this side of the lake."

The constable pointed to the rugged region opposite Nilstad church. "I completely forgot about that," Vahleen said. "Olofsson! Of course. His cabin is actually directly across from the church."

The constable returned quickly to the map and placed his pointed finger on the area where he believed Olofsson's cabin stood. "Look. That's exactly where Olofsson's cabin is, directly across from the church," Sten said excitedly.

"Go check on the orphanage, Sten," Pontilius nodded. "I'll ski over to meet with Olofsson and see what I can find."

Pontilius pulled his jacket over his head, then stopped abruptly. The idea of Solveig leaving his life forever suddenly entered his consciousness like a thunderclap. He left the police office and skied with reckless abandon in the direction of Solveig Olin's cottage.

Chapter Thirty-seven

Valåkravägen was one of many peculiar little streets on Nilstad's northern boundary. The unusual road meandered in corkscrew fashion past single-bedroom cottages serving as summer retreats for Nilstad's more affluent families. The street was a continual garden of carefully tilled parcels producing great quantities of fruits, flowers, and vegetables. Some families planted small orchards of apple and pear trees while others specialized in berries of different varieties. Everything grew abundantly in Jamtland's summer of continuous light. Fragrances of flowers and fruit perfumed Valåkravägen with a rich, sensuous aroma. But now in midwinter, the entire lane lay buried beneath deep drifts of snow and looked no different from the rest of Nilstad's snowbound landscape.

Solveig Olin's family owned two parcels adjacent to one another at the end of the lane. Here, Valåkravägen came upon the first trunks of a large stand of white birch trees that gradually mixed with the thick forest of conifers covering most of Jamtland County.

When her father died, Solveig's mother sold their city house without hesitation; and the girl, sixteen at the time, approved of the decision. Solveig loved Valåkravägen. She enjoyed working their gardens once the land was free of frost, and she met Fredrik Pontilius there two years later on Midsummer's eve.

He had climbed onto one of her pear trees, intent on stealing some fruit. When she discovered him, she told him he was trespassing and threatened to call the police. Pontilius was caught red-handed, but he was also quick-witted. He jumped to the ground and presented her with the fruit. "I wanted to offer you flowers," he fibbed, "but I couldn't resist these pears." Solveig accepted the offering and smiled demurely when he told her she was beautiful when she was angry.

Her mood changed instantly. She had intended to scold the young man with the curly honey blond hair, flashing blue eyes, and devastating smile, but fell in love with him instead. Pontilius later confessed he had also fallen in love with her the moment they met.

They dated through high school and the two years of their precollege gymnasium course. Upon graduation, they both received their traditional white academic caps. Solveig entered nursing school in Nilstad while Pontilius pursued a teaching degree at the local college.

At age twenty-two, Solveig was an accredited registered nurse, assigned to the trauma section of Nilstad's general hospital. She and Fredrik became engaged and announced a midsummer wedding. Her mother granted permission for them to live in the cottage next door to her.

When war between Russia and Finland broke out in 1939, Pontilius stunned her with the news that he and a group of friends had answered Finland's call for Swedish volunteers to help them fight the hated Russians. She remembered their last night together, lying next to him as he slept and holding him tightly, sick with worry. She had exhausted every conceivable argument to get him to change his mind but to no avail. The following day, three weeks before Christmas, Fredrik boarded the train that would take him to war.

"I'll be home soon. I promise." Pontilius laughed. "We'll get married at midsummer. I love you . . . I love you with every fiber of my being," he declared. The train pulled away, vanishing within the pine forest, its forlorn whistle echoing across the valley foretelling the disaster that was to come.

Five months later, a very different Pontilius returned, his right leg missing at the knee, his handsome face scarred and his spirit crushed. Months went by before the muscles in his face strengthened allowing his jaw to move sufficiently to speak.

Many more months of rehabilitation included learning to walk with the aid of a cane. His dashing smile was gone, replaced by grim tight lips hidden behind the tangled mass of an unruly beard. Pontilius spoke through clenched teeth and ordered the doctors not to allow anyone to see him, including Solveig. The distraught woman could only look on silently throughout his rehabilitation, hidden from his view without his knowledge.

Solveig endured ten months of frustrating patience when she finally received a note from Pontilius asking her to visit. Euphoric with the invitation, she rushed to his bedside and was devastated once again. Pontilius ended their engagement and told her to find someone else.

She desperately sought to escape the painful memories of Nilstad and searched for alternative places to go. Leaving the country was out of the question as all of Europe had become enveloped in war. Then a steady stream of wounded Swedish volunteers from the fighting in Norway arrived at Nilstad's hospital, interrupting any private thoughts she had of her needs. She worked long tiring hours, usually together with Gretha Vahleen; and they became fast friends. Solveig joined Gretha's church choir as a substitute for a social life in spite of the many invitations she received.

But Valåkravägen became her sanctuary. She devoted her time to caring for the garden and fruit trees during the summer and moved in with her mother, abandoning the cottage where she and Pontilius had lived. Shortly afterward, her mother met a professor from Lund University in southern Sweden and remarried. Solveig was invited to move to Malmo with them, but chose to remain in Nilstad, holding on to the hope that one day, she and Pontilius would be together again. Within a week, she discovered her decision was a mistake and found herself more alone and heartbroken than ever before.

Solveig decided it would be best to leave Sweden entirely. The first opportunity for a new life came in an unexpected letter of invitation from her married cousin in the United States. She had received the invitation in the autumn but decided now was the time to accept the offer.

If there had been any hope regarding Fredrik's interest in her, it was extinguished when he dismissed her in church on Christmas Day. Finally, after nearly two years of self-imposed denial and suffering, there was a faint stirring with the thought of a new beginning. Solveig left for her work schedule at the hospital with an optimism she had not felt for months.

The skier swooped down the hill expertly, dodging trees through the stands of white birch, and Solveig recognized Pontilius at once. The man skied fluidly, without any sign of his handicap; and for a moment, the memories of their exuberant skiing together rushed through her entire body. She steadied herself on her ski poles as Pontilius neared.

"Hi, Solveig," Pontilius's strong voice surprised her. He braked to a stop, sending up a plume of snow in front of him.

"Hi, Fredrik!" she answered.

"I saw you in church," Pontilius said. His overheated face was wet with perspiration, matting his curls against his forehead.

"I know," she replied.

Pontilius waited for her to continue, but Solveig said nothing more.

"I came because . . . I . . . I wanted to . . . wish you a Merry Christmas," he stammered.

"Thank you, Fredrik. You're a little late. Christmas was last week"

"Solveig, I'm sorry. I tried to speak to you at church . . ." His voice trailed off.

"Well, Merry Christmas, Fredrik. I'm sorry too, but I don't have time now. I'm due at the hospital in fifteen minutes."

"I came to apologize," Pontilius said quickly. "I'm very sorry for what I've done to us. I was wrong . . . so very wrong."

"Thank you for the apology, Fredrik." Solveig strapped on the thongs to her skies.

"Wait, Solveig!" Pontilius grabbed her arm. "Don't you understand? I'm here to tell you I'm sorry."

"And I told you I'm sorry too!" Solveig shouted, her voice angry. "I've been sorry for too long."

Pontilius was desperate. "I heard you'll be leaving for America. Please don't leave! I was selfish. I want us to be together again. That's why I'm here,"

Solveig could no longer withhold her pent-up frustration. "You're too late, Fredrik!" she shouted. "Too late! I waited nearly two years for you to say just one small promising thing to me."

"I felt I had no right," Pontilius protested.

"*You* had no right?" she repeated, lowering her voice in disbelief. "You had no *right*? Did you ever ask *me* . . . about *my rights* . . . or how *I* felt? Did you ever give a thought to what *I* had to say, or how *I* pleaded with you not to go?" She absently swept a strand of hair from her face as tears streamed down her face. "You were willing to sacrifice everything for what *you* felt was right. *You* had to go to war in Finland, *one month before our wedding*! No matter how I pleaded, *you* had to go. *I'm* not the one who sent you, Fredrik, but *I* was the one to welcome you back with all my heart. It was *I* who did everything I could to keep us together. *You* rejected that. *You* rejected me, and now you talk to me about *your rights*!"

Pontilius allowed his grip on her arm to relax, his face confused and hurt. Solveig pulled away, satisfied to have finally spoken her mind to the person who had caused her so much unrelenting grief. She took a deep breath to gain control of her emotions and lowered her voice.

"No, Fredrik! I've already agreed to go to America. I have given my word. A family is sending a contract. I'll join them in California."

"California . . . ," Pontilius echoed in astonishment. "That's so far away."

"I know, Fredrik . . . and you're too late."

Solveig pushed on her ski poles and glided away from Pontilius. She skied strongly along the snow-covered corkscrew lane of Valåkravägen, unable to control the tears that Pontilius could not see.

Chapter Thirty-eight

Aimo lay quietly on his side, his eyes fixed on Olofsson who was deeply involved in whittling on a piece of wood. Aimo stared curiously for several minutes, unwilling to leave the comfort of his bed. His interest piqued as Olofsson maneuvered his knife over the wood expertly. He held the object in front of him scrutinizing it carefully.

"That looks like a fishing lure," Aimo said weakly. Olofsson turned in surprise.

"You're awake! Thought you were gonna sleep right through lunch."

Aimo stepped out of bed and tightened the blanket around him. He made his way over to Olofsson, sat on the bench, and reached for the object Olofsson held.

"How you feelin'?" Olofsson asked.

"OK," Aimo answered. "What's this supposed to be?" Aimo fingered the object gently.

"A fishing lure. You got it right, first time," Olofsson answered.

"Balsa wood, right?" Aimo asked again.

"Yep! Gonna use it for pike. Sometime I get walleyes or big perch on a lure that size."

"Do you have more wood? I know how to make lures, but I don't have my own knife anymore. Do you have one I can use?" Aimo asked hopefully.

"Sure, kid! Tell you what. I'll get you your own knife. You can try to make one yourself." Olofsson fetched a small wood-handled knife and handed Aimo a molded section of raw wood from beneath the bench.

"Thanks, Magnus," Aimo said. "Do you have wire?"

"Wire comin' up," Olofsson answered. He rummaged through his toolbox and returned with a roll of thin-gauge wire and a pair of wire cutters.

Aimo took the roll, snipped a length of wire and placed it in the fire. Working his knife swiftly, Aimo reduced the balsa wood to a tapered oblong shape. Then he lifted the heated wire from the fireplace and carefully threaded the glowing white metal through the center of the wood from one end to the other. Thin wisps of smoke rose from the soft wood, threatening to consume the entire experiment in flames, but Aimo deftly extinguished the fire each time it flared.

"You've done this before," Olofsson said, genuinely impressed.

"My dad taught me. But I'm not done yet," Aimo said, fully concentrated on what he was doing. Olofsson took the break in the conversation to step over to the Victrola and look among his records.

"Play something where somebody sings," Aimo called. Olofsson plunged into the stack of records with renewed vigor.

"By god! You want to hear singing? Just wait to you hear this," Olofsson shouted. A moment later, the rich tenor voice of Jussi Bjorling singing "Che gelida manina" from *La Boheme* filled the room.

Aimo eyed Olofsson warily, a sign of his disapproval of the opera. He had had something more contemporary in mind but quickly returned to his task. He whittled at the middle of the wood mold to create a thin waist in the form until he exposed the wire.

"Now it's a jointed plug," Aimo said. "Do you have any swivels and hooks?"

Olofsson reached beneath the bench again and returned with a number of small boxes. He opened two, one with ball bearing swivels and the second with treble hooks.

Aimo placed a swivel over the forward end of the lure and, twisting it into place, and knotted the wire around the treble tail hook. Olofsson was fascinated by the boy's dexterity. Like a surgeon's assistant, he responded to the boy's every request without question.

"Almost done," Aimo said. "I need a thin piece of shiny metal about this big." Aimo separated his fingers half a centimeter.

Olofsson searched among the boxes.

"Nothing here," he said. Suddenly the old man received a thought. He jumped from the bench and, fetching a hammer, found a silver spoon from among his meager utensils. The old man hammered the spoon flat. Using tin snips, he cut away a small oval section, which he handed to the boy.

"What the hell you gonna do with that?" Olofsson asked.

"You'll see," Aimo said, slicing a deep mouth in the front of the lure. "You cut a mouth like this . . . then fit the piece of metal into the mouth like this and"—Aimo displayed the lure, holding it up by the nose—"when you pull it through the water, the nose dives, the tail wiggles, and the pike go crazy."

"Your father taught you that?" Olofsson said admiringly.

"Yep! Save the spoon, 'cause I'm gonna make a spinner lure out of it. Pike love spinners too. Do you have more spoons?"

"Yeah! But we need 'em unless you want to eat with your hands."

"That's OK," Aimo said happily. "I prefer makin' wooden plugs." Aimo handed the finished lure to Olofsson who nodded his head in approval. "I'm gonna have to paint it. You've got paint here, right?" Aimo asked.

"I got everything we need," Olofsson said with enthusiasm. "Soon as the ice breaks, we'll try this out."

Aimo left the bench and shuffled back to bed, suddenly weakened. The simple effort of making a fishing lure was too taxing of his energy. He pulled the blanket tightly around him.

"I hafta lie down for a while," Aimo said.

"You feel OK?" Olofsson asked worriedly.

"A little tired, that's all," Aimo yawned.

"Go ahead and take a nap. I'll wake you in an hour. We can have some lunch, OK?"

Olofsson waited for a reply, but the boy had already closed his eyes. The old man rewound the Victrola and decided it was time to replenish the wood stack. He quickly stepped outside but did not notice Pontilius until the teacher skied to a stop several meters from him.

"Hi there!" Pontilius called, breathing heavily.

Olofsson spun around in surprise, his bundle of logs tumbling to the snow. He eyed Pontilius warily.

"Who the hell are you?" Olofsson asked threateningly.

"My name is Fredrik Pontilius. I'm looking for Magnus Olofsson."

"That's me," Olofsson said. "Pontilius? Where did I hear that name? Oh, yeah, you're the ski jumper."

"And that's me, Herr Olofsson," Pontilius replied respectfully. "I stopped ski jumping a few years ago."

"That's smart," Olofsson replied. "Ski jumping is a damn fool sport. It's an easy way to break your neck."

"I could hear the voice of Bjorling out on the middle of the ice," Pontilius said. "He's my favorite tenor."

"Mine too," Olofsson replied, his guard slackening. "They can say what they want about Caruso. He's good, but he just sings in Italian. He can do Italian better than anyone. Wagner's operas were made for Bjorling's voice. He's perfect in German. What brings you out here, Pontilius? Can't just be the music."

"I'm looking for a Finnish boy named Aimo. He ran away from the home where he was staying. They thought he might have run out onto the ice. I'm afraid he didn't survive."

Olofsson edged closer to the door, listening to Pontilius with one ear and hoping not to hear Aimo stirring in the cabin with the other. "Can't see how anybody could survive for long out there," Olofsson added.

"I'm afraid you're right. Could I trouble you for a drink of water? I've been skiing pretty hard, and I'm thirsty."

"I can't invite you in," Olofsson lied. "Been skinning a moose. It's a mess inside. Wait here. I'll come out with some water."

Skinning a moose in his house did not sound right to Pontilius. He watched as Olofsson retreated inside and strained his eyes to search the old man's property. There, in full view and less than ten meters from the house, stood a hand-winch mount fastened to a crossbar. Its purpose was for lifting heavy farm machinery or for hanging big game animals, such as moose. Olofsson was not telling the truth. No one in his right mind skins a moose in a house.

Olofsson appeared with a flask of water and offered it to the teacher who drank thirstily.

"Thanks! If by chance you see the boy and find him, he'd need immediate medical care," Pontilius said.

"There's little chance anybody could survive too long out there," Olofsson said conclusively.

Pontilius returned the flask to Olofsson, then looked directly into the old man's eyes. There was no doubt that he was hiding something in his cabin. Pontilius was determined to find out what that was. The teacher immediately thought the worst. Suppose Aimo had found his way to the cabin. He probably was in need of medical care. Then Pontilius was struck by a new and frightening thought. How safe might the boy be in the care of such a recluse? The old man could be mad.

"Well! So long," Olofsson waved his hand in a farewell gesture.

"So long," Pontilius said without moving. He had to do something fast. If the old man returned to the cabin, Pontilius would be at a disadvantage.

"Better get going before you freeze yourself," Olofsson continued.

"I'm the boy's teacher. I'm also his friend," Pontilius blurted.

Olofsson remained silent, and Pontilius decided to lie. "I haven't told you the whole truth, Herr Olofsson. I'm actually with a party of searchers under the direction of Constable Vahleen. They will want to know if the boy is in the cabin. If I don't see for myself, they'll be here in an hour."

The lie worked and Olofsson lost his temper.

"The boy is not going back to that goddamned priest. He's gonna stay with me. You can tell Vahleen I told you so." Olofsson picked up a log and held it menacingly. "I'll smash the skull of anybody who tries to take him away," Olofsson shouted.

Pontilius was overjoyed. Aimo had survived after all and was inside the cabin. "All right, Olofsson. Tell me the condition of the boy."

"He almost died of pneumonia. He's weak, but he'll survive."

"Any frostbite?"

"No! That poor kid beat all the odds. It's a miracle he's alive! My cabin is the only safe place on this side of the lake. It's a miracle he found me."

There was no longer any question in Pontilius's mind that Olofsson was telling the truth. More importantly, it was obvious the old man genuinely cared for the boy's best interest.

"Olofsson, I've got to see him for myself. I'm alone. Only Constable Vahleen and I are officially searching for him. I'm desperately concerned for the boy. Not just as his teacher but also as his friend. Perhaps the constable and I can help you with some of Aimo's needs."

Olofsson realized he had to bring himself to trust the young man. There were a number of things, medicine, clothes, and food items that Olofsson needed but had no way of getting them himself. The boy required Olofsson's around-the-clock care. The old man studied Pontilius carefully and concluded the schoolteacher appeared trustworthy. But Olofsson wanted to establish certain conditions before he would allow Pontilius inside his cabin.

"I'm not going to let you take him away. You understand that, right?" Pontilius nodded his head that he accepted the old man's conditions. "OK!" Olofsson said. "Come in, but be quiet. He's sleeping."

Olofsson led Pontilius into the cabin and walked him to the bed where Aimo lay. The boy slept peacefully, and Pontilius nodded in recognition. Olofsson gestured the teacher to the table. "Have a seat. I just made a fresh pot of tea."

Pontilius sat and released the prosthesis with its customary loud snap. Aimo's eyes flashed open at the metallic sound. The boy lay absolutely still, keeping his back to the men and listened to their low voices in the background.

Olofsson explained Aimo's condition the night he arrived, describing the welts on his back where Blixdal had struck him.

"He was delirious with fever, but he kept repeating something about the reverend. If that son of a bitch tries to lay a hand on him again, I'll personally rip it off." Olofsson's face reddened with emotion.

"He's gone through a great deal more than that," Pontilius added. He told Olofsson the details of the Russian invasion at the boy's home at Lake Jarvii as well as the difficult train trip to Sweden and the boy's care of his sister.

"I know all about that," Olofsson added and recounted how Aimo and Anna had hidden in his truck. "Now I feel guilty for bringing the poor kid back to the church. I'm telling you . . . he's not going back! Not if I have anything to say about it."

Pontilius drained his cup of tea and offered his hand to Olofsson.

"Herr Olofsson—"

"Call me, Magnus," Olofsson interrupted.

"Magnus, I need to tell Sten Vahleen. The boy's sister is staying with them, and she thinks her brother has died. They should know. I promise to keep it secret only among us. Is it a contract?"

Olofsson took Pontilius's hand. "A contract!"

"You know," Olofsson continued, "I was at the Vahleen's at Christmas. I met a beautiful young woman there, Solveig Olin. They told me she's your fiancée. Where the hell were you?"

"It's a long story, Magnus. I've been lost in my own world of self-pity. I just learned she's leaving for America and doesn't want to see me anymore."

"Too bad! She's a beauty. I don't mean just pretty but beautiful inside, you know?"

"I know! I know!" Pontilius shook his head despondently.

"Hey, don't feel bad," Olofsson said. "You still have time. My fiancée left me while we were in Göteborg . . . making plans for our honeymoon. How about that? She sailed away with some Portuguese guy. Know what I did? Nuthin! . . . and I never got over it. I let it kill me. Never let anybody get close to me again." Olofsson nodded in the direction of Aimo. "Then I see a boy like this and I wonder how it would have been to have kids of my own . . . and grandkids. When I saw your fiancée, young and beautiful . . . and me, an old man . . . boy! I knew. I let life pass me by."

"I wish I had hope, Magnus. She said it's too late," Pontilius said sadly.

"Women! They're strange and special at the same time. When you get 'em just right though there's nuthin' softer in the whole world. I mean you just go crazy over 'em."

Olofsson was enjoying the company of an adult guest at his cabin for the first time in months. It felt wonderful to tell someone about how he felt and why he felt the way he did. He got up from his chair and allowed his arm to sweep across the room in a broad gesture. "See this room? I like it just the way it is. But if a woman came here, she'd want to clean it even though I just did. Know what I mean?"

"I know what you mean," Pontilius nodded.

"Then they'd want to put curtains over the windows even though I prefer to look outside 'em just the way they are, know what I mean?" he repeated.

"I know! I know!" Pontilius replied.

"And then . . . know what?" Olofsson stared at the teacher curiously.

"What?" Pontilius asked.

"I'd get to like the damn curtains too. In fact, I'd miss 'em if they weren't there. See what I mean? Women are strange."

"Somebody said you can't live with them, and you can't live without them." Pontilius was finally able to interject a full sentence.

"You know what else they do? Talk! A woman *has* to talk. I think it's the way they breathe. If they stop talkin', they die."

Pontilius laughed loudly. "I'd better get going before it gets too dark. I'm glad we met, Magnus. I promise to tell only the Vahleens . . . *and* . . . the boy stays here with you." Pontilius pushed himself from the table and reattached his prosthesis.

"Thanks, Fredrik. I gave the boy my word I'd take him back to Finland in the spring. I'm going to keep my promise."

Pontilius shook Olofsson's hand and left the cabin. The time was not yet 2:00 p.m., but darkness was rapidly closing in. Olofsson waved farewell as Pontilius skied away.

The news to Aimo was both reassuring and welcome. Olofsson and Pontilius were two adults he could trust, and both were unaware that Aimo had overheard their entire conversation.

Chapter Thirty-nine

Vahleen maneuvered his motorcycle cautiously on the snow-cleared single-lane passage leading to the Nilstad Orphanage. Deep lines of concern furrowed the constable's brow, and he gripped the handlebars tightly with both hands. He felt afraid and was no longer thinking of the cold air whistling around him.

He felt uneasy about his decision to visit the orphanage alone, and the thought genuinely disturbed him. He shifted his concentration momentarily to glance at his police cap on the sidecar seat next to him. The golden three-crown emblem reflected its image of authority onto the mirror-polished bill. It bolstered his resolve but did nothing to stifle his gnawing fear.

He could simply turn around and return later with an assistant, certainly better than going to the unsettling place alone, but Sten knew that time was of the essence. He feared for Aimo's safety, particularly if the reverend had secreted the boy there in the first place. This was both the constable's territorial jurisdiction and his sworn duty to protect everyone's interest within it. Most disturbing was this might become the first possible felony of his career.

In fourteen years of service as county constable, Vahleen was called upon to provide a law-and-order presence to a Swedish society that embraced law as common civil sense and who practiced order to a fault. He had visited a variety of accidents, numerous fires, and three suicides. He had also delivered two babies during his tenure. He never had a robbery, break-in, or anything resembling a felony. The job of the Jamtland county constable was benign, and Vahleen preferred it that way. He liked the routine and disliked complications.

To keep from being bored when making his rounds, the constable volunteered his knowledge of updated tax law to those requesting help with tax return preparation. Additionally, his hobby of stock investments kept him up to date with this ever-changing subject. As a result, visits by the constable were usually a welcome event.

Vahleen drove on ignoring the cold wind that swept over him. The business with Aimo presented many complications. Uppermost was the personal responsibility Vahleen felt as a Swede who had given his word to the Finnish people to care for their children. He thought aloud, rehearsing how to begin the conversation with the orphanage director.

"Fröken Elsa . . . what the hell *is* her last name?" Vahleen asked himself aloud. "Kulander!" he remembered, shouting aloud. He began his speech anew, throwing his voice to the wind: "Fröken Elsa Kulander, I'm Constable Sten Vahleen. I'm looking for a runaway Finnish boy named Aimo."

Vahleen shook his head in disapproval. *No need to tell her who I am,* he thought. *She knows who I am. And no need to tell her immediately why I've come, so what do I say? Hi! I was in the neighborhood . . . Merry Christmas?* "Won't do! Won't do!" he admonished aloud.

But something about Fröken Elsa had always disturbed him. Now, the thought of being alone with the woman brought on a fear he had not felt before. Vahleen felt his skin prickle with goosebumps, and he became silent, the muscles of his concerned face tightening.

The motorcycle reached a section of road where the wind swept the snow clear, providing an unobstructed view of the southern horizon. The sky glowed in kaleidoscopic reddish colors, creating both a beautiful sunset and ample light. In spite of the snow-altered landscape, Vahleen knew exactly where he was; and five minutes later, he brought the motorcycle to a stop behind a high snowdrift.

Vahleen removed his goggles, then replaced the leather helmet with his official police cap. He opened the storage compartment of the sidecar and retrieved a six-battery dry-cell flashlight from a leather satchel.

A new thought struck him, and he reached for the satchel again and located his five-shot service revolver in a buttoned pouch. He examined the weapon cautiously, making certain the pistol was loaded. This would be his first investigation involving the use of a firearm, and the cold metal in his hand, as clear a harbinger of death as anything he could think of, made him uneasy. He gave a thought to return it to the hiding place, but the thought of confronting Elsa Kulander alone in *that* haunted-looking house, reentered his mind with a disturbing warning. He stuck the revolver in his pocket and scrambled over the snowbank toward the Nilstad orphanage.

The large Victorian home was bathed in long purple shadows, heralding the approaching night while the aurora borealis danced its enigmatic patterns of light overhead. A warm pink-hued glow illuminated a peculiarly shaped octagonal window at the top of the building.

Vahleen fixed his gaze on it. He looked for movement, saw none, then glanced at his wristwatch. It read several minutes before three. There were no other lights in a house he knew was filled with at least nine children. *Something's not right*, Vahleen thought. It was too early for the children to be in bed. Stealthily, he moved toward the darkened building and reached an area directly in front of the verandah. There he noticed the snow on the steps had been flattened. A drag trail next to the house led to the back yard. Curious, Vahleen decided to check on it.

The area of the orphanage property between the house and main road was well cared for in summer by the orphaned children. They labored long hours to maintain the neatly cut lawn and zones of cultivated flowers. However, the wilderness encroached on nearly everything else.

Vahleen moved cautiously against the building, searching for footprints, but found none. Whatever had flattened the snow was clearly done by *something* creating a drag trail. Vahleen heard sounds coming from the octagonal room above him. A popular American tune was being sung by the Andrews Sisters, suggesting Fröken Elsa was inside, listening to the radio over the BBC.

But the drag trail intrigued him, and he followed it to the back of the house and to an outhouse shack some twenty-five meters away. Vahleen again looked at the trail near his feet. The windswept snow was much lower here, enabling him to see a set of human footprints. They had been made after the blizzard and led back toward the verandah.

A half-moon ventilation opening identified the shack as an outhouse. Vahleen knew from prior visits that the orphanage had indoor plumbing. If something had gone wrong with it, there would have been dozens of freshly made tracks. Instead, there was only a drag trail leading to the structure and a single track coming back. Someone had taken something to the outhouse, unburdened themselves of whatever it was, then returned to the main building.

The man's breathing came faster as he moved quickly to the small wooden structure. A two-meter-long length of iron bar, used by farmers to pry rocks when tilling their land, lay at an angle against the door to keep it closed. Vahleen pulled it away, and the door swung open.

The undulating glow of the aurora borealis reflecting off the snow illuminated the interior and revealed a large light-colored shape standing upright in a corner. Vahleen switched on his flashlight and played the beam over a rolled up handmade rya rug. Unable to control his curiosity, he stepped into the outhouse and closed the door behind him.

Sten was now driven by his police instincts that demanded he discover whatever lay wrapped inside the stiffly frozen rug. He lifted the edges to his chest and yanked mightily. The small emaciated frozen body of Pehr dropped onto the wooden floor with a loud thud.

Vahleen leaped backward through the door and tumbled out onto the snow. Fearing he might have been discovered, he turned to face the orphanage and held his breath, listening intently as clouds of hyperventilated breath billowed in front of him. The happy voices of the Andrews Sisters resonated unnaturally from the pink-hued windows and onto the macabre scene of the dead child lying in the shack. Vahleen jumped to his feet and returned to the outhouse. Once again, he pulled the door closed behind him, certain he had found the body of Aimo.

The constable played the flashlight beam over the nude body on the floor.

He was of Aimo's age, the same height and coloring, but his body was emaciated. Welts and bruises were clearly evident over much of the child. The body was frozen solid, and Vahleen guessed the boy had died a week earlier. That timing would coincide with the end of the blizzard and the footprints he had seen near the house.

The case became clear to the constable. The reverend had somehow managed to secret the boy to the orphanage and had either killed him or left him outside to freeze to death. Whatever the case, for the first time in his career, Vahleen had a felony murder on his hands.

Vahleen backed out of the shack, his eyes fixed on the frosted body in the small dark outhouse, glowing weirdly from the flashing northern lights in the night sky. He closed the door and absently reached for the iron bar he had placed against the wall. It was missing. Sensing imminent danger, the constable spun around to a nightmarish sight.

Fröken Elsa stood directly behind him. She was holding the spearlike iron bar rigidly above her right shoulder with both hands. Her facial epxression was blank, devoid of any human expression. It was a sight Vahleen had never seen. Her countenance was a frozen mask with only the eyes revealing a suggestion of life. There was no question however of her intent. Her watery eyes projected unbridled hatred.

In a blur of motion, she thrust the bar at Vahleen's head with full force. At that same instant, the constable switched on his flashlight. Blinded by the light, Elsa's strike was thrown off course and missed the man's skull by millimeters. The weapon splintered into the door of the outhouse. Reactively, Vahleen struck out with his flashlight, shattering it across the side of her head. The woman dropped unconscious into a crumpled heap on the snow without a sound.

Sten struggled to gain his composure, trembling from his close call with a violent death. He managed to secure the unconscious woman's hands behind her back with his handcuffs and dragged her by the jacket collar to the house. He hauled the large woman through the front door and leaned her inert body against a wall. Finally, he allowed himself to take a deep breath; and immediately, the acrid odor of human waste assaulted his olfactory senses. The entire building permeated with it, and he gagged for breath. Above him, Glen Miller's popular tune, "In the Mood," played from a radio somewhere on the uppermost floor.

Worried that he might find Blixdal up there waiting for him, Vahleen drew his revolver and moved cautiously up the stairs, leaving the unconscious woman behind. At the second-floor landing, he switched on a floor lamp and exhaled in relief as the warm comforting light erased the dark gloom. However, a new sound, one of whimpering from within two rooms on the landing, drew him to one of the doors. He opened it cautiously.

The foul odor of human waste was overwhelming. Vahleen covered his mouth to keep from throwing up and gazed in disbelief at the horrific sight. Frightened eyes stared at him from within the cots. He moved across the hall to the second room, which presented a similar scene. Vahleen switched on a room light and gasped. Fully illuminated, the constable saw the inhuman squalor of the Nilstad orphanage.

Bed-wetting had become a chronic problem for several of the children and, as punishment, Fröken Elsa made the children sleep on urine-soaked mattresses. Because the bed-wetting did not end, Fröken Elsa forbade the use of toilets altogether and forced the children to use metal buckets placed in the corners of each room. Dissatisfied with those results, she added to the punishment. Since they seemed to enjoy living as animals, they would be treated that way. Clothes were not allowed to be washed or hung in closets. Instead, they were stuffed beneath their cots, adding to the overwhelming stench within the children's rooms.

Spasmodic coughing from phlegm-congested chests greeted the constable, and he feared he may have arrived too late to save the children.

"Listen to me," Vahleen announced loudly. "I'm a police constable. I'm going to take you away from this place."

"Go away," a boy hissed in a forced whisper. "Fröken Elsa will punish us."

Vahleen walked to the boy's cot angrily. He was freeing these children from their tormentor, yet they remained cowering under their blankets.

He looked down at the boy's face. Dark rings encircled terror-stricken eyes, shrunken within the gaunt grey skin of his face. Twin streams of mucous trailed from an abnormally shaped nose and collected on the unruly black hair matted against his face. The countenance that stared back at the constable was not that of a child but of an ageless, dispirited being crushingly subdued. Vahleen pointed to his police cap.

"Do you recognize this?" Vahleen asked and the boy nodded that he did.

"And this?" Vahleen held out his revolver. The boy nodded again.

"Do you believe I'm a police officer?"

"Yes," the boy replied timidly.

Vahleen lowered his voice. "When I tell you I'm going to help you, I need you to trust me. You need not fear Fröken Elsa ever again, all right? Tell me your name."

"Jounnii," the boy said haltingly as though he had forgotten. "But everybody calls me Mooseface."

"OK, Mooseface. You're now my deputy. Is there anyone else beside Fröken Elsa in this house?"

"Sometime Reverend Blixdal comes over," Mooseface answered.

"Is he here now?"

"No," the boy replied

"All right then, let's get moving. Get all the children to dress in their warmest clothes and to cover themselves with their blankets. You're all going to leave this place."

Dutifully, Mooseface crawled from bed and followed his instructions with a newfound enthusiasm. For the first time in months, the boy heard an adult tell him he was useful and necessary.

Vahleen left the room and climbed the stairs to Fröken Elsa's chambers and discovered in awe the contrast with the rooms below. Compared to the filth and squalor of the floor below, Elsa's private living area was an exaggerated, otherworldly chamber resembling a French brothel.

Frilly pink lampshades cast a sensuous glow over the walls. The room itself was dominated by a ceiling-high canopy bed. Smoldering incense countered the foul odors of the house with a heavy musky scent. Negligees of black, pink, and red hung from a freestanding clothes rack on scented cloth hangers. Scented candles of varying shapes and sizes stood in an array of candleholders throughout the room.

The brassy sounds of Tommy Dorsey's Orchestra blared from a radio, filling the room with incongruous gaiety. Angrily, Vahleen turned off the music and discovered a photograph atop the radio within a floral designed pewter frame. A photo of Reverend Blixdal, bearing the inscription, "To my darling Elsa, with love, Bjorn," did not surprise him.

"Pretty stupid, Bjorn," Vahleen said to himself, stuffing the photo into his pocket. He picked up the desk telephone.

Gretha Vahleen pressed the telephone tightly to her ear, muffling the moans of wounded soldiers within the acute center of Nilstad Hospital. Solveig stood next to her, trying to make sense of the guttural responses Gretha made into the receiver. Gretha hastily scribbled onto a pad then lifted her eyes, her face masked with disbelief. She stared hard at Solveig, clearly conveying that something serious had happened. She spoke into the phone.

"We'll be there as soon as possible. Take care of yourself," she added, then hung up the phone. Suddenly Gretha began stuffing medical supplies into her nurses kit then exploded. In a string of excited sentences that all ran together.

"We've got to get to the orphanage. Fröken Elsa may have killed one of the children. He thinks it might be the Finnish boy who ran away. She even tried to kill Sten! We need help. We have to get an ambulance. And a doctor. Sten said more of the children could die."

The women left the acute center, hitting the hallway at a dead run and calling loudly for help.

Sten herded the children together on the second-floor landing. He tersely issued instructions while Mooseface scurried about, making certain the constable's orders were carried out. The children were now dressed in their warmest clothes and had draped woolen blankets around their shoulders for added warmth as instructed.

"Mooseface! Go upstairs to Fröken Elsa's room and tell me when you see lights at the road," Vahleen ordered. The boy did not move. "Mooseface! Did you hear me? Go upstairs," the constable ordered with urgency.

The boy stood fast. Tears streaming down his face, and he shook his head. Vahleen understood.

"Did Fröken Elsa take you to her room?" the constable asked.

"Yes," the boy answered.

"All right. Stay here and watch the others. I'll be right down."

Mooseface nodded and watched as the constable raced up the stairs, two at a time, before disappearing into the third-floor room where Fröken Elsa kept her cat-o'-nine-tails. He shuddered from the memories of his visits and turned away to look over his pitiful orphan mates, their blankets clutched about them. Suddenly, a noise from downstairs caught his attention. The creaking sounds of a heavy body climbing the stairs from the first floor brought the boy to the railing. He looked down.

Fröken Elsa, her face streaked with blood and her hands clasped behind her back, climbed unsteadily. She neared the second-floor landing and stared directly at the boy, her gaze terrifying. Mooseface froze in place, unable to move or speak, the sight so horrific that urine splashed in his pants. When he finally screamed, the sound was more animal than human.

Vahleen bounded down the steps as Fröken Elsa reached the landing amid the children's terrified shouting.

"Hold your tongues," the woman ordered. In practiced obedience, the children's voices subsided to stifled whimpering.

Vahleen moved forward, putting himself between the children and Fröken Elsa. He was relieved to see the woman's arms remained manacled behind her back.

"That's far enough," Vahleen ordered.

"Why are you doing this?" Elsa asked with her best effort to sound injured.

"Why did you kill the boy?" Vahleen demanded.

"He died from pneumonia," Elsa declared, her eyes expressing sadness at the thought. "What was I to do? We've been snowbound. Who could come to help me? I couldn't leave him in here, could I? Think of what it would do to the other children." She took a step closer.

Vahleen studied the woman's face. The gash from the flashlight blow to her forehead continued into her hairline and blood had splashed freely over her coat.

"Why did you try to kill me?" Vahleen asked.

"I saw someone at the shack. I didn't know who it was and went to investigate. The door was closed when I arrived. I heard someone inside and thought it might be an animal. I took the bar to protect myself. When you came out, I was startled. I didn't recognize you. I thought you meant us all harm."

She had worked her way closer to the constable.

Vahleen was beginning to think he had made a major mistake and sheepishly buried the pistol in his coat pocket. He knew the Swedish justice system. No matter how she may have mistreated the children, the rules would not tolerate police brutality. It was his word against that of a woman living in an isolated, snowbound orphanage. The constable could see his career unraveling. The thought was so overwhelming he did not see the woman's right foot kick out swiftly into his crotch.

The constable doubled over in pain, unable to cry out as sharp flashes of light erupted in his head. Fröken Elsa's second kick caught the side of Vahleen's head. He pitched over the railing and frantically clutched for the banister. He heard the shouts of both the children and Fröken Elsa as he tumbled down the stairs, rolled to the floor below, and came to a jolting stop against the wall.

He tried to focus on the blurred form of Fröken Elsa rushing down the steps toward him. Her voice raged unintelligibly. The constable tried to move, but the kick to the groin had immobilized his legs. Gasping for breath, he tried to lift his arm and felt the hard metal of the revolver in his coat pocket pinned beneath his body. Elsa was nearly upon him.

Vahleen twisted violently to his side in a move that allowed his right hand to fasten around the grip of his revolver. He tugged at the weapon but was unable to free it from his pocket. Elsa reached the bottom step. Desperately, Sten pulled the trigger. The bullet tore through his coat, splintering into the banister next to Elsa's legs, stopping her in her tracks. She stared malevolently at the man, frozen in place, contemplating her next move. She was totally unaware of the heavy galvanized pail that Mooseface had just dropped from the second floor.

His aim was perfect. The pail struck the orphanage director directly on her head, and she dropped in a moaning, slop-covered heap in front of the constable. Mooseface peered down from the balcony, grinning through his green/yellow teeth broadly, triumphant at his handiwork.

The door to the house flew open as Gretha, Solveig, and several hospital staff members stumbled inside. The sound of the gunshot brought the group into the house with such urgency they nearly fell onto the prone form of Fröken Elsa, awash with the foul contents of the pail.

Gretha ignored the mess and rushed to her stricken husband in panic, her voice shrill, "Sten! Are you all right?"

"I think so," Vahleen answered shakily. "I think I dislocated my shoulder."

"We heard shots," Solveig announced.

"No one got shot. It's a long story. I'll explain later. Let's get these children out of here." Sten struggled to his feet. "I'll take care of her," Vahleen nodded toward Froken Elsa's inert body lying on the soiled floor.

Gretha and Solveig began the task of quieting the traumatized children before leading them into the rear of the waiting ambulance. Dr. Nathan Gotfrid rushed inside but stopped in his tracks at the chaotic sight. He saw the constable and approached grimly.

He and Sten were the same age, had grown up in the same community, and both had courted Gretha. She chose Sten when Gotfrid left to study medicine at Lund University in southern Sweden. When Dr. Gotfrid returned to Nilstad, he arrived with a wife of his own and the one-time rivals remained good friends. The doctor put his hand on the constable's left shoulder, which drooped forward at a peculiar angle.

"You're right, Sten. The shoulder's dislocated," Gotfrid told him. His practiced fingers found the bump caused when the bone separated from its socket. Gotfrid placed his right arm across Vahleen's back and, with his left palm beneath the errant bone, shoved it firmly back in place.

Vahleen howled in pain, glowering at the doctor through watering eyes. "Djaklar!" he swore. "You're a bad loser, Nathan."

"Sorry, Sten. The shoulder's going to be fine. How do you feel?" Gotfrid asked.

Vahleen shook his head slowly. His groin throbbed. His elbows and knees ached. His shin was badly scraped from rolling down the stairs, and the shock of relocating his shoulder nearly caused him to faint.

Vahleen managed a weak smile. "Just remember, I've still got a gun," he quipped. Then he became serious. "There's a body of a child outside. I think it's a Finnish refugee boy who was living with the Blixdal's. I'm nearly certain the reverend brought him here. I'll need you to help me find out how he died."

Vahleen cast a glance at the inert form of Fröken Elsa who had begun to stir. "Right now, both the reverend and . . . that . . . *woman* . . . are under arrest for suspicion of murder."

The constable led Gotfrid to the outhouse where the doctor rewrapped the frozen body of Pehr within the rya rug and carried it back to the ambulance. "We have a dilemma, Sten. We can't put the body back there with the children."

"You're right," Vahleen answered. "I'm not going to put Fröken Elsa back there with them either. I can promise you, you don't want to be alone with that woman."

When the ambulance finally drove off to the hospital, Gretha and Solveig huddled together in the rear of the ambulance with the orphanage children. Fröken Elsa lay in a befouled stupor, manacled to the passenger door, the rug-covered body of Pehr propped against her.

Chapter Forty

Sten plopped wearily into the armchair in front of the fireplace and plunged his bare feet into the basin of hot water Gretha had prepared for him. He closed his eyes and sighed deeply, trying to forget the day's traumatic events at the orphanage.

His body ached from multiple bruises, and the slightest move brought a sharp pain to his groin. But the combination of heat from the crackling fire and hot water embracing his chilled feet soothed him into instant drowsiness. Home never felt more welcome.

Gretha emerged from the kitchen with her usual energy, seemingly unaffected by the events of the day. She carried a tray bearing a pot of tea and several open-face cheese sandwiches. She poured tea into the cups and offered one to her husband.

"Feeling better?" Gretha asked gently.

"A lot better, thanks. I was shaking so badly I thought my teeth would break," Sten answered.

"You've had quite a shock," Gretha offered while draping an arm over his shoulders. Sten swallowed a mouthful of tea and raised his eyes at his wife, a smile of contentment spreading over his face.

"You put some aquavit in this," Sten said.

"It's from my bottle Olofsson gave me at Christmas. Now is a good time when I think we both can use it," she answered.

"What's going to happen to those kids?" Sten asked.

"We'll take care of them in the hospital for the next couple of weeks. Dr. Gotfrid converted the storage room into a temporary ward. Solveig is staying with them tonight. We'll have to find truly good homes for them when they get well." Gretha sipped the tea and winced from the strong flavor of alcohol.

"How bad off are they?" Sten asked.

"They all suffer from influenza. Two of the oldest children may have pneumonia. She made them walk barefoot in the snow. Can you imagine? All have been beaten, some with a cat o' nine tails whip." Gretha's face twisted into a scowl. "What's going to happen to her?" The anger in her voice demanded some sort of drastic punishment be meted out to the orphanage director for her crimes.

"I need to get a report on the boy's death from Dr. Gotfrid before I can file or suggest anything. He's going to determine the exact cause of his death. Elsa probably is psychotic. How tragically unfortunate no one knew that about her. I wouldn't be surprised if she's committed to a mental institution," Sten replied. "What's her physical condition?"

"A concussion and two lacerations on her head, one from your flashlight and one large gash from being hit with the pail."

Sten shuddered as he recalled the terrible helplessness he experienced as he lay at the foot of the steps. Elsa was intent on stomping him to death.

"Did you manacle her to the bed?" Sten asked anxiously.

"By the feet," Gretha smiled, "and in a straightjacket."

"When Dr. Gotfrit releases her, I'm going to formally charge her with child abuse as well as suspicion of murder. I'm also going to recommend incarceration throughout her trial."

"Don't forget attacking an officer of the law," Gretha injected, withdrawing her arm from Sten's shoulders.

"Take a look at this," Sten retrieved the floral-embossed photo stashed in his leather satchel. "I found it in Elsa's bedroom."

Gretha read the inscription aloud, "To my darling, Elsa . . . with love . . . Bjorn?"

"Blixdal's an idiot. His clerical career is finished," Sten said flatly. "He has much to answer for, including secreting Aimo into the orphanage, then lying to me about the boy running away from the church. He's also a strong suspect in having a hand in the boy's death. I'm probably going to officially charge him with murder."

"How do we tell Anna about her brother?" Gretha asked.

"Let's not say anything to anyone until we learn what Dr. Gotfrid has to say."

Gretha returned the picture frame. "What will you do about the reverend?"

"Bishop Levander needs to be informed. He's groomed Blixdal to succeed him. He's certain to be tarnished by this scandal as well. I feel sorry for Levander."

"How about Karen Blixdal? *That's* who I feel sorry for. What's going to happen to her? She's as victimized as those poor orphan kids." Gretha raised herself from the armchair. The thought of Karen Blixdal's predicament coming into focus for the first time. "I've got to talk to the girls in the choir about offering some support."

A loud knock at the door stopped Gretha in midthought. She looked at Sten questioningly.

"Who can that be?" Sten asked. "It's nearly nine."

"I'll see," Gretha said, crossing the room. "If its Blixdal, I'm not letting him in. You stay put." She opened the front door cautiously.

"Fredrik!" she shouted in surprise. "What are you doing here? Come in."

Gretha led Pontilius into the living room and took notice of the man's flushed face. Whatever brought him to the Vahleen household was of considerable urgency.

"Constable Vahleen. Fru Vahleen. I'm sorry to disturb you, but I have great news." Pontilius was unable to conceal his excitement, but Gretha interrupted him.

"It's about Solveig, isn't it? I told you she still loves you, didn't I? And *please*, don't call me *Fru Vahleen*, it's Gretha."

Pontilius raised his hand to stop the excited woman from continuing and made his announcement.

"The boy . . . Aimo, is alive and well! I found him living across the lake with Magnus Olofsson."

The constable jumped from his chair, nearly spilling the basin of water in the process. "My god! It's a miracle, Fredrik. What good news! How did Aimo survive the storm? Come, join us." Sten offered Pontilius a position against the fireplace. "I have some news of my own from my visit at the orphanage. I found a dead child. I thought it was Aimo."

"I'll get you a cup for some tea," Gretha added.

She moved toward the kitchen, embarrassed by her presumptuousness about Solveig. But the news of Aimo's survival was a welcome substitute for the reconciliation with Solveig. She knew little of the feisty Finnish boy called *Aimo*, yet there was something about his indomitable spirit that made it seem the boy had always been a member of their community. Gretha turned to the men as she reached the kitchen door.

"Then who can that poor child be at the morgue? Wait! Don't say anything until I return," she said to Pontilius. "I want to hear how you found Aimo, and you'll want to hear Sten's adventures at the orphanage today."

Pontilius nodded his agreement, disengaged the prosthesis, and sat down on the floor against the warm chimney piece. "You found a dead child at the orphanage, Sten?"

"A boy of Aimo's age. I found him in an outhouse, wrapped in a rya rug. The child was frozen solid. Dr. Gotfrid confirmed the body showed visible signs he had been abused but isn't certain of the cause of death. *The outhouse*, that's where Elsa first attacked me but . . . let's wait for Gretha to return. I guarantee you the story's worth the wait."

Both men recounted their day's experiences in riveting detail, capturing Gretha's attention so completely she remained uncharacteristically quiet. Finally the grandfather clock chimed its eleventh hour from a darkened corner in the living room and ended the storytelling.

"It's already eleven," Gretha said quickly. "Tomorrow will be a busy day for all of us." Gretha's announcement served as the signal for the evening to come to an end, and Sten automatically raised himself wearily from the armchair.

"Why not stay with us tonight, Fredrik? It's late," Sten offered.

"What a good idea," Gretha agreed enthusiastically. "I'll fix the sofa for you."

"Gretha! Wait a moment," Pontilius's voice was urgent. "You said Solveig is on duty at the hospital tonight."

"Yes," Gretha recognized Pontilius was seeking her advice, and she cocked her head curiously inviting the man to continue.

"She alone is caring for the children, correct?" Pontilius continued and Gretha nodded.

"What would you say if I surprised her there . . . to volunteer my help?" Pontilius's face expressed hopefulness. A corner of Gretha's mouth twisted upward, and she placed a hand to her chin giving the idea her deepest thought.

"I don't know, Fredrik. I suppose it would be allowed . . . especially under the circumstances."

"That's not what I mean," Pontilius searched for the correct words. "What would *you* do if *you* were Solveig? Would you forgive me?" The expression on the man's face revealed his uncertainty.

Gretha searched the teacher's handsome face. The hardened lines around the corners of his mouth were gone, and the unsmiling eyes that had made up his daily countenance for nearly two years were now wide and moist.

"Solveig still loves you, Fredrik, but you have to regain her trust."

"How? If it were you . . . suppose you were in the hospital with the children, and I just showed up . . . after how I've behaved . . . irretrievable things I've said . . . what would you do?" Fredrik groped for the words that would convey his dilemma.

Gretha moved to the fireplace and stared at the glowing embers. "I'd give you chores to do there, I think. Yes, I'd welcome your help."

"I'd do them gladly," Pontilius said.

"Of course, you would," Gretha smiled, "but you asked specifically what *I* would do. I would be so overjoyed to have you back, I think I'd burst. Solveig is another matter."

"Would *she*?" he repeated.

"Yes," Gretha answered, "I think she would. But don't give her too much to think about. Don't ask her to make decisions. Don't talk about the past. You're starting anew."

"A new beginning?" he mused, thoroughly beguiled. He exhaled and swept back the locks from his brow absently, then straightened himself suddenly as a thought came to him. "I have an idea. Do you have any fresh fruit? An apple, or better still, a pear?"

"We have both," Gretha said, offering a bowl of mixed fruit. Pontilius selected a pear and placed it in his pocket.

"What are you going to do?" Gretha asked curiously.

"Just an idea, that's all," Pontilius smiled. Gretha gave the man an unexpected hug.

"Have courage. Remember what I wrote you: *Life can only be understood backward, but it must be lived forward.*"

Pontilius stepped into the winter night and fastened his skis. He took a deep breath to summon his resolve and glided onto the snow toward Nilstad Hospital.

Occasional puffs of clouds drifted over the electric-charged sky, spilling flurries of floating ice crystals earthward. Countless stars comingled with the wavering lights of the aurora borealis creating a magical winter scene. The undulating light formation bathed the snowscape in ever-changing flashes of green, red, and violet hues as Pontilius's shadowy silhouette glided urgently between patches of dark forest and dales of glowing snow.

Nilstad Hospital stood in the center of town on the shores of Lake Valdemaren. In summer, the green lawns leading to the lake attracted hundreds of grazing snow geese and their goslings. An underwater fountain system within the lake spouted small waterjets in an ever-changing pattern of spray, hurling plumes of water thirty meters into the air. The island of Gröno served as a natural backdrop to this man-made spectacle. It was beautiful at any season but spectacular in winter when the torch-bearing skiers coursed down the mountainside, creating a breathtaking scene.

Pontilius stopped to admire the view. The scene was spellbinding. He inhaled the frosty air deeply, filled with a renewed purpose, the memory of Gretha's words of optimism repeating themselves over and over again in his mind. He pushed off again with renewed purpose.

Pontilius reached the hospital and entered the building. A spasm of uncertainty swept over him as he recognized the familiar corridors he had grown to loath during his months of rehabilitation. He breathed deeply, gathered his resolve, then hobbled up the stairs leading to the second floor, moving quietly along the dimly lit hallway toward the storage room.

The door to the converted children's ward was closed, but to Pontilius, it was like some formidable barrier. He reached into his pocket and took the pear Gretha had given him. He thought to knock and announce his presence but changed his mind. Steadying himself, he slowly opened the door with trepidation.

Heated humid air, pungent with the familiar odor of isopropyl alcohol, wafted over him. Pontilius did not move but allowed his gaze to search the darkened space the size of his classroom. Against the wall to his right, he distinguished a line of cots occupied by sleeping children. The wall opposite faced the lake where four large windows provided an uninterrupted view of Gronö. The moist air had coated the windows with a feathery frost, allowing the pale glow from the skiers' torch lights to appear dimly through the frozen window panes as meandering patterns of glowing light.

Pontilius discovered Solveig, her head resting against a window casing. She appeared deep in thought, observing the lights on the mountain through a small clearing on the frost-covered pane. Unknown to him, she was still struggling with the conflicting emotions made when Pontilius had come to her home earlier. He was so sincere and had become the love of her life once again. Somehow, she had to meet with him again, she concluded, unaware that Pontilius had entered the room.

A wave of excitement coursed through Pontilius body. He again thought to make an announcement of his presence but chose to say nothing. Solveig remained totally absorbed with the mesmerizing display of the torch-bearing skiers on the slope. Pontilius limped quietly toward her.

Solveig's eyes focused on the skiers, but her mind had drifted back to memories of Fredrik when they had been among the skiers themselves. Just a few hours earlier, Fredrik had finally emerged from his self-imposed exile, and he stood within reach. He asked for a reconciliation, words she had longed to hear for months, but she reacted by speaking harshly. She felt justified rationally, but emotionally, she was miserable. Once again, she found herself alone and allowed herself to fantasize the glorious moments of their past.

In summer, she trained by running on trails that interlaced the breadth of Gronö, the woodchip-covered paths muffling the sounds made by her spiked shoes. Fredrik often ran behind her, saying he preferred the view; and she knew he did, feeling his gaze on the rhythmic movement of her hips, creating ripples of sensuous sine waves. The vision acted as an aphrodisiac on the man, and many jogging sessions were interrupted by passionate lovemaking.

Solveig heard the approaching steps before she was fully aware of them, a soft, hobbling sound that stealthily closed the distance to her. She turned to face the sound. An approaching shape neared her in the darkened room. She uttered a short cry of alarm.

Pontilius answered in a whisper. "Solveig! It's me, Fredrik. I'm sorry I startled you."

Instinctively, Solveig put her hand to the side of the man's face in relief but withdrew it quickly. "What are you doing here?" she whispered. "You frightened me half to death."

"I'm volunteering again. I just came from the Vahleens. They told me you were here alone with the orphanage children tonight. I hoped you could use some help."

Solveig fidgeted nervously in the corner of the room. Only moments before, she had been recalling passionate memories with her lover, wishing she could relive that time again. Now, quite unexpectedly, he stood within arm's reach. For a brief moment, she considered a hostile response to Fredrik's unexpected appearance. But her anger was no match against the hunger for this man that had consumed her thoughts for months. A surge of warmth flushed over her, awakening an arousal that made standing difficult. Every pore in her body opened, and beads of perspiration appeared on her face. She placed her hands against the wall to steady herself, absently offering a garbled whisper.

Fredrik stepped closer. "What did you say? I couldn't hear you." His face was nearly touching hers.

"I said yes . . . you can stay." He was so close she could feel the warmth of his breath, and his blue eyes reflected the glow from the frosted windows hypnotically.

"I have something for you," Pontilius said. He reached into his pocket and retrieved the pear. He thrust out his hand to present it to her but inadvertently rested his clutched fist against her breast.

Solveig reactively brought her chest forward, the action pressing the man's fist into the softness of her bosom. She focused on Fredrik's lips, now framed by his well-trimmed beard. He had obviously prepared himself to look his best and she leaned closer to him.

Pontilius finally became aware of what he was touching but unsure of his next move, if indeed there should be a next move. His arm remained rigid in front of him.

"When we first met," he said throatily, "I stole a pear from you. I've come to give it back." He paused momentarily, his balled fist still clutching the fruit as he absently moved it forward and back across her turgid nipple. He stared deeply into Solveig's eyes. "And to tell you again, you're the most beautiful woman I've ever seen!"

Solveig lowered her eyes to her chest, and Pontilius followed her gaze, discovering his hand totally buried in her blouse.

"I don't see a pear," she said.

Pontilius smiled guiltily, and Solveig returned his smile, slowly at first. "You can give me the pear later," she said, thrusting her hands to Pontilius's face. She pulled his mouth to hers, her lips fastening to his hungrily.

Pontilius returned the kiss and plunged both his hands into her chest. The pear tumbled to the floor with a thud as he hurriedly unbuttoned her blouse. He reached into her brassiere and felt the soft warmth of her flesh yielding itself willingly to his probing caress. Cupping her breasts with his fingers, he kissed her strongly. Solveig responded by taking Fredrik's shoulders and pulling her fingers across the muscles of his back. She extended the tip of her tongue between Fredrik's lips and kissed him with abandonment.

A deep, congested cough from one of the children interrupted the moment abruptly. Solveig took Fredrik's hands, still firmly cradling her breasts, and pushed herself away. Exhaling a loud sigh, she struggled to gain her composure. She buttoned her blouse then whispered hoarsely.

"You wanted to volunteer? Tonight we have to take care of these children."

But Pontilius's ardor was aroused, and he brought his face closer to the woman. She kissed him quickly. "Not now," she said, her voice promising a passionate reward if he behaved.

"I love you," Fredrik said breathlessly. "God! How I love you."

"I love you, too. I never stopped loving you. But right now, I'm on duty, and if you're serious about being my assistant, then you're on duty as well."

Pontilius breathed deeply and straightened himself into a military position of attention. "Fredrik Pontilius at your service, madam. What are your orders?"

"There's a sink in the far corner of the room. Wash your hands, and put on one of the white smocks that hang on a clothes tree next to the sink. Then join me."

Pontilius offered a snappy military salute and smiled broadly. He limped to the far end of the room as a second child, then a third joined in with coughing spasms.

Solveig followed Fredrik's figure as it moved deeper into the darkened room. For a brief moment, the pain of being abandoned again swept over her, nearly causing her to panic. But the taste of the man's lips still lingered on her mouth, and her breasts still tingled from his touch. Her body ached for his fingers to discover all of her again.

Pontilius followed her instructions and slipped into a white smock, then limped back to her. His broad smile describing the man's unbridled joy. She leaned against the wall as tears of joy spilled from her eyes, and she watched him approach. Once again, her entire being welcomed her life's love; and she felt lightheaded, the heavy, sorrowful weight from months of unhappiness suddenly replaced with a rapture that overwhelmed her.

Chapter Forty-one

Aimo was bored. He yawned lazily as he made his way to the fireplace, stoked the burning wood, then idly scanned the walls of the cottage. He cast a glance at Olofsson snoring loudly in his soft armchair, his right arm hanging loosely at his side, and a partially made balsa wood fishing lure on his lap. There was no adventure there. The boy's eyes scanned the cabin looking at his surroundings.

A shotgun and rifle hung from wood pegs on one wall together with several canvas backpacks. The boy looked above him. The entire ceiling was an open crossbeamed storage area bearing a number of wooden crates. Aimo's interest focused on an obscure corner where he discovered two sets of rowboat oars, a carefully folded gill net, and two extraordinary looking fishing rods. Like a bolt from the heavens, the boy had discovered Olofsson's fishing equipment and was overjoyed.

Aimo immediately climbed to the rafters and crawled along one of the log beams leading to the equipment. There lay two of the most beautifully handcrafted split-bamboo fishing rods he had ever seen, glistening from a thick coating of shellac. Translucent agate-stone eyelets were bound to the rods with ornately designed thread. Aimo seated himself on the beam, his legs dangling. He lifted one of the rods carefully, allowing his fingers to pass over the smooth finish. He gripped the rod butt by its cork handle and studied an elaborate reel he had never seen before. Several levers and buttons puzzled him.

A thin green linen line passed through a level wind, which Aimo correctly guessed had something to do with distributing the line evenly over the spool. He explored the star-shaped drag of the reel and the metal button on the opposite side but had no clue regarding their purpose. He pushed a button forward, and the line flowed silently when he pulled it from the reel. When it was pushed backward, the reel emitted a clicking sound.

Aimo's interest was piqued. He threaded the line through the eyelets of the rod, then dangled the line below him, exploring the functions of the drag and the button to the line lock. He fantasized being hooked up to a big pike to test the wonderful rod but, lacking a fish, looked for a suitable substitute. Anything at all that could offer a little weight or resistance. Below him, Olofsson still snored loudly, the balsa wood lure on his lap. Aimo found his target.

He maneuvered himself across the pine beam on the seat of his pants, stopping directly over the sleeping man. He formed a loop on the end of the line then released the button, allowing the reel to operate silently. He lowered the line to Olofsson's lap then set the brake button on the reel. The boy fished the loop until it reached the narrow waist whittled into its wooden center. Aimo gently snapped the rod tip upward, the subtle action tightening the loop into a knot that closed around the lure.

Success! He had snagged the lure firmly. Totally delighted, Aimo cranked the reel, but the balsa wood lure did not come straight up as the boy had planned. Instead, it swung out into the room, then swung back directly into Olofsson's open mouth. Things happened fast.

Olofsson's jaws slammed shut, his teeth sinking into the soft wood. His dangling right hand flashed up from the floor, smacking his bearded face hard, and his fingers tore at the thing that had violated his mouth. He jumped to his feet, yanking hard on the fishing line.

"HELVETTA FON!" he shouted.

Aimo pulled back on the rod, reeling furiously. The old man's arm lifted into the air, and Olofsson jerked his arm back. The fishing reel screeched loudly above him, and the old man looked up into the rafters.

There was Aimo, peering down guiltily. A long moment of silence followed as each regarded the other in astonishment. Then Aimo laughed, the fishing lure still hanging from the corner of Olofsson's mouth. He looked so absolutely ridiculous, and the boy could not contain himself. Aimo laughed hysterically.

For the first time, the old man saw a side of the child that could express itself with joyous abandonment. Olofsson spat out the lure and joined in the laughter, then collapsed onto his chair, roaring out loud. Aimo giggled uncontrollably until he lost his perch on the crossbeam. He twisted backward but lost his grip on the fishing rod. The old man caught the rod in midair as Aimo, now free from the fishing pole, clutched desperately at the crossbeam. His body dropped off into the room below, but he held fast to the beam. The jolt loosened the folded legs of the oversized long johns, and the material flailed emptily in the air. Now it was Aimo who looked ridiculous.

Olofsson pointed a finger at the spectacle, his laughter even louder. Once again, he collapsed into his chair. Tears rolled down his face, and he gasped for breath. Finally Olofsson rose from the chair and clutched Aimo by the waist. "You can let go. I've got you," Olofsson laughed. Aimo fell into the old man's arms. "So! You're well enough to play jokes on me," Olofsson said.

"I'm sorry. I didn't mean that to happen . . . to go in your mouth"—Aimo giggled—"like a fish."

He threw his arms around the old man and laughed anew, the laughter so contagious that once again, Olofsson joined in. He hugged the boy strongly and stroked his head. Finally, the laughter died down.

Olofsson lifted the fishing pole from the floor. "These are the best fishing poles made," Olofsson said proudly. "See how sturdy it is at the base? Then up here at the tip, it's very thin, so there's a lot of spring. It's made by the best fishing manufacturer in Sweden." He offered the rod to Aimo. "It's yours."

Aimo held the rod in disbelief, and Olofsson smiled.

"I've got two of them. I only need one. We'll try 'em out as soon as the ice breaks."

Aimo handed the rod back to Olofsson.

"I can't take this, Magnus," the boy said. "You promised I would go home."

"And a promise is a promise," Olofsson said. "But there's no way you can go back to Finland until the winter ends. Then I have to contact your parents somehow so we can make the arrangements. That's not going to happen until summer at the earliest. But I'm going to do the best I can."

He placed the rod in Aimo's hands. "I'm giving you this because you're my best friend. You can take it with you when you go home."

Aimo shook the rod several times, testing its flexibility. "Thank you," he said, throwing his arms around the old man again. "This is the second best thing I ever got in my life."

"What's the first best thing?" Olofsson asked.

Aimo went to his bed and returned with the military medal he kept stashed beneath his pillow. "My mom gave me this. It's my Dad's. He wore it on his uniform." He held his hand open. "Do you know what it's for?"

"I don't know, Aimo," Olofsson said studying it closely. "I never was in the military. I never liked war, so I don't know much about these things." He gave the medal back to Aimo who returned his prize to its safekeeping place.

Olofsson shook his head in dismay. The boy looked pitiful in his ill-fitting long johns. The old man could only guess as to how much the boy had suffered before arriving in Sweden. It was a shame, Olofsson thought, but then again, there was nothing about war that was fair. At least, the boy's courage and tenacity had brought him this far. Best of all, he was alive and well. At that very moment, lives were being lost, including those of children, throughout the countries surrounding Sweden.

"What's wrong, Magnus? You look sad," Aimo said.

Olofsson's mind had drifted off. He ran his hand over his bearded face. "Nothing's wrong with me. It's the damn world that's wrong. There should never be war. Never!" he said emphatically. "Did you see war in Finland?"

"Yes!" Aimo replied.

"Do you want to tell me what happened?" Olofsson asked.

Aimo nodded his head and recalled every detail of the horror at his home, but no longer mentioned his feelings of abandonment at the Jyväskylä train station. He talked of the train ride through Finland, the terror of being attacked, and his arrival in Haparanda. The boy's voice grew angry as he expressed the injustice he felt when his head was shaved and his arm injected with needles.

Then Aimo said there was something about the *Sunpath* itself, the modern electric-driven train that had taken him to Nilstad. He admitted it was beautiful and a thrill to ride. But it also had given him a feeling that the Finnish children were entering a different world where they didn't belong. Returning home was something he had to do, Aimo explained, not only for him but also for his sister.

"She's with the Vahleens, isn't she?" Olofsson asked, already knowing the answer. Aimo nodded yes.

"As I remember, she likes it there," Olofsson added.

"I guess," Aimo said thoughtfully. "She told me she wants to stay, but I know my mom and dad want her back."

"Well, the Vahleens are good people, Aimo. They're taking very good care of her. All Finnish children are supposed to go back to their families when the war is over anyway," Olofsson added.

"We should have all stayed home," Aimo said, his voice rising. "Nobody asked us if we wanted to go."

"Your parents did a brave thing, Aimo. Sending you to another country is a very brave thing if you think about it. The war must have been terrible for your parents to do that." The old man's eyes expressed his feelings.

"It was," Aimo admitted.

Olofsson changed the subject. "I'm gonna get you some better clothes. There's some stuff in some of those boxes up in the rafters. Feel like going up there again?"

Olofsson purposely halted the talk of war somewhat satisfied that the boy finally could tell him how he felt. There was a lot more Aimo had hidden deep inside of him. There would be more to come if the boy were given time.

Chapter Forty-two

Pontilius set the pace as he and Constable Vahleen skied across the frozen lake toward Olofsson's cabin. The temperature beneath the lowering cloud-covered sky was only a few degrees below freezing, causing the constable to perspire freely. He called out to Pontilius, energetically skiing in front of him.

"Slow down, Fredrik. I'm going to melt at this pace."

"Sorry, Sten," Pontilius answered. "I didn't realize I was going too fast. I was deep in thought." Pontilius slowed the pace.

"About what?" Sten asked.

"Solveig. I stayed with her last night at the hospital."

"That's great," Sten shouted.

"Not really. We worked all night, and I fell asleep in a chair. Gretha woke me in the morning and told me Solveig had gone home." Pontilius unconsciously increased the pace again.

"Poor woman must have been exhausted."

"I wish she would have told me she was going off duty. She might have left a note," Pontilius complained. "I was going to see her at her house, but Gretha told me you needed to see Aimo."

"How did everything go between you two?" Sten asked. The pace had once again reached a competitive speed. He was dropping farther behind.

"I love her, Sten. I told her so. She said she still loves me."

Pontilius skied strongly, increasing the distance between them with each stride. "That's first class," Sten called out with difficulty.

"But we never had time to talk . . . or do anything. I don't know what she's thinking."

"Probably about a lot of things, Fredrik, same as you. Don't push her though. You'll scare her away."

"That's what your wife advised," Pontilius recalled.

"I know. Gretha told me." Sten panted. Vahleen came to a stop, cupped his hands to his mouth, and shouted, "Listen! Will you please slow down a bit?"

Pontilius came to a halt and waited for the constable to reach him. "Sorry, Sten. I guess my mind is somewhere else.

"I can't compete with you when your energy juices are going, Fredrik. Now, if you don't mind, I'm going to set the pace." The two skiers moved forward again, and Sten continued, "To change the subject, how did Olofsson sound when you talked to him? Sometimes he can be crotchety."

"He sounded fine," Pontilius answered. "As I told you, he was uncooperative at first, but once he felt comfortable, he confided in me. He definitely wants the boy to stay with him. I told him it probably would be fine."

"A hell of a lot better than living with the reverend," Sten agreed. "I'm going to meet with Blixdal tomorrow. I thought I could squeeze in a visit tonight, but I didn't count on a cross-country race this afternoon. By the time we ski back home, I'm going to be too exhausted."

"Just as well," Pontilius added. "It's already starting to snow so we don't want to stay too long."

The men reached Olofsson's snowbound cabin, identifiable only by a bank of low hanging smoke from the chimney. The constable called out, "Hey, Magnus. It's us, Sten Vahleen and Fredrik Pontilius. May we come in?"

Olofsson opened the door warily and scanned the area beyond the two men. Seeing his visitors were indeed the constable and the teacher, he invited them in. "Damn! It's starting to snow again," Olofsson said." I hope it's not like that big one at Christmas."

He followed the men into his cabin and closed the door behind him. Vahleen's eyes searched the room in disbelief. "What the hell did you do here, Magnus?" Vahleen said. "I've never seen the place look so neat. All you need now are some curtains."

Olofsson smiled knowingly at Pontilius. "See what I mean? After you live with a woman for a while, you start to think like one." The old man invited the men to sit at the table. "What can I offer you, gentlemen?"

"Two things," Vahleen said. "A glass of water because I'm very thirsty. I also understand Aimo is here. I thought we could arrange for him to stay with you legally. I brought some papers that state you'll take proper care of him and be totally responsible for the boy. You must also promise to see to it that he gets home when the war is over."

Vahleen pulled the papers from a knapsack and placed them on the table. "You'll have to sign. Fredrik will be your witness." Once again, the constable searched the room curiously. "By the way, where is the boy, Magnus?"

"You sound worried, Constable," Olofsson joked. "He's right here. Aimo! Say hello to our guests while I get them some water."

"Hello, Herr Vahleen. Hello, Herr Pontilius."

The men looked to the ceiling. There was Aimo, lying as flat as a cat on a crossbeam, an impish grin across his face. Olofsson laughed out loud.

"Believe it or not, we were practicing fishing. Come on down, Aimo," Olofsson called. Aimo swung down from the ceiling, and Olofsson gathered the boy in his arms before placing him on the floor, then joined the constable at the table. Olofsson signed his name to the documents; Pontilius signed as a witness, and with the deed done, the constable returned the papers to his knapsack.

"Actually, we were looking through some of my old clothes up there so the boy can dress in something better than my long johns. Tell 'em what you found, Aimo."

"Mice," the boy answered excitedly. "All the boxes have mice nests. Some even have babies."

"So," Olofsson continued, "we can use some clothes for Aimo, and a cat for our mice."

Pontilius extended his hand to the boy. "Hello, Aimo. I'm glad to see you're all right." Aimo took his teacher's hand and bowed courteously. "Thank you, Herr Pontilius." Aimo extended his hand to the constable. "Hello, Herr Vahleen." The constable shook the boy's hand, and once again the boy bowed respectfully.

"I want you to know Anna is doing very well. My two daughters treat her like she's their sister. She was very worried about your safety when she learned you ran away," Vahleen explained.

"Reverend Blixdal was going to kill me," Aimo said.

"I promise you he'll never get that chance," Olofsson answered resolutely.

"I can also make you that promise," Sten added. "Herr Pontilius and I both think it's a good idea for you to stay here with Magnus Olofsson. We don't want the reverend to learn of your whereabouts just yet. Both of you have to hang around here for a while. Stay away from the church, and don't go into town."

Aimo and Olofsson nodded in approval as Pontilius retrieved several books from his knapsack. He placed them on the table.

"Here are your schoolbooks, Aimo." Pontilius shifted his gaze to Olofsson. "I'll expect you to see the boy puts these to good use."

The old man smiled weakly. "I will," Olofsson promised.

"Well! Since you're both going to be here for a while, what do you need, Magnus?" Vahleen asked.

"Clothes for the boy, that's the first thing," Olofsson answered quickly. "Boots, shoes, socks, underwear, pants, sweaters, a few shirts, gloves, ski cap."

"Didn't Fru Blixdal have a lot of clothes for you?" Vahleen asked.

"Yes," Aimo replied worriedly. "What are you gonna do?"

"I don't know just yet. I'll try to think of something. I didn't ask you, Aimo, but I take it you want to stay here with Herr Olofsson?" Sten queried.

"Yes, sir, if it's OK. He said he'll help me get home," Aimo answered.

"I promised the boy I would try to get him back to his family as soon as possible. Could you help us, Sten?" Olofsson asked.

"I can help arrange it. But there won't be a train to Finland for some time. Things are pretty bad there." Vahleen patted the boy reassuringly on the head. "Don't worry, Aimo. Everything will turn out fine. I'll ask my wife to write a letter to your parents. They'll be happy to hear you and Anna are both doing well."

Aimo could not contain his happiness. He jumped wildly into the air then crawled back up into the crossbeams.

"Thank you, Sten," Olofsson said, extending his hand.

"Can you think of anything else the boy needs?" Vahleen asked.

"We could use some milk, eggs, bread, things like that. Otherwise, we've got plenty of food. As soon as we get the boy some clothes, we'll start doing some ice fishing. Thank you both."

Olofsson offered his hand to Pontilius. "How have things progressed with your girlfriend . . . what's her name?" the old man asked.

"Solveig," Pontilius replied. "I don't know. I told her my true feelings . . ."

"Don't *tell* her," Olofsson roared. "*Show* her! That's what a woman wants. Let her know she's the most beautiful woman you've ever seen. Can't live without her. You know, all those things."

"Thanks," Pontilius said shaking Olofsson's hand. "So long, Aimo. We'll see you soon."

"So long and thank you, thank you, thank you," Aimo repeated.

Pontilius and Vahleen stepped out of the cabin and into their skis as dry snowflakes fluttered quietly around them.

"Is it all right if you ski home alone, Sten?" Pontilius asked.

"Of course," Vahleen replied. "I may even take my time. Where are you going?"

"Back home. I'm really tired. Didn't get much sleep last night. I've got to think about what I can do about Solveig."

"She'll make her own decision, Fredrik. You've done what you can, now let her make the next move."

"I'll talk to you tomorrow, Sten. Say hello to Gretha."

Pontilius skied in the direction of his school, disappearing in the gray mass of falling snow. His route took him across the lake to the hill leading to the schoolhouse. Climbing the hill in the deep snow was exhausting, and when he reached the summit, he was bathed in perspiration. He lathered his head with snow to cool down and rested against a tree, totally fatigued. The combination of physical exertion, lack of sleep, and emotional stress was suddenly catching up with him.

He continued in the direction of the school, his synchronized stride allowing him to glide easily through the curtain of softly falling snow. Reaching the open area in front of the school, Pontilius was startled to find a light glowing from his apartment. The hair on his arms rose in fright. Someone had broken into his home and possibly was still inside. It had to be Blixdal, Pontilius concluded. The clergyman had been searching for Aimo, and Pontilius wondered if Blixdal had somehow learned the boy was with Olofsson. The clergyman might be lying in wait inside Pontilius's home.

Pontilius removed his skis and stealthily approached his apartment window. He tried to peer through the glass, but the frost-covered pane distorted his view. Fresh footprints tracked directly to the schoolhouse entrance, but the falling snow obliterated most of the impressions. There no longer was any doubt that someone waited in ambush inside. He had to arm himself.

Pontilius opened the door as quietly as possible then eased it shut. He hobbled silently to the desk and grabbed his gnarled walking cane. He felt reassured by the stout weapon. The sound of Jussi Bjorling's tenor voice softly crooned a melodic recitative from Wagner's *Tristan and Isolde*. It came from his radio in his apartment.

Pontilius was thoroughly baffled. Why would someone break into his apartment, then alert him to their presence by playing the radio? He resumed his stealthy approach to the door of his apartment. Pontilius opened the door sufficiently to peer inside holding, his cane at the ready.

There, in a mound beneath the covers of his bed, lay Solveig, fast asleep. A flickering candle on the night table cast a pattern of light shadows dancing across her face. Pontilius's mouth dropped open in surprise. He was frozen in his tracks as he drank in the dear sight he never again expected to experience.

Solveig lay on her side, her hands pressed together beneath her face. Her long blond hair fanned out over the white pillow. An open book lay next to her, and the radio played softly next to the bed. Pontilius could not remember seeing a sight more beautiful. A surge of energy rushed through his body, replacing his fatigue. He lay the cane against a bureau and moved quietly to the edge of the bed, unable to take his eyes from the woman. Gently, he placed his hand lovingly on her temple and allowed his fingers to comb through the hair that splayed across her face. She stirred briefly then opened her eyes. A smile of recognition spread slowly from her mouth, and she reached up to take Fredrik's hand.

"Surprise," she said sleepily.

"My god!" Pontilius stuttered. "My god . . . you're so beautiful. I love you, Solveig! Do you know how much I love you?"

"Enough to never leave me again?" she asked.

"I'll never leave you! Never . . . I was so stupid . . . never!" Pontilius stammered.

"Then you may come in," Solveig said, pulling back the covers.

Her naked body twisted provocatively on the warmed white cotton sheets. Pontilius's eyes bulged, and he collapsed onto her.

"Not yet," Solveig said, pushing him away. "Take off your things first. Hurry up, I'm getting cold." She pulled the covers up to her neck.

Pontilius undressed as quickly as possible, no longer able to think of anything except the beautiful woman he loved so desperately, lying naked next to him, wanting him as hungrily as he wanted her. He removed his trousers, but the sight of the leather straps binding his prosthesis to his thigh struck a blow to his heart. It never looked more ugly. Pontilius stood transfixed by his deformity, unable to move.

"Take it off," Solveig coaxed while gently pulling him onto the bed. "I have to get used to it, and I want to start now." She turned Fredrik's face to hers and kissed him passionately. The man returned her kiss feverishly as the prosthesis clumsily dropped to the floor.

Solveig could wait no longer, her sexuality out of control. She pulled his underwear down over his legs and drew Fredrik against her body. Then, wrapping her legs tightly around his waist, kissed him furiously. "Make love to me, Fredrik. Please make love to me," she pleaded.

Chapter Forty-three

Meggan was six years old when her parents brought home a two-burner Huskvarna electric hot plate. From that day onward, she took over the chores of making breakfast. Sten installed it on a counter in the kitchen next to the wood-burning stove, and Meggan fell in love with the contraption at first sight. She cooked everything imaginable on the small range.

Gretha willingly allowed the girl to prepare the breakfasts but only after she had precisely explained the rules she expected her daughter to follow. Meggan performed her new chore with enthusiasm. The girl had so much fun she even invented a game involving her sisters, and breakfasts for all of them were a much sought-after sport.

She placed two pots of water on the burners, brought them to a boil, then used the water to preheat the teapot and coffeepot. Then she boiled more water. She poured that into the sink for washing the morning dishes. Finally, she boiled water for coffee, porridge, and tea. Meggan's purpose for boiling so much water were twofold; in addition to warming the kitchen with clouds of heated air, the steam fogged the windows. There it froze immediately, creating fantastic patterns of ice designs on the windowpanes. The game everyone played followed the rules made up by Meggan, of course.

Each morning the girls searched for frost-figures, flowers, or animals on the windowpane. The best discovery of all were ice fairies floating among the ice clouds with their translucent wings.

With morning porridge and tea finished, the younger girls cleared the table and placed the dishes into the hot, water-filled sink. Then it was up to the bathroom to brush teeth and get Mama Gretha's help to place bows in their hair. Meanwhile, Meggan finished the dishes and set them on a wooden rack to dry. The end result of Meggan's industry was that by the time her parents came down for breakfast, the girls were ready for school. That pleased everyone, particularly her mother. Today, however, was going to be different.

The girls studied the ice patterns on the window. Two ice fairies had just been discovered, and an earnest search for more was in full swing when Gretha and Sten arrived together in the kitchen. Papa Sten wore his most formal policeman's uniform, and Meggan wondered if she had forgotten some special occasion.

"We found two fairies," Lisa shouted. Anna pointed to the windows. "Look! They're beautiful."

"Good morning, girls," Gretha said.

A chorus of "Good morning, Mama and Papa" sang out in return.

"Papa Sten has some good news. Very good news, especially for you, Anna," Gretha smiled broadly.

Papa Sten came right to the point. "Aimo has been found. He's alive and well."

Meggan leaped from her chair, throwing her hands over her head. "Hoorah!" she shouted. "I knew he would be all right. Every night, we all said a prayer for Aimo. Hoorah! Hoorah! Hoorah!" she yelled.

Lisa joined, clapping her hands wildly. Meggan clutched her arms around her father's waist in genuine joy.

Anna remained strangely quiet. Her eyes filled with tears, and Gretha took the little girl into her arms. "Don't cry, Anna. Your brother is safe," Gretha said.

"I want to see him," Anna sobbed.

"Where is he?" Meggan asked, her eyes pleading. "Is he back with that awful Herr Blixdal?"

"No!" Sten answered swiftly. "Aimo's never going back there again. I can't tell you where he is now. We just wanted you to know he's well. I saw him myself yesterday. You cannot tell anyone else about this. Is that understood?"

The girls nodded their heads and Sten turned his attention to Anna. "You'll soon get to see your brother, Anna. Aren't you happy?"

Anna's lower lip protruded. She rubbed her eyes with her fists but could not stem the flow of tears spilling down her face.

"Anna, now what's wrong?" Meggan asked, thoroughly baffled.

Gretha stroked the girl's hair. "Aren't you happy with the news?"

"I don't want to go away," Anna sobbed. "I want to stay here with you." The room became silent. Then Mama Gretha spoke, "You *never* have to go away." She turned her attention to her daughters. "What do you say, girls? Do we want Anna to stay with us?"

"Yes!" they shouted.

Using her most serious face, Lisa declared, "You're my little sister now, and you're gonna stay with me."

Gretha took her husband's hand, overtaken by a flood of relief until she noticed the time on the wall clock. Instantly, her mood changed to pragmatic decision making.

"All right, everyone. Finish your breakfast, and get ready for school. Girls, don't forget to put some cream on your faces, it's snowing. Papa has already put new wax on your skis. Meggan, make sure all of you brush your teeth." Gretha called out instructions with a rapid-fire delivery, and everyone fanned out to their duties with practiced precision.

Gretha and Sten brought their breakfast to the dining table out of earshot from the girls. Gretha leaned forward and spoke quietly so as not to be heard from the kitchen. "Be careful when you meet with Herr Blixdal today. Something's not right with the man," Gretha warned.

"I will," Sten replied. "I'm not taking any chances. I'm going to *wear* my pistol so it's visible. I don't want any more surprises. I want to learn what he knows of the dead boy. We know he was Aimo's cousin. We'll have to bring Aimo the tragic news."

"Will you tell Blixdal about Aimo?" Gretha's face reflected concern. "All of this is so unfair to Karen. She truly loves the boy."

"I'm going to speak to Blixdal alone. Maybe he'll incriminate himself. He had to know everything that went on at the orphanage."

"Oh! Sten!" Gretha mocked. "He visited the orphanage regularly. Of course, he does. For all we know, he may have had a hand in the abuse himself."

"That's possible. I'm going to try to find out. I hope to get him to *admit* what he's done. I have a plan."

Sten adjusted his woolen hat, pulled the ear flaps down, and gave Gretha a quick kiss on the mouth. He strode out to his motorcycle and took off in the direction of the rectory.

Vahleen's first task at the church was to check the surrounding area for footprints. The undisturbed waist-high snow around the residence struck Vahleen as being particularly strange. Blixdal always kept the walkways around the church free from accumulated snow even if he needed to call on volunteers to help him. Tracks from the reverend's parked sedan leading to and from the road indicated he had driven in and out several times.

Vahleen arrived at the church, the reverend's car in full view. He tried the door handle, found it unlocked, and made a chilling discovery. Lying in full view was the cudgel Aimo described as having been used on him.

Blixdal obviously kept the cudgel in his car, intending it as a weapon. The boy was right. Blixdal did intend to do harm! The constable was worried as to what other weapons Blixdal might have hidden somewhere. He left the cudgel where it lay, walked back to the church entryway, and stepped inside.

"Here we go again," Sten whispered to himself, his eyes adjusting to the darkened room. He searched among the shadows, his entire being alert. The empty room was in sharp contrast to the inviting place of worship it had been on Christmas Day. A single candle glowed vaingloriously within its red glass votive holder at the altar. The dark room seemed to be sulking silently in heavy gloom.

Vahleen made his way down the nave, his gaze flitting from among the stern-faced statues lurking within the shadows, then to nooks and crannies where darkness was impenetrable. When he finally reached the doorway to the living quarters, he was breathing excitedly. Vahleen rapped his knuckles hard against the door but never took his eyes from the frightening room.

"Pastor Blixdal, this is Constable Vahleen." He waited several seconds then pounded again at the door. "Pastor Blixdal! Fru Blixdal! Is anyone home?"

The door opened slowly, and Vahleen lowered his gaze to meet the figure of Karen, a heavy wool shawl draped over her shoulders. She opened the door sufficiently for Vahleen to step inside then closed it quickly behind him.

"Come in," Karen said softly. She led the constable to her husband's study in silence. Certainly out of character with her usual talkative nature, Sten noted. He followed closely behind, choosing to remain silent himself as their footsteps echoed across the stone floor. When they reached the study, Karen opened the door and faced the constable.

"Please have a seat, Constable," she said weakly. "I'll tell Bjorn you're here."

The image of the woman, now in full view was startling. Illuminated in the light, Karen Blixdal was unrecognizable. Gone was the flighty personality; the high-pitched, excited voice; and the pretty face with its affected smile. She had aged dramatically, her unkempt hair held in place by several unmatching combs. Her ashen grey skin accentuated the dark hollows of her eyes. When she looked at Vahleen, he saw only darkened orbs.

"Are you all right?" Sten asked with genuine concern.

"Yes," Karen replied. "Please go inside." She turned without saying another word and ascended the stairs to the second floor with measured steps.

Vahleen sought the warmth of the fireplace. A single log crackled as several small tongues of flame licked weakly about its edges. The sound of footsteps falling heavily on the stairwell announced Blixdal's approach; and moments later, the reverend entered the room, a happy expression on his face. He jauntily crossed to Vahleen, his hand extended and his demeanor in sharp contrast to that of his wife.

"Hello, Sten! Good New Year. Good New Year," he repeated.

"Good New Year," Vahleen answered, accepting the handshake.

"What news do you bring today, my friend?" Blixdal asked.

Vahleen withdrew his hand from Blixdal's grasp and studied the man's disheveled appearance. His manner was brisk, but his normally well-groomed grey hair reflected the haste with which he had combed it. His wolf eyes were bloodshot, and his breath carried the strong odor of alcohol. Vahleen noted the transparency of Blixdal's behavior and increased his guard.

"You look ill," Vahleen said.

"Do I? I feel fine . . . tired perhaps, but fine." Blixdal offered the constable a seat, but Vahleen chose to stand with his back to the meager flame.

"Karen doesn't look well." Sten observed. "In fact, neither do you."

"Life has not been the same here since the tragedy," Blixdal said. He retreated from the fireplace and sat in a chair behind his desk, the darkness shadowing his face.

"What tragedy is that?" Sten asked.

"The boy!" Blixdal answered quickly. "Karen is devastated. The boy should never have run away." He fumbled for a package of Turkish cigarettes in the desk drawer and continued his banter. "I have Bishop Levander to thank for taking up his bad habit of smoking. It must be the stress of these last days."

Blixdal put a cigarette to his lips, lit it, then drew the smoke deeply into his chest, this time without coughing. "What brings you here, Constable? Do you have news of the boy?"

"I have some questions. I noticed you've been using your car. The driveway has been cleared, but not the path to your residence."

"Why is that strange?" Blixdal asked flatly. "I have many responsibilities and no longer have help with tasks like snow shoveling."

"Someone shoveled the drive?" Sten responded.

"I did. I told you, I have responsibilities in the community." Blixdal's voice was stronger.

"Ah! Responsibilities in the community," Sten repeated. "Tell me, Reverend, does that include the orphanage?" Sten straightened his body.

Blixdal nodded his head and answered with a grunt.

"When did you last visit there?" Sten continued.

Blixdal rose from the chair in agitation. He moved to a cabinet at the far end of the room and fidgeted among the bottles of alcohol on a tray. Ignoring the constable, he poured himself a glass of Bishop Levander's Irish whiskey. Blixdal took a long swallow, keeping his back to Vahleen. He then refilled his glass and sighed audibly. "Sometime before Christmas, I believe," Blixdal answered.

"Were you alone?" Sten asked.

"What do you mean, Sten? Of course, I was alone. It was official business."

"Are you certain there was no one in the car when you went inside? Someone who was told to wait until you returned?"

The clergyman remained in the shadows, staring intently at the constable. Once again, he drained the glass of whiskey. Vahleen could feel his steely gaze from across the room.

"He's alive, isn't he?" Blixdal stated softly.

"Who's alive?" Sten asked.

"The boy, damn him! Aimo! You know who I'm talking about." Blixdal's voice rose in agitation.

"Why don't you tell me about it?" Sten asked calmly.

"Where is the boy now, Vahleen?" Blixdal's tone turned menacing.

"Constable Vahleen, Pastor Blixdal," Sten reminded him. "And today, I'm on official business. Perhaps you should sit down."

Blixdal returned to his seat behind the desk and lifted his cigarette from the ashtray, regarded it dumbly, then ground the butt into the ashtray. "Bring the boy here and have him tell his story in front of God. Then you'll know the truth."

"I didn't say Aimo was alive, did I?" Sten continued.

"How did you know he was in the car when I was at the orphanage?" Blixdal's self-incriminating answer was exactly the information Vahleen sought. Now he had Bjorn Blixdal exactly where he wanted him.

"Perhaps Elsa Kulander provided me with that information. You know her quite well, don't you?" Sten queried.

"What did she tell you? She's a spinster. She lives a lonely life filled with fantasies. What has that to do with me?"

"'*To my darling Elsa, with love, Bjorn.*' I think that's how I recall your photograph's inscription," Sten said.

"Get out!" Blixdal erupted. He jumped to his feet. "Get out of here *now*." He crossed to the door of his study, turned swiftly, and faced the constable. Vahleen stood unmoving and ramrod straight at the fireplace.

Blixdal knew he was trapped. "I'm sorry, Sten"—Blixdal's voice became conciliatory—"I didn't mean to lose my temper." He crossed the room, stood in front of Vahleen, and lowered his voice to a whisper. "I beg you, please! Don't let Karen know about this. I ask you as a friend."

Vahleen was not yet finished with the man. "Do you know about Elsa's abuse of those orphans?" The constable kept his position, consciously measuring the distance between himself and the clergyman. He was not going to allow any more sneak kicks or punches either. He hooked his thumbs into his belt, his right hand in front of the holstered pistol.

"I knew she hated them, especially the Finnish."

"Enough to kill one of them?" Sten asked.

"The boy died of pneumonia. I know that as God is my witness," Blixdal answered.

"He died *after* Christmas, Bjorn. You said you were last there *before* Christmas."

"I wanted to keep our relationship a secret," Blixdal admitted.

"And that's why you lied?" Sten asked quickly.

"Yes!" Blixdal answered.

"And you've lied before, haven't you, Bjorn? You beat the boy with a club. I found it in your car. You *chased* him out into the storm. You lied to me about that, and when the boy testifies against you, we'll show you contributed to the abuse of those children just as much as Elsa did."

Blixdal stood thunderstruck. He stared at the floor as Vahleen lowered his voice to a whisper. "The only reason I'm not placing you under arrest now is my concern for your wife. She's a decent person who deserves much more from life than what you've given her."

"Please! Don't tell the bishop," Blixdal pleaded.

"I'll let Aimo tell his story to the bishop. The boy *is* alive, and he'll testify against both you *and* Fröken Elsa Kulander."

Vahleen yanked open the study door. He marched smartly through the hallway and back into the church, reflecting on the tragedy the reverend had brought on himself. He deserved the shame and punishment certain to befall him, but the clergyman's wife was another matter entirely. Vahleen forced it from his mind as he reached the frosty air. He retrieved the wooden ladle that lay in Blixdal's car and placed it as evidence in the sidecar of his motorcycle, then drove back to his office.

Neither he nor the reverend were aware that Karen Blixdal had kept her ear to the study door, completely overhearing the conversation between the two men.

Chapter Forty-four

Blixdal paced the floor of his study, steadily draining the bottle of Irish whiskey. His life was ruined. A few months ago, he had wealth and was assured the post of bishop. Now his future was hopeless, destroyed by his own foolishness. He cursed Aimo, faulting him for being the source of all his problems, then cursed his wife for insisting they take the Finnish boy into their home. Finally, he cursed himself for agreeing to the exodus of Finnish children into Sweden in the first place. His father had told him years ago the Finns were a heathen race. The Russians had finally been on their way to eradicating them, and Sweden had no business interfering.

The greatest fault of all was the reverend had allowed others to decide for him. That is what had brought disaster to his life. He dropped drunkenly into his chair, placed his elbows on the desk, and cradled his head in his hands. "What is going to happen?" he said aloud. "I'll never become bishop. That's over."

He took stock of whatever positives were left in his life, his mind deep in thought.

I'm still the pastor I have my church . . . I have my home . . . I still have my wife. What must I do to keep it all? What must I do to keep it all?

He repeated the perplexing question several times praying for any a solution, regardless how meager.

Do not admit to an affair with Elsa. That would doom him. Deny there was anything between them. Who would believe the word of a lonely, sadistic spinster, possessed with sexual fantasies, against the word of a man of the cloth? He pushed himself away from the desk and settled back into the chair. "Deny everything," he slurred aloud. "Her word against mine."

Unless his word could be contradicted by someone who could point a finger at him in front of witnesses and confirm they saw the pastor and Elsa together. He dismissed the idea of the orphans testifying. They were so terrified of the woman they could not possibly be aware of the tryst involving Elsa. Aimo was another story. He always feared the boy had survived his escape into the storm, and he prayed he be the one to find him. This time, he would not fail to personally kill the boy and hide his body so no one could find him. Aimo was his most serious threat. There was no escaping the fact that Aimo *was the* witness who could deliver damning information and destroy him.

Blixdal tried to remember if Vahleen had provided any clues to the boy's whereabouts. "Whatever the costs, the boy must be gotten rid of," he said aloud.

The reverend attempted to stand, but the alcohol had taken firm hold of his senses. Blixdal placed his head on the desk, consumed with thoughts of finding the boy. His fading mind dismissed the likelihood that Aimo was with the Vahleens because the constable would not have told him the boy had survived.

Blixdal concluded the boy had to have been found shortly after running away from the church. But where could he have gone? He had headed toward the center of the lake, running blindly across the ice. He lay his head on his desk, wondering where the boy have could have gone, and fell into a drunken stupor, snoring loudly.

Karen Blixdal also had thoughts of Aimo. In fact, she thought of little else. Initially, she was elated at overhearing Constable Vahleen tell her husband the boy was alive, but was devastated to hear Vahleen say he would not allow Aimo's return. Her only opportunity of raising a child dashed, she sadly set to the task of assembling Aimo's clothes, new skis, and ice skates. She placed the clothes in a steamer trunk, dragged it in front of her husband's study, and placed a note with instructions on the lid.

Blixdal discovered the steamer trunk early the next morning by falling over it on his way out of his office. He noticed the note which simply read, "Please see that Mikael gets his things."

Blixdal regarded the trunk without examining the contents. A smile slowly crossed his bearded face as an idea came through his alcohol-clouded brain. *The boy's teacher* had to know of Aimo's whereabouts, and if he didn't, one of his pupils would. The solution could not be more clear. He would deliver the clothes to Pontilius, wait to see who took them, and follow that person to where they were delivered. Then he would finish the job with Aimo.

Chapter Forty-five

January thirteenth was the day families gathered to sing and dance around the Christmas tree prior to removing all the decorations and signaled the official end to the Christmas season. Nowhere was there a more joyous celebration than at the Vahleen household when Solveig and Fredrik announced their wedding plans for midsummer at Grönö church. To make the day even more festive, Solveig asked Gretha to be her matron of honor.

The celebration at Olofsson's cabin was considerably more sedate. A recording of Christmas music played on the Victrola while Olofsson and Aimo removed fishing lure ornaments from the old man's tree. Olofsson confided to Aimo of a New Year tradition he always enjoyed, a barbershop haircut. Going to a barber in Nilstad with Aimo dressed only in long johns was out of the question. So the old man produced a pair of scissors and a comb. He placed Aimo on a chair and gave him a haircut to the best of his abilities. When he finished, any irregularities were hidden as Olofsson splashed aquavit on the boy's hair, his own substitute for a witch hazel astringent, and liberally massaged it over the boy's head. Then he created a center-part directly down the middle of Aimo's head.

"Did you see what I did?" Olofsson asked.

"I think so," Aimo answered.

"Good, 'cause now you're gonna give me a haircut."

"You're supposed to teach me my schoolwork," Aimo reminded. He postponed his barber's apprenticeship by fetching the books Pontilius delivered.

"Oh! Yeah! I forgot," Olofsson said.

"You forget a lot," Aimo observed.

The old man's memory was, in fact, beginning to fail. Occasionally, he stopped his conversations in mid-sentence. At other times, he would move through the room with a task or destination in mind only to stop and contemplate for long moments before asking Aimo what it was that he had set out to do. There were other hints of the old man's approaching senility that occurred, but Olofsson was unaware of the problem. Aimo's statement came as a surprise.

"No, I don't forget a lot," Olofsson said defensively.

"Not a whole lot, but a lot," Aimo hoped he was being diplomatic but feared he might have offended the old man.

"You know why I forget? Because I have important things on my mind. Anyway, when you get older you will too." Olofsson announced.

"Why?" Aimo asked.

"I'll tell you why . . . suppose there was ah, ah . . . *a dragon* in the forest, and you saw it. What would you do?" Olofsson looked Aimo in the eye and the boy shook his head.

"There's no such thing as *dragons in the forest*," Aimo remonstrated.

"That's not the question. The question is, *suppose* there was. What would you do?" The old man looked serious.

"I dunno," Aimo shrugged. "I think I'd tell you if there was though."

"Of course, you would," Olofsson thundered. "That's *exactly* what you would do. And you'd want me to do something about it. And that's what I think about all the time. It's what all people do when they get older. They have to worry about a dragon that might suddenly show up, and they're the ones that have to do something about it. That's what it's like to be old like me. Someday you'll find out for yourself."

Aimo was convinced the old man had just said something quite profound, but was not quite sure what that was. He trudged to the window and studied the forest across the lake trying to imagine a dragon living among the conifers.

Blixdal waited until the last of the children disappeared from sight before he drove to Pontilius's school. He removed the steamer trunk from the backseat of his car, dragged it across the snow to the schoolhouse doorway, and knocked loudly.

"Come in," Pontilius called.

Blixdal stepped into the room looking worse than he had during his previous visit, the odor of alcohol stronger than ever. There was no doubt the reverend was drinking heavily. His voice, however, was far less strident; and he certainly didn't appear or sound drunk. In fact, the man sounded civil.

"Good afternoon, Herr Pontilius. I hope I haven't disturbed you?" he asked politely.

"Not at all," Pontilius answered with equal politeness.

"I have something for you. Constable Vahleen visited me yesterday and told me the Finnish boy who ran away from us has survived. Do you, by chance, know where he is?"

Blixdal knew Pontilius would never admit to anything but felt the question appropriate anyway. "I've not heard a thing," Pontilius lied, his body stiffening.

"Ah! Well, I think eventually you will. Fru Blixdal has gathered the boy's things, his clothes, skis, things like that. They're outside in a steamer trunk. May I bring them inside?"

"Yes!" Pontilius's quick answer caught the preacher completely by surprise.

Blixdal pulled the steamer trunk inside, placing it next to the teacher's desk. He went out a second time and returned with Aimo's skis and skates.

"Karen and I want the boy to have these. Hopefully you can see to it that he gets them. Good day, Herr Pontilius."

Blixdal offered the teacher his hand, and Pontilius accepted the handshake.

"Good day," the teacher answered as Blixdal left.

Pontilius examined the windfall that had been delivered to him. He was overjoyed. It was exactly the request Olofsson had made. Now it was a matter of getting the heavy trunk across the lake. His toboggan, Pontilius thought. He was confident the chest could be secured to his toboggan and that he could tow it across the lake to Olofsson's cabin.

The clock on the wall showed it was nearing four in the afternoon and a three-quarter moon was on the rise. There would be enough light and more than enough time to deliver the chest and return to the cabin before Solveig's expected arrival at six. Pontilius set to the task of preparing the sled.

Blixdal sat in his parked car a short distance away out of sight of the school. The black-garbed pastor waited several minutes before leaving the warmth of his seat and walked back through the snow to a vantage point where he could view the school clearly. He stood shivering within a cluster of pine trees and stamped his feet from side to side to increase his blood circulation already compromised by the alcohol in his system. He prayed that Pontilius would soon show himself.

Blixdal swayed within the shadows of the trees as the moon rose, its glow sending spears of light through the conifer boughs and illuminating the alabaster landscape in gauzy glow. There was no certainty that anything at all would happen, but Blixdal had a hunch. As his luck would have it, he did not have long to wait.

The schoolhouse door opened, and Pontilius stepped out, dragging the chest behind him. He returned to the building and came out a second time, carrying a flat-bottom toboggan together with Aimo's skates and skis. He placed everything on the toboggan, lashed them tightly to the sled, secured the toboggan rope to his waist, and skied off in the direction of Lake Valdemaren.

Blixdal was giddy with the success of his guile. The schoolteacher never suspected the reverend's treachery, having no idea he was being watched. The reverend never felt smarter, nor had he had a higher sense of self-achievement. Pontilius was heading in the direction Blixdal felt was logical. Aimo was somewhere across the lake. He hurried to his car, restarted the motor, and turned onto the main road. He traveled a short distance to where the road curved toward an open area on a high bluff, providing an unbroken panoramic view of Lake Valdemaren. He pulled the car to a stop and waited.

Pontilius skied down the hill and onto the lake. Ten minutes later, Blixdal spied a small dark figure moving between the myriad of small islands that stretched from one shore to another. The teacher was bathed in bright moonlight and easily recognizable.

Blixdal stared anxiously as Pontilius angled out toward the wider portion of the lake. The skier reached a peninsula of land jutting out from the opposite shoreline, and he disappeared from view behind the point. The reverend returned to the car to warm himself, then waited to allow sufficient time for the skier to return to view. Blixdal moved back to the bluff and returned his scrutiny to where he had last seen Pontilius. He saw no one.

The teacher's trail had taken him in the vicinity of a point directly across from his church. The reverend was now fairly certain he knew Aimo's general location, but was puzzled because he knew of no homes in that area. Nevertheless, the reverend now had a trail to follow. He drove back to his church, ignoring the shivering chill that shook his body. He was very pleased with his day's work. Tomorrow, he would follow the trail before the wind or new snow could obliterate it.

Pontilius's visit was brief but welcome. Anxious to be on time for Solveig's arrival, the teacher skied swiftly back toward the school, leaving the steamer chest on the toboggan in front of the cabin and the surprised Olofsson.

"Where the hell you going in such a hurry?" Olofsson shouted.

"Solveig." Pontilius laughed.

"Can't live with 'em, can't live without 'em," Olofsson replied. He tousled Aimo's hair, the inadvertent gesture destroying the boy's neatly parted hairstyle.

"Can't live with who?" Aimo asked innocently. He attempted to restructure his hairstyle with his fingers.

"Women! That's who. And we better get this stuff inside, or we won't live at all," Olofsson said. He and Aimo pulled the toboggan and all its cargo directly into the cabin and closed the door behind them. The old man threw a new log into the fire and set to the task of examining the chest. Olofsson stepped back in amazement at the contents.

Aimo was overjoyed to get his clothes and his skis. The skates were another matter. The memory of his disappointment when he received them as well as the chaos that followed were too great for him to bear. Aimo opened the door to the cabin and hurled the skates out into the snow, then slammed the cabin door shut.

Olofsson placed an arm around Aimo's shoulders.

"Dragons, Aimo. That's what we always have to watch out for," Olofsson said, leading the boy to the steamer chest. "Did you bring all this stuff with you from Finland?"

"Fru Blixdal bought me these so I could look good in school."

"Well, let's see what you've got that's gonna look better than my long johns."

Karen Blixdal had packed the clothes carefully, keeping suits and ensembles together on hangers. Aimo quickly unpacked the chest and laid the clothes on his bed. He stopped when he reached the Lord Fauntleroy outfit.

"What in hell is that?" Olofsson asked in disbelief, fingering the wide white collar with the black velvet bow tie.

"I don't like it, do you?" Aimo asked.

Olofsson shook his head. "Tell you what," he said, fetching one of his favorite plaid shirts. "Put this on instead of whatever that is. We'll use that white thing for dryin' the dishes."

Aimo dressed himself in his knee stockings, knickers, and Olofsson's plaid shirt. Finally, he pulled on his seven-button jacket, ecstatic to be dressed in his clothes again.

"Is this OK?" Aimo asked.

Olofsson smiled broadly. If ever he had wanted a son, or a grandson, he wanted one to look just as Aimo did at this moment.

"You look fine, Aimo," Olofsson said approvingly. "Now, we have to make a clothes closet for these things." He pointed to his toolbox. "Bring that over to the table while I get some lumber from my storage shed. Now that I taught you how to be a barber, I'm gonna teach you how to be a carpenter. That OK with you?"

"OK with me," Aimo said with enthusiasm.

Chapter Forty-six

Aimo sat on the edge of his bed, admiring the fishing pole Olofsson had given him. Light from glowing embers of the previous evening's log cast a red glow through the early morning darkness, providing heat throughout the night to every corner of the cozy cabin. Living with Olofsson was fun, Aimo thought. There was always some exciting thing to do. The old man never raised his voice or ordered him around as his parents had done. Instead, he *asked* Aimo to perform duties, usually with a smile. That was another thing Aimo never experienced with his parents. He took the time to explain things whether it was cutting hair or working with building tools. Quite a difference from his life at Lake Jarvii, the boy thought.

Aimo was devoted to his parents, and nothing was going to prevent him from going home, of that he was determined. But as he reflected on his last year at Lake Jarvii, he never once remembered any of the adults enjoying life. Food had been scarce, and people shouted at each other, constantly arguing about the coming war. The boy's only escape was the forest, but even then, he had to keep one eye on his baby sister. Now Anna was with the Vahleens, safe and happy.

Then, like a recurring nightmare, Aimo's reverie took him back to a darker time and his last months at Lake Jarvii. Aimo's eyes darted to the darkened window, the blackened glass revealing the shape of a man's face staring menacingly at him. He dropped the fishing pole and rushed to Olofsson, crawling frantically over the old man, his terror-stricken eyes glued to the window.

"Grandpa! Grandpa! Wake up!" Aimo shouted desperately.

"What's going on?" Olofsson asked groggily, not yet fully awake.

"Somebody's at the window. Grandpa! Get your gun!"

Olofsson jumped from bed, grabbed his shotgun. "Do you still see him?" Olofsson asked in a whisper.

"I don't think so," Aimo answered quietly.

"Who the hell was it?" Olofsson kept his eyes riveted to the window.

"I don't know. I think he looked like a Russian soldier. He was gonna shoot us."

Olofsson shifted his gaze to the boy, realizing that Aimo had imagined someone at the window. Most significantly for the old man, the boy called him grandpa. He unloaded the shotgun and sat next to Aimo.

"Do you want to tell me what happened the day the Russians came," Olofsson asked softly.

Aimo nodded and proceeded to detail the events of the last minutes in his house at Lake Jarvii. He spoke haltingly, recalling the terrible atrocities of that horrific day, each of the stories in vivid detail. The old man was held spellbound.

"I think I did see somebody at this window though," Aimo said.

"But you're not sure, are you?" Olofsson asked, placing a hand on the boy's shoulders.

"I'm not sure," he answered.

"But you got scared, right?" Olofsson tightened his grip on the boy's shoulders, and Aimo nodded.

"Tell you what," Olofsson said cheerfully. "You can call me grandpa any time you want to. Even when you're not scared."

Aimo nodded his head in agreement. "OK," Aimo agreed, "but I can call you Magnus sometimes too, OK?"

"Just don't call me late for breakfast. If we're gonna go ice fishing, we'd better get up and get started."

Before leaving the cabin, the old man fetched the books Pontilius had left. Aimo stared at the old man quizzically. "What are you gonna do with those?"

Olofsson stuffed the books in a knapsack and secured it on Aimo's back. "Your teacher told me to put these to good use. That's exactly what we're gonna do."

Olofsson questioned the wisdom of an ice-fishing trip, worrying whether to risk taking the boy into the cold or disappoint him with a postponement. Today would be Aimo's first venture outdoors since running across the lake to escape from the reverend, and the old man did not want to jeopardize the boy's health.

"How do you feel?" Olofsson asked.

"Good," Aimo replied.

"Warm enough?"

"Yes," Aimo answered, eager to leave.

"Got the fishing stuff?"

Aimo nodded, anxious to get started.

"You sound healthy enough to me," Olofsson said, stepping out of the cabin. He picked up an ice auger in one hand and grabbed a snowplow-shaped wooden shovel in the other.

"We're gonna go out to the point," Olofsson indicated. "That's a good spot."

"I know," Aimo replied. "I met you out there, remember?"

"Sure! Sure I remember," Olofsson said, trudging through hip deep snow. "By the way, I looked for tracks outside the window, but I didn't see any. Know what I think you saw?" He asked.

"Dragons?" Aimo replied.

"That's exactly right. Dragons." Olofsson laughed.

"How do you know that?" Aimo's curiosity was genuine.

"'Cause you called for help. I told you that's what happens when you see dragons."

Aimo laughed at the silly thought, yet the old man behaved just as he said he would when Aimo needed help.

"Now I know what you mean," Aimo said.

"Stick around me, kid. You'll learn a lot," Olofsson said.

Nearing the point, Olofsson gazed at the southern skies. "Look," he said, pointing to the sun. It hung in the morning sky, a full orb after nearly six weeks of being nothing more than a glow on the distant horizon. "Won't be long before it comes up high enough to start melting all this snow. A few more weeks, Aimo, and it'll be spring."

"When does the ice break here?" Aimo asked.

"Mid-April. May, sometimes."

"Well, it's gonna be more than a few weeks before spring, 'cause it's still mid-January," Aimo answered smartly.

"Yeah," Olofsson answered. "That's another thing you're gonna learn. The older you get, the faster the time goes by."

Olofsson reached a position off the point. Beneath the spot, an underground spring rose from the bottom of the lake. The fresh current attracted schools of yellow perch, and their larger cousins, walleye pike, like a magnet. He plowed a large section of ice with the wooden shovel creating a snow wall that also served as a windbreak. Next, he augered two holes, three meters apart, through the thick ice and instructed Aimo to take out his schoolbooks.

Aimo pulled the books from his knapsack and read the subject titles aloud. "History! . . . Mathematics! . . . Science! . . . Literature! . . . And, hey, look," Aimo called, "Herr Pontilius gave me a Bible."

"Give me the Bible and the history," Olofsson said and placed them near one of the augured fishing holes. Then he carefully sat on top of the stack.

"Your teacher wanted me to make certain we put these to good use. You can sit on those three. The Bible's gonna give me some good luck."

Aimo smiled. He sat on his stacked books and immediately started fishing. After several twitches of the wooden rod, he set the hook into a fish and pulled the first perch onto the ice amid shouts of encouragement from Olofsson.

Neither of the engrossed fishermen was aware that Blixdal had followed the drag trail made by Pontilius's toboggan or that the reverend heard Aimo's voice together with Olofsson's blustery laughter. Blixdal reached the peninsula point where the two fished and hid from view.

The reverend's preoccupation with passing judgment on heathens and sinners had narrowed his vision to the mundane occurrences of life. He never observed the cabin, lying at the water's edge, directly across from his church. Now that he knew, he no longer was concerned about finding Aimo. Eliminating the boy was another matter. But he had a plan. Wooden cabins burn all the time, Blixdal thought to himself, sometimes with tragic consequences.

Chapter Forty-seven

As weeks passed, Aimo's health returned fully. He regained the weight he had lost, replacing it with sinewy muscle resulting from his daily efforts in and around the cabin. Meanwhile, Olofsson was taxed with inventing various chores simply to harness the boy's energy. Happily, he arrived at a solution that held Aimo's interest while keeping him busy at the same time.

Olofsson divided the month by odd and even days. On even days, the old man conducted his version of a classroom, but with a twist. Olofsson himself volunteered to study together with Aimo, declaring one was never too old to learn. Each gave the other exams, and the plan was an instant success. Learning became fun, and Aimo's schoolbooks no longer were used just for ice fishing forays.

Every odd day involved household chores, and the repair of various pieces of furniture suffering from years of neglect. Best of all, for Aimo, the old man turned repair sessions into woodworking classes during which Aimo was taught to use the old man's carpentry equipment. The boy's instinctive woodcarving skills were being turned into the ability to do useful work.

Ice fishing held a special priority however, and it was agreed they would go whenever the spirit moved them. Perch and walleye fillets, sautéed in a hot, greased skillet became common fare; and the desire for this savory dish often justified a divergence from Olofsson's planned schedule.

Cross-country skiing was a challenge for Olofsson, and he proved to be poor company for the boy. However, once on skis, Aimo's nature caused him to behave like a thoroughbred colt turned loose on an open field. The boy bolted in ever-widening circles in a celebration of youthful energy until he skied out of the old man's sight.

Aimo remained on Olofsson's side of the lake as he was told, and he avoided contact with others, including his former classmates, until Constable Vahleen completed his investigations of the events at the orphanage. Vahleen reported that Blixdal was unpredictable and not to be trusted. There was no telling what problems he could cause if he learned Aimo was living with Olofsson at the cabin. Based on the reverend's recent behavior, Vahleen believed Blixdal might be a danger to the boy.

Aimo never considered the cabin confining and Olofsson's sincere attention made the boy feel welcome. He had learned to respect the old man and genuinely sought his counsel. More than anything else, Aimo was having fun. More fun, in fact, than he ever remembered having and he accepted Olofsson as a good friend.

The months of January, February, and March held northern Sweden in an icy grip familiar to the people of Jamtland. There were frequent snowfalls, but they were spared the type of blizzard they had at Christmas.

April brought welcome changes, each passing day heralding more long minutes of increased sunlight. By midmonth, the sun was high enough in the sky to warm the frozen countryside. The dark bark of pine trees absorbed the sun's strong rays and radiated its warmth into snow-laden branches. Eventually, each limb shook free of its burdensome load, allowing white plumes of snow to cascade down to shower onto the forest floor.

On every open meadow, the sounds of water freshets beneath the mantle of white foretold the approach of spring. Ice-covered brooks reflected the increased volume of water within their banks with loud gurgling. Each hour of sunlight added to the pressures on the thick lids of ice that covered the streams. Rushing water pushed upward incessantly, creating multiple fissures on frozen surfaces. The liquid turbulence beneath every creek, brook, and river seeped to the surface, soaking the drifts of powdery snow above them into heavy masses of slush. Finally, the unstable ice shattered, sending heavy chunks of frenziedly driven ice blocks adrift in swift currents.

Every stream flowed into Lake Valdemaren, increasing the pressure there as well. But the thick lake ice, measuring nearly half a meter in depth, would be a formidable task for the new season. At least, two more weeks of flooding streams and abundant sunshine were needed before Lake Valdemaren's ice would break.

Aimo and Olofsson stood in shirtsleeves against the lee side of the cabin, soaking in the warmth of the April sun. The dark red-painted wood heated their backs while sunlight reflected brightly from the snow, radiating its heat across their faces. Above them, a wooden ledge below the cabin's eaves was crowded with dozens of chirping finches, their blue gray feathers fluffed in excitement.

"Look at all the birds, Magnus," Aimo observed.

"They can tell spring's coming," Olofsson declared.

"How?" Aimo asked.

"The sunlight. They see there's more of it every day, just like we can. That gets their juices going, and their bodies produce hormones. That's how they know when it's time to build a nest and mate."

Aimo was always impressed with Olofsson's storytelling, regardless of the subject. If the old man had an interest in something, he was an encyclopedia of knowledge.

"How do you know that?" Aimo asked.

"I read about things like that. Did you know most birds stay together for life?" Aimo shook his head. "Well, the ones with the brightest colors are the males, and the less shiny ones are females. Once a pair mates, they stay together."

"Why do you read about birds?" Aimo wanted to know.

"To learn, Aimo! I love all of this," he said, gesturing to the wilderness that surrounded them. "Birds, fish, animals, the forest. They're all part of my life. Somebody wrote, 'We love what we understand but understand only what we're taught.'"

Aimo eyed the old man quizzically. Olofsson had a sense of humor that he often blended into his conversations. The boy wanted to be certain of the old man's sincerity because what he just said sounded very important.

Olofsson continued, "If you can learn just one new thing every day, think how smart you'll be when you get to be my age." Aimo's face contorted into a confused scowl as Olofsson laughed. "Now, how about we dig my truck out of the snow? I'm gonna teach you something new."

"What's that?" Aimo's voice was expectant.

"I'm going to teach you how to drive!" Olofsson said enthusiastically. "You have to learn sometime, right?"

Aimo's face lit up in excitement. "Wow!" he exclaimed. Unable to say anything more, he rushed to fetch two shovels.

Olofsson received several visits from Constable Vahleen during the winter and one memorable visit from Solveig and Pontilius. The young couple treated Aimo to a spirited ski run, and Aimo fell in love with the woman at first sight. He took special pains to put on an exceptional skiing demonstration and felt his cheeks flush when she stroked snow across his heated face. Solveig confided to Aimo that Pontilius strongly admired his skills and believed that with proper training, he himself could develop into a competitive skier.

A big surprise for both Aimo and Olofsson was an invitation to the couple's midsummer wedding. Pontilius confounded the boy further by asking him if he would agree to a role in the procession, but Aimo balked. He had never been to a wedding before having no idea what to do.

Solveig told him he would be the ringbearer and Meggan Vahleen, the flower girl. "Everyone will do just fine," she promised. "We'll rehearse beforehand so no one will make a mistake."

Aimo looked at his teacher dumbly, not knowing what to say until Pontilius offered Aimo his hand. "You're one of my best friends, Aimo," the teacher said. "You would honor us if you agreed."

Aimo glanced over to Olofsson who smiled proudly. The boy felt especially lucky to have three adults whose friendship he respected. Aimo extended his hand to Pontilius and shook it vigorously, then bowed to Solveig. "It's a contract," he said and became an official member of the wedding party. Aimo smiled, proud to be considered a grown-up.

Constable Vahleen's weekly visits to Olofsson's cabin were especially welcome since he brought with him an array of varied prepared foods, including Aimo's favorite, Meggan's cinnamon muffins. He also brought news of Anna. She was doing well, and Vahleen promised to arrange a meeting between them.

But not all the news was pleasant. Gretha had written two letters to Aimo's parents at their address in Jyväskylä, but had heard nothing from them. The constable said the turmoil within Finland made delivery of mail difficult at best. Gretha intended to write the Red Cross representatives in Jyväskylä in the event she did not get a reply soon.

Aimo was thoroughly frustrated with the unsettling information. It underscored his lack of power to do anything himself. He trusted the Vahleens and knew they would follow through as they promised, but nothing assuaged his yearning to have some control over his efforts to reconnect with his parents.

Equally disturbing was news of the war. Vahleen had intended it for Olofsson's ears only, but the boy overheard the constable say there was no certainty who might be winning. The Americans were more involved than ever, but German shortwave broadcasts claimed the Americans were foolish warriors because their bombers flew daytime raids against German targets at a terrible cost to their planes. Vahleen said he did not know how much credence he could give to those broadcasts, nor could he guess whether or not the Yanks could make much of a difference in the outcome of the European war because so much of America's resources were directed at fighting the Japanese half a world away in the Pacific.

Olofsson reminded him that the Germans still controlled most of Europe and all of Scandinavia except Sweden. "We're next!" Olofsson shouted and pounded his fist into his hand. Vahleen, suddenly aware of Aimo listening nearby, changed the subject.

Vahleen revealed the former orphanage director, Fröken Elsa Kulander, had been committed to a mental institution. The decision was politically motivated to stifle news of the mishandling of Finnish children by a Swede. Officially, the death of the child at the orphanage was a result of illness, and there the matter ended. As soon as he said this, Vahleen could have bitten his tongue.

Aimo was instantly alerted. "Who died?" Aimo asked in a panic. "My cousin Pehr is at the orphanage. So is my best friend, Mooseface."

"I don't know who died, Aimo," Vahleen lied.

At some point, Vahleen intended to tell him about his cousin but decided it was kinder for the moment to wait. But of Aimo's friend Mooseface, the constable had good news indeed.

"Your friend is with a nice family in the next county. They own a bakery, so I think Mooseface is going to do very well," Vahleen reported.

"What about Pehr," Aimo insisted. "Where is he?"

Vahleen paced uncomfortably, not really prepared to reveal the death of Pehr just yet. He stared at the lake from the window to avoid Aimo's scrutiny. When Vahleen finally answered, he spoke with deliberation, his eyes fastened on the world outside the awkward room.

"He was very sick, Aimo. The doctors think he may have died from pneumonia."

Olofsson put an arm over the boy's shoulder in comfort. "I'm so sorry, Aimo."

Aimo's face strained in grief. He looked up at the old man, trying to find the words to express his feelings.

"Why?" It was all Aimo could manage.

Olofsson and Vahleen regarded one another, each searching for a proper answer to give to the boy. Then Olofsson replied.

"I don't know," he said softly.

Chapter Forty-eight

In spite of rationing, war brought limited hardships to the community of Nilstad; and with the exception of the Christmas blizzard, the winter was uneventful. Even food was not a pressing problem since every family had summer gardens from which vegetables and fruits had been preserved. Added to this daily fare was the abundance of big game within the local forests. A caribou or moose provided many months supply of meat for an entire family.

The reappearance of the sun, with its blessed light and warmth, transformed Swedish dispositions to nearly uncontrolled gaiety. The season of new life had arrived and everyone's attention focused on the eve of April 30, Valborsmässoafton, the night the witches returned to Sweden. Bonfires would light the sky, and graduates of the *gymnasiet* would wear their traditional white graduate's caps. Celebrations would carry on throughout the night.

All of Nilstad prepared for the annual event with the exception of Bjorn Blixdal. He had another type of bonfire in mind and had waited many weeks for the opportunity to ignite it.

The reverend paced nervously across the cold stone floor of his study, clutching his head in his hands. He tried to regain some sense of his life, which had spiraled downward ever since Aimo had entered his house six months earlier. He cursed the boy anew and added the name of Constable Vahleen to his wish list of eternal damnation. Blixdal had never before experienced such a deep depression. He hated Aimo, he hated Vahleen, he hated the Finns, and he hated his county's government with his entire being. He questioned God if he was going mad.

Vahleen's latest visit had been devastating. The constable announced he had sufficient evidence to bring formal state charges against Blixdal. To make matters worse, Karen had confronted him after Vahleen left. His wife declared that she did not care about his infidelity because sex no longer interested her. Her greatest injury was that Blixdal had wantonly risked their station in life, single-handedly destroying all they had built through years of dedicated labor.

The loss of their combined hard work was *unconscionable*; destroying their reputation in the community, *unforgivable;* and driving the boy from their home at the risk of his life, *sinful.* The issue of the boy alone made his other failings irrelevant, she said. Then she delivered the most crushing blow of all. How tragically ironic, she told him, the only opportunity life had given her to raise a child should be destroyed by her husband.

Karen remained in a deep state of despair, spending countless hours in prayer, frequently falling into an exhaustive sleep at the altar rail. Visits from Gretha Vahleen and other church members offered well-intentioned solace, but Karen's feelings of depression and shame were total. She unequivocally concluded her world had come to an end. Optimistic thoughts of her future were inconceivable. She avoided contact with her husband and tuned out his frequent drunken ravings entirely.

When the reverend left the church on Valborsmässoafton, the night the witches returned to Sweden, she did not ask where he was going or when he intended to return. She no longer cared. She lay asleep on the chilled church floor in front of the altar, unaware the reverend had set out on foot to cross Lake Valdemaren and Olofsson's cabin, a box of stick matches in his pocket.

The terrain above Olofsson's cabin sloped gradually upward, then flattened into a ridge of dense pine trees. There, the elevated landscape swung an arm back toward the lake, creating a hundred-meter-high cliff over Valdemaren. The vantage point provided Aimo and Olofsson an uninterrupted view of the city, glowing from dozens of large bonfires.

Olofsson gazed at the sight wistfully to a time long past when he too wore his white graduate's cap and sang with his friends, bidding farewell to winter and welcoming the spring on this special evening. He lowered his gaze to Aimo who stared wide eyed at the vision in front of him. The boy was trembling.

"What's wrong, Aimo? Are you cold?" Olofsson asked.

Aimo shook his head, unable to remove his eyes from Nilstad. It was almost the same scene he remembered when the *Sunpath* pulled away from Haparanda as dozens of fires burned in the Finnish village of Tornio.

"I want to go back to the cabin," Aimo mumbled.

Olofsson returned the boy to the cabin without question. Aimo lay on his bed without removing his clothes and curled into a ball facing the wall.

"Do you want to tell me about it?" Olofsson asked.

"No," Aimo replied. "Maybe tomorrow."

"Good night, then," Olofsson said gently.

"Good night," the boy murmured.

Olofsson placed the evening's log on the embers in the fireplace, then searched among his records for suitable music. The sight of the bonfires in Nilstad had a special significance to him. To Olofsson, it went beyond being a harbinger of spring or a special reward to all Swedes for excelling at school.

His memory raced back to the Valborsmässoafton when he met his fiance-to-be. She was with a group of friends, singing one of their school songs. Olofsson simply walked up and kissed her. She didn't seem to mind, and neither did her schoolmates who cheered them on enthusiastically.

The memory was painful. Olofsson became melancholy and that called for music by Sibelius. He chose the composer's "Fifth Symphony" and placed the record on the turntable.

The first chords of the symphony swiftly returned the old man to the bittersweet time with Dagmar Sommarfelt, the love of his life. He cast a glance at the bottle of aquavit he kept on the mantle of the fireplace. He had not had a drink since Christmas, but he was hurting with sadness. A drink might help. He put the bottle to his mouth and shuddered as the potato brandy burned its way into his stomach. He downed another drink for old time's sake but resisted the urge to finish the bottle and returned it to its place on the mantle. Olofsson lay on his back on the bed, cradling the back of his head in his hands while staring blankly at the dark rafters above him. He blinked his eyes a few times, then fell soundly asleep with dear memories of Dagmar and the one glorious summer they had shared.

Aimo had been asleep for nearly two hours when he unexpectedly awakened. He listened intently but remained in a fetal position facing the wall of the cabin. Olofsson's snoring, the crackle of the slow-burning log in the fireplace, and a mouse that scampered quickly across the wood floor were ordinary noises. He knew they were not the cause of his being fully alert. He sensed something else, something threatening and sinister. It was lurking in the darkness just beyond the window.

The idea of again being watched from the outside crept into his brain and raised the hair on the back of his neck. He thought to cry out for Olofsson but remembered how foolish he felt some weeks earlier when he had done the same thing. He remained silent, certain that someone was at his window, staring at him, someone who hated him. He dared not make a move. Slowly, he turned his head as though moving in his sleep and ventured a peek from beneath his arm.

The window reflected the soft glow of the fireplace. That was normal. But there appeared to be another glow, just outside the building, coming from the direction of the woodpile against the cabin. Alarmed, Aimo shifted his gaze and noticed light wisps of smoke curling from beneath the door. A movement at the window caught the boy's attention as a tiny pinpoint of a glowing red light floated past the pane quickly followed by several more.

Aimo swung out of the bed, recognizing the floating red lights as burning embers. The area in front of the cabin was bathed in orange. He darted to the door and pulled it open. The acrid odor of smoke and crackling sound of open flames from the woodpile was unmistakable. A fire was burning dangerously close next to the house.

Suddenly, a horrible nightmare emerged from the darkness. The black figure of Reverend Blixdal floated inexorably forward. He loomed in front of the boy, and Olofsson's story of menacing dragons living in the surrounding forest came true. The clergyman's eyes blazed wildly. He held one of Olofsson's shovels in his hand and lunged forward, ramming the shovel at Aimo's face with a deadly thrust.

Aimo leaped backward into the cabin and slammed the door shut, screaming in terror. A moment later the blade of the shovel thudded several times against the wood in rapid succession, rattling the door against its hinges from repeated thrusts.

Olofsson jumped upright in bed, trying to make sense of the din invading his unconscious mind. Aimo's yelling voice brought the man to his feet, and he discovered the boy pushing mightily against the door as strikes of the shovel blasted repeatedly from the opposite side.

Now totally alert, the old man realized someone was indeed outside and trying to break in. Olofsson jumped to Aimo's side in a flash, his adrenaline-charged body prepared for battle. The old man yanked the door open as Blixdal again thrust the shovel forward. The blade swooshed past Olofsson's nose, narrowly missing it, but the momentum carried the reverend directly into the cabin. He collided heavily against the old man's chest.

Aimo scrambled back against a wall as Olofsson grabbed the reverend by the lapels, preventing him from tumbling into the room. The two men regarded each other in momentary surprise, their heads close together. Then Olofsson exploded into action with a fury. He shoved the reverend against the doorframe and swung his left fist directly into Blixdal's face. His knuckles smacked loudly against Blixdal's cheek, driving the reverend's head hard into the wooden door.

Blixdal exhaled a cry of pain and staggered out into the snow. Olofsson was on him instantly. Seventy-one years or no, his backwoods life had kept sinew where a city dweller his age would have gone to fat. Worse for Blixdal, he was weakened from weeks of physical depression and alcohol while Olofsson's rage had thrown the old man out of control.

Olofsson caught Blixdal by the arm, turning the reverend's face directly into the old man's right fist. This time, it burst against Blixdal's mouth, splitting his lips against his teeth. The clergyman slid on his back across the snow.

"Bastard!" Olofsson shouted. "You can hit kids but can't do shit against a man." Olofsson stood over the beaten minister groveling to pull himself to his knees. He tried to crawl away, and Olofsson planted a swift kick to his rump, sending him gliding on his face like a black toboggan.

"Grandpa!" Aimo shouted behind him. "The house is on fire."

The burning woodpile was totally ablaze, threatening to set fire to the timbers of the house. Olofsson grabbed the shovel that lay near his feet and hurled scoops of snow onto the blaze.

"Aimo . . . help me!" Olofsson yelled. "Get the other shovel!"

Aimo stepped out of the house carefully, taking a precautionary look at Blixdal who had managed to get to his feet. The beaten man hurriedly staggered away from the cabin toward the lake. Frantic shoveling soon suffocated the fire under a high mound of slush. Satisfied with the job, Olofsson led Aimo back into the house.

"Put on your boots and coat," he said, grabbing his shotgun.

Olofsson stalked out of the cabin with Aimo at his heels. The reverend's trail led directly to the lake, and Olofsson scanned the white surface of Valdemaren.

"Can you see him out there?" Olofsson asked.

Aimo's eyes strained to penetrate the darkness. "What are you gonna do, Grandpa?" the boy worried.

The old man's rage was ferocious, a side of Olofsson the boy did not know existed. His face reflected the same rage his father displayed when shooting the Russian soldiers.

"I'm gonna shoot the bastard," Olofsson huffed.

"Wait!" Aimo said. "I heard something."

They stood in poised silence, controlling the sound of their breathing. Seconds passed, and Olofsson regarded Aimo quizzically.

"What did you hear, boy?"

The answer to Olofsson's question came suddenly. A low moan sweeping across the vastness of the lake, followed a moment later by a high pitched *ping* that echoed in the night. Then, a new and much stronger moan rumbled, and Olofsson smiled broadly.

"The ice is breaking! She's gonna go tonight. Maybe it's gonna swallow that bastard before he gets to the other side," he said hopefully.

Aimo and Olofsson trudged their way back to the cabin amid a background of growling sounds made by the heaving ice. Like some gigantic living thing, the entire lake groaned a symphony of strange and varied noises reverberating throughout the valley. Inside the cabin, the old man sat on the edge of Aimo's bed and allowed the boy to nestle against him. He stroked the boy's hair then heaved a deep sigh of relief.

"Your grandpa did OK tonight, didn't he?" Olofsson asked. Aimo grunted to say he agreed and the old man continued, the feelings of being victorious overwhelming. "I've waited years to kick that pompous bastard's ass."

Olofsson made a humming sound to mimic the noises coming from Lake Valdemaren's wakening. The daylight would reveal large leads of open water, and in one week, the lake would be ice free.

Blixdal staggered across the frozen lake and onto his church property completely out of breath. He grasped the cold timbers of the boathouse, steadied himself, then allowed a final glance over his shoulder at the lake moaning loudly behind him. He was momentarily relieved to see he was not being pursued, but his relief was short lived. He suddenly realized he had failed again. Now there was no escape to his fate of a lifelong prison sentence. He was totally defeated. He stuffed a handful of snow into his mouth to rinse away the taste of his own blood, then swiped his face with moist fingers to control his hair.

Blixdal entered the boathouse. He scaled a ladder leading into the catacombs and stumbled painfully past the cobweb-coated caskets, mumbling incoherently while gasping for air. He pulled open the door leading to the church and steadied himself against a wall. He was greeted by a pitiful sight as another loud moan from the lake echoed loudly among the walls.

Stretched across the floor in front of the altar railing lay the limp form of his wife. She had removed the barrettes from her hair allowing it to spill across the stone. Her long white dress was spread casually around her. She slept in exhaustion.

Blixdal stared at the woman for a long moment. He intended to wake her and tell her the damnable boy—the cause of all their problems, but whom she so desperately loved—was alive and well, living directly across the lake; but he changed his mind. He knew he looked a mess, and his mouth tasted of blood from his broken lips. Above all, the reverend did not want to tell her of another of his failures.

Blixdal climbed the stairs to the second floor, stumbling into the bathroom. He rinsed his bloodied mouth in the sink, then splashed water over his sore face. What was he to do? Instead of killing Aimo as he had planned, he made matters worse by being discovered by Olofsson. The thought brought a stab of panic to the man's brain. What if the old man was on his way to the church at that very moment?

Blixdal bolted to Aimo's former room to get a better view of the lake. Outside the window, the heaving ice hurled new sounds that rose in a tumultuous crescendo as solid sheets of lake ice rippled, sending splitting seams swiftly from one side to the other. Blixdal's concentration was on the opposite shore where he was certain Olofsson would come. He stared in that direction for several moments, then became aware of a widening lead of open water in the middle of the lake.

He sighed in relief. The old man would not risk his life under such treacherous conditions. Just then, a new movement on the church side of the lake caught his attention. A ghostly figure, its light-colored form just a shade darker than the snow, was moving toward the middle of the lake. Blixdal looked on curiously. He brought his hand to his forehead to better focus his sight then gasped in horror. Karen, clad only in her white dress and seemingly oblivious to the sounds of heaving ice around her, walked steadily forward, in bare feet.

Blixdal understood her intentions immediately. *Suicide!* She was heading directly for the open water and she would soon reach it unless he could stop her. He yanked the window open and screamed.

"Karen! Karen!"

His voice was swallowed by the loud sounds of the groaning lake. Again he shouted as loudly as he could.

"Karen! No! No!"

Blixdal ran through the church and down the steps leading to the catacombs. He reached the boat opening and unhesitatingly jumped onto the ice and toppled forward. He rolled forward several times coming to a stop on his knees . Blood spilled from a head laceration over his forehead and spilled down his face in meandering rivulets. Dazed from his injury and Olofsson's beating, the reverend pulled himself to his feet and shouted Karen's name continually. He could see her in the distance, a hundred meters in front of him. He raced after her, sprinting wildly, fueled by raw adrenalin alone.

"Karen! Karen!" he shouted her name over and over again.

Finally the woman stopped. She stood with her back to him as Blixdal ran with all his strength. Fifty meters, then twenty-five, and finally ten meters separated them when suddenly, the woman stepped forward and disappeared from view.

The reverend ran ahead savagely reaching an open lead of water in time to see his wife floating away from him just below the black surface of the frigid lake. Blixdal fell to his knees and stretched his hand far out in front of him. His wife's hair waved tantalizingly in the current, so near but just out of reach.

Blixdal leaned outward to his extreme limits. He groped for the strands of floating hair that would enable him to pull the woman to safety and shoved his fist forward. Flexing his fingers wildly, he struggled to grab the handful of hair that would allow him to pull her toward him. Suddenly, his wife's slender white arm thrust itself out of the black surface of the lake. Her hand closed over her husband's wrist in a talonlike grip.

The Reverend Bjorn Blixdal cried out once, then relaxed his body. Devoid of all energy, his spirit gone, he returned to a time when, as a boy, he awaited yet another beating from his father. He bowed forward and without a struggle, surrendered himself to the sensation of sinking into the wet, cold, stygian blackness of icy Lake Valdemaren.

Chapter Forty-nine

The constable scribbled in his pad while searching the area around Olofsson's cabin. The old man spoke animatedly, describing the details of the encounter with Blixdal while they both surveyed the damage the fire had done. The blackened wall, scorched firewood, and charred timbers in the eaves testified to an event that could have been much worse.

"You're both lucky," Vahleen declared. He pointed at the damage. "A little longer and the roof would have ignited."

"I was sound asleep, but the boy wasn't. Thank god he saw what was going on." Olofsson said.

Aimo trailed behind silently except to answer yes whenever the old man needed reassurance of his recollections.

Vahleen turned to Aimo. "That's when you opened the door and saw Blixdal?"

"Yes!" Aimo replied.

"He didn't know the bastard was out there," Olofsson interrupted. "Son of a Bitchdal didn't say anything . . . he just tried to hit the kid with a shovel. Isn't that right, Aimo?"

"Yes!" Aimo replied.

"We had a feeling something was going to happen here," Sten admitted. "Gretha's been worrying over Fru Blixdal for some time. She even had a premonition last night, insisting we visit the church this morning. That's how we discovered their tracks leading onto the lake."

"Are you sure he didn't fall through the ice when he left here?" Olofsson brought the little group to a stop. "We heard the ice breaking, but it was too dark to see. Right, Aimo?"

"Yes!" Aimo answered, again without elaboration.

Constable Vahleen cast a troubled glance at Aimo, then directed his words to Olofsson carefully. "The woman's tracks showed she left the house in bare feet, heading straight to the center of the lake. I can only guess she wanted to commit suicide. The reverend's tracks are unmistakable. He was running after her. Their trail ends leading to open water." Vahleen turned his attention to Aimo. "I'm sorry you had to hear that, Aimo. I think you know Fru Blixdal cared very deeply for you."

"Yes! I know," Aimo said, devoid of emotion.

Olofsson took the boy by the shoulders. "Aimo, war does terrible things to people. The reverend believed himself to be a man of God. He was not always bad. We can never tell anybody about this, do you understand?"

Aimo nodded that he did. It was not enough to satisfy Olofsson.

"No! Tell me that you understand. Say it," he commanded.

"I understand," the boy said, and Olofsson embraced him strongly.

Olofsson turned to the constable and changed the subject. "Well! Let's go inside. I can smell that your wife has warmed some cinnamon buns."

Gretha had busied herself within Olofsson's cabin since her arrival, treating the place as though it were her own. She set the table for four with placemats, mugs, spoons, and sections of Aimo's Fauntleroy shirt as napkins. A plate of Meggan's warmed cinnamon buns sat at the center of the table, and a delicious aroma wafted from them.

When Gretha had first entered the cabin thirty minutes earlier, her most pressing thought had been to shake off the chill from riding in the open sidecar of Sten's police motorcycle. She stoked the fireplace, added new wood, and stood as close to the flame as possible. In fifteen minutes, she had a roaring fire, radiating extra warmth up to the ceiling. The men entered the cabin and closed the door. At once, an avalanche of snow cascaded from the steeply angled roof, exposing its sod-covered timbers for the first time in six months.

"There goes winter," Olofsson shouted. "Now it's official."

"It's official when I see my first flowers," Gretha answered, placing a bowl of them on the table. Olofsson and Aimo gawked at the tiny blue and white anemones.

"I'll bet you got these on the side of the hill. It always gets green there first," Olofsson declared.

"And that's just where I found them. Aimo, would you mind picking some more to give to the girls?" Gretha asked.

"Yes! Sure!" Aimo replied with enthusiasm.

Gretha handed him a bowl. "See if you can fill it up. The stems are short, so try to nip them as close to the ground as possible."

"OK, Fru Vahleen," Aimo replied, a cinnamon bun in his hand.

"I'll tell Anna you picked them yourself," Gretha said as the boy opened the door. "And, Aimo, Meggan loves flowers, so pick some extra for her to let her know you appreciate her cinnamon buns."

Aimo nodded in embarrassment then left the cabin quickly, his cheeks flushed. Gretha sat at the table together with Olofsson and her husband. No one spoke a word as she poured coffee into their mugs. Gretha's voice broke the silence, shaking her head sadly.

"I feel responsible for Karen's death. I should have done something."

"There's no way you can blame yourself, Gretha," Sten sympathized.

"It's the goddamned war," Olofsson added. "Look what it's done to us here in Nilstad, and we're not even fighting in the war. God knows what it's doing to the rest of the world."

"I can tell you, it's not good in Finland. The first of the retreating Germans are the SS death squads. They're as bad as the Russians. The Finns are being wiped out," Sten added.

"I haven't heard from Aimo's parents nor from the Red Cross in Jyväskylä," Gretha said. "You may have to take care of the boy for some time, Magnus. Can you manage?"

"Fru Vahleen," Olofsson answered incredulously, "you mean you can't see the difference in me? Or in this house? Of course, I can take care of him. Ask Aimo. He's happy here."

"I apologize, Magnus. I didn't mean that. I mean, you live alone and have no family," Gretha added quickly.

"I *am* family! The forest around us, even the lake, there's family all around. I'm better than a thousand Blixdals, and the boy's future is more positive with me at this moment than it would be in Finland, wouldn't you say?" Olofsson stood from the table and looked around the cabin, marveling at the order he had achieved since Aimo's arrival. "The only thing missing are curtains. That's all," Olofsson said, defending himself. "And I don't like curtains."

"We didn't mean to upset you, Magnus. The boy is lucky to have you come into his life," Vahleen added.

"I'm lucky he came into mine. He saved my life twice, but he's given me something more. He's given me a *future*. Can you imagine that? I'm seventy-one years old . . . and I finally have a future."

Olofsson returned to the table and sat down, facing Gretha. "That boy is the best friend I've ever had. I promised him I'd personally see that he goes home to Finland even if I have to take him myself."

The room grew quiet.

"Gentlemen!" Gretha announced. "It's time we brought Aimo together with his sister. It's been more than four months since they've seen each other." She regarded Sten closely. "We missed Valborsmässoafton and the First of May, but we'll all celebrate together this Sunday." Gretha rose from the table. "What do you say? We'll come over on Sunday and bring the girls. They'll go crazy when I tell them the flowers are blooming."

"What about Solveig and Fredrik?" Vahleen reminded his wife. "You invited them to the house this Sunday, do you remember?"

"Bring 'em all out here." Olofsson jumped up from his seat. "I want Aimo to see he has a family with all of us."

"Great idea, Magnus," Gretha answered. "We intended to do some planning for the wedding anyway. I don't see why we couldn't do that right here."

Aimo burst through the door excitedly, his bowl brimming with anemones. "Look how many," Aimo said. "Every place there's green grass, there are flowers."

Gretha accepted the bowl from the boy. "We'd like to come to your house this Sunday together with your sister and my girls. We'll all have dinner here, and you can show the girls where you picked flowers. Is that all right with you?"

Aimo's face brightened. He had accepted the fact that Anna was happy and safe, living with the Vahleen family. Much had happened in his life since he last saw his sister, and he was confused at the prospect of seeing her again, but Olofsson's broad smile signaled it was all right with him.

Aimo extended his hand to Gretha. "It's a contract."

"A contract it is," Gretha agreed. "We'll bring the food."

"Maybe Aimo and I can row out and catch some fresh fish for the smorgasbord," Olofsson added.

"We can go fishing in a *boat?*" Aimo's eyes widened.

"If it's in a boat, we've got some work to do," Olofsson answered.

"Speaking of work, I've got more forms to fill regarding the Blixdal's. We've got to get back now anyway," Sten said. "We'll see you on Sunday."

"See you on Sunday," Aimo shouted.

"It's a contract," Gretha laughed.

Aimo and Olofsson set to the task of preparing the cabin for visitors. They swept every corner of the house and hung bedding on lines to absorb the fragrance of the fresh air. Everything that could be dusted was wiped down with damp cloths, and nothing escaped their attention, including the rafters.

Down came fishing equipment, knickknacks, and crates filled with mouse-infested clothes. One of the crates still housed a mouse family, nested cozily in a pair of the old man's long johns. Olofsson carried the crate to a low-lying, steep-roofed shed, then handed his burden to Aimo and swung the door open.

Aimo's mouth opened wide in surprise. In front of him lay Olofsson's deeply shellacked rowboat, resting upside down on pine logs that elevated it off the damp ground. The boat measured four meters in length with a meter-wide beam that curved widely before pitching downward to a metal-reinforced midseam. Both ends of the vessel rose peculiarly into identical bows, similar to that of a canoe, and Aimo marveled at the expert craftsmanship. "Wow," he exhaled reverently at a loss to find more words to express his amazement.

To emphasize the rowboat's seaworthiness, Olofsson had painted a wild-looking white mule over the bow, its rear hooves kicking to the sky. Beneath the mule, Olofsson had printed the name *BRONCO* in white letters, providing a final touch.

"What a beautiful boat!" Aimo exclaimed admiringly.

"My father built it before I was born, so it's more than seventy-one years old. We have to seal the seams with tar before we can take it out. It's a big job, so let's get started."

Aimo placed the mouse family's crate in a corner of the shed, then helped Olofsson roll the boat into the sunshine. Olofsson fetched two pairs of heavy duty leather gloves and a pail from the shed containing a wooden trowel and several hunks of suet-treated pine tar. The remains of Aimo's Fauntleroy shirt hung from Olofsson's pocket. He put on a pair of gloves and handed the second pair to Aimo.

"Put these on and fill the pail about three quarters full with hot coals from the fireplace."

Aimo returned with the pail of coals and watched the old man demonstrate the application of heated pine tar into the seams of a boat. Aimo understood the task immediately, and they both set to working tar into the seams, repeating the motion continually until a seam was filled with the molten paste. The trowel scraped excesses from the wood surface; and, with the tar still warm, they towel-wiped the wood clean. When the exterior was complete, they righted the boat and climbed inside.

The warm May sun quickly heated the interior of the rowboat, and soon, Aimo and Olofsson shed their shirts. When the task was completed, the sun had dropped low on the horizon. They pushed *Bronco* onto the lake, and the cold water hardened the tar paste into a watertight seal almost instantly.

"That was a lot of work," Aimo said.

"Hard work makes the rewards greater," Olofsson recited. "Look how beautiful she looks."

Olofsson scanned the northern horizon where an extraordinary sunset reflected colorfully on the still waters. The early evening sun tilted northward with each passing day, returning life-giving light to the northern latitudes. Each new day was brighter than its predecessor. The white landscape rapidly replaced with vanguard patches of green from new grasses. Tiny blue and white anemones created a colorful carpet, and white birch trees sprouted ethereal colored buds of pastel green.

Almost magically, a landscape that for six months had lain beneath an unbroken mantle of white transformed itself into a north-woods scene of lakes, rivers, and forests, all within a two-week period. The phenomenal powers of nearly continual sunlight accelerated the floral growths. In two more weeks, wildflowers of every size and color would bloom to blanket the emerald green countryside in a dazzling sight. It was a time of new life. The midnight sun and its twenty-four hours of continual sunlight was fast approaching.

Aimo was impressed by what he had learned about boat care from Olofsson. In Finland, everyone sank their row boats in a lake for the winter, the cold water preserving the wood while expanding the seams. When boats were lifted from the water in the spring, the vessels were already watertight but appeared weatherworn. The superiority of Olofsson's method was measured by the gleaming result floating majestically in front of them. Aimo threw an arm around the old man's waist, and they stood together admiring the wonderful boat until the *Bronco* became a dark silhouette against the blood-orange sky.

"Listen, Grandpa!" Aimo said. He turned to face the southern sky. "Over there! Can you hear them?"

"I don't hear so good. What's out there?" Olofsson asked.

"Geese! Listen! The geese are comin' back."

Aimo pointed in the direction of the sound, and Olofsson followed his gesture. Columns of high-flying geese, each group flying at a different altitude, followed their own peculiar V formation heading toward Lake Valdemaren. They descended to the water by the hundreds with a cacophony of excited calls reaching a crescendo as they splash landed.

"That's the official sign of spring," Aimo said.

"I still think it's snow falling from my roof," Olofsson joked.

"Even more official than flowers?" Aimo continued.

"Nope! It's still the snow on my roof."

"You know when it's officially, officially spring?" Aimo asked. "It's when we go fishing in a boat." He pointed in the direction of the *Bronco.*

"Well, boy! Let's get something to eat and get some early sleep. If spring is goin' fishing in a boat, then it's gonna officially, officially start tomorrow."

Aimo awakened with first rays of morning light. Olofsson snored peacefully, but as far as Aimo was concerned, the time for fishing had arrived. He prepared a porridge breakfast and a pot of coffee before shaking Olofsson awake.

"Get dressed, Grandpa," Aimo announced. "It's time."

"Did you make breakfast yet?" Olofsson asked sleepily, hoping the boy had not so that he could stay in bed a while longer.

"Everything's ready. C'mon, get up," Aimo's voice was eager.

Aimo sat at the back of the *Bronco,* preparing the fishing poles as Olofsson rowed. Billows of dense mist hovered over the entire lake, and Aimo cast a wary eye at the cold, enveloping gray mass.

"Do you know where we're going?" Aimo asked.

"Sure," Olofsson replied without breaking his rhythm. "We're gonna go around the point. There's a sandbar above a drop-off along that whole edge where we should find some good walleyes. We'll use those spinners and white jig rigs."

Olofsson turned the boat when he judged they had passed the rocky point of the small peninsula. The old man stopped rowing and peered down into the clear water. Satisfied there were no rocks, he resumed his course in the dense mist. Suddenly the plaintive eerie call of a nearby loon broke the silence of the lake, and Olofsson dug the oars in the water to stop the forward motion of the boat.

"Damn!" Olofsson muttered. "Scared the hell out of me. I thought we hit a rock."

"It's only a loon," Aimo answered.

"I know it's only a loon. I'm just glad it's not a rock. I'll betcha we'll hear another one answering him," Olofsson promised.

"How do you know that?" Aimo asked.

"They're always in pairs. They call to each other so they don't get lost." Almost on cue, the call of a second loon answered from a distance. "See what I mean? In a few minutes, this mist is gonna burn off, and we'll see 'em swimming next to each other."

Olofsson stopped rowing and reached for his fishing rod. "OK, Aimo. Drop in your line. It's about five or six meters deep. Keep the lure bouncing on the bottom."

Aimo lowered the lure into the dark water before Olofsson had finished his instructions. Finally, he was fishing with the gift Olofsson had given him. Once again, he admired the smooth working function of the equipment as the line slipped effortlessly from the spool. When the lure touched the sandy bottom, Aimo snapped the drag lock on. If line were to leave the reel now, it was because a fish was pulling it off. Aimo was impressed. Six meters of line had left the reel before it touched bottom just as Olofsson had told him.

The cold swirling gray mist enveloped them. There was no sign of land or sky in sight. The air was still, and no waves were striking the shore that he could hear. Yet the old man knew exactly where they were. "*How does he do that?*" Aimo wondered. Meanwhile, Olofsson repeatedly snapped the tip of his baited fishing rod diagonally over the water.

Minutes passed, and finally the veiled form of the sun became visible through the gray overcast. It warmed the air in minutes, lifting the mist entirely, leaving pockets of white fog to drift over the water until they too dissipated. Olofsson had rowed them into a large bay, positioning them just off a rocky ledge. The boat drifted slowly; and as Olofsson predicted, the two loons swam side by side, a short distance away. Suddenly, Olofsson snapped back on his rod and released a noise from his open mouth, a combination of animal growl and orgasmic pleasure.

"Aaarrrggggghhhh! Fish on!" he shouted. Olofsson reeled steadily as the tapered end of the rod quivered into a bow. Aimo stood up to look, but Olofsson barked at him to stay still.

"Walleyes swim in schools. There're more down there," he said. He brought the fish to the surface and scooped it up with a long-handled net.

"The captain always catches the first fish on my boat," Olofsson boasted.

"How big do you think he is?" Aimo asked.

"A kilo. Maybe a kilo and a half. Good eating size. Let's see if we can get a few more."

Aimo's rod tip snapped downward even as he admired Olofsson's catch. Unskilled with the new rod, Aimo allowed the fish to run as it pulled lengths of line from the reel in its panic to reach deeper water.

"Watch your line, Aimo. Don't let it touch the boat or it'll break. Tighten the drag, and let him fight the rod." Olofsson issued his instructions rapidly, and Aimo responded to each one of them. He tightened the drag, and his rod tip dipped into the lake, reacting as Aimo had dreamed it would. Gradually he reeled the tiring fish to the surface. Aimo netted a walleye twice the size of the one Olofsson had brought in earlier, and his excitement was out of control.

"Wow! Look at the size of him! The captain may catch the first fish, but I'll catch the biggest," Aimo shouted.

"We'll see about that," Olofsson challenged, unhooking the catch. He sent it flopping to the bottom of the boat to join its companion.

The fishing continued at a hectic pace until after an hour, two dozen walleyes lay in the bottom of the boat. Then, as suddenly as it began, the school of walleyes disappeared. Olofsson allowed fifteen minutes of fruitless fishing to pass, then announced they had caught enough fish for the day.

"Do you like smoked fish?" Olofsson asked.

"Sure," Aimo replied.

"Well, let's get this bunch home and stick 'em in my smoker. It'll take about an hour. They should be ready by the time your sister and the Vahleens show up."

"Can't we try just a while longer?" Aimo begged. "I want to see if we can catch a pike."

"Now's not a good time for 'em. They're all up the streams spawning in the bogs."

Aimo surveyed the wide bay. The mouth of a small river poured into the lake a short distance in front of them, surrounded by a heavy growth of reeds. It appeared to be a perfect pike habitat. "Can we try just one time over there?" Aimo pointed toward the reeds hopefully.

"OK!" Olofsson said. "Put on a wire leader 'cause a pike will bite right through this line. Use both poles. You'll double your chances."

"Don't you want to fish?" Aimo asked.

"I'm going to row. We'll troll along that edge of grass out there."

Aimo replaced the spinner-jig lures with the jointed balsa wood plugs that he had made, preceded by a length of flexible wire. Olofsson rowed, and Aimo allowed first one and then the other lure to drift behind the boat, keeping a rod on either side of him. When the lures were some twenty-five meters behind the boat, he locked on the reel brakes. The lines tightened as Olofsson continued rowing, and the wobbling plugs dove beneath the surface, causing both rod tips to vibrate from the wiggling action of the lures.

Olofsson dug the oars through the current caused by the entering stream, bringing them into a parallel course alongside the reed patch. Aimo held the rods anxiously, switching his focus from one tippet to the other. Ahead of them, a gaggle of geese launched themselves noisily into the air to graze on new grasses growing rapidly in the nearby meadows. Aimo followed the flight of the birds as they formed their familiar V-shaped column.

Suddenly, the rod in Aimo's right hand bent backward into a deep bow, and the reel brake clicked loudly as line left the spool. Olofsson dug his oars into the water, bringing the *Bronco* to a stop. He grabbed the free rod and reeled in the lure to prevent the lines from tangling.

"Do you have him?" Olofsson asked.

"I dunno," Aimo answered. "I think I'm stuck."

Olofsson rowed backward toward the snag.

"Reel in, Aimo! . . . Keep the line tight! . . . Do you feel anything yet?"

Olofsson followed the action on the tippet of the rod, still arced in a deep bow. Then suddenly, the tippet throbbed several times before bending savagely into the water. "A Swedish crocodile," Olofsson shouted. "You've got a big one on."

The pike's method of feeding was to lie in ambush among the grasses, its large eyes ever aware of the flashing scales of prey fish swimming near the surface. Once it discovered its quarry, it stalks it silently, closing the distance on its unwary victim. Then it attacks in a flash, snatching prey, varying from fish to young water fowl, within its razor-sharp, tooth-filled jaws. The predator's dim brain that had just grabbed Aimo's lure finally announced the thing fastened in its mouth was not a food item. In a panic, it raced for the safety of the reed bed.

"Yeeow!" Aimo yelled. "You're right. I've got a big one!"

As the line curved toward the shoreline, Aimo leaned back on the rod heavily, and the fish reacted to the pressure. It rushed upward to the surface and vaulted itself into the air in an explosive plume of water. The pike was huge, at least a meter long and weighing well over ten kilos. Its gill plates flared widely as it shook its head violently. With a loud snap, it flung the top half of Aimo's lure free from its mouth, then crashed back into the lake, leaving a swirl of turbulent water in its wake.

Aimo's line lay limply on the lake's surface as the boy trembled uncontrollably, his eyes fixed to the spot where the largest pike he had ever seen in his life had disappeared.

"That's a shame," Olofsson said. "He was a monster. It's good to get rid of those because they'll take baby ducks and geese."

Aimo was crushed. He said nothing and slowly reeled in the slack line. He inspected the lure and saw that the deeply gashed wobbler had snapped off at its waist. He held the lure for Olofsson to see.

"He cut the wire!" Aimo said in shock.

Olofsson inspected the lure, fingering the wire Aimo had used to create the jointed wobbling plug. The huge fish had twisted the metal to its breaking point when shaking its massive head. The weakened joint broke when the pike left the water.

"That's my fault," Olofsson said. "I should have told you to use flexible piano wire."

"I'm gonna get him the next time," Aimo added with a defiant promise.

"The next time it is, Aimo. Now let's get back. We have some work to do."

Aimo gave a backward glance at the reed-covered shoreline, growing more distant as Olofsson rowed away.

"I'm really gonna get him the next time, I promise."

Olofsson opened the rusty metal door to a small mound-shaped building made of river stone sealed with sod. Constructed by his father many years earlier, the seventy-five-year-old smoker worked as well as it had when it was first built. To enter, a tall man had to crawl in on his knees, and Olofsson knelt on the dank earthen floor as Aimo arrived with the cleaned walleyes.

"Are they salted?" Olofsson asked, his voice muffled within the chamber.

"All ready," Aimo answered.

Olofsson took the fish and placed them on metal racks that stretched over a pit dug within the center of the smoker. He ignited a stack of fast-burning, split birch wood then flung juniper tree shavings into the flame, filling the mound instantly with billowing, pungently sweet smoke.

Olofsson backed out of the smoker coughing loudly.

"I brought soap and towels down by the boat, Grandpa," Aimo announced, and Olofsson followed the boy to the water's edge. They pulled off their clothes and stepped into the warm shallows. Aimo stared through the mask he had carved from the soapy lather on his face. "Ready?" he shouted, then dove out into the lake, leaving a trail of soap bubbles to rinse from his body.

"Fee Fon!" Olofsson shouted loudly then hurled himself into the lake. Olofsson's head broke the surface in a swarm of bubbles. "Shit! It's cold," he yelled, swimming rapidly back into the shallows. Aimo was right behind, a towel draped around his shoulders, and handed a towel to Olofsson. They nearly completed drying themselves at water's edge when Constable Vahleen's voice called from the forest road.

"They're here!" Olofsson shouted, leading the boy in an all-out sprint to the cabin. Olofsson and Aimo dressed frantically as the sounds of approaching boots trudging through the loamy path announced the arrival of their guests.

"Aimo! Aimo!" Anna shouted.

Her little girl's voice penetrated the cabin, stopping the boy in his tracks. It was a familiar sound, one that had always irritated him when they were together at Lake Jarvii. Now it sounded musical. A plethora of confusing images flooded his mind, and he was uncertain what to do next. Completely flustered, he looked to the old man for something to say, but Olofsson shrugged his shoulders and remained silent. Then, as though receiving some unseen bolt of wisdom, the boy erupted.

"It's my sister!" Aimo exclaimed sprinting for the door. "Anna! Anna!" he shouted. He ran pell-mell from the cabin, then came to a sudden stop in front of the group of visitors who faced him.

Anna stood a step ahead of the others. She was dressed identically to Meggan and Lisa, her grown-out hair held in place with a wide bow. She stood in a pair of mud-splotched yellow rubber boots and a new velvet-collared spring coat. All three girls carried small bouquets of freshly picked flowers held primly in front of them.

Constable and Gretha Vahleen held a large wicker basket of food. Next to them Pontilius and Solveig smiled broadly.

Anna approached and offered her flowers. "These are for you," she said, and Aimo accepted the bouquet.

Meggan followed quickly with her bouquet. "These are for you too," she added.

"Thank you," Aimo said. He stood rooted to the spot, a bunch of flowers in each hand.

"Give your brother a hug," Gretha instructed, and the little girl threw her arms around her brother's waist. She clutched him tightly, then released her grip when Meggan stepped forward. Meggan looked into Aimo's face.

"I'm glad you're not dead," she said, bringing a loud round of laughter from the adults. Undaunted, Meggan threw her arms around Aimo and hugged him dearly.

"Welcome, everybody," Olofsson shouted. "Come on inside."

Gretha entered the cabin first. Immediately, she and Solveig set to the task of preparing a smorgasbord on the dining table.

"Let's put some spring music on your Victrola," Pontilius said, and the room filled with requests.

"Try the *Pastoral Suite* by Lars-Erik Larsson," Pontilius suggested.

"How about Tchaikovsky's 'Waltz of the Flowers'?" Gretha called.

"You can't do 'Waltz of the Flowers.' It's too synonymous with Christmas," Pontilius corrected

"But it's flowers," Gretha protested, preparing the table.

"Pontilius is right!" Olofsson announced. He enthusiastically dug through his stack of records. "Look out the window at those kids and tell me if that's not what Grieg had in mind when he wrote the 'Spring Passage' in the *Peer Gynt* suite."

"Just look at them," Gretha called.

The group assembled around Olofsson's curtainless window, watching the children romp around the cabin in an impromptu game of tag. Someone discovered a new patch of wildflowers, and the children descended upon them, picking in a frenzy. Meggan wove a mixture of flowers into a small wreath and placed it on Aimo's head. Her craft was an instant success. Amid a continual commotion, she taught everyone the art of laurel-weaving with great sincerity.

Within the cabin, Edvard Grieg's symphonic depiction of spring captured the unbridled joy of the human spirit. After emerging from six long months of cold and darkness, every living thing in and around Olofsson's home seemed to revel in the returning warmth of sun, light, and life.

Chapter Fifty

Pontilius pedaled his bicycle furiously, focusing on Solveig's rump in front of him and oblivious of the leather thongs binding the prosthesis to his right thigh. Her long legs pumped rhythmically, but try as he might, the man could not overtake her lead. Solveig turned down the gravel lane leading to the Vahleen household, a trail of long blond hair streaming in the breeze behind her. Their bicycles skimmed swiftly beneath branches of blossoming apple trees, humming with the drone of hordes of honeybees busily flitting among the pinkish white flowers. Solveig reached the front of the house first and braked to a dusty stop.

"The war is over!" she shouted happily to whoever was inside the house.

Pontilius skidded to a stop beside her, cupped his hands to his mouth, and called out, "The Americans have landed in France!"

The door of the house opened. Sten Vahleen stepped out, his somber expression a contrast to the two lovers beaming at him. Pontilius spoke first.

"We just heard on the shortwave the Americans have invaded France. The war will soon be over."

"Not soon enough," Gretha answered, emerging sadly from the house. She held a lengthy yellow paper in her hand, and her eyes glistened with tears. "Anna's parents are dead," she declared and offered the telegram to Pontilius.

"How horrible," Solveig exclaimed. She stepped away from her bicycle and allowed it to clatter to the gravel, then embraced her friend as Sten offered his hand to Pontilius.

"Hello, Fredrik. What did you say about the war?"

"The news just came over the BBC. Allied forces are in Normandy." Pontilius's voice trailed off as he became fully engrossed in the telegram. The paper contained a list of people killed in the area surrounding Jyväskylä,

Finland. The Red Cross message simply stated the region had been overrun by Russians. Pontilius looked up. "Have you told Anna?"

"No," Sten replied. "This just arrived."

"Meggan has the girls out gathering flowers," Gretha added.

"I'd better tell Olofsson," Sten said somberly.

"I'd like to go with you," Pontilius volunteered.

"So would I," Solveig joined in.

"Why don't you all go?" Gretha suggested. "I'll tell Anna. It will be good for her to have the girls close by."

Pontilius turned to Sten. "Let's try to arrive together at Olofsson's cabin. I want to show him the telegram."

Olofsson stood bare-chested and deeply tanned in the midst of his potato patch, admiring the neat rows of flowering plants. His trousers were stuffed into a pair of black knee-high rubber boots. Beads of perspiration ran down his brow and dripped off the end of his nose. He dug his gnarled fingers gently into the warm earth beneath a plant to expose the developing tubers. Satisfied he could soon begin his harvest, he tenderly covered the new potatoes with soil, salivating at the thought of enjoying his favorite dish of pickled herring served with dill-flavored new potatoes. The sound of Vahleen's approaching motorcycle drew his attention to the road, and Olofsson discovered the constable was accompanied by the two bicyclists.

"Hello," Olofsson shouted and waived at the approaching trio. He made his way through his potato patch, carefully stepping over the rows of plants as Vahleen pulled up. Moments later, he was joined by Solveig and Pontilius.

"Hello!" Sten answered.

"You all look pretty warm. Anyone want to join me in a dip?"

"No thanks, Magnus. We've come with bad news," Vahleen answered. "Is Aimo around?"

Olofsson did not find a smile among the familiar faces. Something was obviously wrong, and Olofsson's first jolting thought was that he was losing the boy. The grin left the old man's face. "He took the boat early this morning to go fishing," he answered. His heart pounded strangely.

"His parents were killed. We just got a telegram," Vahleen stated.

"Bastards!" Olofsson spat out the word. "How? Germans? Russians?" He dropped wearily onto a stump and cupped his hands to his face. "What's the difference? Bastards! All of 'em."

"We'd like to be with you when he hears the news. Aimo will need some support." Vahleen offered.

"All right," Olofsson agreed, "but let me be the one to tell him."

"Good enough," Vahleen answered.

"Is there anything I can do?" Solveig asked eagerly.

"Give him some motherly hugs. I still remember my mother's hugs. Nothin' in the world like 'em."

"I know," Solveig answered solemnly.

Just then, Aimo's voice rang out loudly from the lake, his call booming from the bay behind the rocky point.

"Hey, Grandpa! Grandpa! I got him," Aimo shouted.

The rowboat rapidly rounded the point, with Aimo pulling mightily at the oars. The *Bronco* moved swiftly toward the beach and Olofsson led the group to the water's edge. Aimo dug his oars into the water and allowed the craft to glide into the shallows. He got up excitedly and maneuvered himself to the back of the boat. Grinning broadly, he lifted a large pike, still very much alive, beneath a mound of iridescent green seaweed. Aimo cradled the fish in his arms, its toothy mouth gulping air.

"I got him by the weeds. It took me an hour to get him into the boat."

With considerable effort, Aimo held the fish up proudly. He was unable to contain his excitement and oblivious to the fact the fish was covering his arms and abdomen with its slimy, protective mucous.

Aimo was particularly aware of Solveig's presence and took the opportunity to impress her whenever possible. Now, with the trophy pike in his grasp, he especially wanted some recognition. Solveig obliged.

"He's beautiful, Aimo. Don't let him bite you."

"He won't bite me," Aimo scoffed. "Whew! He's heavy, at least ten kilos." Aimo turned his attention to Olofsson and addressed him by his first name.

"Magnus, can you help me get him on shore?"

"Sure, lay him on the bottom of the boat first and cover him with wet seaweed. That'll quiet him down."

Olofsson stepped into the shallows and pulled the *Bronco* onto the sandy shore while Aimo followed the old man's instructions.

The boy regarded the slime on his arms with disgust. He was dressed in shorts, his tanned skin glistening with a deep bronze color. His sinewy frame foretold the athletic body that was to come when he reached manhood. The boy stepped onto the rear seat of the boat, and dove into the deeper water, then swam back to shore. Dripping wet, he stepped up to the group, a huge smile etched on his face.

"Hi!" Aimo said and was met with a chorus of greetings while rubbing water from his eyes. Something is wrong, Aimo thought. Everyone looked at him with unsmiling expressions.And they were all strangely quiet. "What's wrong?" Aimo asked.

"Come over," Olofsson invited. Aimo walked over to the old man.

"Are you cold?" Olofsson asked, knowing the boy was not. He rubbed the boy's shoulders, and Aimo became alarmed. Pulling away from the old man, Aimo asked the question again, this time with authority.

"What's wrong?" he demanded.

"Constable Vahleen came over . . . and he asked . . . Herr Pontilius and . . . ," Olofsson stammered, became silent, then turned to Vahleen for help, but it was Pontilius who stepped forward.

"Constable Vahleen received a telegram from Finland, Aimo. Your parents have been killed."

Everyone grew silent as all eyes settled on Aimo, awaiting his reaction. Olofsson's heart ached. Not knowing what he should do, he stood impotently, still looking on sadly. The boy stared at the ground, his head shaking slowly side to side.

Are you sure?" Aimo asked, his voice nearly a whisper.

"I have the telegram here, Aimo. Quite a number of people were on the list. You may want to read it." Pontilius handed the boy the paper.

Aimo peered through the list and stopped when he reached his parents' names. He gave the telegram to his teacher and returned his stare of the ground. Pontilius made an effort to sound hopeful.

"There could be a mistake, Aimo. Things are very confused in Finland now."

"There's no mistake," Aimo said. "My aunt and cousins are on that list too. So is my grandmother. I saw them all get killed."

Solveig moved to embrace the boy, but Aimo turned away and waded into the lake. He reached the rowboat and looked at Pontilius.

"I knew it was going to happen. I told them I wanted to stay and help, but nobody listened to me. I knew it was going to happen."

Aimo jumped into the boat and stared at the huge pike, its eyes wide and watery. The fish gulped for air pathetically. Aimo lifted it from the bottom of the boat and dropped it over the side. The fish lay near the surface for several seconds before sensing its freedom. It gulped great mouths of lake water over its gills, allowing the oxygen-rich liquid to revive its nervous system. Then it slowly sank and swam away.

Aimo dug the oars into the lake and began rowing furiously toward the distant shoreline. Olofsson shouted, "Aimo! Come back!"

"Let him be," Pontilius said, understanding the boy's pain well. He took the old man's arm. "Give him his space. He knows you care for him. He'll be back."

"We'll wait together with you," Solveig volunteered.

Olofsson watched the rowboat grow smaller as it moved away and shook his head sadly. "He didn't even cry. After all he's been through, he never cries." Olofsson leaned against a nearby white birch tree. "If it's all the same to you, I'd rather be alone with the boy when he comes back." Olofsson regarded his friends sadly, not wanting to offend. "Please, if it's all the same to you," he repeated.

The time of the midnight sun had come, its glow of never-ending sunset rolling across the northern sky until it lifted again into a new sunrise and a new day. Olofsson sat alone, his back against the birch tree, staring at the expansive beauty of Lake Valdemaren. Families of water birds swam to and fro, exuberant participants in the return of life to the north country. The high-pitched peeping of ducklings and goslings mingled with the mature calls of adult birds. Overhead, dozens of newly arrived swallows swept across the golden sky.

Olofsson guessed the time to be near midnight when he finally heard the squeak of the rowboat's oarlocks. Aimo had been taught to splash water on them to prevent the noise, but the boy had more important things on his mind now. The boat drifted silently to shore, and Olofsson silently waded into the water, grabbed the bow and pulled the *Bronco* into the shallows. He tied the rope to a birch tree and waded back to Aimo. The boy remained seated in the boat, his eyes fastened on the glowing horizon.

"Why doesn't the sun go down in the summer?" Aimo asked.

"Same reason it doesn't come up in the winter," Olofsson answered. "Something about the earth's axis . . ." Olofsson caught himself. He climbed into the rowboat and sat opposite the boy. "The world's a fun place sometimes, full of life and light, and sometimes it's shit."

"I still want to go back," Aimo said, fixing his eyes on Olofsson.

"I made you a promise, son. I'm gonna take you back." Olofsson extended his right hand to Aimo. "It's a contract!"

Aimo took the old man's hand in his and nodded silently.

Aimo returned to the cabin, climbed into bed, and retrieved the military medal beneath his pillow.

"I'm gonna throw this damn thing in the lake," Aimo declared angrily.

"I don't think you should, Aimo. Remember how important you told me it was? Sometimes, we do things without thinking, only to regret it later. Why don't you put it away for a while. Then if you want to get rid of it, I think I'd like to have it. You know, like a reminder of our friendship."

Aimo gave the proposition his deepest thought, then nodded and returned the medal to its place beneath his pillow. He lay on the bed, his back to the room, and curled his knees to his chest.

"Do you want something to eat?" Olofsson asked.

"No, thank you," Aimo replied quietly.

"Do you feel like talking?" Olofsson's tone was hopeful.

"No," Aimo said without emotion. Nothing more was said that evening.

Two weeks went by, and still the boy never discussed the event of learning that his parents had been killed, and the old man avoided talking to Aimo about it. Whatever emotions Aimo felt when he rowed off alone and heartbroken, he now kept to himself.

Aimo's silence on the matter frustrated Olofsson. He accepted the behavior with understanding but was prepared to listen whenever Aimo was ready. The boy seemed normal otherwise, continuing with his life with two exceptions: Aimo used the term *grandpa* exclusively when addressing the old man, and he no longer went off alone for any length of time. Olofsson wished for something that would crumble the wall Aimo had built around himself.

If he would just cry and release the sorrow locked inside of him, Olofsson thought. He was unaware of the dramatic events soon to come that would finally lead to such a release and of the part he himself was to play in it.

Chapter Fifty-one

Midsummer dawn swept over the Swedish countryside like a magic elixir, eradicating the normally shy behavior of the populace. No other holiday in the calendar year held as much gaiety or freedom from social discipline as did the long-awaited national holiday. Midsummer Eve, the one day of the year when inhibitions were set aside, simply to celebrate the joy of being alive.

The next twenty-four hours would bring couples together to sing, drink, and participate in an athletic dance called hambo, followed ultimately by passionate, lusty lovemaking. The infectious upbeat music played by various fiddlers and fifers seemed to be inspired by the forest god Pan himself. Even the most timid of souls took part, well fortified with extra amounts of aquavit, just to get into the swing of things.

Olofsson awoke and sprang from his bed with a burst of energy. He rushed out to the lake and howled wildly with a yell that echoed to the distant shoreline before hurling himself naked into the chilly waters of Lake Valdemaren.

The startling noise brought Aimo to the window. Olofsson splashed in the water like a playful otter. He was obviously having a lot of fun, and the boy decided to join him. He ran to the water's edge, tore off his nightclothes, and swam rapidly to the old man with whooping shouts of his own. After some horseplay, Olofsson pulled himself from the lake and improvised a bare-butt jig back to the cabin. Aimo mimicked his every move.

Over breakfast, Olofsson decided to expound on the significance of the midsummer holiday since Aimo had known nothing like it in Finland. Olofsson's countenance took on a quizzical expression as he decided on a new tack to explain why the entire country behaved as it did.

"Remember back in March when this place was covered with snow? It was bone cold, but when we stood against the barn in the sun, it was warm?"

Aimo nodded his head that he remembered, and Olofsson continued, "Well, birds were above us, in the eves, getting warm like we were. The males had bright attractive colors. Even though the females looked plain, they had something else goin' for them . . . hormones! The males could smell 'em, and it made them go crazy . . . then . . . well . . . the males and females . . . they had *their* midsummer celebration . . . so the females could lay eggs."

Aimo was totally confused. "You mean everybody makes babies in midsummer?"

Olofsson got up from the table and crossed the room to the clothes closet he and Aimo had made during the winter. He pulled two folk costumes from their hangers and handed the smaller costume to Aimo, all the while giving thought to Aimo's question.

"Put these on, and let's get going, or we'll be late for your teacher's wedding. Solveig brought these especially for your part of the ceremony."

Aimo followed Olofsson's instructions. He pulled on a pair of black woolen knickers. Then came a black woolen vest worn over a white long-sleeved shirt. He completed the outfit with black knee-high stockings, cinched to the knickers by two spectacular scarlet-tasseled garters.

"These look funny," Aimo said, kicking up his feet.

"No more funny than mine," Olofsson answered. "How do I look?"

"Like a male bird smelling hormones," Aimo laughed.

"You got that right. Let's go! We've only got half an hour to get there," Olofsson said, hurrying out to the *Bronco*.

They rowed rhythmically, side by side with steady strokes, gliding smoothly over Lake Valdemaren. They passed a series of islands that marked the way to Grönö.

"About makin' babies," Olofsson said, "female birds find male birds with the best colors and send the male signals. That's why us guys dress like this. Females see us, then they make us chase after them."

"And make babies!" Aimo declared.

"Not right away. We'll chase a girl because she's pretty. She knows we're chasin', and maybe she'll let us catch her or . . . maybe she won't. Same with birds."

"That's how they make babies?" Aimo was confused.

"No! Not yet. While we're chasin' her, she's got one eye peeled to see if there's somebody else out there that she likes better. The females buzz around the new guy to see if he gets interested. Then things get complicated."

"That's not fair. If you saw her first, she's supposed to go with you."

"That's what makes it interesting. Because while you're chasin' her, you've got your own eyes peeled. Maybe there are more attractive females flyin' around. Then everything gets to be fun."

"Sounds like a lot of work," Aimo said. "I'd rather go fishin'."

"You'll see when it happens to you. I've already seen how that Vahleen girl looks at you."

"No, she doesn't," Aimo protested . "We just pick flowers."

"You have time. Look over there!"

Olofsson pointed to an island barely large enough for someone to have built a summer house. A long blue-and-yellow streamer, displaying the Swedish colors, twisted gently on a flagpole as a group of revelers chased one another on a well-trimmed lawn. Peels of laughter and shrieks of delight erupted as a young man caught up to a buxom young woman. They kissed furiously before falling to the grass in a tangle of arms and legs. Olofsson had a huge grin on his face.

"Now that's the way to catch a girl," Olofsson said. Then he turned serious. "But it's not the way to keep a girl. Something has to happen inside of you, here." He held his hand to his heart. "It's called love. You feel funny and sometimes, even a little sick."

Aimo studied the old man's face, but Olofsson was too occupied with the couple on the grass to continue the conversation. He had come to know the old man well, better in fact than anyone he had ever known. Olofsson certainly seemed to be acting strangely. There definitely was something special about this day, and the boy believed he was beginning to feel it himself.

The *Bronco* reached the shallows of Grönö Island among a group of similar craft already moored. They jumped ashore and lashed the rope to a small birch tree. A crowd of people on a hill had gathered in a clearing around the bride whose bright white dress shone in splendid contrast to the red and green folk costumes of the other women. The skirts of their woolen jumpers billowed out at the slightest turn. Long sleeved white blouses, scarlet sashes, and white kerchiefs completed their colorful attire. Aimo noticed the men in the group wore outfits identical to his own.

A group of fiddlers struck up a lively tune, and Aimo looked to Olofsson for instruction. "What do we do now, Grandpa?"

"Well! We'd better get up there, 'cause the march to the church is about to start," Olofsson replied.

Meggan's voice rang out above the revelry. "Aimo!" she shouted. She ran down the hill to greet him, her knee-length pink dress rustling with each fluttering stride. Aimo stood mesmerized by the sight.

White bows were bound to her wrists that matched those at her ankles. White patent leather shoes completed her formal outfit. But something else caught Aimo's attention. She wore a crown of white daisies on her head, and her lips showed a blush of color from her mother's borrowed lipstick. His eyes fastened on her flaxen blond hair, which swung freely beneath her flower crown. He had never before seen her like this. Meggan was absolutely beautiful!

"You're almost too late," she said breathlessly. She handed the spellbound boy one of two small bouquets of bluebells. Then she placed a wreath of newly opened green birch leaves on his head. "You have to wear this," she instructed.

Aimo stood quietly, too enchanted by the girl's proximity to speak. Impatient with his inaction, Meggan took the boy's hand and pulled him up the hill while excitedly chattering instructions.

"We have to be in the front of the procession, and we have to skip step the whole time," she said while demonstrating it for him.

The fiddlers' strains of "Entrance to a Summer Meadow" by Jamtland's own composer, Wilhelm Peterson-Berger, signaled the wedding party to begin its march toward Grönö church. Exhilarated, Aimo remained firmly fastened to Meggan's hand, and he skipped happily behind a bevy of fiddlers.

"We have to do this sometimes," Meggan instructed, and she pirouetted without releasing her grip of his hand. "If you do it a lot, everything spins around. It's fun!" she laughed, then pirouetted three times in a row. By the time the procession came to a halt, Aimo had become as dizzy as Meggan.

Gul-Brit Davour, the newly appointed reverend of Nilstad church, welcomed the wedding group when it reached the rustic red-timbered church on the crest of Grönö Island. Clouds of pink Cecil Bruner roses fulfilled their annual promise and embraced the wooden trellises against the building, filling the air with a deliciously sweet aroma.

Anna and Lisa, dressed as identical twins, held small bouquets of bluebells and joined Aimo and Meggan at the front of the procession. The fascinated girls focused on the little white veil over the bride's face and strained to see if they could see her eyes. Pontilius stood tall and straight in his black tails, and Aimo was pleased to see the bridegroom wearing a wreath of birch leaves on his head identical to his own.

At the conclusion of the short ceremony, the bride and groom exchanged rings, placing simple gold bands on each other's fingers. Then Pontilius lifted Solveig's veil from her face and kissed her firmly on the lips.

Meggan reached for Aimo's hand and squeezed it tightly in hers. He reacted to the pressure and shot a quick glance at Meggan who smiled back coyly. Aimo's face grew warm. The church filled with applause at the kiss, and a group of Pontilius's friends shouted his name.

"Fredrik! Fredrik! Fredrik!" they chanted, and Pontilius responded by kissing Solveig passionately. The guests erupted in lusty applause.

"Did you ever do that?" Meggan whispered.

"No!" Aimo replied quickly.

"Do you want to?" she asked again.

"OK!" Aimo said. He innocently moved his face toward hers, but Meggan pushed him back peremptorily and he recoiled in confusion.

"Not here!" Meggan whispered urgently. "Only the bride and bridegroom can do that inside a church. We'll do it outside when we're dancing."

"I don't know how to dance either," Aimo admitted worriedly.

"It's easy! I'll show you," Meggan said confidently. The boy was hers, and she happily squeezed his hand again.

The wedding procession moved toward a green meadow where a group of men raised a large midsummer pole bedecked with wildflowers. Fiddlers played gay music as well-wishers cast wildflowers at the newlyweds while throngs of revelers danced around the decorated pole.

Meggan cupped her hands behind Aimo's neck and instructed the boy to place his hands on her waist. She tapped her foot to the ground, synchronizing her step to the throbbing beat of the hambo music. Aimo felt her body tense to the rhythm.

"Hold tight and follow me We're going to dance . . . now!" she shouted.

Aimo was launched into a series of swiftly spinning circles. He caught a glimpse of Olofsson and a happy-faced, slightly overweight woman as he and Meggan whirled around the flower-decorated pole. The old man's fingers were buried in the woman's hips, and he stomped his foot into the turf. He spun his partner wildly around then kicked a leg high in the air. The scarlet tassel flailed wildly. The woman shrieked with delight before Olofsson led her into the next dizzying spin.

"I can do that," Aimo told Meggan. Up to then, she had been doing the leading.

"Do it!" Meggan shouted.

Aimo grasped the girl's waist tightly, stomped the ground, and kicked his tasseled knees to the skies, then swept the girl into the air so quickly he had not known he had done it. Meggan rewarded him with a loud screech.

Aimo felt the girl's body anticipate the move before being raised high into the air a second time.

"This is fun!" Aimo yelled, his foot stomping the ground.

"I told you it was," Meggan answered, allowing Aimo to fling her skyward once again.

Dance followed dance, accompanied by a continuing dissonance of fiddlers, laughter, shrieks, squeals, and nonstop gyrations. Aimo perspired through his shirt and desperately needed to quench his enormous thirst.

Meggan led him to a long smorgasbord table covered with an array of food. At either end were chilled bowls of wild berry punch. One, decorated with a large white bow, was surrounded by a cluster of adults who drank and laughed uninhibitedly, and Aimo again discovered Olofsson. This time he stood beside the plump lady, one arm fastened around her waist. In the other, he held a tall glass of punch, which he drained swiftly. The woman spoke animatedly to the group, which included Meggan's parents. They all burst into raucous laughter over something she told them.

"We can't drink that," Meggan indicated the ribbon-wrapped bowl. She offered Aimo a cup filled from the second punch bowl.

"The ribbon means there are spirits mixed in." She glanced over at her parents, satisfied to see they were very involved with their friends. Aimo drained the cup, refilled it, and offered it to Meggan.

The girl drank thirstily, smoothing the berry juice on her lips with her tongue. She returned the cup to Aimo.

"You have to do this," she said, moistening her lips.

"Why?" Aimo asked.

"So it will taste good when we kiss."

"When are we supposed to do that?" Aimo asked, but Meggan was interrupted before she could reply. She viewed three boys who dashed up to them with an acid stare.

Arne and Lenne raced up to Aimo breathlessly, calling out a series of queries. They were joined by a familiar face with an unforgettable nose. Mooseface! None of them had seen Aimo since his disappearance six months earlier and they fired their questions in a rapid-fire series of shouts.

"Aimo! How are you doing? I thought you were dead. What happened to the reverend? When are you gonna come back to school?"

Aimo was delighted to see his friends again but was unable to focus on any of the myriad of questions being hurled at him at one time. Even if he could, the happiness of once again seeing his friend from his carefree days of adventures in Finland filled him with unbridled joy. He launched himself at Mooseface and grasped him in a tight embrace. His old friend happily returned the hug.

"Where are you stayin'?" Aimo asked.

"With the Rydels. They own a bakery. I even work there. How about that?" Mooseface made no effort to hide his good fortune or the two partially eaten sausages he held in each hand. He flashed his somewhat whiter teeth.

"Want to go see somethin'?" Arne yelled loudly, a lascivious smile crossing his face.

Mooseface put his cupped hand to Aimo's ear, his sausage-filled fingers nearly on his friends face. "Some people are doin' it back over there," the boy whispered. He indicated a forested grove near the lake. "We're gonna watch." A huge grin appeared below his remarkable nose. Arne and Lenne smiled a smirk telling him they were ready to join in the devilment.

"He can't!" Meggan answered firmly. She grasped Aimo by the hand. "We have to stay here 'cause we're in the wedding party."

Aimo looked at Meggan. Her eyes fastened to his, unspoken promises transmitted by her gaze.

"I've got to stay in the wedding," Aimo said apologetically. A large smile lit up the girl's face.

"OK!" Mooseface shouted. "We'll see you later." The boys ran off in the direction of the grove.

Meggan kept Aimo's hand in hers. She led him away from the meadow and onto the woodchip-covered trail. Following a path that took them to a large bluff high above the lake, Meggan brought them to a stop. Taking his hands in hers, she entwined their fingers and pulled the boy closer to her.

"Are you sure you didn't do it before?" Meggan asked.

"I never," Aimo answered.

"OK! We have to do it like this," Meggan instructed. She leaned forward and offered the boy her lips.

"You have to keep your mouth like this. Then you wet your lips like this," she continued. Her tongue glided over the lipstick. "This will make our lips stick together. It's more fun like that."

Aimo leaned forward. "Did you ever do it?" He asked.

"Never. But I know a girl who did, and she told me. This is my very first time. Now, wet your lips . . . then . . . close your eyes . . . we'll lean forward at the same time, OK."

Aimo closed his eyes, moistened his lips, and flexed his face forward until he felt the gentle touch of Meggan's mouth on his. The girl pressed her lips tightly. Long seconds went by before Aimo dared to take a peek. Meggan's eyes remained closed, and she kept her head cocked to the side.

"When are we supposed to stop?" Aimo mumbled, his mouth still connected to hers. Meggan pulled her head back in shock.

"Don't you like it?" she asked.

"Yes! I like it a lot. But I don't know when we're supposed to stop."

"The girl is supposed to tell you when to stop. Now close your eyes, and do it again until I say stop."

Aimo closed his eyes, and he again felt Meggan's mouth contact his. This time he concentrated on her lips. He tasted the berry fruit drink and became aware of her warm breath as she exhaled softly through her nose. His fingers released their grip from hers and instinctively took hold of the girl's waist.

Something strange was happening. He felt funny and even a little sick, just as Olofsson had forecast. His mouth remained glued to Meggan's, and she kept her hands fastened to her side. Finally, she moved her face away. Aimo looked deeply into the most lovely set of blue eyes he had ever seen. The glow of the early evening sun, bathing the northern sky in an array of golden colors, framed Meggan's flushed face a bright scarlet. Aimo moved forward, eager to resume the new and wonderful experience and very ready for another kiss. Meggan moved away and regarded him coyly.

"I'll race you back," she shouted.

Meggan took off in the direction of the party, laughing loudly. Aimo raced right behind her in full pursuit. They reached the midsummer pole, and the fiddlers' music continued unabated. "We can dance this slow one," Meggan suggested.

Aimo returned his grip on Meggan's waist. She placed her hands on the boy's shoulders and led him into a gentle two-step. "My mother said that if you get your first ever kiss on midsummer, then that's who you'll marry," Meggan softly informed.

Aimo stopped dancing suddenly, his face desperately serious. He released his hold of the girl, then turned away wordlessly, walking swiftly down the hill toward the rowboat.

Meggan was both baffled and heartbroken. She watched the boy move steadily toward the lake, then kicked the ground angrily in frustration. Summoning her resolve, she walked purposefully down the slope to the moored boats and found Aimo sitting in the midsection of the *Bronco*, looking seaward.

Meggan stood silently at the shore for several seconds, gathering her thoughts.

"What did I say that was so wrong?" Meggan asked.

"Nothin'," Aimo said without turning his head.

"Would it be so bad to marry me?" she demanded, choking back the overpowering urge to cry.

"No," Aimo said tersely.

"Don't you even like me?" Meggan pleaded.

Aimo turned quickly and stood on the boat's seat. "Yes! I like you! I really like you a lot! That's the trouble. Every time I like somebody, something bad happens to them." Aimo returned to his seat and resumed facing the lake.

Meggan climbed into the boat and sat silently next to the boy. She put her arm around his shoulders and thought of something to say but was unable to find the proper words. They sat quietly beside each other, their eyes following the changing patterns of light reflecting on the mirrored surface of the lake. The rowboat stirred occasionally on gentle currents while fiddlers' music floated down from the meadow behind them, and calls from waterfowl echoed over the water.

Finally, Meggan broke the silence. For two hours, she dominated a conversation wherein she described her best friends, her favorite hobbies, her most anticipated events, and her interest to either become an architect or a super detective who solved incredible mysteries. When Aimo finally spoke, he admitted that he had given no thoughts at all to his future and could only vaguely remember his friends in Finland.

Meggan asked him about the train trip to Sweden, and it was then that the boy held her spellbound as he described his harrowing experiences in minute detail. Their attention was diverted by the sight of Solveig's white dress as the bride and groom stole away from the celebrants. The newlyweds climbed into a rowboat moored a short distance away. The new bride chatted happily from her seat in the stern while Pontilius rowed off across the lake, the sound of the oars rolling softly in the water.

"I'm not supposed to tell anyone where they're going," Meggan said, "but I can tell you. Promise to keep it a secret."

"I promise," Aimo said.

"I heard Solveig tell my mother they're going to Valåkravägen."

"Where's that?" Aimo asked.

"It's where they first met. Isn't that romantic?"

"I guess," Aimo replied.

Meggan tried to understand what sounded to her as a very perfunctory answer, but Aimo simply stared blankly. Neither of them heard Olofsson walk up behind them.

"Oh, ho!" Olofsson said drunkenly. "Look who I found!"

Both Aimo and Meggan spun around to face the old man swaying unsteadily on the shore. His shirt was unbuttoned and bits of grass debris clung to his knickers and vest. Olofsson bowed exaggeratedly.

"Hello, Fröken Vahleen." The old man shifted his glassy-eyed gaze to Aimo. "I told you the Vahleen girl had her eye on you." His words slurred, and he laughed loudly.

Abashed, Meggan angrily jumped from the boat and rushed toward the meadow, separating herself from Olofsson as swiftly as possible. Aimo moved to follow, but Olofsson's strong grip held the boy back. The old man lowered his voice to a slurred whisper.

"Never, ever run after a woman. Always let them chase you instead." He steadied himself on Aimo's arm and staggered into the boat, plopping down by the oars. "Untie us, Aimo. We're gonna go home. I don't feel so good."

Aimo was angry. It was the first time he had seen the old man drunk, and it mortified him. Olofsson had no right to behave so insultingly, but the boy's loyalty to his adopted grandfather stifled the urge to voice his displeasure. Aimo did as he was told and untied the boat. He jumped into the *Bronco* and took a seat in the stern.

"Lie down for a little while," Olofsson said working the oars. "I've got a bad headache . . . need some fresh air . . . Get some sleep, Aimo . . . I'll wake you if I want you to take over."

Even in the midnight light, Aimo could see the old man was not well. Frothy spittle dripped from the corners of the old man's mouth, disappearing in rivulets into his beard. His eyes appeared glazed and unfocused. Aimo was having considerable difficulty understanding the old man's disjointed sentences.

But the boy was exhausted. It felt good to sit down, and he decided to save his criticism until Olofsson was sober. He curled up on his seat and quickly fell asleep to the rhythmic groan of the oarlocks together with the gentle wash of lake water washing over the bow.

Aimo slept soundly until his pleasant dreams became a nightmare. His unconscious mind struggled to make sense of the confusing signals he was receiving. He was uncomfortably warm, and some unseen object rubbed irritatingly against his calf. Aimo's eyes blinked open. It took a few seconds to become aware he was still in the rowboat.

The warm sun on his face told him several hours had passed since he fell asleep, but the sound of oars rowing had stopped. Aimo noticed a white object in the water trailing along the side of the boat. He raised his head sleepily, then sat up suddenly, startled by the piercing call of a nearby loon.

Aimo's gaze fixed on Olofsson. He lay slumped against the side of the boat, his right arm hanging limply in the water. The old man's eyes were open and wet with moisture. His mouth opened and closed. The boy did not know if Olofsson was trying to speak or had difficulty breathing. The old man had been trying to awaken him by weakly moving his right shoe forward and back on Aimo's calf.

Aimo reached forward and tried to pull Olofsson into an upright position, but the old man was unable to support himself. He plopped forward into Aimo's arms. Aimo was terrified. Something serious had happened to the old man. The boy searched the surrounding vastness of the lake for help. His eyes focused on the community of Nilstad in the distance, the fountain of spouting water in front of the hospital, a beacon. Aimo maneuvered Olofsson to a reclining position, took the oars, and rowed furiously.

Aimo sat alone on a hallway bench in the hospital, listening to the unfamiliar sounds of sick and injured people coming from behind the closed doors that lined the corridor. He had no idea of the passage of time, and no one appeared to give him information about Olofsson's condition. All he knew was when he brought Dr. Gotfrid to the boat, he was told that he had done "the right thing" in recognizing the seriousness of Olofsson's illness. The boy could then do nothing more than wait as the stricken man was placed onto a stretcher and taken into the hospital.

Finally, a door from one of the rooms opened; and Dr. Gotfrid, dressed in a white smock, an operating mask hanging beneath his chin, approached.

"Is your name Aimo?" Dr. Gotfrid asked.

"Yes," Aimo replied.

"Who is the old man?"

"Magnus Olofsson. He's sort of my grandfather."

The doctor recognized the Finnish accent. "He can't speak very well, but he could say your name."

"He got drunk at the wedding," Aimo admitted.

"That's not what's wrong with him, Aimo. He's had a stroke, an injury to the brain. I found a problem here"—Gotfrid pointed to the right carotid artery in his neck—"I hope I was able to fix it. He's asleep now, but I won't know his condition for several days."

"When will he get better?" Aimo asked.

"I don't know, Aimo. His condition is critical. If he survives these next few days, he probably will have difficulty talking, walking, or doing anything normally again, at least for a while. But I don't know. We'll have to wait and see. Where are you living?"

"With him," Aimo answered.

"You're one of the Finnish children, aren't you?" the doctor asked. Aimo nodded.

"Well, we'll have to find someone you can stay with. Do you know anybody else?"

"The Vahleens. My sister lives there."

"I know them well. I'll call Constable Vahleen for you."

"No!" Aimo said strongly. "I'm supposed to go home to Finland."

Aimo turned from the doctor and ran into the recovery room where Olofsson lay, an oxygen mask over his face and IV tubes attached to his wrists. Aimo placed his hand on Olofsson's forehead. He whispered softly.

"Magnus . . . Magnus. It's me, Aimo. Can you hear me?"

The old man stirred then slowly opened his eyes. A weak smile of recognition twisted onto his face as he tried to mouth a few words.

"Aimo," he said quietly, but clearly. "Is that you?"

"Yes!" Aimo placed his face closer to the old man.

"I love you, boy," Olofsson rasped.

"I love you too," Aimo sobbed.

The old man tried to lift a hand then closed his eyes. His head slid to the side of his pillow, and he became silent. Aimo blinked his eyes swiftly, holding back tears. He could not bring himself to believe the old man had passed away.

Aimo ran out of the hospital, sprinting through a flock of grazing geese on the lawn that sent them honking angrily into the air. The boy jumped into the boat and rowed determinedly toward the cabin. He brought the *Bronco* to a jolting stop against the shore and raced into the cabin. There he found the suitcase Pontilius had delivered and hurriedly stuffed it with his clothes. He fetched his identity card and placed it around his neck.

Finally, he remembered his mother's gift still stashed beneath his pillow. He clutched the military medal in his hand, the action bringing him to an abrupt halt, and he plopped wearily onto his bed. He opened his fingers to study the object through tear-filled eyes. The article seemed to be making an effort to communicate with him. The shiny brass metal winked with bursts of reflected sunlight. He twisted the medal continually, and each time it flashed a bright shard of light signalling images of his parents, then the image of Olofsson swiftly in his mind.

Aimo's throat knotted tightly. He coughed several times to clear it until finally, a groan from deep within his chest rushed to his mouth and exploded in an anguished cry. The boy's body convulsed, his chest heaving spasmodically. He cried savagely, fighting to catch his breath, but like a volcanic explosion, the months of contained uncertainty had erupted with a violent emotion, shaking the boy free of his suffering. After several long minutes, his cries subsided to a whimper, and he lay his head on a pillow sobbing quietly.

Gretha held the phone to her ear and listened intently to the voice of Dr. Gotfrid describe Olofsson's condition. Sten stood nearby, reacting nervously to the troubled expression on his wife's face, then she lowered the phone. "Olofsson had a stroke."

"My god!" Sten exclaimed. "He was jumping around like a wild man just a few hours ago."

"Dr. Gotfrid said Aimo probably saved his life by bringing him to the hospital soon after the attack," Gretha continued. "Then the boy went to see Olofsson in the recovery room. Dr. Gotfrid said Olofsson's condition improved dramatically."

"That poor kid. Nothing seems to go right in his life. Gretha, we're going to have to try to make room for him here."

"Where?" Gretha asked. "There's no room left in this house. I don't see how we can do it. Even if we could, Aimo told Dr. Gotfrid he's leaving today to go back to Finland."

"The train *is* scheduled to come in today," Sten said.

"Who's going back to Finland?" Meggan asked. She stood in the doorway, rubbing her eyes sleepily with her sleeve.

"Aimo!" Gretha answered. "Magnus Olofsson is in the hospital."

Meggan's mind raced over the news. She struggled to form thoughts into sentences but stuttered over all of them. Finally she blurted out her worst fear, "Aimo is going to Finland? . . . When?"

"There's a train today, but I don't know where Aimo is," Sten said. "I suppose he went back to Olofsson's cabin. I'll go and fetch him."

"We can't stop him if he wants to go, Meggan. You know that." Gretha tried to be of comfort.

"He doesn't want to go back. I know he doesn't! I know he doesn't!" Meggan shouted. She ran up the stairs to her room.

Sten took hold of his wife's shoulders. "Gretha, I'm going to the cabin to get Aimo, and we *will* make room for the boy here with us. I want you to come with me and tell him yourself," he said with authority. Gretha nodded her head approvingly.

Sten sped off on his motorcycle in the direction of Olofsson's cabin with Gretha occupying the sidecar. Moments later, Meggan left the house and sprinted across the field toward Valåkravägen.

The pear trees on Solveig's property were in full blossom. Except for the humming of bees among the flowers and the calls of song birds in the yard, the house was quiet. Meggan flew up the steps and pounded loudly on the door.

"Help me! Please help me," the girl called in despair.

The door flew open. Solveig, her face flushed, stepped outside anxiously, a hastily thrown blanket pulled tightly around her neck.

"What's wrong, Meggan?" Solveig demanded.

"Aimo! He's going back to Finland," Meggan sobbed.

"When?" Pontilius asked, materializing behind his new wife.

"Now! Right now! There's a train coming. I heard the whistle."

"What happened?" The teacher asked.

"Herr Olofsson might die. He's in the hospital right now." Meggan cried disconsolately. "Please don't let Aimo go. He doesn't want to go back. I know he doesn't. Please! Please!" she begged.

"I'll go," Pontilius answered. "I'll put on some clothes right now."

Meggan sat on the bar of Pontilius's bicycle as the teacher pedaled wildly toward the Nilstad train station with Solveig bicycling beside him. They reached the station, dropped their bicycles, and climbed onto the platform.

The *Sunpath*, its polished sides reflecting brightly in morning sunlight, towered above the groups of people milling about on the platform. A dozen Finnish children, their identity cards around their necks and their suitcases at their side, embraced their Swedish families amid tearful farewells.

Pontilius limped along the platform, peering into the windows of the waiting train. Most of the cars were occupied, and the teacher nearly missed seeing Aimo, slouched on a seat, staring at his hands. Pontilius signaled to Solveig and Meggan that he had found the boy and indicated he wanted them to remain on the platform. Having done all that was possible, Meggan leaned against Solveig's shoulder, and the woman pulled the girl tightly against her.

Pontilius made his way through the coach toward Aimo's seat. Shards of sunlight slanted through the windows filling the room with a warm, gauzy haze. Pontilius waited a moment before he spoke.

"I just learned about Olofsson," Pontilius said softly. "I'm sorry."

Aimo turned his head toward his teacher, his swollen red eyes filled with sorrow. White rivulets traced down his grimy face as evidence that he had been crying. Pontilius looked at the boy's hands folded on his lap. They held something that he continually flipped from one side to the other.

"I wanted to say good-bye. Solveig is waiting outside with Meggan. We all would be very sad if you left without saying good-bye to us."

"I know," Aimo said, his voice barely audible. "I have to go back."

"I can understand. It's a terrible thing when all your hopes are shattered. When I lost my leg, I felt so ashamed I wanted to die."

"Nothing good ever happens to me. I'm supposed to take care of my sister and got her in trouble too. At least she's happy where she's staying."

"She has a home, Aimo. She lives with people who love her and care for her. Do you know what you'll find by returning to Finland?"

"I didn't want to come here," Aimo protested, his voice becoming louder.

"But you couldn't have stopped war from coming if you stayed, could you?" Pontilius waited for an answer, and the boy slowly shook his head.

"You couldn't stop your family or your cousins from being killed either. In fact, you and your sister probably would have died as well. Am I right?"

Aimo slowly nodded his head again as tears once again flowed down his cheeks. He stared at his hands, his focus on the military medal more intense.

"Aimo! Look at me," Pontilius commanded. The boy lifted his sad face to his teacher. "I did this to my leg. I made the choice to go to war, and it nearly cost me my life. Had I listened to those who loved me, I would have stayed home, and this would not have happened to me."

Pontilius paused as several more children entered the coach. He lowered his face and whispered.

"It's not your fault. You didn't want to leave, but you didn't want war either. There is no guarantee you'll be allowed to go home, Aimo, because there still is a war in Finland. In fact, you not only have no home, you have no parents. There's a good chance you'll be sent to an orphanage."

Pontilius straightened himself and glanced nervously around the coach. Every seat was filled. He had little time left.

"Don't make the same mistake I made. I'm here at this moment because I'm lucky. More importantly, I'm here because I'm with people who love me and care for me. That's what's here for you, Aimo. Love, hope, and a promise for your future."

"There's also bad people too, like the reverend," Aimo injected bitterly.

"There is good and bad everywhere. You've seen the worst and the best. Olofsson is not dead."

Aimo's eyes flahed open in surprise. He searched Potilius' face for more welcome information and the teacher continued.

"In fact, he improved when you visited him, Aimo. Do you see what I mean? He certainly loves you. If you were to leave, it would break his heart. You have your family here in Sweden . . . with us . . . a new family, new friends, and a future."

"Where would I stay?" Aimo asked.

Pontilius had agonized over his decision to go to war. His decision to break off the relationship with Solveig had come only after weeks of lying in a hospital bed. His decision to ask her to come back into his life likewise came after months of thought and prompting. Like a true Swede, his ability to make a spontaneous decision was almost nonexistent. He was astonished then at the thought that came into his head and transferred itself onto his lips at almost the same instant. Somehow he knew Solveig would approve.

"With me," Pontilius answered quickly. "With Solveig and me. You can teach me to fish, and I can teach you things to help you become whoever you want to be. When Olofsson recovers, you can return to him if you like. He certainly could use your help. We'd all be so happy if you agreed. I'm offering you a choice."

Aimo's eyes returned to the medal in his hand as he considered Pontilius's offer. He turned the medal in his fingers, continually causing the brass emblem to flash in the sunlight.

"Do you know what this is for?" Aimo asked. His eyes turned downward.

Pontilius nodded that he did and offered his hand to Aimo. "I know it well," the teacher said. "It's a Finnish Army medal. I have one that's identical."

"But what's it for?" Aimo insisted, again lifting his face to his teacher.

"Courage," Pontilius answered as the boy took his hand.

Epilogue

The Finnish War Children's Movement of Word War II resulted in the flight of nearly one hundred thousand children from Finland to Sweden. It remains the greatest exodus of children in the history of mankind.